The Drag Clan: Book I –

Rebirth
of Courage

The Dragoon Clan: Rebirth of Courage By Brandon Rospond
Cover by Tommaso Dall'Osto

Zmok Books an imprint of
Winged Hussar Publishing, LLC,
1525 Hulse Road, Unit 1, Point Pleasant, NJ 08742

This edition published in 2017 Copyright ©Winged Hussar Publishing, LLC

PB 978-1-958872-36-9
EB 978-1-6201814-7-8

Bibliographical references and index
1. Fantasy 2. Epic Fantasy 3. Action & Adventure

For more information on Winged Hussar Publishing, LLC, visit us at: https://www.WingedHussarPublishing.com
Twitter: WingHusPubLLC
Facebook: Winged Hussar Publishing LLC

Thank you to everyone that has helped me to get thus far in my writing endeavors and supported Winged Hussar Publishing in our foundation years. A special thanks to Mark Barber for helping me in the editorial process of this novel and for always being a sounding board for ideas in all of my projects. Even the editor needs an editor!

This book is dedicated to anyone that has ever taken part in The Dragoon Clan's adventures. Our stories have finally become so much more than fantasy.

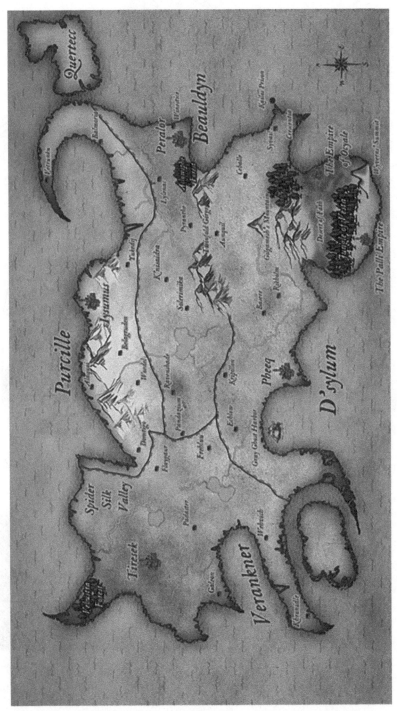

Prologue

Dreams, as the humans know the word to mean, are fragments of life that are both created and extinguished in the vacuum of the mind that is called sleep. They can be extravagant fantasies of quests that span distant journeys or small steps on familiar pathways to the market, ecstasies of forbidden love or a romantic moment with someone close, and they can even be lusts for acquisition of untold power or even the meagerness of strength to get through a daily struggle. Beyond the false sense of satisfaction that they can give, dreams can deceive the mind by twisting the scene into something more sinister. Vast nightmares that ravage the dreamer with terror also lurk within the mysterious void of consciousness; failing one's duty beyond redemption in front of respected peers, skittering multi-legged insects infesting every orifice, standing helplessly as everything that is held dear slips away, or even something as devastating as watching a loved one perish can all shake the dreamer to the core. All dreams, no matter how comforting or painful, are fragments of a fantasy unfilled, a moment in time reachable only in that instant.

In the Dreamscape, one of the realms beyond the living, a dream is more than just what the mind conjures in sleep; what the inhabitants there call a dream is a mortal person's entire span of life.

A single, feminine being pondered over these concepts as she sat on her throne and watched over the endless amount of dreams taking place. They surrounded her in the form of bubbles that fit within her cupped hands, hovering as they gleamed with depictions of life. The deity, whose appearance currently resembled that of a young human woman with long blonde hair, parted her lips into a smile as her gaze danced from one sphere to another around her. She looked down at the arm of her throne and her smile widened; the crystal it was made out of was so illustrious and pure that it reflected the scenes she gazed upon and casted a rainbow across the great hall. A red tapestry, made from finer silk than any mortal hand could weave, draped down the middle, separating her slender body from the cold crystal. The hem of her long white dress just barely kissed the floor as she sat proudly examining the dream bubbles.

Some called her the Queen of Dreams, others knew her as the Keeper of Fantasy, with the pious ones she was most reputable as the

Life Breather, and still there was a majority of people that referred to her as the Creator. The name that she called herself, arguably her 'real' name, was Mokiwana; she was a being whose essence spanned a lifetime that knew no beginning or end. She was the caretaker of each dream and had created the life within, watching the soul inside grow until their bubble would eventually pop, signaling the end of their time in the waking world of Vivacidy and the beginning of a new life in her world. Mokiwana had even visited the realm of mortals occasionally, favoring a guise similar to how she appeared now.

There was a soft cooing sound from beside her, and Mokiwana lifted her hand up to where it came from, barely taking her eyes away from the bubble she had been watching. She softly nuzzled the head of the pet on her shoulder. This creature of flight, Vooloo, as she named it, resembled what the living in Vivacidy called a dove; except unlike those birds, it had a flowing tail and its wings seemed to shine like the crystal of the throne as they fluttered in contentment. Mokiwana could not remember a time in her existence where Vooloo had not been by her side. Beyond the companionship the creature provided, Mokiwana would travel to Vivacidy using Vooloo as a spiritual vessel when she needed to directly see what was occurring in the mortals' realm. And right now, with its head slightly cocked, the eyes of Vooloo watched the dream beside its master.

In it was a farmer, hard at work cultivating his land. He was toiling in the bright sun, sweat dripping from his brow, one hand on a back that was clearly sore from the day's labor. Mokiwana's heart ached for his pain, but she knew it best to leave him to his work. Her tasks were to create life and observe it; the most that she could do was ensure he had a well-rested sleep that night. She nodded her silent thanks to the farmer before pushing the dream bubble away and scanning the room for a different orb in this place where time had no meaning.

As her eyes drifted, she sighed. Mokiwana knew that not all dreamers were pure of heart. Her people could be easily corrupted; after she created them, they had to make their own choices on how to live their lives. It was one of the most painful things for her – to watch one of her creations be twisted by the vile, sinful minions of Hades, the God of Death and Destruction. Once the dreamers who had lost all hope of redemption woke up, they were sent to eternally suffer within The Pale – a realm that she created specifically for beings of tainted heart and soul, and a dimension in which one of Hades's most loyal followers, Sairephir, Lord of Demons, reigned supreme.

Mokiwana, distraught by the thoughts that began to linger in her mind, pushed a dream bubble away just moments before it nearly bopped her in the nose. She stood up and slowly descended the dais, her bare feet pitter-pattering ever so quietly. She stared up at the deep violet and royal blue swirls of Dreamscape's sky beyond the translucent veil of a roof.

A name clawed its way through her mind and then sundered all other thoughts like a bolt of the fiercest lightning. Just the thought caused her chest to feel heavy. He had been Hades's greatest human pupil. He had succumbed to the dark whispers more than any other being she had brought life to. His darkness was so overwhelming, that using the strength he borrowed from the God of Death and Destruction, this being became stronger than even Sairephir. She thought such a thing impossible, especially with a mortal she had imbued with so much love and capacity to change the world.

She stopped when she came to an orb as black as night. As it hovered there, silent and still, she could feel the hate and the madness radiating off of it. The corruption of those once noble ideals hung pungently around the sphere.

It belonged to him. *Graymahl Vulorst.*

She didn't need to touch the orb to cause it to move; just putting her hand up near it caused it to swirl in the opposite direction, away from her aura of light. Sighing once more, she continued walking the length of the chamber.

When Graymahl finally ascended to claim his place as the herald of darkness, Mokiwana realized she had to right the wrong she had unintentionally made and realign the balance between good and evil. At that time, there had been none in Vivacidy strong enough to stand on even footing with Graymahl, so she made sure a child was born who could combat the darkness. She chose several souls to imbue with the capacity to do great things, in hopes one of them would be strong enough; but as the years passed, there was clearly one more advanced than the others. It was no coincidence that the mother and father that she had given the soul to were both warriors fighting for the side of good, strong people who wanted to change the world for the better, and had encountered Graymahl before he achieved his apex of darkness. She could ask for no better candidates to raise the savior of light, but she feared what potential the child could have as he grew older, as well as what dark temptations Sairephir and Hades could offer him. Despite the trials he faced, the child remained pure of heart with every passing year.

He continued to prosper, where the other destined children faltered or gave up on their soul's calling.

And now... events in Vivacidy were starting to align themselves.

"It is almost time, Vooloo..." Mokiwana's voice airily echoed through the long chamber. "A little more than two decades ago in the living world, I blessed a child with the courage to stand up to darkness, to have the heart of a lion, and the empathy to understand anyone's pain. I created a being strong enough to do battle with my greatest mistake, and soon – so soon – his power will awaken. I have sensed a storm of darkness gathering, and Odin has assured me the boy will soon be ready to embrace his destiny."

Vooloo cocked its head once more, as if to show its confusion. Even though the bird uttered only a light cooing, Mokiwana understood it perfectly.

"Unfortunately, yes. It is inevitable. Graymahl will return." She hesitated and glanced at the black orb that was slowly drifting down and across the chamber. "His tainted dream remains intact. His supporters gain numbers by the day, and Hades continues to deceive those who have faltered on the path of light. This dreamer though... I have steeled his heart with all that I could. I have tried to shape his soul to be stronger than any evil. However, I cannot control whatever happens in his realm. He will have to make decisions that not only affect him, but everyone; those in the living realm of Vivacidy, as well as those here in the Dreamscape. Choices that even impact the very fate of you and I, Vooloo."

Mokiwana paused, staring at the black orb that floated closer to her crystal throne, and she forced her eyes away. She inhaled through her nose slowly.

"I have taken a gamble, and I must trust it pans out, for the sake of us all. His story – his dream – will be larger and more perilous than any other, but it will have the biggest implications and impact across the realms."

She stepped forward and cupped one of the orbs in her hands. Much like with how she felt the negativity from the black bubble, she could feel the heat from inside this one warming her cheeks as she pulled it close. She intently watched the inferno that took place within the dream for several moments before speaking again.

"He will need our help more than any have ever needed it before."

Chapter I

Flames fueled by hatred licked the corners of stones and rubble, enveloping strewn and motionless bodies in a blanket of cleansing fire. Chaos and destruction reigned in every direction. A town that once stood resolute behind its fortified walls and illustrious gates now lay in ruins. And what of its people? They had either fled or succumbed to the sea of flames that danced across the cremated corpses of the countless fallen. Among the ruins, a woman lay collapsed and trembling. She clawed at the ground, trying to frantically crawl backward; her voice was nothing more than a frightened whimper. Her eyes, blurry from tears, wavered on the aggressor that strode slowly toward her; a malicious terror with a soul as cold and as black as the soot that clouded the orange glint of the dusk's sky above. A pair of power-hungry eyes, submerged within a glow of blood red, leered out from a helmet with two large horns that stretched from ear to ear, and the fury and disdain within that gaze felt as if it was staring right into the woman's soul. The evil entity towered over her as it stalked forward like a great beast ready to claim the last fleeting breath of life of its prey.

The aggressor raised his arm, exposing the scythe that dripped with the blood of the slain. Six feet tall and with a two feet wide cleaver, the vitriolic black metal seemed to split the sky as it was lifted into the air that was rank with death. The young woman gasped and, as the blade began its descent, her mouth opened wide to let out from deep within a bloodcurdling...

* * * * *

Darkflare bounded up to a sitting position in his bed and gasped for air as icy beads of perspiration trickled down his pulsing temples; his lungs frantically heaved in and out cool bursts of rejuvenating air, despite feeling on fire. The young man listened intently to the soundlessness of his room, his eyes darting around the familiar four beige walls. It was as if he was waiting for the torturous nightmare that had been plaguing him off and on throughout the past few months to become reality this time.

There was nothing. Just the heaving of his breath echoed in his eardrums, which had reduced significantly since he had awakened.

Once Darkflare felt calm enough, he let out a heavy sigh and threw back the blankets into a mess of cloth. He swung his feet over the side of the oak bed and stood cautiously. Despite the fog of confusion that still latched onto his brain, he made his way to a dresser across the room.

He had to shield his eyes as he approached it, as the light of the sun shining in through the cracks of the curtains threatened to blind him. He exhaled, trying to calm his heartbeat as he searched through piles of folded clothes, examining each piece to make sure he picked the right attire.

Once he was content, the young man walked out into the hallway, past the two rooms used for storage, and made his way down the staircase. He paused in the welcoming room and thought about making breakfast as he stared into the kitchen, but he shook his head.

Darkflare waited before moving toward the front door. Something caused him to poke his head in each of the rooms downstairs. The thought was silly; he lived alone and had for as long as he could remember. There was no noise, and certainly no one else was here. He supposed he was still trying to shake off the lingering thoughts about his dream. Sometimes the empty rooms in the house his parents had left him got the better of his nerves; especially mornings after he had the nightmare.

His mind returned to the dream, and he could not ignore the uncomfortable chill through his bones. This particular dream kept recurring on and off for at least the past four months. It unfolded a little more every time his mind played it, as if piecing together a forgotten memory. It had slowly evolved from a scene of a raging inferno, to one of the corpses caressed beneath the flames, to the one now of the heavily armored man shrouded in darkness standing before the screaming woman. It was the first time that he had seen either one of them, and besides the scream, there had been something about the woman that made him wake in such a fright. He felt like he knew who she was. Even though the details of her face were a blur in his memory, her name was on the tip of his tongue.

Darkflare shook his head once more, dispelling the lingering thoughts, and he stepped out onto his porch. He closed his eyes as he soaked in the warmth of the sun on his skin.

"Finally," an icy voice said.

He didn't need to look at the person to know who spoke.

"Morning to you too, sunshine," Darkflare responded before descending the few stairs of his porch and continuing over to a roofless, wooden shack that was attached to the side of his house.

As the door closed behind him, Darkflare disrobed and hung both pairs of clothes on a hook before stepping past a curtain. With a loud creak, he turned a metal handle and a cascade of cold water washed over the front of him; he shivered from the numerous tiny icy pinpricks as his eyes focused on changing the gauge by the handle to warmer water. As the hotter water reddened his skin, he slouched from the relaxing feeling. He didn't want to think about a world where magic didn't power everything. Bathing, heating a house, the lighting in a room; anything used as either a necessity or accessory, magic was the source of power. The handle in the shower had wires that led to the back where a small orb was centered. Depending on if he wanted cold or hot water, he'd turn the handle in either direction to cause the fire-embodied crystal or the ice-embodied crystal to change the temperature. That, at least, was the basic principle that Darkflare understood. The inner workings and details were still a mystery beyond his understanding.

Wiping the water from his face, Darkflare slid open a face-high window and peered out at Attila, the person who spoke moments ago. The man with lightly tanned skin and long black hair that fell on both sides of his face was leaning with his back against the porch, staring up into the morning's mostly cloudless sky.

"You do remember what today is, correct, Darkflare?" Calm and collected, the murmured question was almost lost in the hissing of the water.

"Right, right. We're heading to Ceballe for the tournament. I know. Cut me some slack, I didn't sleep *that* late!" Darkflare called back, pulling the window shut once more. "We've still got plenty of time to make it there before dusk."

"That may be, but by the time *you* are finished getting ready, dusk will have long since settled."

Darkflare chortled lightly as he turned off the water.

"We've waited a long time for this one, old friend." The shower head hissed to silence as a few last droplets of water crawled out. "In all of the years we've known each other, have you ever known me to cower from a challenge? And now, here we are, the day before the biggest tournament Ceballe has ever hosted! Getting the opportunity to test my sword skill against new opponents from across the land is all I've been able to think about, night and day!"

"Right, just as long as you don't go showing off for that girl you swoon over."

Darkflare threw open the window and glared at Attila. "*Gloria* and I are just friends, I don't know how many times I have to tell you this. The Despils have been more than kind to us every time we see them, and it would do you well to actually remember her name." He shut the window once more as he reached for his clothes. "I'm more focused than ever, believe me."

"Good. It shouldn't need to be said, but the stakes have never been higher."

Darkflare nodded as he began to dress himself, aware the gesture wouldn't be seen. The two men were no strangers to tournament fighting, nor were the events a rarity to the hustle and bustle of the ever-busy town of Ceballe. But the fact that the four kingdoms' rulers would be overseeing the event was a shocking addition. The King of D'sylum, Lazelus Corsius, made a decree that too many years had passed since the last 'royal' tournament, and then invited the rulers of the three other kingdoms, Verankner, Beauldyn, and Purcille to come and behold the spectacles.

This was the opportunity of a lifetime – especially for a young man whose only reputation was being a fancy sword fighter, living on the edge of a ruined town, depending on the meager winnings from each fight – to make a name for himself. Not to mention the prize money the rulers would be contributing would easily be more gold than Darkflare had ever held at one time! People all over the continent of Caelestis would be flocking to Ceballe to either take part in the contest or witness the festivities. Darkflare couldn't help but smile, thinking about the surge of people that would be filling the stands to bursting capacity.

Darkflare finished putting on his clothes – casual for the trip – and moved to a shelf just before the door. He grabbed a small bottle and squeezed a few drops over his head. Working the tips of his fingers through his short brown hair, he managed to get most of it to form into a messy assortment of spikes. To finish the look, he grabbed two more items: a pendant he hung around his neck and a red bandana that he tied across his forehead, the tails floating down to the top of his back.

Darkflare emerged from the shower with a toothy, almost sarcastic grin toward his friend. Compared to Attila, Darkflare was the leaner of the duo, but the short-sleeved blue shirt he wore showed off his toned arms. Though slender, his body was taught with muscle on his five foot, ten inch frame. Even though he was no brute, Attila was broad-shouldered, only further accented by a black shirt, frayed where sleeves had once been.

Both men wore similar black breeches and belts, but Darkflare's jet black knee-high boots differed from Attila's more natural tan ones. Resting by his feet was a leather sack that Darkflare knew contained a sun-splotched leather brigandine, along with whatever other various items Attila brought with them – which was ever hardly much at all.

Darkflare fixed his fingerless gloves in place, pulling slightly where a cross-design was sown into the backhand, before giving the other man a thumbs up.

Attila nodded back with his chin. "Might want to tuck that in."

Darkflare's hands scurried up his chest as he looked down.

"Oh, right! Family heirloom. Don't want to lose that." His fingers wrapped around the pendant dangling from his neck and held it up to admire it. It was a cross-handled sword, intertwined and coiled by the bodies of two dragons that formed closed-mouth heads that pointed away from the top of the blade's hilt. The bodies of the dragons had tiny letters scrawled on them, but it was in a language Darkflare did not understand. In the middle of the cross gleamed a ruby; the only thing of color on the otherwise silver item. He smiled as he tucked the pendant underneath his shirt, feeling the metal against his chest. "The Drachenfaith. Last time I had it showing in Ceballe, I had merchants nearly trying to pry it off my neck. Must be the gem."

Attila pushed long black strands of hair away from his cerulean blue eyes; his brooding face now clearer to see, Darkflare felt the weight of Attila's icy glare. Beside him, a sword almost as tall as he was rested against the house.

"Glad to see you're all set," Darkflare walked by, patting him on the shoulder as he passed, and then ascended the steps of his porch again.

"At least one of us is."

Darkflare heard the words just before the screen door shut behind him once more. He retraced his steps, sprinting up the stairs two at a time, but he stopped at the entrance to one of the storage rooms and looked back to his own room. Everything seemed just the way he had left it when he awoke, but... something still felt awry; as if something *had* changed in the short time he had left. Perhaps it was nothing. Perhaps it was that accursed dream that haunted his waking mind and swayed him to paranoia.

Whatever the cause, Darkflare tried to shake it off as he entered the room he liked to call the armory. Several sets of rusted or chipped armor were displayed on human-like wooden fixtures, buckler and kite shields missing chunks of their metal were hung across the walls, and weapons were scattered about both in sheaths and without. Everything in this room had belonged to his parents, their various spoils they had collected through their many years of being warriors. How or where they obtained each piece was a mystery to Darkflare.

He smiled as he passed through the room, coming to a black trunk he'd taken as his own. He bent down, gently opened the lock, and reached inside of the coffer lined with red silk to withdraw a thin longsword that was sheathed in a black scabbard. This particular blade had become Darkflare's weapon of choice for several years now, favoring it more than a spear, axe, dagger, or bow. It would be the perfect weapon to place his trust in going into such a monumental tournament.

Darkflare stood, hooked the sword onto the frog of his belt, and turned to one of the closest armor displays. The wooden humanoid wore only a well-maintained brigandine, which Darkflare carefully inspected for damage before stripping it and donning it himself. He made sure to pull out the bandana tails from underneath as the armor caressed and hugged his body, clamping the light shirt in place underneath.

He did not wield the most illustrious set of armor or weaponry, but Darkflare made use of the tools at his disposal. As far as he saw it, it was not the gear that made the warrior – it was skill – and he honestly believed he had a lot of that at his young age of twenty-two. Darkflare stretched his arms out wide and rolled them in a circle, making sure he could maneuver around easily enough with the armor clasping his frame.

He looked around the room at the collection of disheveled and damaged arms. He closed his eyes, and in his mind, he could see it all shining and new. The centerpiece would be his own set of armor, his *knight's* armor, and the crest of a kingdom, maybe Beauldyn's, in the center, beaming proudly for his accomplishments. The first step toward that dream would be winning this tournament. And to do that, he'd need to have the utmost of…

Courage.

Darkflare's breath caught in his throat and his body froze in place. His head swiveled as he looked frantically around the room. Someone had spoken. He *swore* he had heard a voice. The strangest part was that the voice was *familiar* to him, and there were very few people whose voices he could associate that word with. A name was on the tip of his tongue, but his voice failed to utter what his brain was trying to put together.

He kept looking around the room. No one was visible, and he knew there was no place to hide. So then, how in the Pale did he just hear a crystal clear voice say the word 'courage' in his ear, finishing his thought?

He felt a chill pass through him. He tried to convince himself that he was just on edge still from the nightmare, but something in the back of his mind kept nagging him that the voice sounded all too real. It almost felt like this had been what he had been anticipating when he woke up.

Darkflare rubbed his chest from outside his armor. On his right breast was a birthmark that resembled a helmet with horns protruding from both sides; and at that moment, it burned something fierce. From time to time it ached, some days, like today, more intense than others. Especially mornings after he had the nightmare.

"It's just anxiety... Today's a big day after all," Darkflare murmured out loud to no one in particular, as if still trying to force himself to believe that he *was* alone in the room.

Now that he started thinking about it, he wasn't even really sure he *had* heard anything in the first place. Maybe it was the wind, or he had stepped on a creaky board, or perhaps it was the chest he had closed making a last noise. It was probably nothing more than a habitual sound of the house. After all, it was impossible for him to hear another voice inside his own house.

Darkflare exhaled forcefully and shook his head. He took the brigandine off, marched over to the door, and grabbed his own travel bag. He had already packed the necessities, including a waterskin and some fruit, and he carefully stowed the armor. Slinging the pack over his shoulder, he started out the door. He did not have time to sit and ponder the mystery.

It was time to leave.

Chapter II

Returning outside, Darkflare hurried down the porch steps and found Attila just as he had left him, leaning against the house and staring up at the clouds. Darkflare was almost envious of how Attila was able to keep himself from getting worked up. It would have been more likely to see a man skipping naked into their deserted town than to see Attila get excited about anything. It was only in the heat of a fight that Darkflare saw the occasional hint of a smile on Attila's face. If he had any worries about the tournament right now, there was no such glimmer that Darkflare could sense.

"Sorry," Darkflare mused quickly, resting his arms on his hips. "I got a little distracted. Let me just call Oboro and we'll be on our way."

Attila nodded, grabbed his sword, picked up his bag, and pushed away from the wall. Darkflare placed his index finger and thumb to his lips and whistled loudly. Silence followed for a few long seconds, but it was broken by the sound of flapping wings. Darkflare looked up to see a creature roughly the size of a hawk flying toward him and Attila.

The royal blue scales on the wyvern's body glimmered softly in the sunlight as it approached from above. The bright color was a stark difference from the dull white with a hint of orange of Oboro's underbelly, wings, and crescent ear-frills. Darkflare smiled as he watched the wyvern approach, and he allowed himself a moment of recollection.

Darkflare had nurtured the wyvern from as early an age as he was able to grip its shell in his hands. Even though the memories were vague, something in his mind told him that his parents had found the mysterious egg in their travels. Once Oboro had hatched, it was the young Darkflare that his bulbous black eyes had locked upon, concluding the boy to be his parent. If the great intellect of wyverns allowed Oboro to make the connection that Darkflare was not his blood kin, he showed no difference in the way he treated the young man.

Darkflare patted his companion lightly on the head as he hovered beside him, and then he turned and nodded to Attila. The nod, as brisk and as wordless as it was, was all that they needed to begin their march for the city of Ceballe, a journey that he knew would mostly be in silence. As they walked the hidden path through the trees that stood as Crescentia's borders, Darkflare knew better than to force conversation; when Attila was silent, such as he had been, every answer he would give to any topic would be single words or grunts. Instead, the peace gave Darkflare time to dwell on his own thoughts and to mentally prepare for the coming tournament.

He waited until the silence became unbearable, and then Darkflare decided it was time to play a game he enjoyed – one that he knew Attila couldn't stand.

"Padaster?" Darkflare smiled slyly without turning his head.

"No," Attila responded flatly, his gaze fixed ahead.

"Basere? Ravenshade? Alaquoi? No, wait. I think I've asked you that one before. Oh, what about Galeon? I've read it's supposed to be very warm there." When Attila stopped responding, Darkflare knew the game was up. "Ah, well. At least that narrows one more town down."

Though Darkflare had known the scowling young man for most of his life, Attila refused to speak about before they met. Darkflare was the only person left alive to call Crescentia their birthplace – or at least he thought so. Everyone else had died from, what the scorch marks on buildings and piles of dark ash revealed, to be some sort of giant fire that ravaged the entire town – save his parents house, for some strange reason.

Darkflare's positivity helped him to move forward and live a life of his own, but at times like this when he really began to think about the devastation, the sorrow could not be kept at bay. He felt some of his exuberance dissipate as the thoughts clawed their way into his mind. The day of the catastrophe and anything before that were practically absent from his memories. He could remember blurry snippets of his mother, father, brother, and sister, but he could not focus on details of what they looked like. He knew he should have been old enough to remember what happened and who his family was, but the more he thought about the day of the destruction, the hazier the memories became, and the more his head hurt.

Whoever or whatever had destroyed the town – which had once been a fortified stronghold, Darkflare had noted from the aftermath of broken walls, towers, and a massive gateway – had to have known exactly where and what Crescentia was. No one had come in the days since; and while the town was nothing of note anymore, not even the older, more dated maps Darkflare had seen marked the area as inhabited. There was very little reason for anyone to come this far southeast; thick woods secluded Crescentia from the north and the coast that was in walking distance from the town's south had no harbor. The road bypassed Crescentia, and the end of the path led to only one destination: Kailos

Prison, which sat on an isthmus east of the forest. No one that Darkflare met had known or even heard of a town named Crescentia.

Attila had been the first and only visitor. Darkflare recalled that he had to have been seven or maybe eight at the time; far too young for two boys to be on their own.

He had never known fear like what had seized him when he saw something more human than animal make its way past the forested border. He had no idea what to do – how to react, how to interact with the person. With balled fists, he had rubbed his eyes several times, but none of it shooed away what he saw. He thought the person to be a boy, but the view of something dragging itself with him made Darkflare question the assumption. The something had been a blade, much bigger and longer than its owner.

Its size did not stop the startled boy from standing defensively behind it when Darkflare made himself known to the youngster.

"No, no! I don't mean to hurt you." Darkflare shook his head frantically and then started to fish inside his tattered pants' pocket to bring out a piece of sweet bread he had been saving. His hand trembled as he held it out to the boy. "Here… F-For you."

The stranger, in equally ratty clothing, looked back and forth from Darkflare to the bread several times before letting go of the sword and cautiously approaching him. He reached his hand out and curled the chunk of bread in his shaking fingers before recoiling away. He looked at Darkflare with uncertainty, to which Darkflare anxiously smiled and gave a nod. In an instant, the bread was devoured.

"You look really tired. If you don't have anywhere to go, you can make this town your home. It's called Crescentia. I'm the only person that lives here anymore… My name is Darkflare Omni."

The boy cleared his throat uneasily, trying to structure the right words. "At… Attila. Attila Laise."

* * * * *

"Attila?"

The dark-haired man cocked an eyebrow toward Darkflare but said nothing. The silence was only broken by Oboro's beating wings.

"Remember the day we first met?"

"Hard to forget. You saved my life that day. Why do you ask?"

"Just thinking. Reminiscing, really. It made me curious. I'm sure there were countless towns on your journey from… wherever it is that you came from. What brought you to Crescentia of all places?"

"There was no reason. I was determined to follow the road as far as it would go, but once I got to the forest, it felt like the right decision to make the turn."

"Like something was calling you? Like... fate?"

Darkflare raised his eyebrows as he said the last word, to which Attila turned and narrowed his eyes.

"I don't be-..."

"Don't believe in fate, I know. You don't like the idea of some greater being pulling the strings."

Attila stared for a few more moments before he turned back to the road. "My intuition told me to turn away from the path. I was starving and needed rest."

"Good thing I was there then, eh?" Darkflare smiled slyly. "Wouldn't it have been a surprise if I had gone foraging, only to come back to find a dead boy lying in my bed? It would have been a pain to lug your body down to the ocean."

"Burial at sea? I wouldn't even get a spot in the graveyard?"

"Too much effort! Your thick skull would have ensured you would have sunk right to the bottom."

Darkflare laughed heartily and jokingly shoved Attila, who snorted in return. Oboro cooed lightly at the exchange, presumably all too used to this sort of interaction between the two.

Darkflare looked at the berry bushes they passed, thinking about those bygone days of foraging. Attila, Oboro, and himself relied on each other to survive for many years, but they could not take all of the credit for it. Some things had survived in the wreckage of the town such as stored food, leftover coin, and trinkets that they could sell; and somehow, they always seemed fresh. Darkflare suspected Attila had a hand in that, but his stalwart companion always denied his involvement.

Yet, those meager morsels that they found were not enough to sustain them indefinitely. It had been a certain chance meeting that had saved the then children. Merchants made quite the plump profit selling various food and items to the guards at Kailos Prison, who rarely ever left their posts.

Intrigued by the horse-drawn vehicles – creatures that Darkflare had only ever read about and was amazed to see in person – they had witnessed countless carts' travels from the edge of the forest, but they were one day spotted by a majestically dressed merchant from within his pavilion. Yelling a command at the driver, the carriage rolled to a stop and the man hopped down.

"Ho? What have we here? Prisoners who have escaped from Kailos? No… you both are far too young for that. What in blazes are you doing here?"

The boys had been startled at first by the flamboyantly dressed man's approach and remained silent for a time. It was Darkflare who worked up the nerve to answer him.

"We, um… We live here."

"Where? The forest?"

"No…"

The man stared at the two boys and sighed, scratching his bearded chin as he looked past them.

"You boys are lucky that it was I who you encountered. There are soulless fiends who dare to call themselves merchants who would not think twice on selling two young boys into slavery. I would never stoop so low to such a foul thought." He looked back down at them and smiled genuinely, a suspicious and strange sight for the two. Seeing them still keeping their guard, the man shook his head. "Are you lads hungry? My main purpose for traveling this road is to bring the guards at the prison leftover food for the convicted. I'd rather give my overstock to two children than guilty murderers and thieves."

Darkflare's eyes widened as he looked to Attila, then back at the man.

"Yes! Th-Thank you, uh…"

"James. James Liraef."

Darkflare remembered that they would often wait for Liraef's trip once every month; at first, Attila was hesitant, but once he bit into a fresh cut of meat, he abandoned his staunch resistance. It wasn't long until Darkflare felt the need to repay the merchant for his kindness, and he often brought the man relics from Crescentia that seemed they might fetch a fair amount of gold. The man always accepted their gifts thankfully, and they continued to trade for nearly a year.

However, there came a point that the boys felt that they needed to learn to fend for themselves again, as they could not always depend on the man's kindness for the rest of their lives. They had considered becoming merchants themselves in Liraef's company to repay him, but the idea never took flight. While they could manage money well enough, Attila did not have the charisma to hawk wares to people. They also realized they might be doing the opposite of their intent, by taking potential customers from the others in Liraef's troupe. They had come to a mutual agreement that they were not fit to be merchants but instead were far better with swords.

Two things that were in abundance in the remains of Crescentia were weapons and armor. As they grew up, not one day was spent without a weapon in their hands, practicing with them against one another. At first, they tried to mimic the techniques Darkflare found in books in his house. They trained vigorously, honing their swordplay in duels by making up new, intricate, and sometimes ridiculous techniques. Darkflare also began to study the complex system of penmanship by analyzing the surviving books and notices found on the roads. The two taught themselves everything that they had learned, and they lived as if each day was their last, undaunted by any challenge.

The one dream that still went unfulfilled was becoming knighted, and that thought brought him back to the present.

"What do you think our chances are of being noticed by one of the rulers?"

"Not likely," Attila shrugged.

"Not likely? Surely watching us duel with combatants from across the four kingdoms bare all on their blades, the rulers would find interest in one of our skills – if not us both! In royal tournaments like this in the past, they've recruited entrants right off the field!"

Attila turned his head, narrowing his eyes. "How would you know that?"

"Read it in a book I picked up in Ceballe about tournament histories."

Attila rolled his eyes. "What a waste of time."

Darkflare shook his head. Despite Attila's sarcasm over his reading material, both men had dreamed of one day raising their swords under the glorious green and gold banner of the benevolent Queen Faïne Ragwelv, the ruler of the eastern kingdom of Beauldyn. The young queen's generosity and warm heart were often a popular subject of conversation among the people they met in Ceballe. They heard many accounts of the queen who often held council with her people, doing her best to help their everyday lives. Her kingdom was also renowned for its beauty, as people often described the lush fields of green, abundant dense forests, and the beautiful blooming flowers.

The artists' depictions Darkflare had seen of the kingdom in his books made it look like a fairy tale wonderland compared to D'sylum's rather bleak landscape. He looked around at the wild grass; while this part of the continent had nature as its caretaker, other, more civilized areas of the kingdom were walled in with tall buildings, and human construction obscured the wonders of green.

Even Queen Ragwelv's personality was a stark difference from King Lazelus Corsius, the ruler of their kingdom. Darkflare had never met the man personally, but the king had a reputation for being cold and militaristic. This was even reflected in so many of the towns' thick walls and little if any agricultural space.

Darkflare hadn't had any particular issues with the ruler, but people of Ceballe were often divided on their opinion. King Corsius had come to the throne after the former capital, Syvail, had been destroyed. Even though the king seemed to have his people's best interests at heart, the change in policies left many unhappy.

Darkflare snapped out of his thoughts as he noticed the road ahead splitting into three directions. To the west was the Crescentia Forest, as Darkflare called it; a woodland so dense, that the duo had only ever gotten a few feet in before turning around. As with Crescentia, most maps did not have a good grasp of what lay beyond the trees; only that it was an expanse of desert and smaller forests within. Often, he found his inquisitive nature nagging him to someday explore what lay west of the dense woods. To the east lay...

Kailos Prison. Just one look at the building in the distance with its looming spire gave Darkflare shivers. The last stop for all travelers on this road. From what records Darkflare could find from his parents' belongings, it seemed that those living in Crescentia held watch there before the destruction. The lack of wardens in the aftermath must have been noticed, and now it was said to be run by mercenaries.

Darkflare had never ventured inside the prison himself. Word was that those convicted had a fate awaiting them worse than death. People at Ceballe would tell stories about the ways prisoners would be tortured, but they were all second-hand accounts, told to them by someone else who had *supposedly* been to Kailos. But the screams... those were real.

The trio had dared to take the eastern fork once, leading them on a long, narrow gravel road with an ocean view on both sides. They got about halfway down the winding path to the dark-bricked building before they heard three blood-curdling screams. Darkflare remembered them very vividly, and another chill ran through him.

Darkflare shook his head as they continued on north, following the path that wound west past the forest, and onward to Ceballe.

"We're making good time today," Darkflare remarked as he looked up toward the sun's spot in the sky.

"Going too fast for you?" Attila teased.

"No way in Pale. A brisk walk like this will definitely help to unwind for tomorrow."

"Nervous?"

The question caught Darkflare off guard, but such was the nature of Attila's inquisitions. "What? Why do you ask?"

"Because you're playing with your necklace."

Darkflare glanced down at his hand which had unconsciously pulled the Drachenfaith out.

"Heh, I guess so," Darkflare gave the pendant a last look before tucking it back under his shirt. "You know that it's my good luck charm. I guess I'm just lost in thought... The past and my parents and the like. This necklace is the only thing that helps me remember them. There's the stuff in the house, sure, but nothing feels as comforting as this."

Attila nodded, having heard the story so many times prior. The Drachenfaith had been bestowed upon Darkflare when he was very young, from what he could remember, and he always treasured the heirloom with tender care. He had never been sure how his parents had come across the exquisitely crafted item or why they had not given it to Darkflare's older brother, Terra.

"You know how I am when I get lost in my head. This tournament's a lot different from all the others that we've been in before. I've heard and read so much about my mother and father, and all of the great things they did over their lives. I just want to make them proud and honor their memory by making something of myself. If we were to be recognized for our talents and recruited into knighthood, we could help make the world a better place under the banner of a king or queen."

Attila didn't speak for a few moments. From what little memories Darkflare had about his parents, the spoils and trinkets, and the worn weaponry, he had always believed them to be great warriors – and from the size of Crescentia's destroyed portion, there had to have been a score of other warriors that once lived there. They had to have built something grand before... Before...

"We have to win this," Darkflare eventually said, feeling a lump in his throat. "I have to, at least. To honor my parents legacy. I have to make the world a better place – like I'm sure they tried to do."

Atilla stared at Darkflare for another silent moment, and then he nodded.

"Relax. How many years have we been fighting in tournaments? We are at the peak of our swordplay, and the succession of victories over the past few years is a testament to that. Our losses from past bouts give us strength. Do not let the hype daunt your resolve. Yes, we will be fighting opponents from across the four kingdoms, but we've been training our skills and technique for years."

"True enough," Darkflare muttered. "How long have we been doing this for?"

"What? Tournament fighting? Since we were fifteen and able to pass the age check."

"I can't believe it's been seven years, and only the past three have we truly begun to reap rewards."

"I'm surprised they still let us enter the ones this year."

"We put on a good show when it's just you and I at the end," Darkflare shrugged. "The people get their money's worth, even if our sparring sessions are more intense than what they see. We fight and dance a bit, then one of us takes the 'finishing blow' in style. It works for all parties and we don't risk getting injured." A smile formed on Darkflare's face as he let out a light chuckle. "Maybe this will finally be the time we go all out."

"That's if we both make it."

"Right." Darkflare nodded. "I don't know how we managed before we started winning tournaments. The oddjobs were nice and all, but those rewards pale in comparison to tournament earnings."

"Not to mention the fighting was less painful than interacting with people."

Before they had been old enough to compete, the two boys offered their services out to the townspeople of Ceballe whenever they could. Whether it was just simple errands they needed help with, finding something of rare value outside of the town, some sort of escort or delivery duty, or finding a lost pet that had scampered away; whatever the case, they always tried to help out if they could. They never asked for anything in return, but the townspeople would usually offer a reward of some sort for the aid.

Offering their help was also how they had met the Despils – chasing after a pickpocket who had stolen Gloria's broach. They had been so thankful and invited the boys to dinner that night. Gloria had even called Darkflare a hero and kissed him on the cheek…

All in all, ever since they started venturing to Ceballe, their lives had started changing for the better; and that thought helped bring back some of Darkflare's peppiness.

After following the path for some time, the grass slowly began to wither away, leaving this patch of land barren and dead. Darkflare could see a stretch of stone wall coming up to greet them; blackened and decayed, it was reinforced by newer looking stone and timber in areas where it was crumbling. Even though they were decrepit, the walls still stretched high. A thick-barred gate, stemming from a broken portcullis, that had several chains and padlocks wrapped around it ensured no one would enter the ruins again.

This was the former capital of D'sylum – Syvail.

Darkflare shook his head as he continued west, past the all-too-familiar sight. He turned to say something to Attila, but his friend was standing still, facing Syvail with his arms crossed.

"Attila? Everything okay?"

The raven-haired young man glanced at Darkflare out of the corner of his eye and then started walking forward, toward the ruins.

"Attila, hello? What are you doing?" Darkflare spread his arms out wide before letting them drop to his sides. He glanced at Oboro, who cocked his head. Darkflare jogged after Attila, who was now at the gate with both hands clasped firmly on the bars and looking inward.

"We've both always wanted to get a closer look as to what lies in the ruins. Tomorrow is a day of great importance; we shouldn't be held back by anything at this point."

"Uh, yes, that's great and all, but now's not the time for this."

"Scared?" Attila's blue eyes seemed to pierce through Darkflare as he turned to look at him. "You don't actually believe what is said about this place being cursed, do you?"

Darkflare put his hands in the air, backing away slightly. "No, I don't think it *is* cursed, but it *is* forbidden to trespass here. I don't want to face the wrath of King Corsius and his guards instead of fighting in the tournament tomorrow."

"How would anyone know if we were to enter?" The bars rattled as Attila held them tighter, pushing his head in for a closer look. "Why do you think he's sealed this place off? What is he hiding in there?"

"How do we know someone's not watching us right *now?*" Darkflare put his hand on Attila's shoulder, causing the tanned-skin man to pull his head back from the bars and stare down at the ground. "The tournament is the most important thing for us right now. It can and hopefully will change our lives dramatically if we get noticed. But in order for that to happen, we need to get there and *not* get thrown in shackles.

And if we win, with the prize money you can pay King Corsius yourself to take you on a guided tour of the ruins." Darkflare paused, and his gaze darted into the ruins and back to Attila momentarily. "Besides... If there really is anything haunted in there, would you really want to disturb it?"

Attila rolled his eyes and shook his head, relinquishing his hold with a clatter. As he walked back toward the trail, Darkflare moved into the spot at the gate. He couldn't see much, but there were huge piles of rubble and destroyed buildings scattered all over the place. The whole town had been devastated, save for maybe the entranceway of a few buildings in the far back; at least, that's what it looked like when Darkflare squinted.

Syvail, although a husk of its former glory, did not look unusual for a set of ruins, but Attila's question nagged at Darkflare heavily: why did King Corsius seal Syvail off? Was there something that lurked deep within that the king did not want out? Was there some dark reason for Syvail's destruction? Could it possibly be linked to whatever happened in Crescentia?

"Darkflare!"

He dismissed his thoughts once again as he turned to the call of his name. He must have been standing there for at least a minute and did not realize how far Attila had walked. Oboro nudged his head against Darkflare's shoulder consolingly. Darkflare smiled uneasily at his wyvern, tickling him under the chin, and jogged back over to Attila.

"Sorry... I guess I... kind of got caught up in the moment as well," Darkflare murmured.

His eyes moved to the road ahead, but his mind was still back in Syvail.

* * * * *

"Only a little further now," the calm voice of Attila spoke.

Their journey toward the southern hub of trade and commerce was drawing near its end, and the sky reflected this. The sun's brilliance now drooped down into the embrace of the clouds and slunk closer to the horizon. The land was covered by an amber hue that the shadows seemed to stretch in as the light continued to fade.

A journey that had once taken them two to three days they had cut down to almost half of one. When they first began venturing to Ceballe, the biggest concern had been camping in the fields overnight. Monsters and bandits roamed the area more prominently under the concealed veil of the moon's shadow. It was very rare for the duo to ever set out past the sun's peak anymore, knowing what lay in store for them, but occasionally they would encounter a ferocious creature from out of the forests. Not all animals that inhabited the area were monstrous; there were still small creatures that had not yet mutated into their carnivoric counterparts. But that did not mean that safety was to be taken for granted.

"Quite an uneventful trip." Darkflare looked around them as he spoke, making sure nothing suddenly popped up from the shadows at his cue. "It seems fortune smiles upon us today."

"Yes, quite a shame. It means we don't have to worry about fighting for our lives today," said Attila with obvious sarcasm that was followed by a frown.

"We'll have enough of that tomorrow. Toughest opponents in the land – can you believe it? I'm excited at the prospect of studying some foreign techniques."

"Study all you want, but it won't help you when we are put against one another. I'll almost feel sorry about beating you."

"What the Pale is that supposed to mean?" Darkflare stopped to glare at Attila, who just kept walking, undaunted.

Darkflare hurried up the hill after Attila, and a grin spread across his face as he stared down below. He was able to make out the large wooden gateway of Ceballe and the hundreds of people that were still flocking in. Scrambling down the rise to follow the path below with Oboro close behind, they hurried to their destination that was illuminated by a row of torchlight along the road.

Sighs escaped both of their lips as they had once again approached the familiar sight and then returned to a slower pace of walking. A wide, arched gate into the city was guarded by four heavily armored men in the royal purple armor of Pheeq, D'sylum's capital. Darkflare was impressed with just how seriously this tournament was being taken; there were usually local militiamen that kept an eye on the entrance, but to actually have soldiers watching over who was coming and going was a step above. To top it off, a banner floated between the two gates high above the ground that read,

"CEBALLE WELCOMES FIGHTERS TO THE ROYAL TOURNAMENT!! BECOME A HERO – EVEN IF JUST FOR ONE DAY!"

As they got closer, the buzz of people and the resonant melody of instruments flooded their eardrums, overpowering any thoughts in Darkflare's head. The guards at the gate checked them over from head to toe, gazed at what arms they carried with them, checked their bags, and nodded once to each young man to give them the go ahead. Oboro landed on Darkflare's shoulder, perched like a bird, so he would remain close to his ally.

The excitement as they stepped past the gate was unlike they had ever seen before. Clowns, jugglers, bards, and all sorts of entertainers were singing, dancing, and performing up and down the street. Children and adults alike were enthralled by the characters. Beautiful women with long hair and beautiful silk dresses were spread out, handing out laurel wreaths of good luck to anyone that appeared to be a tournament fighter. A buxom blonde woman threw one over Darkflare's head as he passed, and he felt his face redden when she smiled at him. She went to do the same to Attila, but he took her hand and kissed it before she finished; and then it was her turn to blush.

Darkflare forced his mind back on the crowd as he continued to stare in awe. It wasn't just the *kind* of people that came to Ceballe – it was the *races* of people! Sure, there were plenty of humans like himself walking around, but he could spot people with scales and tails, peaking high over six feet; lithe, almost frail looking people with pointed features and oddly colored hair; short and stout little humanoids that seemed to sway from too much alcohol; and then even those with feline-like snouts and manes! There was no shortage of different races that came from far and wide to Ceballe, and Darkflare recognized them from his books. The scaled ones were called Ocyalean and Palli – the first being more lizard-like and the latter being more dragon-like – and they did *not* get along. Attila had made the mistake of confusing the two, once, and nearly got thrashed for it. The tall magical beings were known as the astrelites, while the small ones were known as dwellers, and the felines were called the leofer.

The further into the city that they walked, the more electric the energy was. Even though dusk would soon settle, the swell of people seemed ready to continue their merriment until the morning. The smell of ale was pungent, and Darkflare had a feeling that it was the catalyst behind the wide smiles and the hearty laughs, as well as some of the squinting eyes and wobbling legs. Vendors still had their stalls open, lining the streets like walls, calling to every passing person to come see their wares. Darkflare couldn't help but smile at most of the other people foreign to the excitement; their mouths hung open, their eyes wide, and their heads moved in all directions to take things in.

And they moved slower than a slugnar crawling through fresh soil. On streets built wide enough to allow people to walk side by side with carriages coming and going simultaneously, Darkflare and Attila had to dodge and shove their way through countless gawkers. In the time it took them to move from one corner to the next, they would have been halfway through the city on a normal day.

Oboro clung onto Darkflare's shoulder, his claws grasping the material of his shirt and not his skin, as they huddled their way through the crowds. His spade tail smacked the shoulders and heads of people they passed, snapping them out of their awe. Their faces were a mix of amusement and terror as they looked at the small creature leering at them with flaring nostrils. Oboro normally did not like strangers, and Darkflare could only imagine how infuriated his wyvern was to be surrounded by so many more than normal.

To say that Ceballe was a large town would have been a grand understatement, as it was widely renowned as the center of trade in D'sylum. The city had three main paths from the gate forking just south of the center of town. The left path was the main hub of business; not only were there more stalls, shops, and the town's colossal armory, but it also housed the Merchant Guild that was home to auctions for the world's richest and most dignified buyers and sellers. Just beyond that was the warehouse center where all of the guild members stored their goods. Day and night, mercenaries stood watch on every side of the building. It housed extremely expensive relics, and the merchants paid the town a great premium to always have guards posted.

The northern path winded west to where the arena stretched out and towered over a fifth of the town. Not only did it have a central pit where the fighting took place, but inside was also a mini-carnival, lined with games and live events to entertain the noncombatants – especially at points during the year when there were no tournaments being held. The seats took up a great portion, as they were elevated at least a hundred rows high; and because of that, the arena could be seen from the town's entrance, and it was indeed a sight to behold.

As they passed the various vendors, Darkflare did not see anything that caught his eye. Many of the dealers had supposed rare items from all across the reaches of the world, but the majority of what they sold was just refurbished, fancied up junk that the merchants gave a different name to in order to turn a profit. It was always good for a laugh to see what was on sale at a 'one time special price.' One day it would be the 'Hullaballoo Flask of Everlasting Life brought from Eenky-Peenky-Doodleville,' then the next it would be a 'Mushroom of Super-Duper Strength and a Half! from Shazalbazal.'

As far as Darkflare could tell, merchants must have thought that if a name sounded exotic and hard to pronounce, and where it was from appeared on no map known to man, then it would make others believe the item must be worth hundreds of gold. He and Attila knew better though. After traversing the same shops with the same merchants for years, it was obvious who sold what at a reasonable price and who the frauds were.

The further the trio followed the eastern path, the more the herd of bodies thinned. Most of the people gathered around the vendors and shops; the residential area was the quietest side of the town, if such a thing could be found.

Darkflare turned to Attila to say something, but he stopped when he heard someone call his name. He turned back, and the big man with short blond hair he saw coming his way brought a big grin to his face.

"Darkflare, Attila!" Rai Despil came running up to them, a big pearly grin beaming beneath his eyes of blue. He and Darkflare shook hands with a fierce grip, and Rai and Attila nodded to each other.

"Hello, my friend. It's been far too long. Is the rest of your family here?" Darkflare asked, casting a quick gaze behind Rai.

"Yes, we've just arrived! The cart is right up the street — we hadn't even gotten a chance to unload into the house yet."

Rai led them toward a large boxy shape stopped along the side of the road. Rai's father, Hal, and his brother, Angelus, came down from the driver's seat upon seeing the boys. Angelus smiled meekly, pushing back strands of his long blond hair from his face, and the portly Hal embraced the boys one at a time — somehow pulling Attila in for a hug that he clearly did not want.

"Sir Des-... Hal," Darkflare caught himself as he was prone to do, "it's so great to see you all again."

"And you both as well. Can you believe all of the people here? Insanity, I say! This shall surely be a show like no other."

"Yes, and I can't wait to engage in the excitement," Rai beamed beside his father as he leaned against the cart.

"You're actually entering this one, Rai?" Darkflare's eyes grew wide with surprise, but Rai nodded with a shrug.

"This is different from the other tournaments. Plus, you've both grown a great deal since we last squared off."

Darkflare smiled, but it felt like there was a knot in his stomach. Rai had been the reigning champion for several years before meeting the duo. They had both fought against him and had never successfully won; but after hearing their story, getting to know them, and the timely aid they provided to his family, Rai stepped away from tournament fighting. The Despils were a successful farming family from the town of Lylenac in the Beauldyn kingdom; even though they did not need the tournament winnings, they still liked to come and watch the festivities.

"I look forward to it," Attila said, tilting his head. Rai narrowed his brows slightly, but he laughed and tapped the darker-skinned man on the shoulder.

"I say though, this is nearly as impressive as our Harvest Festival, wouldn't you agree, Angelus?" The sheepish boy looked up at his father to say something, but before he could, Hal looked around, puzzled. "Gloria? Where are you? Come on out, Darkflare and Attila are here!"

He rapped his knuckle on the carriage a few times and the door opened. Darkflare could not help but smile as a head of shoulder-length brown hair emerged. Her jade eyes locked with his and returned the smile entirely. He thought a hint of red emerged in her cheeks, and he could feel some in his, but it did not stop him from reaching for her hand and helping her down. Her mother, Pearl, poked her head out from the window and smiled.

"Hello, Madam Des-... Pearl. Pleasure to see you! Gloria, you look elegant as ever, if I do say so myself."

This time the red was evident as she straightened out her dress; it was long white-sleeved with a red bustier and a long flowing blue skirt. Pushing her sandy brown hair behind her ear, she smiled at him.

"And you are as gallant as ever, Darkflare. And hello to you too, Oboro!" Gloria put her hand out toward the wyvern, which Oboro sniffed but turned his head away from, which slightly dismayed Darkflare.

Attila nudged Darkflare in the back with his knuckle, causing him to nearly jump. "Uh, right! We better get going to check in and settle into our room."

"Right, right, on you go, son." Hal clasped Darkflare on the back. He held Darkflare by both shoulders at arm's length and smiled broadly at him underneath a caterpillar brown mustache. "Come stop by the house sometime in the next few days so we can catch up with how you boys have been, eh?"

Every time that Darkflare had entered the Despils' Ceballe home, he had never walked away without a heavy pouch of gold and an even heavier stomach. "I look forward to a delightful evening with even more delightful company."

Hal laughed and jumped back onto the cart. Rai waved goodbye, and Angelus looked as if he were to say something else but never got the chance. Gloria smiled with one last longing look at Darkflare before boarding the carriage, and Pearl waved goodbye as she closed the window.

Darkflare watched them drive off, but his merriment was cut short from the glare he was getting from Attila. "What?"

"I'm hungry."

"I apologize for wanting to greet our friends," Darkflare responded, fixing him with a pointed stare.

"You mean for wanting to see your darling Gl-..."

Darkflare held up a hand. "Yes, yes, onward to food, alright?"

From where they were, the path split once more into three. The furthest one was sealed off by a gate with two armed men standing before it; this was for the people that actually lived in Ceballe. The housing ranged from the upscale mansions of merchants, to the smaller and more rundown shacks of the less-fortunate. The Despils had a rather large mansion, and Darkflare swore he could see the spires of their abode as they walked by.

The middle path led up almost adjacent to the townspeople's gate, and the large white building at the end belonged to the doctor. For as large of a city as Ceballe was, only the best of doctors could call it home – or so Darkflare had heard. He had suffered his fair share of cuts and bruises in tournaments past, but he had never been injured badly enough to seek aid. Many tournament fighters had spoken highly about being stitched up and recovering from injuries quickly, thanks to the doctor.

The closest path, and the one they turned down, brought them toward lanes of musty brown, brick, windowed buildings that were all linked together, wall-to-wall, to create one of the largest inns on the continent of Caelestis. This seemingly droll area of the lavish city was their long awaited destination.

Having been out on the road all day, Darkflare started feeling dizzy from his roaring stomach. The succulent aroma of spices and cooked meals began to deluge his senses; it caused him to salivate, reminding him of exactly why he hadn't eaten breakfast. Ceballe's grander tournaments always had some sort of banquet to prepare their contestants the night before, but the pamphlet given when they signed up informed them it was going to be a *buffet* this time! Between the sizzling smell of meat roasting, the tantalizing tang of boiling stew, or the sweet scent of moist desserts, Darkflare couldn't decide which smell enticed him more!

It looked like they would not have to wait long for food; the lines of people at the three rows of long tables were moving quickly, and smoke steamed high from the fire crystals heating the morsels from beneath.

"So, um... I say we just grab all we can and head to our room," Darkflare mouthed, trying to control the drool from slipping out of his mouth. "Because, well... I don't know about you, but all this food is kind of..."

"Yeah... About that..." Attila nodded in agreement, beginning to move toward the tables before he even finished his thought. Darkflare was right behind him, and of course, so was Oboro.

* * * * *

Darkflare rested the knuckle of his right hand on the front door of the inn. He gave it a slight tap, feeling it give way with nothing behind and no lock to hold it in place. Sneaking his right foot in, he pushed the door fully open, quickly stepping in to catch it with his back.

Above Darkflare's head, a bell rang, causing his eyes to dart toward the desk. A man was sitting there, his elbows propped up and face in his hands. He slowly dropped them from a face that looked ragged. Both his open mouth and his red-rimmed eyes only widened when Attila and Oboro waddled in before the door shut.

Darkflare figured his response would be the same if he saw two young men with their arms stacked with plates – let alone the wyvern or the plates it carried in its clasped wings.

Darkflare's mouth had been stuffed with food, but he licked the gravy off of his lips as best as he could before he spoke.

"Um... Herro!" Darkflare swallowed hard, trying to make room in his mouth for words. "My apologies. Long day. We're Darkflare Omni and Attila Laise, checking in. What room, please?"

The clerk moved his mouth several times, but no noise came out. Eventually he peeled his eyes away from the piles of food and looked up and down the list.

"R-Room Twelve… Omni and Laise. Try not to make a mess, *please!*" The young man collapsed into his palms once more. "We have enough going on as is!"

Darkflare tried to smile as best as he could but almost risked a chunk of potato escaping. So instead he nodded at the man who wasn't paying attention anyway, and the trio sashayed up the stairs, precariously balancing the plates of food.

Darkflare led at a slow pace, inspecting each door as they walked, until they found theirs. There was a golden number twelve nailed to the top of the frame that shined as if it had been polished many times over. Darkflare looked at the handle, slowly brought his right hand down, and extended his pinky finger. After that didn't work, he carefully balanced his plates of food on top of each other and turned the knob with his free hand.

The room was no bigger than if the boys combined both of their bedrooms together. An oak bed was positioned on each side, a round table to rest their things on in the middle, and a chest to store whatever else they needed sat in the corner. Darkflare cautiously placed his plates onto the table, making sure nothing spilled over, unhooked his sword, placed it and his bag on the floor, and then proceeded to plop down onto his bed, all the while still clutching one plate that towered with food. The bed's plaid sheets heaved out with a sigh of exhaustion as Darkflare's rear bounced hard on the springs. Attila did not take the same approach as his friend. Setting his plates, bag, and weapon down, he carefully went to lie down on top of the sheets, as if not wanting to ruin the neatly folded blankets quite yet. Attila stared up at the ceiling for a few moments before expelling a loud belch.

"… That was a good meal."

"Best meal I've had in ages!" Darkflare managed to make out between bites. "Mostly because it's a free buffet!"

He was carefully nibbling on a haunch of meat as Oboro leaped onto the bed and curled himself into a ball. Just looking at the wyvern settle down and begin to rest peacefully made Darkflare yawn.

Attila's boots hit the floor with a loud thud as he kicked them off his feet. Before Darkflare could finish chewing to say something, Attila was already under his blankets, turned toward the wall.

"Sleep? Already? What sort of jest is this? You rushed us here and away from the Despils just to sleep?"

Attila groaned, waving at his friend, as if motioning for him to go away.

"I was hungry. And how many times must I repeat tomorrow is a big day?" he muttered just loud enough for Darkflare to hear. "Go to bed... You wouldn't want..."

Darkflare waited for Attila to finish his sentence, but the rhythmic rising and falling of his body had suggested he had already fallen asleep. And Darkflare knew how much Attila valued his sleep above all else – second only to training!

Darkflare placed the tray of scraps on the table and swung his legs onto the bed carefully, as to not wake Oboro. Laying his head down, he decided Attila was right; sleep did sound like a good idea. As the slender slivers of light from the moon trickled in through the glass pane of the window, Darkflare felt himself drifting away into that beam and leaving to dance with the stars of the night. Tomorrow was going to be a good day.

* * * * *

Darkness swirled away into a blazing inferno as Darkflare's eyes adjusted to the vibrancy of the orange light and a heat that was almost palpable. Everything around him was a haze, which he wasn't sure if it was from the billowing smoke or the nature of this nightmarish landscape. Flames crawled along the corners of rubble, blurring and vibrating like some abomination of a candle; faces of the dead seemed to shift from pain, to peace, to a featureless mask. But the details on this battlefield were clearer than they had ever been – and that worried Darkflare more than any of the chaos that surrounded him.

His first thoughts were to run as far away from the flames as he could, screaming for help. But despite every instinct in his body, no sound escaped and his legs were forced onward. Something, some voice in his mind, was urging him forward, to let the events play out. The message was hard to interpret, but when he finally grasped it, the voice was repeating one word:

Courage.

He stopped trying to fight the dream's forced progression. Despite the overwhelming fear and the urge to flee, there was a part of him that wanted to know what was going to happen and who the mysterious people in the dream were.

The flames curled away from him with every footstep, as if his presence commanded them to move. He reached out a hand and the heat surged as he drew close, but the fire retreated. He thought that this held some significance, but he could not dwell on it, as his attention was drawn to something else.

One house stood apart from the others. There was a stretch of land that had still been perfectly intact, as if the fire did not have the chance to tear it asunder yet. He tried with all of his dreamy might to pursue the image he was seeing, but every time he tried to focus, the house's details blurred more. Darkflare began to taste the cinders inside his mouth, burning his cheeks and tongue. Remaining staring at the house, the heat swelled almost beyond bearing, and his vision blurred intensely. He shook his head and forced himself away from the untouched building, trudging through the sea of dead and the trail of rubble.

There she was. His vision a hazy blur, the earlier clarity was completely gone; but he still could make out that woman on the ground. And her attacker, slowly stalking over his prey. The moment he had feared was about to come again. He could hear her frantic panting, he could just see the tear-and-ash-stained cheeks, and he could feel the fear in her trembling frame as she crawled backward. Why? Why had this... *thing* destroyed her whole town? And why did it leave a single piece of land untouched? He could feel his fist clench as he thought of how helpless he was to do anything.

There it was - the raising of the blade.

Darkflare felt like his heart would leap out of his chest as he watched on helplessly. Her lips parted wide, and Darkflare braced himself for the scream; the piercing cry of a woman about to die. The grip his fist made on nothing tightened as the fire swelled; just like the high tide on Crescentia's beach, the flames rose as Darkflare's rage and agony grew. As the blood-curdling shriek resounded in his ears, it began to blur and fade into one long drawn out pitch – and the blade did not claim her. Instead, the cold steel found a different target.

A man jumped in the way to engage the cruel weapon with a sword that glinted red off both the fire's reflection and the color of his armor. Darkflare tried to focus on the stranger's facial features, but they blurred intensely the more focus he put on them. Besides the heavy armor, the only details he could pick up were his shoulder-length brown hair that seemed to be held back by some sort of headband or bandana similar to Darkflare's own; but nothing of his face registered as concrete. Darkflare was confused about this new twist in the story, but the aggressor turned to look at him, and the young man felt cold and a dreadful fear like never before.

Tears streamed down Darkflare's face and he started screaming; he could now hear his voice, and it came out the same piercing pitch that the woman's had. His eyes were wide open and he could see the flames swirling high around him, hiding the dark figure's baleful gaze.

Then the flames which had graciously parted at his presence rose and engulfed Darkflare within a sweltering, bloodthirsty roar.

* * * * *

Darkflare's whole body was drenched in sweat as he awoke. Panicked, he gazed around the room, taking in every inch and every corner, his breathing heavy. There was nothing. No fire, no bodies, no forces of destruction. There was simply a confused wyvern staring at him, sleepy-eyed, from the end of the bed.

Darkflare tried to figure out what time it was as he returned to his senses. It had to still be relatively early in the morning. The sun's golden rays were just creeping in through the windowpane, similar to the moon beams last night; and Attila had not awoken yet. Sighing, he pet Oboro on the head and then dropped his face into his open palms.

The only thing that resonated in his mind was:

What the Pale does this damn dream mean?

Chapter III

Darkflare sat with his back against the headboard, one hand massaging Oboro's earfrills, while his eyes absently stared at the sunlight splayed across the wooden floorboards. He wasn't sure how long he had been awake for. He had just been sitting, rubbing Oboro's head, alone with his thoughts, since he awoke from the nightmare.

The silence that he'd grown accustomed to was broken by the dull hum of activity outside the closed window, which brought him back to his senses. Darkflare turned his head at a noise inside the room and noticed Attila's body shuffling direction. When their eyes met, Attila's opened wide and a curious look worked its way into his aggressive features. Attila shook long black strands of hair out of his face as he sat up and draped his legs over the bed.

"You dreamt again last night."

Darkflare did not respond for several moments. After being alone with his thoughts, contemplating the meaning of his lucid dream for several hours, it felt as if there were rocks in his throat. He exhaled deeply, ran a hand through his spiked hair, and shut his eyes.

"Yeah. It was... even more unreal this time." Darkflare finally said, his eyes fluttering back open.

"Tell me about it," Attila must have noticed that Darkflare was already wearing his armor and was ready to go, as he wasted no time jumping up and throwing his gear on.

"It's that same damn one that I've been having lately. There's fire everywhere – fire and death. It's like... like someone started a fire that swelled into an inferno and swallowed a town whole, belching up dead corpses and ash and rubble. I don't know where it takes place or what caused the carnage, but the dream shifts to a point where there's a woman trying to escape a murderer. I tried to help her this time, but I couldn't do a thing. I felt so... helpless. And her scream, Attila..." Darkflare took a moment to exhale an audible, slow breath. "It's the most piercing and terrible thing I've ever heard. Maybe it was the dream that made it so vivid, but everything was just so real."

Attila had simply nodded after a brief period of time, listening still as he had bent down to buckle his boots.

"Does anyone actually die in your dream? Do you see it firsthand?"

"No... I see corpses strewn all around, but I don't actually witness anyone dying. Maybe the woman dies, but my vision becomes too blurred to tell or even see her face. I know she was crying though; I could see the tears on her cheeks but nothing else. When I look quick enough, I can see pieces of the puzzle, but if I try to focus, she just becomes one giant blur. The new element of the dream was that there was a male figure that stepped in the way of the blade this time. He was wearing some sort of demonic helmet, so I couldn't see his face either. But as they clashed blades, it felt like a great surge of emotions and raw power ran through me. And then the flames swarmed upon me."

"What sort of power?"

"I'm not sure." Darkflare looked down at his open palms. They tingled as if he was trying to warm them before a fireplace. "I just felt this indescribable force overwhelming my whole body, threatening to burst from within."

"Right. And how do you feel now?"

"Uneasy." Darkflare paused before continuing on. "Waking up felt weird, but now I just have this sense of... dread. Like something's not right." Darkflare plopped his arms down and shook his head. "I just wish I knew where it was all taking place."

"Well, you said it's in ruins, right? Could it be Syvail?"

"It could be, but I don't think so. It didn't seem to have nearly as many buildings as Syvail seemed to have – in fact, it looked much more open. The walls seemed smaller, not as thick."

"You're into all of that fate rubbish. What if you're seeing a prediction of a future battle to happen there?"

"Ha! Nice try, but no. I just don't get the feeling that it's Syvail."

"What about the old Crescentia?"

Darkflare opened his mouth, ready to say something, but his voice failed him. He had considered the rather obvious choice, but he had denied thinking it possible. At least, he *wanted* to deny it possible. He shook his head, looking away from Attila.

"I have very loose memories about what Crescentia looked like before the fire. I don't even want to think about what it would mean or what this dream is trying to tell me if that's the case."

"Well," Attila stood, slid his claymore's sheath into a strap on his back, and then opened the door, "you might have all of the answers that you need."

As Attila exited, Oboro began to stir. He was still rather sleepy-eyed, after being awoken by Darkflare's state of frenzy earlier. Letting out a yawn, he crawled over to his ally, who met him with a smile and rub of the chin. Darkflare swung his legs out of his bed and equipped his weapon to his waist.

The thoughts of the tournament quelled any restless memories of the dream still wandering in his mind. As he went to follow Attila out the door, he glanced toward the large stacks of plates that still resided on the table. Oboro let out a coo of confusion to Darkflare, tilting his head sideways ever so slightly.

"We'll just leave those right there. The leftovers will serve as a victory feast for when we win!"

Darkflare shut the door behind him and Oboro once he was sure he had everything. Oboro leapt up onto his master's shoulder, much like he had done the day before, folding his wings in. Darkflare gave his wyvern another pat on the head before he turned to jog down the stairs. The attendant from the day before was not at the desk, but the woman who was had a sour expression on her face, as if she hadn't had much better of a night.

"Have a pleasant day!" Darkflare smiled at her as he passed, giving her a wave. He saw her expression rise ever so slightly just before the door closed behind him. Attila was leaning against the wall outside, and once Darkflare joined his companion, they set off.

The aroma of spices and sweets was still as savory as the day before, trailing the boys as they proceeded back to the main path. The further from the inn they walked, the louder the buzz of activity got. Most merchants had already opened their stalls, ready for the people just waking up or making their way back to Ceballe for the day's monumental event. Darkflare's heart fluttered with anxiousness and excitement as they took the northern pass at the cross. He glanced at Attila, but he was as stone-faced as ever, his head held high as he stared at the building ahead.

The arena's entranceway was already swarming with men and women of all shapes, sizes, and races who were conversing and psyching themselves up for the fights ahead. Some wore heavily armored mail, adorned with a crest representing family or kingdom; some wore regular clothing, probably to help with agility; there were those like Darkflare and Attila who wore light armor; and then there were some strange few that wore such *little* clothing that Darkflare had to assume their strategy was to distract the opponent rather than duel them.

Once Darkflare spotted the blond head of hair of the tall Rai, it didn't take them long to catch up to the heavily armored man. He turned to greet them, his brother and sister beside him.

"Morning Despil family," Darkflare waved, looking around. "Where are your parents?"

"Father and mother are off searching for the perfect seat," Gloria beamed at Darkflare with a chipper voice. He couldn't help but smile back.

"Good thing you all got here when you did. I don't know what's going to be worse – fighting for seats above or fighting for entertainment down below!"

"A tough choice indeed!" Rai chuckled and then turned to Attila, throwing some play punches toward him. "How's it going there, bruiser? You ready to try and take me down a peg?"

"Hmph." Attila narrowed his eyes, the slightest twitch forming at the corner of his mouth. "I won't need to try. You've seen how much better I've become."

Rai laughed again, clasping Attila hard on the shoulder. Darkflare turned his attention toward the middle Despil child. "Angelus, you're not going to try and enter?"

"Oh, I would stand no chance." Angelus shook his head with a sheepish smile, pushing aside a strand of his ponytail that had fallen out from behind his ear.

"You've been training under your brother for how long now?"

Rai stepped forward and grabbed his brother with his other meaty hand. "Angelus has as much natural skill with a sword as either of you two do – Pale, he could probably surpass me if he put his mind to it! But he's too busy trying to follow in my father's footsteps."

"It's honestly just a hobby," Angelus shrugged off Rai's grip. "One that I only pursue because you pushed it onto me, brother. I really have no intention of doing anything serious with wielding a weapon. I can make a better impact on this world by taking up father's craft. The fighting and showmanship is all your area of expertise."

"Angelus, we should probably get going," Gloria butted in, grabbing her brother's arm. "Mother and father will begin to worry if we don't hurry."

"Indeed. Good luck, you three."

"Try not to get hurt!" Gloria looked at Darkflare as she said that, and he nodded back to her.

"You have my word that I shall not maim your brother – but no promises on Attila. Depends on how broody he gets."

The darker haired man shot Darkflare a glare that was almost as threatening as his sword, and Gloria and Angelus departed from the trio.

"Come on," Rai inclined his head. "Let's get going, my friends."

As they made their way past all of the other combatants and entered the arena, there were two paths that split at the gateway. To the left was the ascension to the seats, and Darkflare caught one last glimpse of Gloria and Angelus as they searched for their parents. Soon enough, that whole area would be filled to capacity with people cheering and hollering for their favorite competitors. In all of the years he had come here, he had never seen the arena sell out – it had filled up tremendously, but never to capacity. It was astonishing seeing the seats already as filled as if a normal tournament was underway.

Turning his attention back to the more important matters, he followed Attila and Rai to the right – the path that led to the fighter's pit. As they approached the stairwell down, they were stopped by a bald dweller with a long matted beard and smudged glasses. He was sweating profusely and kept wiping his shiny dome with a handkerchief.

"Names?" he questioned the boys, looking them up and down.

"Rai Despil," the charismatic man said, holding out a piece of paper, sanctioned by the town of Ceballe, as his fighter's registration.

"...Attila Laise," said the brooding one, pulling out his own paper.

"Darkflare Omni," he chimed in last, fishing his identification out from beneath his brigandine. Before even looking over the information, the dweller glared at the wyvern on Darkflare's shoulder.

"Woah, wait a minute! What is that? Do you have authorization for that thing?"

"Mave, is it?" Darkflare held back a sigh and forced a smile as the dweller stared blankly at him. "Yes, I do. Bottom half of that paper you have in your hand. While I'm sure you see so many people come through here, how many do you see come bout after bout with a wyvern?"

The dweller squinted hard for a moment, and then he smacked his head. "Oh, it's you! Drak... Darre..." He looked at Darkflare's paperwork very closely. "Darkflare! I remember you now. Go on, go on. Sorry about that."

He smiled once more as he passed the stout man. When Mave tried to put his hand out to pet Oboro, the wyvern slunk away, turning his snout up in annoyance.

"Every damn time," Attila grumbled under his breath as they headed down a stairwell.

"Expertly handled though, Darkflare," Rai nodded. "I'm not sure if I would have had as much patience as you. Little fellow really does not like other people though, does he?"

"Nope," Darkflare put his hand up to the wyvern, and Oboro rubbed his head against the gloved hand lovingly. "I'm the lucky one."

They descended in a spiral for several feet, lit all the while by torches at intervals where it seemed the shadows were about to engulf their path in darkness. As they descended downward, the noise from the crowd began to soften until they reached the bottom, where it could be heard no more than a faint whisper. The atmosphere below was much more solemn than above, a quiet that Darkflare found unsettling in all of Ceballe's madness. The room that awaited them was a large waiting area that was at least three times Darkflare's house in length. It was lit by candlelight, much like the rest of the descent had been. Several wooden tables stretched out across the entirety of the room, allowing the participants to sit and rest before their fight - but that seemed to be the last thing on many of the entrants' minds.

At least half of the assembled competitors either stood in deep thought or stretched their limbs as they waited for the first round to begin. There was some hushed small talk between different groups of people, but it was resoundingly quieter in the chamber than the excitement above.

To the side of the tables was a square board with a detailed chart drawn on it. The trio made their way toward it, receiving various stares and glances as they passed. Darkflare cautiously scanned the room of faces glaring at him. This time, the attention was not solely because of the wyvern on Darkflare's back. While there were a small number of people he recognized, most were unfamiliar, newcomers to Ceballe's tournament scene. There was usually a general feeling of respect in the pit, especially knowing Darkflare and Attila's continued wins; but the eyes that fell upon him were hungry, no doubt looking to gain a name, and sizing up the trio that walked down the middle of the room.

As they looked over the board, Darkflare felt a mix of excitement and concern wash over him when he spotted his name.

"Ha!" Rai pressed his finger onto the board below the words 'Darkflare Omni'. "First round! You better not choke. You'll be setting the stage for the rest of us to follow!"

"Or do." Attila shrugged. "It'll just make us all look better."

Darkflare nodded as he looked over the board, trying to hide some of the anxiety over being first in a tournament of this grandeur. "Fine by me. I'd rather dive right in and let the adrenaline fuel me instead of letting it play on my nerves. It's you I worry about, Attila. Dead last! What poor luck."

"What are you talking about? That is the best spot. I can let the time pass in silence and wait peacefully while fools like you worry your energy away."

"Well don't get too peaceful," Rai pointed to his own name, just slightly away from Attila. "If we both win our first matches, you and I will be opponents in the second round."

"Oh, good. I was worried you'd knock Darkflare out before I had the chance."

An onlooker snorted his laughter as he overheard the young men talking. Darkflare narrowed his eyes and turned to stare at the stranger. He stood a good half foot taller than Darkflare and had a poof of curly, red-orange hair with a matching chin beard of the same fiery color. His face screamed with cockiness as a smug expression wrapped his features in confidence. He shook his head and smiled toward Darkflare, showing off his putrid yellow, rotting teeth.

"So you're my opponent, eh, boy? Bwahaha! They couldn't even give me someone who'd hit manhood yet, eh?"

Rai seemed ready to charge forward and strike the man, but Darkflare grabbed him by the arm to stop him.

"Rai, it's alright, don't worry. This isn't anything out of the ordinary for newcomers, at least since the last time you entered."

"Are you kidding me?" Rai reared on Darkflare, a look of rage boiling behind his eyes. Darkflare let go of him, and he swung back around into the stranger's face. "This is the sort of scum that has been allowed to enter the *Royal* Tournament? Smug rats who think they can talk down upon and belittle others?"

The man's cheeks darkened to a shade of red as he backed away from Rai. "Wh-Who the Pale do you think you are?!"

"Me?!" Rai nearly roared, looking around at the gathered competitors. "The pit is a place for respect and meditation before a fight. This arena is a place for showmanship and honor. You want to bully someone? Get out on to the streets and talk down to your fellow rats!"

Rai threw an arm out, nearly striking the man, and pointed toward the stairwell.

The aggressor sputtered for words, but eventually he stormed away, cursing under his breath about needing air. Rai ran a hand through his hair as he tried to calm himself down, and he looked around at the others. Some were giving him a nasty glare, but many refused to meet his gaze. He plopped down at one of the empty tables, and Darkflare reluctantly sat next to him, Attila across from them. Oboro leapt off and curled into a ball at Darkflare's feet.

"Thanks, I think, Rai. Not too many of those anymore, but occasionally, we encounter newcomers who think they have to show off. Settling it in the arena usually shuts them up."

"It's usually the quiet ones we have to watch out for," Attila added.

"You mean like the one in the corner over there?"

Rai raised his hand to point, and Darkflare turned his head to look to the right. His eyes glanced upon a figure leaning against the wall, clad in a white hooded cloak. No distinct person could be seen underneath; their face, hands, legs, and whole body were hidden beneath the white cloth. At first, Darkflare did not even believe it to be a real person but instead a hanging coat. It seemed too unrealistic and motionless to be living. As if the mysterious person had taken enough of Darkflare's gawking, the hooded face turned to stare right in his direction. He could not see the eyes beneath, but he felt them fixed upon him. His gaze was forced away, and after a few moments, he leaned forward and hushed his voice to a whisper.

"Attila… Check it out."

Cautiously and very slowly to make it seem less obvious, Attila craned his neck in the direction Darkflare had been staring moments before; he drew back his gaze just as quickly as Darkflare did.

"You failed to mention that it's staring right at us," Attila said, as he narrowed his eyes.

"You able to see a face?"

"No."

"Something about it gives me the chills."

Darkflare could not put his finger on what exactly about the figure unsettled him, but the fact that his usually undaunted comrade seemed perturbed worried him even more.

Rai drummed his fingers on the table as he stared at the figure. "I don't see what the big deal is. Oooh, spooky cloth!"

Just as Darkflare was about to speak, the large brown double doors close to where the mysterious hooded figure stood swung open.

A man with slicked back red hair and a forced smile walked through the door in a long silk robe. He looked around at all of the competitors and kept rubbing his hands together. This man was the owner of the arena, and Darkflare was sure that instead of seeing people around the hall, he was seeing big gold coins. His hands stopped rubbing each other and he swiftly clapped them together in a quick, cheery motion which returned the room to silence once again.

"Hello, one and all, and thank you for coming! The first round in the Royal Tournament is about to begin! The first round will showcase…" The owner, Rafiel, cleared his throat and pulled out a small piece of paper from inside his robe. He held it out at arm's length and stared for several moments, but then he quickly put it away. "Oleander Keefe against Darkflare Omni! Will the combatants please follow me?"

Darkflare stood and was met with cold and calculating stares, just as before. Oboro gave him a nod, as if understanding he would have to remain with Attila. He shook hands with Rai, bumped fists together with Attila, and then Darkflare hurried after Rafiel.

His opponent, Oleander Keefe, still had not returned. Darkflare knew that Rai had a vicious streak, but he was afraid his friend had gone too far; he hoped that Rai had not scared his opponent off from competing. The whole reason for entering the tournament was to put on a good show before the rulers; and how was he supposed to do that if his opponent quit? He reached for the Drachenfaith under his armor, pulled it out, and began to fidget with it as his nerves invaded his thoughts.

The hallway ended at a door and two paths. The owner, who never remembered Darkflare's name despite how many times he'd seen him, gestured him off to the right and disappeared behind the door without so much as a 'good luck.' Rafiel was off to the spectator's box, where the heralds and tournament officials watched, safe and high above the fights.

Following the trail of candles, Darkflare came to a pair of ten foot high wooden doors. These were painted with rich swirls of gold, silver, and blue, and on the other side was the arena. Taking a deep breath, Darkflare put the necklace back under his armor and forced himself to try and relax. He could hear the audience roaring with excitement on the other side. The stands had to have filled up by now.

But the excitement and energy that he could feel reverberating through the floor didn't daunt him. Darkflare closed his eyes and focused his thoughts.

He was ready.

* * * * *

Oleander Keefe grabbed the wineskin from the merchant, throwing a few coins at him as he guzzled down some of the liquid. The brute with the poof of flaming red hair pushed his way through the throng of spectators coming into the arena, moving back out into Ceballe. He needed some air, badly. Needed time to think. Needed to calm himself down from those puny beanpoles.

"Little upstarts think they can embarrass me, eh?" Keefe muttered as he pushed past a group of laughing young children.

He had been walking for a few minutes now and had managed to make his way to the outskirts of the city. It was quiet out here; everyone was at the tournament – some merchants remained open, but the streets were much emptier than when he strolled into town.

Few more minutes, Keefe thought to himself. He needed to drain this wineskin badly. He took a long swig of the liquid within, his lips feeling as if they'd never be satiated.

No sooner than as he started to calm down did he hear a loud gurgling from outside the gates. At first, he did not pay much attention to it. The guards must have been detaining some rabble who had gotten smart with them. While he had no room to talk about back-talk, he knew not to push his luck against anyone with real authority. He just cursed them out behind their backs where he was safely out of earshot.

Seconds later, he heard the same bodily noise again, but this time it was louder and more distressed, and he nearly thought it sounded like someone trying to scream for help. Keefe's heartbeat started to race as he looked toward the gateway. The guards never got so vicious as to kill someone, and besides, these were royal guards – weren't they trained in how to detain people or something? He took several cautious steps toward the source of the noises, curiosity taking the reins from all common sense.

He stopped. Jaw open, some strange high-pitched noise came out instead of the scream he wanted. The wineskin dropped from his hand and hit the ground, right next to the bodies of the soldiers that lay dead before him.

* * * * *

Minutes ticked by and still the double doors remained like a wall impeding Darkflare's path. He crossed his arms, breathing deeply and slowly as he tapped his foot increasingly quicker. Had this Keefe person really not been able to take Rai's verbal lashing, when he was the antagonist originally? Maybe he was playing a mind game with Darkflare. Maybe Keefe wanted Darkflare to try to go find him, and right when he was leaving, Keefe would run in and steal a forfeited victory from Darkflare. He gritted his teeth at the thought of being toyed with like that. He turned around to look down the hallway he had come, but there was nothing unusual.

Just above the roaring of the crowd, Darkflare finally heard the trumpets blaring, and he turned back around. He jumped up and down a little bit, shaking his limbs out, and a smile stretched across his face. Keefe must have finally shown up!

The doors swung open and the fever from the crowd was louder than anything Darkflare had ever experienced, almost forcing him to cover his ears. As he ran out into the illuminated center, his eyes could hardly take in all of the people that sat above him. Rows and rows of spectators were cheering for him, from the young to the old, men and women, everyone stood on their feet cheering. Reaching for the handle of his longsword, Darkflare extracted the blade from its scabbard and thrust it high into the air, emitting a hoot that was devoured by the rest of the screaming fans. He quickly, and in vain, tried to find Gloria among the crowd.

Besieged by the energy the crowd was putting out, Darkflare completely forgot about Keefe. He looked across to the door opposite of him, and it was still shut. His smile began to fade, and he gripped the handle of his longsword even tighter. The massive throng of people began to quiet down to a murmur as they noticed his lack of an opponent.

Just when Darkflare thought he'd grind his teeth out of his head, the doors finally creaked open ever so slightly. The crowd fell to complete silence and Darkflare narrowed his eyes at the unusual sight. He looked up to the owner, who was yelling and pointing at the heralds in the box. They controlled the doors, and if they didn't know what was going on, then something was definitely awry. There was some muttering from the crowd again, and he turned to look back at the gateway. From the darkness that the doors concealed, he managed to make out a shape emerging. It was a short, hobbled man who-...

No; the man was not short, but he was bent over as he hobbled out. The pitiful thing that emerged was a wounded man – a man that Darkflare barely recognized from only minutes earlier – his opponent, Oleander Keefe. People cried out in shock and disgust as the bloodstained man limped toward the center of the arena.

"What in the Pale…"

Darkflare sheathed his sword and ran toward the man. It was obvious that Keefe's strength was about to give way, and Darkflare was not sure what he could do. As he reached Keefe, the man's body frame gave a heave and collapsed into Darkflare's outstretched arms. Darkflare looked him over several times. Five arrows jutted out from his back, blood had begun to trickle from his lips, and his gut had a rather large gash in it that a crimson trail seeped out along the ground where he had walked. It was all fresh, which in itself caused questions to run through Darkflare's mind, but there was no time to ask any of them. As Keefe stared up at him, his brown eyes quivered with fear, trying hard to remain still and focus on the young man that was holding him. His face was pale with terror, but he tried his best to focus one last confident expression. Tears stained his cheeks as he forced open his mouth just enough to whisper to Darkflare.

"Bandits… They… They're everywhere. You're all… doomed."

Darkflare's head shot up as, if on cue, the crowd broke out into panic and bloodcurdling screams came raining down on him. He could see people moving and pushing as they fought to get out of the arena. There were so many bodies moving, he couldn't make out the Despils, nor would he have been able to tell what the four rulers looked like. His stomach heaved as he watched the violent emptying of the stands, helplessly.

He turned back to the body in his hands. Keefe had stopped moving; it had been long seconds since his last tremendous exhale. It was the first time Darkflare had seen a dead person this close, let alone held them in his arms. Even though he didn't know Keefe, he felt himself quivering. A life had just been snuffed out, and he held the remains in his hands. He slowly lowered Keefe to the ground.

"Darkflare!"

Hearing his name, Darkflare leapt up and drew his longsword once more. He exhaled and shook his head when he saw it was Attila with his own sword in hand and faithful Oboro by his side. Attila motioned imperatively to hurry with his free hand. Oboro cooed anxiously as he witnessed his master returning.

"We've got to move," Attila motioned down the tunnel as Darkflare followed. "The others already headed back up. Rai went with them to find his family. An attendant came down and was screaming about bandits, so all Pale must be breaking loose above."

"I hope Rai gets to them." Darkflare paused before he continued. "That guy, Keefe. He's dead."

"What?" Attila shot Darkflare a sideways glance as they retraced their footsteps down the passageway.

"He must have used a back passage to come back in... He limped out into the arena with arrows sticking out of his back and a stab wound. It looked like he got sliced up and then got drawn on while he was running away."

"Hmph. Shame."

"Did Rai cause his death? Did... Did we, by just being there? Was he fated to die here either way, or could we have prevented it?"

"Everyone has to die at some point. There's no such thing as fate. His pompous attitude was his own undoing."

"I suppose." Darkflare gulped as they rounded a corner. He was thankful it was clear. "Attila, is this really happening? Bandits? *How?* I can't even remember the last time there was a bandit uprising of this scale; Pale, I thought that the armies still existed primarily to prevent situations like this from happening!"

"I don't know. But it seems like the whole town is in chaos right now."

"But..." Darkflare's eyes bulged as he thought. "How did they get past the knights that were stationed all over town? How *could* they have? I mean, if the rulers are here, and they brought their best soldiers... How many bandits are here?"

"Calm down," Attila's tone was sharp. "We can't assume anything is certain until we get up there and see for ourselves."

"Right," Darkflare nodded, not quite as confident as his friend. "Regardless, it looks like we'll have to put our dreams of knighthood on hold."

"For now. But we can still smash some skulls to make up for it."

Darkflare nodded grimly. As they returned to the waiting room, it seemed much more spacious now that it was empty. However, that solitude lasted no more than a moment before they were joined by others. Like twin embodied specters materializing from the shadows, two bulky men paraded into the room from the stairwell wielding broadswords. Their faces were intense, and something in their dour expressions almost looked inhuman. At first, Darkflare had mistaken them for tournament entrants coming to aid them, but upon closer inspection of their attire, Darkflare readied his blade.

It seemed the two men, covered from head to toe in mismatched, ragged leather armor, slipped past the others. The men had on bandanas that covered their heads and hid most of their long, grimy hair, as well as confused looking wrist guards that could not decide if they were leather or bandaged cloth by their tattered demeanor. Their bodies were barely shielded by frayed leather armor mixed with patches of metal coverings, which exposed more than half of their chest. They wore no armor whatsoever on their legs – simply loose fitting pants that seemed to have been made from a similar tattered material that their headpieces and guards were made from.

Darkflare was more confused now that he saw the men in front of them. If these were the bandits that Keefe claimed to have seen, how could they have possibly beaten the soldiers of the four nations? *These* were the bandits that were attacking the town that was supposed to be filled with skilled warriors? It did not make sense.

The two ruffians locked eyes with the young men and did not stop as they hustled toward them. Attila wasted no time in charging at one of them, bringing his sword up horizontally and managing to push his foe back and pin him to the wall with the blunt side of his weapon. Darkflare was surprised; he knew Attila was strong, but the brutality behind the manhandling was unexpected. He did not have long to revel in his friend's glory, as he was suddenly brought back to the reality of their situation when he refocused on the cold stare from the other bandit.

Darkflare held his longsword low, Oboro sneering at his side. There was something dark and lethal about the way the bandit held himself. His eyes were cold and seemed to be devoid of any sign of emotion. Darkflare refused to back down; if anything, he felt more invigorated than ever to stop them from ransacking a town he had come to call his second home.

Letting loose a guttural battle cry, the bandit ran toward Darkflare, which caused Oboro to rise and take cover in the overhead rafters. Readying himself to counter the man's attack, Darkflare met the bandit halfway and crossed swords in a swift clash of metal that resounded harshly throughout the empty, hollow hall. The strength behind the blow was unexpected and nearly knocked Darkflare off his feet. This bandit was not fighting for show and a surrender – he was fighting to take Darkflare's life.

Both men recoiled with great fluidity and whipped their arms back in attack again. Blade upon blade met and clashed several times, and Darkflare felt himself losing ground, trying to back up from the intense attacks that poured down upon him.

Darkflare did not panic. His mind raced, taking in his surroundings, analyzing his enemy's movements, his brain innately making calculations that would have taken much longer outside of the fight. He felt himself slipping into a completely different, concentrated mentality that was all too familiar to him.

As the bandit began to swing his sword in a vertical motion for the umpteenth time, Darkflare noticed how his aggressor was overreaching his attacks and trying to pursue him with unbridled aggression and ferocity, and there were less well-focused and aimed strikes. He foresaw the incoming angle of the blade and reacted by shifting the weight of his body to the right. With a quick tuck and press of his legs, Darkflare rolled away from his attacker, dodging the attack before his antagonist had a chance to recoil.

By the time that his foe turned, Darkflare was ready to rise to his feet. As he leapt up, his sword soared through the air beside him and stabbed deep into the ribcage of his opponent. Open mouthed, the bandit stared astoundingly at Darkflare, as if mystified that he underestimated his foe so greatly. As black liquid began to ooze from both the wound that Darkflare had created and the man's already suspended jaw, the bandit did not relent.

He rushed forward again, and Darkflare, too surprised at how the man was able to still be standing, took the full force of the tackle that knocked him back, pinning him to the wall under the man's weight. Darkflare gasped as an open hand came up to his throat and squeezed, raising him slightly off the ground. He fought to control the panic as he stared into the red, lifeless eyes of his opponent; no other emotion on his face. The sword arm was being raised, and Darkflare reacted. He grabbed his own weapon that was still lodged in the bandit's sternum with both hands and drove the blade up with all of the might he had in him. His foe's eyes widened, and finally, the grip he had on Darkflare was released, and both men fell to the ground.

A series of coughs racked Darkflare's body as he fought to inhale air again, but he stopped and stared with wide eyes at his opponent as reality began to set in.

He had mortally wounded someone. This was the first time that he had ever fought to kill, and he had taken another person's life. It did not matter whether they were good or evil, right or wrong. Who was he to do such a thing?!

Darkflare stood and yanked the sword out of the dying man. He flew backward with such force that he almost ended up falling onto his rear, only to be caught again by the wall. His sword clattered to the ground by his feet. The shock of his actions had dissolved the polished control he had when fighting, and he had not realized how much effort he put into removing the sword.

He stared at the expressionless look that death wrapped around the bandit's face, and it made Darkflare so sick that he felt the urge to vomit grow stronger with every second he glared disdainfully at what he'd done.

That urge dissipated into something more akin to horror as he watched the body spasm; it stiffened like a board, arms flailed for a moment before righting themselves, and his foe let out an unworldly screech. The skin turned more pale to an almost gray, the pupils' bloodshot red taking over the entirety of the eyes, and there was a strange marking on his neck. Like the snap of two fingers, the man disintegrated into a puff of black smoke that faded away into the shadows.

Darkflare stood still, staring at the spot where the bandit had once been. His jaw hung open, but no sound escaped as he wracked his brain in thought. There was no body and no bloodstain. He reached down slowly with trembling hands to pick up his sword, and he looked at the blade. There was a coat of black liquid on it, the same that dripped out of the wound of the "man," and whatever it was definitely was *not* blood.

The flame of courage burns bright. Do not be afraid to grasp what is rightfully yours. This is your birthright, this is your purpose.

The words came out of nowhere, but he was enthralled the moment he heard them being whispered into his mind. He knew this voice. It was the one from his dream. It was almost as if he was taken out of the moment in time, and the deep voice was speaking only to him. But what did they mean…? Courage…?

He felt a hand grab his shoulder, and Darkflare turned, poised to strike. When he realized it was Attila, he relaxed slightly, but the confusion over the events that just unfolded forced him to keep his weapon up. Darkflare searched Attila's face for any emotion, any sign that he was going through the same thing he was, but there was no remorse for either the dead men or Darkflare's struggle. In the low light, with the same black liquid dripping from his sword, he looked almost sinister.

"Come on. We need to hurry."

Darkflare looked over to where Attila had been fighting the other bandit. There was no sign of him, and Darkflare faintly remembered hearing some sort of wailing during his personal turmoil.

"Are you not at all concerned about what just happened?! I've never killed anyone before, but I'm pretty sure they don't drip black liquid or just vanish into nothingness when they die!"

"Something's not right. We need to figure out what's going on or there are going to be a lot more innocent people dead." Attila turned to move toward the stairs, but he stopped and turned back to Darkflare. "You knew it was going to come to this when you picked up your sword; you knew the day would come when you would have to kill someone."

Darkflare could just barely hear the frenzied crowd far above once he was snapped back to reality. He had heard everything that Attila had said, but somewhere, deep in the back of his mind, he couldn't shake that voice that had been speaking to him. Darkflare stared into his friend's eyes. He nodded his head and a heavy sigh escaped from the depths of his gut which placated the feeling of nausea.

Oboro floated down to nudge his master in the arm. The sign from his wyvern, as small as it was, was enough to make him speak.

"You're right, Attila. It's just…" Words did not feel as much like knives to speak, but Darkflare still had to collect himself. "This was the first time I've ever killed anyone. It doesn't matter if his intentions were right or wrong, nor that I didn't know him; that was still a person I just killed… I think. And it doesn't matter if he – it – whatever just… poofed. How…?" Darkflare hesitated, patting his cooing wyvern on the head lightly. "How has none of this not even bothered you in the slightest?"

"While it was *your* first slain," Attila began to walk away but stopped at the foot of the staircase without turning back to look at Darkflare. "What makes you think it was mine?"

With that, Attila disappeared up the spiral passage. That comment was the last thing that Darkflare expected to hear from him, but he was not in a situation where he could dwell over it. Attila was right, it was either kill or be killed in real fights. Darkflare did not have time to mourn the thing that would have just as easily taken his life had the opportunity arisen, but he would atone for the death later to… whatever deity was listening, Mokiwana or whatever god ruled over the lives of mortals. The most important thing was now focusing on helping the civilians.

Chapter IV

The dialogue with Attila kept replaying itself in Darkflare's mind, distracting him from the strange visceral liquid on his sword. They had been all but brothers for so many years, growing up together and reveling in each other's accomplishments; and at some point in time, Attila could have killed someone without Darkflare knowing.

He couldn't have been more than halfway up the stairwell before the hysteria from the town became more deafening than the cheers Darkflare received earlier, pushing Attila's cryptic words out of his mind. He quickened his pace, taking the steps two at a time, until he came out on top, where the noise was all-encompassing, overwhelming his senses to the point where he could not hear his own thoughts. Mass carnage surrounded him as he rejoined Attila in the main hall; people were trying to flee, yelling and screaming, as both fighters and soldiers alike were trying to fight back against an overwhelming number of the berserker bandits.

Attila stole through the thinnest area of the crowd and pushed his way out of one of the open doorways. Without even thinking, Darkflare pressed through the crowd of people as he rushed after Attila. He stole a glance back at Oboro, who hurried to land on Darkflare's shoulder and hold tight. The last thing either one of them wanted was to get separated in the current madness.

Darkflare had been in the dimly-lit passages for so long that when they finally exited the arena, he had to shield his eyes from the sunlight. He didn't have much time to adjust his vision. Darkflare was jostled forward from the surge of people, and although he nearly lost his balance, he pushed forward after Attila. There was fighting happening everywhere; people were ducking into alleys fighting blade-to-blade with bandits, but some had spilled out into the streets. It seemed contained to backroads and passages between buildings that Darkflare didn't even know existed, but it was clear there was a massive force of raiders attacking Ceballe.

And there was so much blood. And if these 'bandits' didn't bleed red like the ones he and Attila fought...

Darkflare could not help but wonder if the nations' rulers were safe as he fought not to lose Attila in the frenzied crowd. Even more anarchy on a worldwide scale would emerge if any of them were to fall victim here. Whatever these invaders' motives were, it couldn't be a coincidence that they decided to attack the one day all four leaders were gathered. But what *was* the reason? Politics? Gold? The desire for anarchy? This was on a scale too grand for Darkflare to wrap his head around.

And what about the Despils? Even if Rai had gotten to them, would they be safe against... whatever these things were?

A break in the wall a few feet ahead caught Darkflare's attention. Coming up to his right was a thin alley that the crowd seemed to ignore. It was a shot in the dark, but if they could somehow find a way onto the rooftops, they could escape the crowd and get to the heart of the trouble easier.

Darkflare managed to grab Attila's shoulder and then forced his way through to the right. Darkflare glanced back to make sure Oboro was hanging on okay and Attila was still with him; luckily no one else had followed. Darkflare had taken a gamble, and reaching the far end of the alley, he was glad he had trusted his gut.

"A ladder!" Darkflare exclaimed to the other two in great joy, pointing to the wooden ascension at the end of the alley. "We can get up there to get a better v-..."

Attila dashed deeper into the corridor and had one foot on the first step before Darkflare managed to finish his thought. Darkflare sighed as he hurried after his friend, and Oboro hopped off and glided up with a few beats of his wings to meet them on the roof.

As Darkflare reached the top and looked out on Ceballe, his heart sank. Thick trails of smoke wafted into the air from numerous spots in the city. The Merchant Guild was probably on fire, the residential area too, and Pale only knew how many shops and stalls. He could see that the bandits were being fought back to scattered pockets across the city, but their numbers made it seem like they were far from defeated.

His eyes drifted across the street, and he noticed how tightly packed the buildings were to one another. Moving to the edge of the platform he was on, he was thankful for the narrow alleys; the distance to the rooftop ahead made a leap across entirely possible.

"Forward it is then," Darkflare muttered to himself as he ran and then leapt.

As they crossed the tightly-packed buildings, Darkflare couldn't help but keep glancing at the madness below. People were sobbing and clutching family members, some were screaming at the assailants with weapons drawn, and others just stared at the carnage with hands covering their mouths or limp arms hanging at their sides in defeat. The joy of this morning was gone, no trace remained as people fled or fought back.

"What do you think their motives were?" Darkflare called back to Attila, his voice quavering more than he intended as he fought back anger.

"Who? The bandits? To cause fear, plunder a town full of riches, to sow chaos... Just because they wanted to or they are stupid enough to? It could be anything."

"I suppose. It's just that... They're not supposed to be trained fighters, they're *bandits*. If they even are that. These people seem too organized. I didn't even think there was a... a... bandit leader! It sounds just silly saying that."

"Like you said, they're bandits," Attila said, gaining the lead on Darkflare. "I don't think there was some big scheme. The tournament was not a secret. Recruitment and the promise of riches was proclaimed across the kingdoms. It's no surprise that they must have gotten wind of what was going on. Even an untrained mob can overwhelm an army with numbers."

"Yeah, well, they did a good job of disrupting today's events. What do you call what happened to the... bodies? Magic? There's got to be something more at work here."

"Magic is the only explanation I can think of." Attila paused, looking down as he continued on. "It seems they're thinning out or starting to hide."

Darkflare turned to look, and Attila was right; in just a few minutes, there was much less fighting that they could see and much more fleeing. The clusters of colored armor were more visible than before as civilians dispersed; the purple and black of D'sylum, the green and gold of Beauldyn, the crimson and bronze of Verankner, and the teal and silver of Purcille. If the rulers were somewhere among that mix, Darkflare couldn't tell. He wasn't completely sure he *could* even identify them if they were down among the fighting. He had seen pictures in some of his more recent books, but he had never met them personally.

"I bet King Corsius is absolutely furious, especially with how much he focuses on the defenses of D'sylum. I'm sure this is not going to look good for him. The blame for any deaths will fall on his shoulders."

"Maybe that's just it. Maybe Corsius set it up like that purposely. An attack like this only lends support to his stance, and if he's callous enough, he can use any deaths as martyrs for his cause."

Darkflare had a retort, but it was cut short. Instead of continuing onward, Attila had stopped at the edge of the roof they were on. Darkflare slowed as he joined his friend on their perch, and his heart caught in his throat.

The Despils.

Gloria was dragging Pearl by the hand, Angelus took up the rear with sword in hand, and Hal...

"No, no, no," Darkflare moaned as he felt the urge to vomit stronger than before. A limp Rai hung from Hal's shoulder. He couldn't tell if the father was sweating or crying, if not both. A group of bandits was right behind them, and within another moment, the Despils were encircled.

There was no hesitation in Darkflare as he leapt off from the ledge; he only had the burning desire to protect the friends that had taken such good care of him. Darkflare braced himself on one knee as he hit the ground. As he stood up, Attila landed right behind him, standing back to back. One quick look back ensured that Oboro had remained above.

One bandit walked forward, fixing them with a calm stare that was at odds with the bloody swortsword he brandished.

"Darkflare!" Gloria screamed as she ran to cower beside him.

"Are any of you hurt?" Darkflare warily eyed the bandits that encircled them, especially the lead one, and instantly regretted asking the question.

"Rai's dead!" Pearl sobbed, almost to the point of hysteria. Darkflare nearly dropped his sword; the pit in his stomach threatened to pull him to the ground. His friend was *dead*. He had to fight back tears as he steadied his grip.

"You should not fear death," the bandit said, recalling Darkflare's attention. "But instead welcome it. The release from mortal bonds is the greatest bliss."

The chill in the man's tone caused a shudder down Darkflare's spine. "Just what are you fiends?"

The bandit craned his neck, showing off a symbol of some sort that Darkflare was unfamiliar with.

"We are the Marked Ones."

In one swift motion, Attila spun around Darkflare and kicked one of the bandits who was blocking the path in the chest. The force from the strike sent his opponent backward into the surrounding enemies. Using the diversion Attila created, Darkflare motioned for the Despils to move.

"Quickly, while you can! Get out of here!"

"But," Hal gaped, "they have thrice the numbers on you! You're a fool to fight them!"

"We'll buy you all the time that we can, but you must go now!"

Hal did not question Darkflare a second time and hurried forward under the weight of his son's body, pushing Pearl with him. Gloria paused and stared into Darkflare's eyes, but before she could say anything, Angelus jostled her forward and locked eyes with Darkflare. His expression was unlike anything Darkflare had ever seen in him; dark and hollow. As he passed, Darkflare realized that the blade he had in his hands was Rai's.

The foe that had spoken before allowed the Despils to flee, watching them, without a hint of emotion on his face. After a moment, he turned back to Darkflare, locking him in place with an spine-chilling stare.

"To resist or run, it matters not." The bandit's voice deepened, his eyes bulged and filled with an unnatural crimson, and the calm on his face was replaced with a vicious sneer. There was no doubt as Darkflare stared into the monstrous visage before him that this was no mere bandit attack - this was the Pale being unleashed. "Death comes for all!"

Darkflare's looked back and forth as the bandits closed in on them, three from the front and three behind him. He cautiously watched the ones before him, waiting with his weapon held defensively for the first to make a move. The leader finally raised his sword and charged in, causing the other five to come at them in sync.

Darkflare shoved Attila hard on the shoulder, and the two boys split. Darkflare rolled to the right and Attila to the left. The clash of weapons echoed out as the rage of these 'Marked Ones' collided. Darkflare stood and turned to see one of them impaled on the ground. The leader withdrew his blade and turned his baleful gaze upon Darkflare.

Attila rushed at the closest enemy, whose back was to him, and swung the flat of his greatsword up at its head. The creature turned, the impact caught him square in the jaw, and he was lifted off his feet and flew several feet until he hit the wall of the alleyway. The Marked One's limbs sprawled out as he hit the ground, but he didn't dissipate into smoke; which meant, presumably, he was still alive. Darkflare followed the attack by rushing at a different one of the 'bandits,' and he swung his sword low to sweep the legs. A third adversary came at Darkflare as he stood back up, and Darkflare reacted by slamming the butt of his longsword in the ferocious, howling face. Metal smashed into nose with a crunch, causing the creature to double over. Seeing that they could at least feel pain like a normal human made Darkflare exhale in relief.

A fourth bandit rushed in with a flurry of relentless swings, giving Darkflare only moments to bring his sword up to parry. Darkflare barely managed to block the rage-filled swings, but each came with an accompanying backstep; so he forced his fear aside to watch for the right moment to strike back.

He sidestepped the next downward swing, and with a quick step forward, Darkflare thrust his blade into the demonic creature's exposed wrist. His opponent barely flinched as the black blood trickled onto the sword. Darkflare withdrew his weapon and swung his other fist. Even though it was his non-dominant hand, there was still enough force behind it to knock the bandit back. He smashed the flat of his blade into his foe's face, ensuring he would stay down.

Now, having a moment to breathe, Darkflare nursed his hand and turned to Attila's bout. As the next Marked One rushed in to hack at him, Attila swung his sword horizontally, smashing the rival blade aside. Seeing the leader rushing in from behind his opponent, Attila seized the opportunity by bracing his shoulder and hurtling forward. He tackled into the first foe, smashed him into the second, and did not stop moving until he impacted them both on a wall with their heads smacking together loudly. He dropped the unconscious bodies and looked down at them with disdain, but Attila locked eyes with Darkflare, he slowly walked away from them.

After the bandits had been dealt with, Oboro fluttered down beside the two young men. Darkflare found himself instinctively patting the wyvern's head, his eyes locked on the bodies, trying to process what happened. Oboro responded with a confused coo and nuzzled into his master's hand.

"Good job," Attila said as he rejoined Darkflare and Oboro. "That was the whole group as far as I can tell."

Darkflare finally drew his eyes away to look at Attila. "I guess we should at least bind their hands and feet somehow until the guards can get over here. Who knows how long they're going to stay down for."

The sound of footsteps and jingling metal caused Darkflare to look up. Above the archway from which the bandits had originally entered, as well as the ground beneath it, there were twenty additional raiders brandishing bows with flame-tipped arrows.

As the malicious foes brought their arrows up to bear, Darkflare had a sickening realization that there was no escape for them. Even if their opponents were not eagle-eyed bowmen, the odds of twenty flaming arrows missing two targets in a narrow alley were rather slim.

One of the men standing on the ground, whom Darkflare assumed held more rank than the others by his heavier armor, stepped forward.

"What have we here?" He scratched his scruffy chin, looking toward Oboro inquisitively. The wyvern met his gaze and hissed loudly, baring its pointed teeth. "A living, breathing treasure trove. The scales, the hide – Pale, I'm sure even the teeth – will have all sorts of buyers foaming at the mouth. Once we've finished at Kailos, I think we'll be taking a trip west, boys."

Darkflare felt his heart beating in his throat, but he shifted his weight so that he stood in a defensive stance with his sword drawn up diagonal to his chest.

"You will have to go through me before you lay a hand on Oboro!" The words came out of his mouth, but it was almost as if he heard someone else saying it. His brain couldn't wrap around what he had just said. His hands and his body wanted to tremble worse than before, and it took great concentration not to give in. Darkflare's eyes widened, remembering the rest of the man's words. "Wait, Kailos? I... I thought mercenaries had been hired to guard it."

"It's funny how the words bandits and mercenaries can be so closely interchanged when people don't know what they're talking about. I relish the thought of bringing the queen and kings' most loyal retainers under the sway of darkness. Once we mark them, it will shake the kingdoms to the core."

Darkflare shook his head, realizing the bandit had the same strange 'x' tattoo on his neck as the last. "Darkness...? Just what is that mark?!"

The man's answer was raising his own bow. His eyes took on a bloodshot color and his skin paled as he readied himself, much like the others Darkflare had encountered.

Darkflare's mind raced as he tried to figure out how to escape their situation or what they could do to survive, but he could not find an answer. If they screamed, the men would loose their arrows. If they moved, the fire would be upon them in moments. There was *nothing* they could do.

His thoughts shifted to the blazing inferno from his dreams; he could see himself among those corpses all too well. Darkflare could feel the incredible burning sensation of those flames more vividly than ever. Perhaps this was what it was like to die, he thought to himself; worry, panic, and fear formed into a blazing heat that claimed the soul before any mortal wounds could be inflicted. Sweat profusely streamed his forehead and down his bandana as he lowered his sword and grabbed at his chest.

No – the sensations that he felt were real and stronger than any lucid dream he had experienced before. Something was burning through his armor and tearing at him from the inside.

The bandits pulled back on the strings of their bows, in unspoken unison, waiting for their leader to give the sign. Even staring death in the eye, Attila stood unafraid of the possibility that hovered before him. By just glancing at his demeanor – the way he stood stalwart and unfettered as ever – it seemed as if he welcomed the fools to try and attack them, as if he was the one in control of the situation. When he noticed Darkflare staring at him though, his cool broke. His eyebrows furrowed as he looked Darkflare up and down.

"Get up. Pull together and ready yourself."

Attila might have said something else, but it was lost to Darkflare; he could not hear him after that, or anything else for that matter. As if Darkflare had been thrust back into the hysteric crowd, his eardrums were overwhelmed with a blanket of dense pressure and white noise. His eyes remained fixated on the tips of the arrows, but he felt his head swaying; his hand clawed at the leather armor, trying to dig a way into his chest.

He felt as if this was the last moment of his life. He was sure he would burn to death from something internally before the bandits had a chance to fire their arrows. The intensity of whatever was going on within him was more than he could stand.

The burning forced him to his knees and caused his vision to blur. A sound returned to his ears. It was his heartbeat.

The head bandit opened his mouth, but Darkflare could not hear the words; he could only just barely make out the blur of a jaw moving.

He fought back as hard as he could; he refused to die. Not from the flames inside of him, not from the bandits – or whatever these 'marked' beings were! He struggled against all of the intense sensations, fighting to rise against the crippling weight that held him to the ground.

The final images of his dream played out in his mind again and again; the woman screaming, the man dying, and the sea of flames.

That rush of power as the blades collided.

As if Darkflare's mind and body had bore all they could, he shot up to his feet, and he opened his mouth in an attempt to unleash all of the intensity within into a single screeching blast of emotion. He could feel his mouth opening, and he knew something was coming out, yet he could not hear it; he could feel his vocal chords reverberating as the arrows loosed.

He saw the flames coming toward him, but at the same time, fire washed out before him, heading *toward* the arrows. He didn't understand; he couldn't wrap his head around what he was seeing. The moment seemed to stretch into an eternity as the inferno turned the arrows to cinders, and slowly, his vision fell to black.

He wasn't sure if he was alive or dead, but before he lost consciousness, a voice whispered through his mind with great clarity.

You are the bearer of true courage. You are the flame in the darkness. This is not the end.

He could just barely make out a figure in the darkness; it was shrouded in some strange aura of white, a long head of blonde streaming around it. But the face was so clear. It was female; and even though the one in his dream was blonde as well, this was not the same woman. She smiled at him, so crystal clear and warm, and he felt at peace.

This is only the beginning.

Chapter V

Attila struggled to keep his eyes open, finding it hard to keep his gaze focused. He did not have the faintest idea how long he had lost consciousness for, but the world he had awoken in had been so sweltering that he thought at first he had been sent to the realm of the damned. His first instinct was to push his legs into a standing position, but there was no need. The throbbing pain in his head began to die down, allowing his eyes to focus on the fact that he was half-standing, half-leaning against a wall rather awkwardly. The only thing he could figure, by the ruined mess of timbers and splits that surrounded him, was that he had been thrown through one of the buildings in the alley. It took moments for his mind to stop swimming, but he slowly began to piece together with confidence that he was in fact alive.

Using the wall as a crutch to position himself upright, Attila startled when he realized the alleyway was completely in flames. Through the billowing haze, he could see that the archway they had been ambushed from was destroyed and the rubble was strewn across the ground. Their aggressors were nowhere to be seen. He did note that there were some strange dark markings on the ground that seemed more akin to heavy shadows than charred remains.

Attila checked to make sure he still had all of his limbs. Beyond the pain that still lingered in his head, he was somehow intact; he even pinched himself on the cheek and forearm to make sure that he was not in a dream. One moment he had been on the brink of death, and now he stood within what seemed like the heart of a fireball. How his circumstances had reversed in leaving him the survivor and his outnumbering enemies, presumably, the slain still left him baffled. That was when he remembered he had not been alone.

"Darkflare." The name escaped his lips no more than a dry whisper.

"Darkflare!"

He had tried calling louder, but his voice was raspy from exhaustion. Attila looked frantically about the ruins of the alley trying to find some sign of life. What a cruel twist of fate it would have been if that the only person he trusted had succumbed to whatever caused this chaos and left Attila the sole survivor.

Just as he was about to call out again, he heard some faint animal cry. Craning his neck to look deeper into the smoke, Attila finally was able to make out Oboro perched on a heap of stone and timber. Underneath, he could barely make out Darkflare's upper half. He let out a sigh of relief, followed by a series of coughs. He needed to get out of the smoke-filled alley, quickly.

He went to run over to where Oboro was perched but almost fell on his face. It was not until he forced his leg to move so suddenly that a sharp pain surfaced. Attila tried profoundly to remember anything that occurred before he had awoken in hopes of diagnosing the severity of the injury. The last thing he could recall was the bandits notching their bowstrings, ready to shoot – or had they shot? After that, his sight had been entirely blinded by light. He had come out of the dance with death with a leg wound and a throbbing headache; he realized it could have been much worse.

Attila managed to limp to where Oboro was, and he threw himself to the ground beside the cerulean scaled wyvern.

"It's okay… I'll get him out, don't worry."

Oboro seemed to understand Attila's words as he stared him in the eyes for a moment and then pawed out of the way to allow Attila enough room to move the materials under his watchful gaze. Heaving with both arms, Attila forced the wreckage of building materials off of Darkflare until he was fully uncovered. He immediately checked to make sure that he was still breathing and saw his chest moving up and down. Heaving a sigh of relief, followed by another fit of coughing, Attila pulled his friend from the wreckage and propped him into a better sitting position.

"He owes me. You're my witness." Attila pointed at Oboro, who in return bowed his head. Oboro pranced around his master, walking back and forth excitedly. Attila knew of the bond the two shared and let Oboro revel in his joy while he refocused on the bigger situation.

It was impossible to stay where they were, Attila full well knew. The flames were still brilliantly swaying on the sides of buildings, soaring high off the ground, and the smoke was everywhere he breathed. It would not be long before a building collapsed on them or they drowned from the smoke inhalation.

He decided that he would have to move Darkflare, leg be damned, but his eyes widened as he looked back at his friend.

"What the Pale…?"

In the center of Darkflare's chest there was a mark that seemed to resonate as profoundly as the fire around them. It looked as if the flames had crept up to Darkflare and kissed a permanent branding, no bigger than an apple, on his chest. Just like the way the flames swayed naturally, rhythmically, the mark glowed with a fiery crimson; but then it faded softly until it could not be seen. It was in the shape of a horned helmet from what Attila could make out – something that Darkflare had spoken of – his birthmark, was it? Darkflare never made any mention of this supernatural illumination. Even Oboro was noticeably confused as he hissed nervously at it.

"Oboro, he's fine, it's…"

Attila's gaze snapped to where the archway had once been as a figure calmly walked through the thick smoke. Attila rose, cautious of his leg, and withdrew the two-handed sword from his back, crossing it over him in a defensive position.

As the figure drew closer, he saw the long white apparel, which was not a robe, but instead a hooded coat, and Attila's eyes narrowed in recognition.

"You. You were at the arena."

The white cloaked figure stopped, still a few feet away from Attila. It was as if the cinders from the flames dared not to touch the stranger's long coat; the pure white sheen gave it an almost unnatural look, as if it had been polished like armor. The head within bobbed up and down.

"What is your role in all of this? Clearly you're no bandit, but then, they didn't seem to be either. Are you one of… whatever they were?"

The stranger's arms reached up into his hood and threw it back, revealing a head of thick cobalt blue hair. Their eyes stared in a deadlock: Attila's frosted baby blues against the piercing, darker cerulean of the other. The stranger quirked an eyebrow upward.

"I am marked, but my allegiance is not with those creatures."

Attila was unfazed. He held his sword at the ready, not blinking or moving. After a moment, he gritted his teeth, and then his eyes flashed to Darkflare and just as quickly back to the man.

"What is all this talk of markings? What happened to Darkflare?" He gestured with one hand. "Has he become one of them?"

"No." The man shook his head slowly. "He is like me. Please, allow me to help get you three out of this wreckage. It's not safe here, and you both need rest."

The man held his hands out passively, but Attila still did not move. He fought the cough growing in his chest as he weighed his options. "You said you were marked."

The man nodded, pulling up the sleeves of his coat. Etched on both wrists were designs that resembled daggers with jagged edges on both sides. Attila wasn't sure what it meant, but it was not the same, strange 'x' design of the ones who called themselves 'Marked Ones' prior.

"We can talk more about this when we get somewhere safe."

Attila's eyes remained narrowed, his sword unwavering. "Why should I trust you?"

The man shrugged, letting his arms drop and sway at his side.

"Because you've really only got two choices. You can sit here in the flames, pretend I never showed up, and try not to die. Only problem with that is if you somehow manage to limp out without coughing to death, carrying Darkflare's body, what exactly are you going to tell any soldiers you pass when they see the flaming remains? Can't blame the 'bandits;' there are no remains of your opponents. Try explaining that they called themselves the Marked Ones and you'll be believed even less. Instead, you can let me help you, and I'll explain everything once Darkflare awakens."

Accepting the stranger's help was the last thing Attila wanted, but after allowing the weight of his options to sink in, he was right. It would be impossible to explain what had happened when Attila himself had no idea. Relinquishing his guard, Attila saw no other option than to hang his weapon low, which in turn brought a smile to the other man's face.

* * * * *

Darkflare felt light slowly creep into the darkness of his vision. The first thought that ran through his mind was that he was dead. The last thing he could remember was facing a group of bandits that were armed with flaming arrows. Darkflare blinked the blur away from his sight several times, and once his eyes focused, he realized that he was staring up at a wooden roof that reminded him very much of the inn.

Had it all been just a dream? Was today the day of the tournament and could all of the fighting have been an extent of the horrible nightmare? He didn't have the same sense of dread when waking from the scene of flames; no horrible cold sweats and feeling his heart fluttering like a bird.

As Darkflare sat up, the aches across his body reaffirmed that he had not dreamed the brawl; and there was this odd feeling in his chest, right around his birthmark, that he could not explain. The word 'courage' just kept resonating strongly in his mind while trying to remember everything.

"And there he is. Rested enough now, Darkflare?"

The voice that had cut in through his thoughts was not the familiar brooding tone of Attila, nor was it the calming voice from his dreams. Darkflare slowly turned his head to the right; there was another bed that Attila was sitting wide awake upon, but the foreign voice belonged to a man sitting past him in a wooden chair. The stranger was leaning back in his seat with a warm smile behind his steepled fingers.

"Who… are you? What happened?" Darkflare managed, staring at the man's blue hair that was pulled back into a ponytail that was barely visible.

"I'm an ally, let's start there. As for what happened… I can assure you that all of your questions will be answered. For now, save your strength. You've only just awoken and you and Attila have been through quite the ordeal."

Darkflare shook his head, refusing to be placated, and woozily swung his legs over the side of the bed, still trying to adjust to his surroundings. Oboro, who Darkflare just realized had been curled up in the bed beside him, woke at the sudden movement. Darkflare stroked the wyvern on the head to calm him down. He was glad Oboro did not seem to show any signs of injury, but when he looked back over, he frowned at Attila's wrapped leg.

"How do you know my name?" Darkflare's eyebrows arched down as he looked back at the stranger and stifled a nagging headache.

The man's grin slyly spread before he answered.

"I believe an introduction for myself is in order. My name is Kenji Morikuo." The man raised one of his half-gloved hands to his chest and bowed his head. He cleared his throat and placed a hand on his chin, as if thinking and picking over his words very carefully. "I'm trying to think of the best place to begin to make this all seem less… farfetched. Let's start with this. How much do you know of your parents?"

"I know enough," Darkflare said as he eyed the other man warily. He couldn't get a good read if he was actually a warm person, confident, or cocky, but the smile on his face seemed to never leave. "What does any of this have to do with my parents?"

"To be blunt, they have entirely everything to do with this."

Darkflare nearly snorted, holding in a laugh at the audacity of this man to assume his *dead* parents could be linked to the attack created by those demonic creatures. Before he could think of a response, Kenji continued.

"How much do you remember about your childhood? Do you remember your brother?"

"Not much, but yes, I remember Terra and Meredia. Loosely." Darkflare shook away the pain in his head as he narrowed his eyes again at the man. "And my brother certainly did not look like you."

"Hah, no no. I'm not trying to claim I'm Terra. As I said, I'm just trying to see how much you remember."

"I remember enough." Darkflare fought to keep his frustration down, but his words were filled with more steel than he wanted. It didn't daunt the mystery man. "What do you want from me?"

"Come now, is that any way to talk to someone who saved your life?"

There was a bit of ice in the man's eyes as he met Darkflare's. The younger man forced his eyes away and shrugged.

"I apologize," he turned to look at him again, "but between the day's events that are still hazy and this line of questioning, you will have to forgive my hesitation to answer with any sincerity."

Kenji's eyes softened and his smile widened a bit more.

"That's quite alright. I understand these are questions about a sensitive subject. But I do have one more question for you, if you'd humor me. Did you ever consider that Calistron and Sylphe entrusted someone to care for you should something happen?"

Darkflare paused to hold the man's gaze before answering.

"If they did, I've never met them or heard anything about them. My whole life, it's been Oboro, Attila, and myself, fending for each other, defending each other, supporting each other – raising each other."

It was the man's turn to pause before answering, his infuriating smile never fading.

"I know you'd like to think that, but the fact of the matter is that you would never have gotten this far if it wasn't for me."

"You?" Darkflare scoffed, shaking his head. "The only other time I've seen you was at the tournament today. Is this some sort of sick joke to you? Innocent people are dead, some strange evil presence has attacked Ceballe, and I should be out there – helping in whatever way I can! I thank you for saving us, but we are done with this conversation."

Darkflare rose from his bed, but Kenji raised a single hand, the smile on his face dropping slightly.

"Darkflare, please. I understand that a lot has happened. I understand your desire to help people, but if that's truly what you want, then I implore you to listen to what I have to say."

"Why should I?"

"Well, beyond the fact that I saved your lives moments ago, I told you, I'm an ally. You need to trust me. I *am* the one that Calistron and Sylpe named to be your guardian."

Darkflare stared deeply into Kenji's piercing blue eyes. A million thoughts, accusations, and questions filled his mind, causing his headache to almost double in intensity. He had always wanted to believe that someone else survived whatever happened in Crescentia, but he just couldn't bring himself to believe it to be true, here and now. He fought back the pain and managed to bring himself to speak.

"That's a lie. Why would you never once in my life make yourself known and wait until now to reveal yourself? You might have saved me moments ago, but where were you when we were younger, struggling to survive each day by foraging in the woods?!" Darkflare cut the air with his arm furiously. He tried to stifle some of the anger, but his confusion would not let it go. "One moment I was getting ready to fight for my life in the most impossible of situations, the next I'm having a heart attack before I can even ready my sword, and now I'm here. With you! Some stranger I've never met before but claims he's my guardian that has been around me my whole life!"

"Alright," Kenji mumbled at the ceiling as if unfazed by Darkflare's seething anger. He rubbed his chin lightly before returning his gaze to the young man. "I don't blame you for being skeptical or angry, but I can give you a surfeit amount of proof. Allow me to start with the basics. I know you're from a town that has now been reduced to ruins that goes by the name of Crescentia; a hidden haven that won't be found on a map anywhere. It actually used to be a very beautiful respite when your parents were alive. This guy with the brooding look on his face is Attila, your closest friend since childhood, and your wyvern is named Oboro. But those are all just general facts that anyone who's seen your victories at the tournaments could probably find out. Or a very good stalker."

The small kindling of hope that Kenji really did know his parents was ignited in Darkflare's heart, but the broad grin on the man's face challenged Darkflare's pride, and he folded his arms across his chest.

"I give you credit for committing all that to memory, but if you've really been with me my whole life, tell me something more detailed. Recant me a story that no ordinary tournament spectator would know."

Kenji leaned back in his chair, pondering for a few moments, and then sat forward. "You were no older than twelve, maybe thirteen. You and Attila were heading to your usual destination of Ceballe when something had caught your attention off to the side of the forest. Attila said to pay it no heed, but you decided to investigate anyway. What you had seen was a pup that had strayed away from its family. You chased after it, trying to catch it, and it led you right back to its home deeper in the forest. The two of you found a little clearing that had belonged to a carpenter's family. There were two boys outside, and they were relieved that you brought their puppy home to them. They quarreled about whose fault it was, and Attila told them to cherish one another because they never knew when they might be left alone."

Darkflare's doubt was quelled and was replaced by hope - real hope - that maybe, just maybe, this man knew his parents. The memory that Kenji recalled was one of the only times that Attila had conveyed emotion to a stranger. Darkflare's gaze fell toward his silent companion, but instead of meeting it, Attila looked away.

"Alright... Alright." Darkflare sat back down on the bed and exhaled deeply. He ran a hand through his hair and then looked back at Kenji. "What exactly do you know about my parents?"

Kenji smiled and shrugged. "A lot. I fought alongside them for years."

"You fought alongside them? For *years*?" Darkflare's skepticism returned, and he reared back slightly. "But you hardly look thirty years old."

"Age can be deceiving, and it is but a number - one that has no bearing on this story."

"Alright, age aside, no one that lived in Crescentia survived the..." Darkflare's voice trailed off as he recalled the pain in his chest before he blacked out.

"The destruction? Or rather..." Kenji splayed his hands out, as if mimicking the spreading of flames. "The fire? Yes, Crescentia was ravaged by flames. And that word - *fire* - it's a simple word, but the thought it evokes stirs something within you, doesn't it? Maybe memories you don't quite understand?"

"What? How did you... " Darkflare did not know whether he could trust talking to this person about his dream or not. He looked to Attila for advice, and this time the gaze was reciprocated.

"Your call. If you believe everything else he's said, tell him."

Darkflare nodded, swallowing his doubts. "I keep having strange dreams, filled with fire. There are bodies all over, two people are fighting a monstrous entity, and..." Darkflare paused. He knew the answer already, but he had to ask. "Are you trying to tell me... The town in my dreams... is it Crescentia?"

"Yes." Kenji nodded his head, and Darkflare felt a weight drop in his stomach. "Your dream is a snippet in time, tied to your absent memories, your parents' fate, and it all has led up to why you are here, with me, in this inn room. But in order for me to continue, I need to know that you will listen to what I have to say, as absurd as some of it might sound."

Darkflare remained silent for a few moments to let Kenji's words sink in, and he looked toward Attila once more. His friend was nursing his ankle, but he returned Darkflare's glance with a shrug.

"Alright," Darkflare exchanged glances with Kenji once more. "Please, tell me more about all of this. I need to know. Everything - anything."

"Right then." The smug smile remained on Kenji's face, but the tone of voice that he continued with brought a slightly more serious demeanor to the man wearing the long coat. "Today, what happened was that there was a fire that swept over the alleyway right as you blacked out. Attila can attest to that fact, as he woke up to the aftermath of it. What was the last thing you remember?"

"Well..." Darkflare thought for a minute, recalling the events as best as he could. He sighed and put his head in his hands. "I remember that we aided the Despils in escaping the bandits. And Rai – he was dead. Damn the bandits, damn them all."

"Rest assured, the Despils are safe now." Kenji nodded solemnly. "The rest of the family at least. You are correct that the older son, Rai, died, but I made sure to watch over their escape before I found Attila."

That at least brought Darkflare some solace. He exhaled deeply before continuing, trying to push aside the memory of his dead friend; for now. There would be time to grieve later. "Then... more of the – what did they call themselves, Marked Ones? – appeared once we defeated the first group. They had torched arrows. The last thing I can remember is this uncontrollable pain in my chest before I woke up here. It was so strong, I thought I was burning to death. Even though I don't remember exactly what happened, I can recall the heat of the fire so vividly." Darkflare paused again to rub his chest. "But if the bandits, Marked Ones, whatever, did not kill us, what exactly happened?"

"Well, as they loosed their arrows, the Marked Ones were wiped out in a massive inferno – the one that I spoke of that swept the alleyway."

"And what, did it just magically appear?" Darkflare shrugged. When Kenji remained silent, Darkflare stared at him with narrowed eyes. "I know magic is real, it exists in all of the crystals, and I know humans can learn it if they try hard enough. But that takes years of one's life to learn. I didn't see any sorcerers aiding us in that alley."

"You are correct. Normally a spell of that size and power would take an average person a long time to learn... Unless under certain circumstances. There were no sorcerers - the person that conjured a spell of that magnitude was you."

Darkflare's eyes widened and he looked down at his open palms. He could still feel the heat radiating off of them from the dreams he had. It made sense but... "How? How in the Pale could I have possibly done that? I don't know the first thing about how magic works. Did I," his voice suddenly became much weaker than he wanted, "did I kill all of those people?"

"The first thing that you need to understand, Darkflare, is that Marked Ones are not people. They are demons. They are creatures that might have once been human, but they sold their souls to The Pale in exchange for power. They are Sairephir's thralls now, and there can be no redemption for them; no salvation. All good and essence of life has been wiped from them. You should feel no regret for expunging such evil." Kenji's eyes momentarily flared with something akin to zeal, but they softened as he leaned back again. "But there is no doubt, you were the one that made that fire. So yes. You did slay those Marked Ones."

Darkflare again looked to his hands, feeling guilt wash over him as he struggled to bring his gaze back to Kenji as he continued.

"Control over magic does not solely rest in the hands of the astrelite race. While they are the most proficient, being born with the gift of magic inherently flowing through their veins, it is as you said, humans may learn how to use the most basic of spells over the course of many years. However, in your case," Kenji pointed toward Darkflare's chest, "your birthmark is no ordinary scar. It is a rune, and yours in particular grants natural control over the element of fire. Those who bear runes have been chosen by gods of the Dreamscape to be their avatar in the mortal world and wield their magical affinity. Just like your parents were. Just like I am. That mark is proof that you are one of us - a dragoon."

"A... dragoon?" The word just barely scratched the surface of Darkflare's memory. A buzzing feeling ran through his head and he put a hand up to massage his temple. Among the many questions he had, he blurted out the most obvious one. "If that's the case, then... how does my birthmark make me different from the Marked Ones?"

"Dragoons and Marked Ones are different in every way. The only similarity is the fact that both groups bear signs of their gods in the form of markings. Dragoons have existed for thousands of years, but their presence in history depends on what state the world was in. The times they have been most active have been written into obscurity. Most past dragoons throughout history have worked in small groups or on the individual level."

"*Thousands* of years?" Darkflare was trying to wrap his head around what he was hearing, but he couldn't hide the incredulity from his voice.

"Yes. The title has a long, storied origin. As you can imagine, since the creation of our world, evil has always fought against good. As long as there is light to cast a shadow, there will always be darkness to dwell in the shade. In one of the first efforts to stand up against the villainy and evil that ravaged the lands, a man prayed to the gods that protect this world and asked for their divine favor, to free humanity from the shackles of darkness. He swore to overcome any trial, any obstacle, so they would grant select people their symbols to show they were favored, avatars under the guidance of a specific Dreamscape deity.

"As legend goes, this man spoke with the mightiest of the Creator's champions, Odin, who tested the man's resolve. The warrior was said to be trialed for several weeks, if not months, and he would not relent or waver in his dedication; until one day, Odin decided he was worthy. It was then that the first mortal was blessed with Odin's Rune

— the Rune of Courage. He was declared and forever known as the first King of Dragoons."

Darkflare felt his hand rise to touch his chest, the story having a deeper meaning that he realized. Kenji, witnessing this, relaxed, a smug grin on his face.

"And so to answer your original question, the Marked Ones are 'marked' as being claimed by Sairephir as his pawns. Their symbol is that of a disfigured 'x', with another line drawn horizontally down the middle. Like I said, we both have our symbols, but the main difference is that dragoons still have their humanity, their sense of purpose and judgment. As I said, we are avatars. The gods pick who wields their power wisely — as evident by your rune."

Darkflare nodded. "Right. Okay. That puts my mind a bit more at ease. But... I've had my birthma-... rune... since, well, birth. I've never had fire combust out of me before."

Kenji nodded.

"Those that are chosen are born with their runes, given favor before they are even given their first breath in our world. Most that discover their power try to hide it from the rest of the world, terrified of who and what they are. The rune usually won't activate until the wielder experiences an extreme emotional experience or if it's called to by another dragoon in need of their aid. In your case, your rune saved you from a death you were not meant to suffer. Others usually answer the call of a rune with greater power, such as the Rune of Courage."

"Courage," Darkflare's brows drew down as he repeated the word. "And you said that was the King of Dragoons' rune?"

"Yes," Kenji nodded. "Odin has made very few pacts, that I'm aware of, and your father was one of those he chose. Calistron Omni was the last King of Dragoons and wielder of the Rune of Courage." Kenji paused, looked Darkflare over as the young man processed, and affixed him with a grin that seemed slightly warmer. "As you might have already guessed by now, the rune that Calistron had, the Rune of Courage, has been bestowed upon you. What that means is that you've been chosen by Odin to become the next King of Dragoons, and in turn, his natural affinity with the element of fire is at your disposal."

Darkflare looked down at his hands once more. The sensations of heat that had been there before were now registering in his mind as his ability to now conjure the very flames of his dreams. He whipped his gaze back to Kenji, and he was sure his eyes reflected his craving to know more.

"What kind of dragoon was my mother?"

"She bore the Rune of Hope and was attuned with holy elemental magic."

"And yourself?"

Kenji removed the armored fingerless gloves from his hands and rolled back the arms of his coat. Holding up his wrists, he showed Darkflare marks on both that almost looked like daggers.

"I'm the bearer of the Rune of Contempt," Kenji said proudly as he replaced the gloves. "If you still don't believe me…"

Kenji held out his right hand once he had finished fixing his gloves. The palm was faced upward with each of his fingers slightly curled. Darkflare stared at it nervously, quite unsure of what Kenji was about to do. He thought he heard a dull buzzing noise, and then a black ball appeared in Kenji's palm. As if inhaling the air around it, the ball expanded to fit Kenji's entire hand, and he held it up for the boys to stare at. Attila's eyebrows shot upward in awe, and Darkflare gaped at the blackness; all he could see within were gray swirls of energy that vanished as fast as they appeared, as if resembling smoke that faded into the core.

"While you can control the element of fire," Kenji rolled his hand and the ball disappeared just as fast as he had conjured it, "I control the element of void. It's the energy that makes up darkness, and most people mistakenly confuse it to be magic associated with evil. Really, it's just the absence of light."

Darkflare blinked and it took all the reasoning in his mind to accept he had just seen magic – real magic that made up the crystals that he used in his everyday life. He now commanded one of those elements. There was no denying what Kenji had just done, but he really had to question - was he really the master of fire and the king of these mythic warriors called dragoons? The reality of what those words entailed weighed heavily on Darkflare. Would he have to lead people? *Could* he lead people? Would they listen to some nobody from a ruined town?

"Wait," Attila leaned forward, shaking his head. "If Darkflare caused that fire in the alley, how am I still alive? How did I not die from it?"

"Ah, you see, that's magic for you – it's well… magical!" Kenji grinned, waving his hands sarcastically. "Intent is inherent in the use of magic and its user. So if Darkflare had directed the fire spell in your direction, his magic would know you were not the target and simply warm you as it washed past. However, the fire isn't what knocked you out; it was a shockwave from the Rune of Courage. Certain runes, if strong enough, can emit a burst of energy when they awaken; and sometimes, allies can get caught in the crossfire of that!"

"Hmm… Okay then."

Attila's skepticism seemed sated for the time being, and he lay back on the pillow. Darkflare's thoughts drifted back to what started this conversation – his dreams.

"So if I control fire," Darkflare spoke slowly, as if chewing over the words before he spat them out, "did… did I cause the one in Crescentia?"

"No, that wasn't you. Even though you were the sole survivor, you were not the cause of the destruction."

Kenji cleared his throat and dropped the smile. He leaned forward to look harder into Darkflare's eyes, who steeled himself for the story to come.

"Your parents were the leaders of a group of dragoons, and I was among their ranks. We lived in Crescentia and built it into an outstanding town that acted as a sanctuary away from the rest of the world. Our hideaway was a safe haven and training area for skilled warriors. The only people that knew of Crescentia were those that we told, and they kept the secret in order to keep the peace to ourselves. In our tenure together, our group had fought countless vile creatures that threatened the peace of the world time and time again. Nothing compared to the man we fought the day of the inferno… Graymahl Vulorst.

"That was not the first time we encountered him. Graymahl was a warrior who studied the gods' gifts of runes and envied your father for being such a powerful warrior. Calistron had struck him down in combat after the jealousy finally drove him mad, yet your father let Graymahl live, due to his kind heart. Seeking vengeance, Graymahl wanted ultimate power to destroy us, and what better way than to forge pacts for runes of his own? He decided to obtain one his own way – by calling upon the dark gods of The Pale to create his."

"Again, another similarity." Darkflare narrowed his eyes a bit. "Isn't that how the dragoon runes came about, you said? Praying for strength?"

"These runes were different." Kenji closed his eyes for a moment and shook his head. "Dark runes had never existed before; the extent of The Pale lending power to the living world was corrupting them into Marked Ones. This was the first time that runes, similar to the ones that we dragoons bear, came to exist in the living world.

"Tainted from their creation, there was no will to do good associated with them; they were purely evil and granted the bearer strength in return for their mortality. Graymahl made a pact with the God of Death and Destruction, Hades, that if he were to perform the deadliest and most sinister deeds a man could do, he would be granted with a rune of his own. So Graymahl killed, maimed, tortured, stole, betrayed, deceived, and… other heinous acts to gain Hades's favor.

"And Hades, unfortunately for us, kept his promise, knowing that there was no turning back after all the deeds had been acted out; Graymahl was a soul beyond salvation, the perfect manifestation of bane. He and the gods that represented each deadly act bestowed Graymahl and his most loyal followers runes of their own… The Runes of Torment."

"How do you know all this?" Darkflare cocked an eyebrow. "How do you know so much about this Graymahl guy? I can't believe he would have told you all this in the middle of combat."

"Ah, no. He did not. My Rune God, Poseidon, did. I have an, uh… interesting connection with him – a story for another time. He informed me of what Mokiwana had witnessed."

"Can I talk to Odin like that?"

"It's not that simple." Kenji looked like he wanted to say more, but he shook his head and cleared his throat. "Anyway, where was I? Ah, yes. Graymahl and his followers were bestowed the Runes of Torment, and with his newfound power, he was now able to command an army of demons – an unstoppable force that he marched toward Crescentia. Your hometown was not the only one to suffer. On his way, he decided to prove his army's tyrannical might by destroying the capital of the south at the time – Syvail."

Darkflare and Attila exchanged looks and wide eyes. "That's what destroyed Syvail?!"

"Yes, Graymahl and his dragoons were responsible for that. The reason why it's barred off is because King Corsius and his council think that the souls of the slain knights and the late king will come back to seek vengeance if they did not seal it off as a sacred graveyard. Graymahl must have known that the destruction of the capital of D'sylum would send a terrifying message to the rest of the world.

"As you know, from there, it's not far from Crescentia. He must have been able to sense the energy from our runes, because he knew exactly where we were. We were aware that something dark and sinister was coming for us; the destruction shone in the sky and the smell of death wafted down to us. We tried to evacuate the town as quickly as we could, but it was too late. Graymahl and his forces of darkness moved too swiftly for us to counterattack. I urged your parents to protect you and your siblings while I led our allies in a last stand.

"We fought off the demons as best as we could. Hundreds of foes were slain – including the wielders of the Runes of Torment. But we paid a high price. I watched as all of our allies fell, defending your family. And then Graymahl came forth.

"All of my efforts seemed to be in vain as he stabbed me and threw me aside like a rag doll. I…"

Kenji's voice trailed off, choked with emotion.

"I can't begin to explain to you how I survived that day, Darkflare. Once he threw me aside, he left me for dead to focus on your parents. Maybe he thought the flames that they were setting would be enough, I don't know. Your parents had become separated, and Graymahl found your mother. As he went to deal a fatal blow on her…"

"My father," Darkflare nearly breathed the words. "He wore red armor. He jumped in the way to fight Graymahl himself."

Kenji nodded. "As I said, your dream is a snippet of the final fight. Your father leapt in the way to save your mother, and in his hands he held the one thing that could stop Graymahl – a shard of dark matter bestowed upon him during our journeys by Nooremiil Phimtair, the King of the Astrelites. Using the power of the ancient artifact, he sealed Graymahl and his Runes of Torment inside the gem. However, your parents paid the ultimate price for it. Calistron was warned of what would happen – the shard takes life to seal life. Hand in hand, Calistron and Sylphe stood before Graymahl and used the shard's power… In their last battle to save the world from evil, they both gave their lives."

Darkflare shook his head. "Why don't I remember any of this? It doesn't make any sense. Why is it only coming to me in my dreams?"

Kenji sighed. "You had to have been about five at the time this was all happening, Darkflare. With the combined forces of Hope and Courage, your parents placed a barrier over the house you were in, allowing neither good nor evil to pass. As if to coincide with their will, your rune activated prematurely, lending strength to their barrier and scarring your chest with a 'birthmark.' Perhaps due to the power of the Rune of Courage and how young you were, combined with the hope your parents had for you to forget all of the trauma, your memories were locked. Only now, with your rune fully activated and flowing magic through you, I'm sure you've started remembering."

Darkflare rubbed his chest. It was true; the faces in his dream were no longer blurred. He could see his father, with his scruffy beard and long brown hair; and his mother, with her short blonde hair and loving smile beneath emerald eyes. And as he looked at Kenji, he had flash images of a man with a blue ponytail, identical to the one before him. Darkflare wiped a tear away from his eye. "It's all falling into place... But what happened to you?"

"I awoke from my injuries a few days later, surprised that I had been spared my life – either by some cruel twist of fate or some sad smile of fortune. The barrier that your parents had set up protected half of Crescentia, but it faded when their souls did. That's the reason why the land, primarily the graveyard, looks so barren, while the area you live in still looks healthy. I personally saw to burying each body that was left there - allies that I had fought alongside for so many years... It was such a cruel exchange for living."

"I'm sorry. That must have been horrible." Darkflare paused, shaking his head at the thought of having to bury either Attila or Oboro. "But... I do remember seeing bodies and destruction in my dreams. If I was on the other side of the barrier and you had buried them before I left the house, how is that possible?"

"Fragments of the aftermath. Because you and your father bore the same rune, the final memories of the event were preserved as a way to help you recover your memories - should the time arise you needed them. Your rune is *very* powerful - so much so that not even I fully understand what it is capable of."

"I... I see." Darkflare swallowed hard as he thought of the next question. "And... my brother and sister? They weren't in the house with me?"

Kenji hesitated a moment before he pulled away from Darkflare's gaze. He sat up straighter before he looked back at him.

"When I went back to the house to check on you, I discovered your brother and sister were nowhere to be found. I scoured both sides of Crescentia, turned over every pile of rubble, checked as deep into the forest as I dared to venture, and I never found them... I did not find any remains, but I assumed that they passed in the fire as well. I'm sorry."

Darkflare felt nauseous again. Now that his memories were starting to come back to him, he had held onto hope that his siblings were still alive, somewhere; that perhaps Kenji hid them somewhere safe. Even though he counted Terra and Meredia among the dead long ago, to hear it all but confirmed on top of Rai's death hurt him deeply.

"I continued to uphold my duty to watch over you as your guardian, but from afar. I wanted you to grow up on your own, and I felt that if I were to make myself known early on, I would hinder your progress."

"But why?" Darkflare shook his head. "I don't understand why you'd keep yourself hidden from us and never tell us all of this."

Kenji stared for a few moments before answering. "You have to understand that I was in a very difficult situation. I'm a warrior, I'm not a parent. I couldn't pretend to take my friends' child on as my own. I watched your parents care for you since you were a baby. And then as you grew on your own, I continued to see them in everything you did. I saw my failure at letting them die reflect in your eyes and your accomplishments. I couldn't stand before you, claiming that your successes were because of anything I did." He paused again. "They would have been proud to see the man you've become."

Darkflare closed his eyes and exhaled deeply, but he felt a tear escape and drip down his cheek; he was thankful he could now remember the faces of the man and the woman in his dreams with clarity. His parents.

"You too, Attila, have grown much since you first shuffled into the town. Believe me, I was both excited and surprised to see another boy of the same age come to Crescentia. My biggest worry was that he would be socially stunted and that I'd have to step in early, but you alleviated that concern." Kenji leaned back and his smile returned. "Even though I wasn't directly involved, I always made sure you both were taken care of - from a distance, where you would not see me. That stray food or coin you would find? That was my doing."

"T-That was you?! I... Thank you," Darkflare leaned forward, trying to keep his emotions in check. "Sincerely, thank you. There were always things that we couldn't explain, like the trinkets, and I thank you for everything you've done for us. And for explaining everything." He looked at his hands once more before looking back at Kenji. "And for understanding my skepticism. This is a lot to take in, but... I know it's true. I can see my parents' faces now. I remember you and the others that used to live in Crescentia. Thank you."

Darkflare looked to Attila, but he merely shrugged. "Yeah. Thanks."

Kenji chuckled, leaning back with a smile once more.

"So is there anything else you wish to know?"

"I'm not sure." Darkflare shook his head, realizing the tension of his headache was gone with the seal over his memories released. "This whole... dragoon thing... It makes sense why I was hearing a voice. It kept saying something about courage."

"That had to have been Odin communicating with you."

"I honestly thought I was just going crazy." Darkflare chuckled sadly as he stared down at his feet. He placed his hand on his chest, massaging the area where the Rune of Courage was. "Well, what now then? What am I supposed to do if I really am this...King of Dragoons?"

"Well, I suppose we have this whole Marked One situation to deal with." Kenji shrugged. "Before today, I haven't heard of any activity from them since before your parents' deaths."

"That's right!" Darkflare sat straight up. As if the arrow he had nearly suffered earlier had come back to impact him, the message the Marked Ones had conveyed impaled his thoughts. "Kailos! We have to go to Kailos Prison! The Marked Ones said that they were running things there and that they had prisoners from today! What if they captured the rulers?!"

Kenji held out a placating hand, a thoughtful look on his face.

"The last I had heard, the leaders are all safe, but that might explain why several members of their courts have not been accounted for yet." Kenji rose from his chair. Darkflare was taken aback at Kenji standing several inches taller than him. "King Nim Valesti, ruler of the Verankner region, cannot find his sister Aiyell, and Queen Faïne Ragwelv's most trusted knight, Knight-Commander Barrayos, are among the missing. If you wish to go after them, you have my blade at your side."

"I'm going too," Attila rose, still tender on his ankle. When Darkflare moved to help him, Attila waved his hand to ward him off. "My leg is fine. I'll walk it off. Don't even think of excluding me just because I can't cast magic like you both."

Darkflare nodded, a confident smile adorned on his face.

"You know I would never turn down your aid. Your stubbornness would see you at my side no matter what the odds."

"Of course. We just stared death down together; the rest trifles in comparison."

Oboro rose out of the bed, and he cocked his head at his master.

"And of course, Oboro. Wouldn't think about leaving you behind." Darkflare smiled and patted the wyvern on the head. "To Kailos Prison then."

Darkflare stood up and looked out the small window in the room. From the sunlight that filtered in, he figured it still had to be mid-morning, early afternoon. The scuffle with the Marked Ones must have only been over the course of a few hours, and the subtle aches in his limbs reminded Darkflare that he had not slept for very long.

"We could leave now and get there before dusk," Darkflare remarked, rubbing his chin very inquisitively.

Kenji nodded, flashing his smile once again. As the tall man walked over to another chair, Darkflare's jaw dropped at what he saw. Resting against the side was a large black sheath adorned with several characters written in a foreign language, as well as a few strange swirls that must have been for decorative purposes. Kenji gripped the golden handle and slung the curved weapon over his back with great ease. Darkflare went to speak from his slacked jaw, but failing to find words, Attila chimed in for him.

"Nice blade."

Kenji bowed lightly and swept open the flaps of his coat to reveal two daggers poking out from behind him on his waist.

"The katana is called the Izayoi; I've trusted my life to it for more years now than I can remember. These Kukri Knives are simply for backup purposes. I can assure you though that they are more than just for show. Give me some time, and I'll show you why Calistron picked me to be your guardian."

Chapter VI

The Ceballe that they stepped out into was not like anything Darkflare had seen before. Thick clouds of smoke still lingered ominously above scattered parts of the city, but that didn't seem to daunt the merchants. They had taken to their businesses once more, trying to rally people back into purchasing, but the town was the emptiest that Darkflare had ever seen it. The streets once packed with crowds were empty enough for carts to travel in both directions; the groups of people that remained were huddled near buildings. There was a buzz still in the air, but it was dramatically more sullen and deflated than earlier.

Adding to the emptiness was the lack of soldiers. The only nation's troops Darkflare could see were D'sylum's. The soldiers in black-trimmed purple armor were scattered through the streets, helping the injured and those with damaged property. Patrols were also marching quickly through alleys with weapons at the ready, more than likely to make sure no other attackers loomed in the shadows.

"This isn't good," Darkflare mused quietly.

Kenji sighed as he ran a hand through his pulled back hair. "No, nothing that happened today is."

"Right, I agree, but in particular I mean... I don't see any soldiers from Beauldyn, Verankner, or Purcille. Do you think the other leaders are already gone?"

"They wouldn't know where to start searching," Attila said dryly as he shrugged.

"Corsius is very political." Kenji nodded. "He probably had them reconvene at his palace where it's safer."

Darkflare wasn't sure what else to say; he was excited to reconnect with Kenji and keep talking, but he did not want to sound too eager, so he simply nodded and looked at his palms again.

He could control fire! And he was a supposed king... but what did being 'king' of these dragoons entail? He had no land, no subjects, and no money. And he was not about to try and usurp a kingdom. He looked around at the destruction of Ceballe, and it quickly sobered his excitement. How could he use any of this new information to help the people suffering?

Or the Despils. That thought almost made him groan. They needed to find who or what was behind these Marked Ones and put a stop to them. For Rai's sake. Or else he would surely only be the first in a long list of casualties...

"I still can't believe it," Darkflare murmured, as they approached the town's exit. There were soldiers standing guard, prohibiting people from entering but watching closely those exiting.

"Hmm?" Kenji looked over his shoulder to catch Darkflare's gaze as he walked on.

"Everything that happened here today... Was the Marked Ones' attack a sign of things to come?"

Kenji hesitated before he answered, his brows drawing down as he turned back around. "Well, it's certainly not a good sign. Like I said, it's been over twenty years since I've heard of any Marked Ones resurfacing. The fact that they chose to strike on the one day the four rulers were gathered - and then your rune decided to awaken on the very same day... I'd say that things will be interesting moving forward."

"Do the nations' armies stand a chance against the Marked Ones?"

"Surely," Kenji nodded. "The armies are stronger and better organized than how today might have made them seem. Even the greatest of armies can be caught unaware with a well-planned surprise attack. It doesn't matter how high the walls and how trained the soldiers, if an army is caught off guard, they can still be decimated. And despite Corsius's massive walls and highly trained soldiers, they were caught well off guard. But once they realized that they were under attack, it took less than an hour for the armies to slay the invaders."

"Then what makes you think we'll get there before Corsius's soldiers?" Attila interjected. Kenji turned to make eye contact with him, but the stoic man was staring past him, toward the horizon. "As much as I'm looking forward to a real test of my blade, isn't there a very real possibility that this journey is for naught?"

"Sure." Kenji shrugged. "Anything is possible. But I doubt that anyone else is aware that the Marked Ones are holding people at Kailos, and if so, we'll be the ones to have the advantage of surprise, this time. With the strange events that have happened, and who knows what will come next, it won't hurt for the nobles to know it was Darkflare Omni who rescued them. Calistron was known for making as many allies as possible, and that helped us more times than I can count on our journeys."

Darkflare did not respond. The thought of being known by name to the rulers and nobles of the land was another overwhelming thought that piled on the growing list in his mind. Being known for winning a tournament was one thing, but being known as some sort of liberator was a completely different thought. Fame or not, saving the defenseless was something that his heart knew was right to do. He would have done the same even if the captives were commoners.

Once they were out of the boundaries of the city and back on the main road, Darkflare took a moment to appreciate for the first time in a long time just how much of a contrast there was between the secluded city life of Ceballe and the wide open plains of the world. It was soothing to be back where the rolling, green grass stretched for endless miles wherever his gaze turned. A tree, harboring either indigenous wildlife or ripening fruits, occasionally broke the uniformity of pasture every now and then. Darkflare knew that further toward Crescentia there were a few forest entrances scattered along the way, but the majority of the path from Ceballe back to his home was an endless plain of grassland. The weather in D'sylum seemed to usually stay the same year-round, with the occasional rain when nature desired; it was never bitter cold or sweltering hot but always somewhere in between. The sun could be a little overbearing at times on the weary walker, so a cool breeze was always a welcome surprise.

Darkflare found himself staring up at the deepening amber sky. The peace of the afternoon should have helped to calm his nerves, but the orange sky just reminded him of the day's carnage. He wasn't sure how long he was lost in his thoughts, but eventually Oboro flew over and rubbed his head on Darkflare's shoulder. He reached up and patted the wyvern, smiling, despite himself. Kenji turned and smiled as well.

"Wyverns are some of the most empathetic creatures. He's attached to you because he can sense your good heart."

Darkflare nuzzled Oboro's head as the wyvern lovingly nudged into his hand. "He's truly a smart creature."

"Not just anyone can form a bond with them, as I'm sure you've realized. Just because you might have been the first person that Oboro saw upon hatching did not mean that he had to keep obeying you. If he ever judged you unfit, he'd just take off and never return."

"Does… my connection with Oboro have anything to do with my rune?"

"Your connection does not, but there was one other dragoon of note that had a dragon companion. The very first King of Dragoons, the man that I told you won Odin's favor, was supposed to have tamed a dragon. I believe the man's name was Artemis, if I'm not mistaken, and he is depicted being a majestic figure with pride, strength, wisdom, and equanimity. He was considered the epitome of what any leader should strive to be, long before history all but forgot his name. Because he was known by many as the dragon knight, he decided the title of those blessed should be called dragoon, henceforth. Even though taming wyverns and dragons is not the standard for us rune bearers, we all still bear the title."

"Huh, how about that? How do you know so much about the first king, Kenji? I've never read anything about an Artemis that had a dragon, from what I can remember."

"I've been on many journeys. I've learned mostly about him through word of mouth by wise elders and sages. Speech travels where written words cannot. There might be one or two, but not very many, historical books that document his existence. As far as the majority of the world is concerned, we dragoons are just a mythical race developed by storytellers and tale-weavers, because the thought of mortals blessed by the gods seems too unbelievable. But the rulers and their courts – they know of our existence."

"Th-they do?!" Darkflare's eyes widened.

"Of course." Kenji nodded. "They train those that are magic sensitive to create the crystals we use – they aren't blind to magic and its many different users. We've had to seek aid in our journeys in the past. They just don't proclaim it to all of their subjects. They don't want people panicking about what they don't understand."

"So how many people knew that you were dragoons?"

"We told people that we aided what we were, but many didn't believe us. Some were impressed that we could use magic, some were in awe of our martial prowess, when we showed our runes many feared us as if we were Marked Ones, and those that understood the meaning of what a dragoon truly was aided us in every way possible. Like I said, Calistron made many allies, and he always made sure to take the time to show people that we were good natured and to talk about our mission to expunge evil. But still… People fear what they don't understand, and darkness can fester within a fearful heart."

Darkflare wanted to ask Kenji *what* there was to fear, but upon feeling the heat in his palms, he shook his head and swallowed his doubts. Refocusing his gaze toward the landscape ahead, Darkflare watched as the stream of endless green receded. Instead of nature's trail of bountiful grass, the land ahead was corroded with decay. Darkflare stopped at the edge of the scarred line, and he took several moments to stare at the ruins of Syvail, his mind working over the information from Kenji. He saw the damaged walls and broken land in a new light, and the fear and wonder it might have once had was replaced with a deep hurt that made him reach for his necklace.

Attila walked up to the gate, just as he had done earlier, but stopped before reaching the metallic bars. Folding his arms over his chest, he peered into the background of the runic area. Kenji walked up beside him and stared expressionlessly through the slits.

"It's been a while since I've been here," Kenji reminisced as he slid his hands into his coat pockets.

"Is there anything within the ruins that might be of use to us?" Darkflare moved up to join his allies.

"Well... You could say that."

This raised Attila's curiosity as his gaze swerved toward Kenji.

"So then, let's go in. Darkflare and I have always wanted to explore, and with someone who knows their way around, this seems like the perfect opportunity."

"Eh." Kenji turned away, scratching the side of his head, as if searching for a reason not to go in. "Well, despite the tragedy that happened here, now what lies within is nothing but ruins. What I was referencing was that I came here years ago to bury something, but other than that-..."

A high-pitched, very human yelp echoed off the rubble from within Syvail and broke the mesmerizing serenity. Darkflare snapped his right hand onto the hilt of his sword and struggled to look into the ruins.

"Definitely inside," Attila remarked. He had reached for his weapon as well, but he was visibly less disturbed. "They mustn't be far in."

Letting the sword slip back into the scabbard, Darkflare ran up to the metal bars and furiously shook them with both gloved hands.

"C'mon, dragoon powers! Give me the strength to break through these bars!" It was of no use. The gate rocked slightly, creaking from the old rust and chains that secured it in place.

"Please," sighed Kenji as the Izayoi slipped silently from his scabbard with his right hand. "Move."

Darkflare took a few steps back and watched anxiously. Kenji stood in front of the chains that hindered their path and raised the sword high over his head. Gripping the handle with both hands, he brought the blade down with one swift diagonal cut. Kenji's arms moved so quickly and the attack was so silent, Darkflare thought that he had missed; the only noise being a hushed buzz caused by the sword tearing the air asunder with such swiftness. Kenji dropped his right arm, letting the tip of the sword rest upon the ground. He raised the other hand to the metal bars and pushed. The chains had been completely severed and the gate swung open.

Darkflare could hardly believe his eyes as he watched Kenji stroll into the ruins that had been forbidden to them for so many years – with one swift cut! Darkflare exchanged his astonished glance with Attila, and they jogged in after their comrade with Oboro in tow.

As they passed the gate's threshold and took in the full view of the ruins, unhindered by the metal bars, Darkflare found himself stunned in awe. The land was just as decayed inside as it was outside, and the buildings that once made up D'sylum's capital now lay like scattered play toys of children. Not a single thing stirred as far as they could see, but *something* had cried out.

Darkflare caught a brief sad look on Kenji's face before he turned and pointed in two different directions. "One of you go left and the other right. I'll go straight."

Before either could contest, Kenji had already begun running. Further in the back was a large building that Kenji had not taken his eyes off since they had entered; if there was a viable entrance, it was impossible to tell from so far away. Darkflare brought his attention back to Attila and nodded.

"Oboro and I will go left. You'll be alright going alone? How is your ankle?"

"I'm fine."

The biting tone that Attila responded with caused Darkflare to wince as they separated. It was a stupid question to ask; of course Attila would be fine, and Darkflare knew that his friend hated being worried about. Oboro took off slightly ahead, as if trying to scout the area since he had the advantage of flight. As Darkflare ran through the ruins, trying not to trip over the rubble and skeletal remains of creatures that once tried to prosper there, his mind raced with him. What could have gotten inside with the gate still sealed? Was there actually someone still *living* in here - perhaps a survivor? There obviously still had to be *multiple* things still alive upon these hallowed grounds; something that made the yelp and something that caused it.

Coming to a fork in the road, Darkflare skidded to a stop, which kicked up some dust. The right path seemed to lead around to the back of the large building that held Kenji's interest while the left was hidden behind a pile of rubble that blocked the view around the corner. Darkflare was considering his options when he had to double take in the left direction.

"What the...? Oboro, you see that?"

The wyvern growled in response.

Darkflare had seen something dash just out of sight around the corner of the fallen rubble, and even though he barely saw it, the figure seemed short and plump. He followed at a distance, holding his right hand tightly around the grip of his sword. There were several of these creatures, and once Darkflare managed to make out the scraps of armor they wore for helmets, he had a feeling that he knew what he was chasing. Goblins. He had never seen one up close before, but he had read about them in numerous books. They usually covered their putrid olive-green flesh with whatever materials they could salvage to make a semblance of armor.

The path ahead came to an end and Darkflare hid behind a column, carefully hugging it to peek around. His attention darted away from the fiends to the target that they had focused their attention on; a girl who looked around the same age as himself. Her light leather jerkin exposed her arms, but the lack of armor there didn't seem to daunt her as she stood resolute with her weapon drawn. She had a bow made out of simple material, maybe cork, in one hand. She pulled an arrow from the sling on her back and held it and the bow low.

Darkflare did not want to give the goblins another moment to close in on the girl. He turned his head to the left and searched for the first pile of rubble that looked climbable. Without thinking of the dangers, Darkflare quickly leapt onto the ruined mound, trying to make as little noise as possible as he scaled over stones and beams. He pushed himself to move faster as he noticed the goblins lumbering forward with daggers drawn. He hurled his body up and over, and as he reached the edge of the platform, Darkflare measured the distance to prepare himself.

"We have to help her, Oboro." The wyvern nodded his head in response.

Like a lion on the hunt, Darkflare ran and then leapt off the edge, aiming to put himself between the predators and the prey they backed into a corner. Darkflare landed on one knee in front of her and drew his weapon as he stood in one blur of motion. Both parties seemed surprised at the young man's sudden appearance, but the goblins growled and flailed their weapons in the air. Darkflare was sure it was supposed to be menacing, but they looked no more intimidating than children playing knights and castle.

"C'mon! You want a fight? I'm the one you want!"

Giving off a gargle of a battle cry at the man's taunt, the squat creatures rushed forward. Darkflare waited for the first one to swing its knife and then brought his own sword downward with such force that it knocked the dagger out of the goblin's grip. The little creature shrieked as its weapon flew out of its grasp and skidded away across the ground.

The second goblin had rallied its weapon but stood stunned with how easily the first had been deflected. This gave Darkflare an advantage he seized by stepping forward and raising his right leg behind him. With a quick twist of his body, he brought the tip of his boot crashing into the jaw of his opponent. The force of the punt lifted the smaller opponent off the ground and sent him flying several feet back.

The third and final goblin gave out a yelp of surprise as it witnessed its two comrades had been beaten. Darkflare glared a cocky smirk toward his opponent, gripping his sword in both of his hands. He hoped the show would be enough to frighten the third creature off without killing any of them, and he let out a sigh of relief when his efforts paid off.. The final goblin let out a choked cry of distress and fled in the opposite direction. The first goblin regained his wits and followed on the third's heels. It took the second a few moments after the others left, but it awoke in a terrified frenzy and hobbled away quickly.

Darkflare let out a chuckle as he turned around to face the woman he had saved, but he didn't expect the bow to be loaded with an arrow aimed at him.

"Who are you?" The woman growled, her light blue eyes locked on him with a look of anger flashing across her face.

"Hold your arrow!" Darkflare splayed his arms out, keeping his sword low and passive. "I am not your enemy."

"I won't ask again," she said, drawing the arrow back a bit more. "Who are you?"

Darkflare exhaled slowly, letting his arms drop slightly. This was not the thanks he had expected, but he rightly could not blame her; and so he decided to answer her honestly.

"My name is Darkflare Omni."

"What are you doing here?"

Darkflare raised his open off hand in as calming of a gesture as he could manage. "I'd gladly answer your questions, but perhaps you can lower your bow so we can talk a bit easier? And perhaps you could return the favor of a name?"

She stared at him for a moment longer and then dropped her aim, her expression softening as she pushed strands of long blonde hair behind one ear. "My name is Luna Iylvein. What are you doing here?"

"That's a fine question, but I could ask you the same," he shrugged with a sly smile, "especially since the gates were sealed."

She eyed him over for a few more moments before sighing and slinging her bow over her back. "Thank you for the aid, but I could have taken on those goblins by myself."

"Of that, I have no doubt." Darkflare sheathed his sword then inclined his chin toward her as he looked at the bow poking over her shoulder. "I can tell you know how to handle yourself. I didn't like the odds though. And besides, they did have you cornered."

She frowned for a moment and Darkflare thought he saw color rush to her cheeks. "You didn't answer me. What are you doing here?"

"Well, we heard-…"

"We?" she interrupted, looking over his shoulder.

"Yes. I'm traveling with two others. We heard, what I presume, was your yelp?"

This time, he did see red in her cheeks as she turned from him. "Er, yes… I can't believe you heard that! I was startled when I came face to face with those creepy little things."

Darkflare chuckled. "Yeah, I can imagine. They're not the prettiest, which is why I guess they hide behind masks and armor."

She turned back around and cocked her head. A pretty smile formed on her face as she saw Oboro. "Wow! Is that a…? A wyvern? May I?"

"Oh, I don't know, Oboro usually-…"

But as he was speaking, she cautiously approached the wyvern floating beside him, holding one gentle hand out to him. Oboro looked at her, confused at first, but he lowered his head for her to pat him. Darkflare stared at her, at a loss for words.

"He, uh, usually isn't that polite with strangers."

"Well, Oboro! I can assume that you and Darkflare here won't be telling the Pheeq military about our little encounter, hmm?" She turned and winked at him.

"Well, we're just as much to blame as you are," he said, throwing his arms out passively to the sides and letting them drop. "We cut the lock holding the gate."

"That's a relief. I'd hate to try and sneak out the way I came in." She took her hand away from the wyvern and looked toward the entrance, giving Darkflare a wary smile. "Well, thank you for the help - both with the goblins and opening the gate. I'm going to get going now."

"Wait!" Darkflare put his hand up, and he swore he saw Luna reach for her quiver as her hand reached back into the shoulder-length blonde hair. "It's not safe to wander around here alone. There's no telling what other dangers hide in the ruins. Let me walk you back to the entrance. We're both heading that way anyway."

She stared at him for a moment, not saying anything. Luna eventually nodded and motioned forward. "Alright, but you first. I'd rather keep my eye on you, if it's all the same."

Darkflare nodded with a genuine smile before walking forward. Retracing his footsteps, Darkflare returned with Luna to the entrance to find Attila leaning against one of the broken pillars, staring at a rock he was digging into the ground with his foot, and Kenji was sitting on a stone, bent forward, wiping the blade of his Izayoi. Both men turned their heads up to watch the trio approach.

"So this is our squeaker, eh?" remarked Kenji, placing the katana back into its scabbard.

The girl crossed her arms and narrowed her eyes. "I was alone, in a creepy place, and turned around to a strange creature staring at me. I appreciate the concern for coming to find me, but I'm quite alright. Your friend here took care of the goblins."

Kenji looked over to where Darkflare was and raised an eyebrow. "So you found goblins as well? I'm not really too surprised since they love to scavenge in ruins, but they weren't here last I was. I found several in the tower and Attila ran into a few of his own."

"How's your ankle?" Darkflare crossed his arms as he walked over to his brooding friend.

"Working. Nothing I can't handle."

Luna looked at Attila and pointed a dainty finger at him. "So, he's Darkflare, you're Attila... and you are?" She moved her finger toward Kenji, tilting her head sideways slightly, smiling curiously, and cocked an eyebrow.

Kenji returned an amused smile of his own.

"My name is Kenji. And you are, miss?"

"Luna. Pleasure to meet you."

"The pleasure is mine," Kenji said with a deep bow.

"Right," a tight smile painted her face as she spoke, looking at each of them in turn carefully. "So now that the introductions are out of the way, where were you all headed before you stopped here? To my knowledge, there isn't anything this far south beside trees and hills."

"That's a good question," Attila remarked, turning his head to glance at the girl for the first time. "Why don't you start by answering first? What are you doing here?"

She narrowed her eyes again at Attila, but she cleared her throat and crossed her arms. "That's rather rude, but alright, if you insist, since I'm outnumbered. I had gone to Ceballe to see the fighter's tournament, but I left as quickly as I could when all of that chaos erupted about bandits or whatnot. The roads were so clustered with people trying to flee west that I decided to see what lay southeast, since it's not marked on any of the maps I've seen. Someone in Ceballe had told me about the ruins of Syvail, so I decided to see it for myself.

"At first I wasn't sure how I was going to get past the walls. After walking around the outside for a bit, I noticed there was a small hole on one side that I could squeeze through. So I decided to explore for a bit, until those goblins came out of nowhere. The one closest to me had its helmet raised, and I had never seen anything so hideous before. I tried to lose them as fast as I could, only all the debris on the ground made it harder. And that's when Darkflare showed up."

"We know all too well about the bandit attack." Kenji nodded, looking to Darkflare. "We were there when it happened, too. That is why we're out this way."

"Well, you three certainly don't look like bandits." Luna shrugged, looking over the men. "I got a good look at a few of them as I was fleeing. You aren't covered in grime or look like you haven't bathed in months. But beside all that, something about them looked… inhuman."

"That's cause they weren't," Darkflare said as he shook his head.

"What do you mean?" Luna narrowed her eyes. "They're not human?"

"To put it simply, if I understand correctly," Darkflare looked at Kenji, who shrugged to continue, "they're really a form of demons. They're called the Marked Ones."

Luna raised her eyebrows and then let out a chortle. "Marked Ones? Are you sure you're not running on too much of a fighter's high? You might not be a bandit, but you surely went to enter the tournament yourself."

"That's your decision whether you believe us or not. It was hard for me to swallow the information at first, too. Just know that I have no reason to lie to you." Darkflare shook his head, forcing more resolve into his eyes when he looked back at Luna. "But there are innocent people in danger at Kailos Prison. One of the Marked Ones said something about turning them to darkness. We have to get there to stop them before that happens. If anything were to befall the nobles they've taken, it might have a backlash that would be felt by all four kingdoms."

Luna's gaze flicked between the three of them, as if searching for the truth. She eventually settled on Darkflare.

"What did the rulers say when you told them that? There's an army out beyond that gate, right?"

"Ah," Darkflare looked up to the sky, running his hand through his bandana and spikes. He looked to Attila and Kenji, but the first looked away and the latter chortled. "We, uh, didn't tell anyone else. It's just us."

Luna laughed out loud, not bothering to restrain herself. "So that's it? The three of you are going to go storm a prison to save people from supposed demons? Do you understand how farfetched that sounds?" When none of them answered, she shook her head and began to walk off. "Good luck with that."

"We have more than that."

Luna stopped and looked back at Darkflare. When he felt Kenji and Attila's gazes upon him, he wasn't sure what he thought was going to happen. He closed his eyes and held his palm up in front of him. He could just barely feel the flickering heat of the flames in the center of his palm, and he focused on that sensation. It felt like a great weight was pushing down on his hand, and he had to struggle to keep the heat. He heard a gasp from Luna and he opened his eyes. He had seen a ball of flame hover there for just long enough to know he truly did conjure it before it vanished. He felt himself breathing heavily all of a sudden.

"Careful, Darkflare." Kenji was behind him, resting a hand on his shoulder. "You've just awoken your powers. It will take some time before you can properly use them. The physical toll it can take on your body is not to be underestimated."

"What was that?!" Luna cried, and Darkflare realized she had her bow in her hands, but she hadn't nocked an arrow. "Was that...?!"

"Magic." Darkflare nodded. "We have magic on our side, and you've seen it, firsthand. Do you believe me now about the Marked Ones?"

She stared at him for a few more moments before putting her bow away. "Just tell me one thing. Why?"

"Why what?" Darkflare's brows furrowed in confusion.

"If everything you've just told me is true, why are you going to risk your lives to help a bunch of people you don't even know? People that, whether they live or die, don't affect your life in one bit."

"Because it's the right thing to do," Darkflare blurted out, without thinking. "There is significant risk, yes. We're putting our lives on the line. But I've just learned that I have this power, this... magic. And I need to use it to help people."

Luna nodded, at first slowly, but then confidently. "Let me go with you then."

"A-Are you sure?" Darkflare looked at the others nervously. "You have no other pressing business?"

Luna sighed and looked up at the horizon over Darkflare's head. "It's a long story. Let's just say I'm not from around here, and I came east to search for, we'll call it, purpose. And then you three find me here, and someone your age is able to conjure magic? I'm willing to take this as a sign that fate has me on the right path."

"I don't want to hear one more word about fate," Attila nearly spat as he shook his head. "Just tell me you can actually use that bow."

"I'm as sure of a shot as you'll find." Luna grabbed an arrow out from her quiver and twirled it in her fingertips. "I have plenty of arrows, and when I run out, I can fletch more easily enough. I also have a dagger – for just in case."

"And you would be willing to travel to the prison, knowing the dangers?" Kenji put his hands on his hips, that smirk never leaving. "You have no idea who we are, and this is an extremely perilous task we're undertaking. You would have to look out for yourself."

"I know how to take care of myself," she responded, staring at him defiantly. "I don't know you, you're right. But if Darkflare is as noble as his ideals, then I would assume the company he keeps would have to be halfway decent. If any of you try anything, I'll have an arrow in your windpipe before you can blink."

Kenji's grin widened. "You've got pep, that's for sure. Then come along if you'd like to help save the prisoners."

Darkflare nodded as Luna faced him once more. "We're going to need all of the help we can get. I don't even know how big Kailos is. But be warned, we'll be keeping an eye on you too."

"Oh, please. I said you don't look like bandits, but that doesn't mean you have anything that I want. Let's get off on the right foot, shall we? You wanted me to trust you, so trust me in return."

She placed her hand out, and Darkflare grabbed it and shook.

"Alright, Luna. Welcome aboard. I suppose we could do with an archer."

Kenji and Attila took turns shaking her hand before they all walked back to the entrance of Syvail, Oboro hovering behind.

Darkflare stopped as he reached the gates that so long barred his entrance. He stared at the building in the back. Hadn't Kenji said something about coming here in the past? He closed the creaking gates to Syvail and sealed whatever secrets Kenji might have had in that tower.

Chapter VII

Darkflare traversed the path that was so natural to him with quick strides. His heart felt like he was returning home, but his mind knew better. He knew that at the crossroads, he would have to turn east, on a very foreign trail – with a very unfamiliar group.

Ahead of him, the blue ponytail of his guardian bobbed rhythmically with every step; the wary blonde archer walked a few paces beside him, an arrow twirling in between her fingertips; and a glance to his other side affirmed Attila, arms crossed, was keeping pace. Oboro cooed softly as he flew alongside his master, as if trying to soothe his thoughts, and Darkflare raised a hand to his wyvern's chin.

It was not much farther, but night would be upon them soon enough. The orange sky was beginning to darken as the sun drifted toward the horizon in the distance. Hearing the familiar sound of waves crashing on the beach caused Darkflare's heart to beat more rapidly. They veered off the main path, taking a side route where the road began to shrivel, surrounded by water on both sides. In the distance, a large building loomed over the sea, as if it were a giant's hand, beckoning seafarers to false safety. The prison was housed on an island that was separated from the main land – the only way in was from a drawbridge after crossing the narrow peninsula. The group pulled off to the side and hid behind the last large sea rock.

"Well… What are our options?" Darkflare asked, peering around toward the drawbridge in the distance. "This is the farthest I've ever made it to the prison. Didn't really give any consideration to getting across the drawbridge."

"Hmm…" Kenji stroked his chin, and there was a moment's pause before he spoke again. "They are definitely Marked Ones. You were right, Darkflare."

Luna cautiously peered past the rock and shook her head. "How can you tell? They don't look like the 'bandits' that attacked Ceballe."

"Use that archer's sight of yours to look closer."

Luna raised her eyebrows sarcastically, as if about to retort, but her face hardened as she looked back at the men on the two tall, thin structures at the end of the bridge. "I take it back. Armor is different, but they've definitely got that same soulless look you described. And… what is that on their necks? The…"

"The mark?"

She turned back to the men and nodded hesitantly. "That's what gives them their name, I assume?"

"It is." It was Darkflare's turn to nod. "I'm just surprised they're bearing the symbol like a mark of pride."

Kenji leaned back against the rock. "Because it is to them. Their minds are warped; they consider it a great accomplishment to wield such power. Besides, the mark is discreet enough to the average eye. Did you notice it before you knew what the Marked Ones were?"

Darkflare shook his head. "You've got a point. We know what we're looking for now."

"This is ridiculous," Luna said as her eyes bulged. "Are they really demons? Is there any saving them?"

"No." Kenji's voice was harsh. Darkflare had expected as much, but he felt himself deflate just slightly. "Once you willingly sacrifice your mortality, there is no salvation. They are no longer people – just a husk taking the form of someone who once was human."

There was a silence that followed, but Kenji turned and looked back at the Marked Ones.

"Luna, is your aim as true as you claim it is?"

"I'll easily prove it, just say the word." The arrow she had been twirling increased in its speed, as if it were about to fly forth from her fingers.

"Okay. Darkflare, act as if you're bringing Attila in as a prisoner. Distract the guards long enough."

Darkflare grinned at Attila, who stared at Kenji with narrowed eyes.

"Seriously?" The dark haired man shook his head, annoyance flashing in his face. When Kenji nodded, Attila smacked Darkflare on the shoulder. "Let's get this over with. Don't do anything idiotic."

Darkflare stood, chuckling to himself, and as he began to get Attila into position, he stopped. He turned to Oboro, who padded along the ground behind him.

"Sorry, Oboro. It's probably best for you to wait here. Your new friend will keep us safe."

With that, Oboro looked over at Luna, who flashed the wyvern a wide smile. The creature gave Darkflare a longing look before walking on all fours over to the blonde archer. Darkflare made sure to meet her gaze and nodded solemnly.

"Give me your sword," Darkflare said as he turned back to Attila and held his hand out.

"Excuse me?" Attila cocked an eyebrow, but his eyes reflected astonishment.

"You're supposed to be my prisoner. I'll have your sword pressed against your back, looking like I'm driving you forward, so if anything happens, I can just hand it back to you."

Attila reluctantly shoved the handle into the open hand and turned around. Darkflare swayed under the weight of the weapon, forcing himself to rebalance his stance.

"If that blade so much as touches the ground, I'm throwing you at the Marked Ones."

"I've got it! Now, hush and start moving!"

Darkflare made sure to shove the broad side of the blade into Attila's left shoulder, to which he received a dirty look, but no more snide comments.

* * * * *

A pair of guards stood at the end of the path in front of twin, ten-foot poles that signified where the bridge dropped to. Gulping down the last of his worried nerves, Darkflare prepared himself for what he hoped would be the best performance of his life. As they slowly approached, the men that stood in their way drew their weapons. Darkflare did his best to look at the symbol on the left side of their necks only once, but his eyes darted to it a second time.

"Halt! State your name and purpose for coming to Kailos."

They sounded like humans, and they didn't look gray-skinned like the ones that Darkflare had vanquished. Their similarity to what he'd call 'normal' almost gave him pause. He cleared his throat.

"Woah, now! Hold on there, you dimwits! I've come to collect the bounty on this fellow. Don't you know who this is?!"

The guards shared a glance, but they did not relinquish their stances. One of the men simply inclined his head, as if to motion for Darkflare to keep talking.

"Why, this is the Great… Uncle's… Brother of… the, uh, Royal Lord… Wickhamwaddam, who everyone knows is the esteemed Guardian of King Valesti of Verankner!"

Narrowing their eyes, the two guards exchanged confused looks once again.

"Lord... who?"

"Great Uncle's... what?"

Darkflare heard a gurgled cry that was followed by a loud splash. Both guards whipped around to see what caused it, only to jump back from the drawbridge dropping before them. The guard that had been watching over the controls was now floating dead in the water, an arrow protruding from his jugular. Just before he disappeared in a flash of shadow, Darkflare saw the telltale gray skin.

Attila rushed forward and punched both men in the stomach as they turned. Doubled over in pain, he slammed their heads together. A loud clanking of metal upon metal rang out as both men fell over, knocked out cold.

"Lord Wickhamwaddam... Really, Darkflare? Really?" Attila shook his head as he shoved the passed out bodies into the water. Shadows burst forth from the depths a few moments later.

"Is *that* what you said?" Luna asked, fighting back from bursting out in laughter as the trio rejoined them.

Darkflare felt his face redden as he clenched his teeth. "I was just trying to draw time out for you to loose your arrow! Besides, I'm better entertaining with my sword than my words!"

Kenji shook his head, stepping past them all. "I don't want to know how the Pale out of all of the names in the world, *Wickhamwaddam* was the first to come to your mind..."

Darkflare shook his head, and after he handed Attila's sword back to him, hurried after Kenji with Oboro on his shoulder and his allies in tow. As they strode across the drawbridge, his fingers twitched nervously around the longsword at his hip. It was too quiet. He had seen the numbers that the Marked Ones were capable of at Ceballe – and he had to keep reminding himself that they were not just ordinary bandits or mercenaries, but in fact demons.

As they approached the open portcullis, no one came to challenge them from the darkness within; but Kenji pulled them off to the side and leaned against the wall, as if listening to ensure that was the case. Darkflare felt his heartbeat in his ears as the slow moments ticked by, waiting for whatever defenders the prison rallied in its defense.

But still, no one came. Kenji looked back to the group and nodded, ushering them onward. Darkflare moved in and put his back against a wall, allowing his eyes to adjust to the dim light that was cast by muted flames. The waxy candles lined the walls at sporadic intervals, casting just barely enough light for Darkflare to see the outline of his group.

"Alright," Kenji's voice was no louder than a whisper. "There's a large courtyard on the roof of the building that leads to the warden's quarters. If they're being held here, that courtyard would be a perfect place to keep them away from the rest of the... villainy here."

"How do we get to the roof?" Luna asked, looking around. "I don't see any stairs."

"There is a way up at the very back. We'll have to pass through most of the prison to get there though, which includes going around the center work yard."

"How do you know so much about this place?" Luna hissed.

"Because before the bandits took over, Kalios was maintained by the residents of the nearby town - and I used to be one of those residents."

"I see. I'm sorry." Luna shook her head.

Darkflare found himself more excited than he should have been. His studies had been correct about the former wardens of the prison! The joy was short lived and his spirits sank; if only his parents could see how decrepit the place was now.

Kenji peered ahead to make sure they still hadn't been spotted. "Let's get going. We can't afford to waste any more time."

Kenji cautiously stalked forward as he led the group, into the darkness of the corridor, against the wall and away from the light of the torches. Darkflare could not help but steal unseen glances across the hall at the prisoners they passed. He wished he hadn't. Not all the cells were occupied, but the faces that peered out from those that were looked ghostly pale in the dim light of the candles. They seemed more along the lines of specters than living people - specters that, if they spotted the intruders, might cry out to the guards if they thought it would ease their sentence or grant them a morsel more of food. He shook his head as he reminded himself that this *was* a real prison at some point.

Darkflare made sure to stay half a step behind Kenji, and he had Oboro cling tightly to his shoulder to avoid flapping his wings and creating noise. As he covertly leapt from one shadow to the next, Darkflare's breathing fell as close to muted as he could make it. It seemed silly, but in his own head, he thought that if he could hear himself breathing, then that meant that someone else would also hear the sound of his lungs inhaling the raw air. A quick look back showed Luna close behind Darkflare, and Attila trailed in the back.

After a few minutes of rushing down the corridor, Kenji waved his hand backward, as if to indicate stopping. A drop of sweat trickled down Darkflare's forehead, and he could feel his pulse drumming as he looked ahead. A guard was coming down the corridor, probably on a normal patrol route. Darkflare hurried Oboro to wedge between he and Kenji as he pinned his back to the wall between two cells. They were not in the vicinity of any torchlight, but could the shadows really conceal all five of them? If one prisoner leaned out to look into the hall, they would see them, even in the darkness. His fingers twitched nervously once more as they gripped the handle of his longsword. If the guard did spot them, it would take one quick and precise slice to silence him.

Darkflare could hear the footsteps echoing off the stone floor growing closer and closer, and his pulse seemed to match the rhythmic marching. He was only a few feet away now, and Darkflare inhaled silently, keeping the breath sealed tightly in his lungs.

He only let it out once the man passed by Attila without noticing them. Perhaps the darkness was really more concealing than he thought. Perhaps the horrors of the prison they had entered was beginning to fray his nerves. Perhaps Darkflare needed a drink when they got out of there. And he was not a drinking man.

Darkflare heard the breath exhale from Attila and Luna's lips alongside his own, and Kenji was quick to give them a chiding look. He must have known full well that the new 'warriors,' if they could even be called that, must have been scared. They were in a new and intimidating area; darkness, death, and damnation hung all around them.

They could not allow themselves to get caught – after all, they had been harboring safe passage for the closely distant relative of Lord Wickhamwaddam.

Kenji moved forward, and Darkflare swung Oboro back to his shoulder in order to follow his guardian once more. As they continued on, Darkflare could still feel his heartbeat pounding in synchronization with each step he took. The anxiety subsided from making him feel as if his ears were about to shatter from the throbbing of his pulse, but his footsteps did still feel heavier and louder than they actually were. They stopped at an intersection so suddenly that Darkflare almost slammed into Kenji, which would have caused a chain effect behind him. Luckily enough, Darkflare noticed the body right in front of his face and halted on his heels. In front of them was one of many crossroads that they encountered traversing the prison. The patrols were increasing, and a pair of bandits crossed right in front of them. The trick was just being patient and they avoided any contact with the guards.

After a countless series of intersections, a small force of patrolling guards, and many intense moments labored in utter silence, the path stopped just as abruptly as every other time they halted. Forward was barred by a metal gate – much smaller than the one that closed off Syvail. Darkflare felt his stomach lurch as he caught a glimpse at the figures that, if he didn't know better, could have been zombies on the other side of the wall. All of them looked malnourished to the bone, as if they had not more than a morsel a day for years, and each of them had deep scars all over their bodies from lashings; even if they had been criminals, it was obvious that the Marked Ones were abusing them. And who even knew if they *were* criminals? Darkflare had a sick feeling that the prison was being used to torture more souls into joining the Marked Ones' ranks.

"What is this?" Luna's voice was shaky, her repulsion obvious.

"I…" Kenji hesitated, his brows furrowing in confusion. "This was the work yard, but *this*…" His voice took on a dark, almost growling, tone. "What did they do to this place?"

"This is a labor yard," the words fell out of Darkflare's mouth flatly, drained of emotion. "This isn't a prison. It's a labor camp."

"Bastards," Attila mumbled coldly.

Darkflare shook his head and forced his eyes to the ground. He wanted to get away from the sight as quickly as he could. *They* were what cried out screams of terror; there was no mistaking the lash markings that were engraved on their backs and arms. The pain was so visible that it made Darkflare's body throb with tremendous torment. *No one* should be used as fodder in some demonic army. Darkflare gripped the wall, doing his all not to punch it in anger and disgust.

"We can't just let-…"

"Don't, Darkflare," Kenji swung on him with a harsh look. "Don't look at them and don't think about them. Kailos may be run by a group of demons, but don't be deceived. Corsius still sends criminals here to serve. Whether the Marked Ones turn them here, or they die somewhere else, they'll still end up in The Pale. They don't deserve your pity."

Kenji leapt to the other wall, following it left and around a corner. Darkflare forced himself to follow, but he glanced back at Luna. There was a new look of concern on her face, but she reciprocated Darkflare's look with a hesitant nod.

Once they reached the other side of the labor camp, Darkflare
felt for the first time since entering the prison that he could relax his
guard. The doorway that held the passage upward was just a short
distance off; so close that Darkflare could see it under burning torches.
Kenji began to slowly creep over to it, making sure that there were no
guards around to stop them from going upstairs. Darkflare was right on
his heels, letting the adrenaline think for him, until…

Knock, knock. Knock… Knock …

All four of them stood frozen, and with each clattering echo,
they felt more exposed under the light of the torch nearby. Darkflare
whipped around, looking for the initial source of the commotion. One
glance at the horror on Luna's face told him who caused it. The hollow
noisemaker he saw bounce to a stop in front of Kenji was a large, decaying
bone that could not have been of human origin. Footsteps could be
heard pounding in from behind them and around the next corridor.

They could not be caught. Not now of all times. They were
almost to the second floor; Darkflare could see the illuminated passage
not more than twenty feet off. He had to think quickly, the guards would
be upon them in a matter of moments. His eyes frantically swept the
area, trying to find something – anything – that would give them better
cover in the darkness.

That was when it hit him – the candle. Darkflare raised his right
hand to the only source of light around them, focusing on the flame.

"Darkflare, what are you…?" Luna hissed, but Attila placed his
finger to her lips in order to silence her.

Darkflare closed his eyes. He felt through his emotions,
searching quickly within his own mind for the memory of his dreams,
for the heat of the flames. He tensed the muscles in his right arm, forcing
his fingers to reach out, and he began to feel the center of his palm tingle
like before. It was not a burning sensation, but it was warm, soothing,
and gave him an uplifting sense of power. He felt as if the flames were
listening to his thoughts, ready to obey his commands in recognition of
him being their master. It took more energy than when he summoned
the ball of fire in Syvail, and he almost thought he would faint from the
exertion.

His eyes snapped open, and with one fluid thrust of his hand
forward and then snapping it back, the flame of the candle faded quicker
than a heartbeat. Once again enveloped in darkness, they waited for
the guards to run by the corridor they had come from, silent and dark
as shadows. If they had said anything, Darkflare didn't hear it; he was

too focused on keeping his balance. He felt a hand on each shoulder as Kenji and Attila steadied him, holding him back against the wall. Once the Marked Ones ran past them, shouting in some dark, guttural tones, Kenji hurried around the corner and across the hallway, leading his allies toward the ascending steps.

Darkflare hurried to catch up to his guardian, but as the pinpricks of stars faded from his vision, the reality of what he just did set in – and he was in awe. He really had used his power to control the flames and doused the light from exposing them. The scene played over and over in Darkflare's mind as he traversed the staircase, so much so that he almost tripped as he and his allies climbed.

At the end of the ascension, Kenji delicately opened the door, making sure not to allow any squeaks or noises to permeate the air. Once he stepped through to the second floor, he paused. When Darkflare led the others through, he noticed the confused look on Kenji's face. Darkflare briefly glanced around and realized that no bodies inhabited any of the cells. No prisoners, no guards; only the flickering lights in the hall welcomed the group. Kenji frowned, obviously distraught with his findings.

"That's odd. There's absolutely no one here."

"Hold on," Luna exhaled a deep breath and then walked in front of Darkflare to look him up and down. "That's the second time I've seen you use magic, and I'm just having a hard time believing it. Are you an astrelite?"

"Er, no. I'm not." Darkflare turned to look at Kenji, who simply shrugged at him. "Kenji and I are dragoons. We've been chosen by deities to be their warriors and wield their magic."

Luna crossed her arms and fixed him with narrowed eyes. "I believe you now about the Marked Ones and the ability to use magic. But chosen by the gods? That's a little bit more… fantastical."

"I don't know how else to-…." Darkflare paused and put his hand on his chest. "Watch. What I always thought was a strange birthmark is apparently the symbol that I'm Odin's chosen warrior."

Darkflare took a steadying breath before he held his hand out, palm up. He caught a warning glance as Kenji took a step toward him.

"Don't worry. I understand it takes a toll on me. I'm fine though."

Kenji did not respond, and Darkflare shut his eyes. He focused on recalling the sense of power over the flames once more, and he felt a warm sensation in his chest. This time, he was able to open his eyes when the ball of fire danced within the palm of his hand, and he could see the mark glowing on his breast, vibrantly above his armor.

"Well now," Luna's eyes were wide, illuminated by the ball of flame. "That's definitely something I've never seen before."

"The Marked Ones have symbols to show that they're given power by Sairephir, and Kenji and I have our own to show our gods' blessings."

Kenji nodded slowly, admiring the orb in Darkflare's hand.

"Impressive. It didn't take you nearly as long to concentrate the fire energy that time. That could be because the power is still fresh from the candle you doused, but you're learning fast."

"I know magic is real, but I thought that things like dragoons and Marked Ones only existed in stories. This," Luna gestured widely at the three men with one arm, "all is going to need more explanation when we're out of here."

"Right, and I can gladly explain after…"

Kenji whipped his head to stare in Attila's direction. Darkflare extinguished the flame with a quick roll of his wrist. Attila had raised his hand, as if to tell the others to be quiet. He closed his eyes, focusing on listening, and Darkflare found himself doing the same. It was hard to hear, but faint noises were coming from one of the corridors. It seemed quite far, and so the guttural cries must have been some sort of quarrel. Kenji nodded to them to follow as he began to cautiously creep down the corridor.

The hallway ended with a room on the right where Darkflare thought he heard three different voices screaming; something about cheating. They were all fighting to be the loudest, so it was hard to make out anything concrete. Kenji slyly poked his head around the corner, and then he waved Darkflare ahead to peek in. Three men sat around a table in front of a single cell that was deeper into the room. He could see cards scattered around as the men pointed viciously at each other, mugs of ale forgotten on the table.

Darkflare's eyes were drawn back to the cell. Why would the only three Marked Ones on this floor be in the room of one single chamber?

Kenji backed up to Attila, his hand wrapped around the handle of the Izayoi.

"I know how much you look forward to whetting your sword."

"Good," Attila grinned darkly as he stepped forward.

Two of the husks sat on one side of the table facing the doorway. One of them sat with his back to them, but he got up just then to walk to the far side of the room. Attila knew an opportunity when it presented itself and he rushed in; the two men, even though volatile and angry, barely had a chance to react. Their hands fled to their weapons, but Attila grabbed the table one-handed and flipped it against them. The two Marked Ones were pinned against the wall, thrashing to get freed. With his sword still in one hand, he plunged deep through the wood several times until he heard the hiss of smoke and shadow.

Darkflare and Kenji swooped in behind him. Kenji let the table drop and then beheaded the second furious demon with a swift flick of his wrist. Before the body vanished, Darkflare met the third one as it rushed at them. Their blades collided, and the demon almost forced Darkflare back. He had prepared for a vicious force from the brute, but he underestimated the foe's tenacity. They traded another two more blows before an arrow struck the demon's arm, forcing him back. Darkflare took the opportunity to thrust his sword forward, stabbing through the chest, but still it would not die. It took a combined effort from Kenji and Attila's blades before the Marked One finally returned to the shadows.

One, two, and three, the Marked Ones had been disposed of and the fight ended in a heartbeat; a beat that droned dully in the back of Darkflare's mind.

"Hmph. That was hardly worth bleeding my blade," grunted Attila as he shook off the black substance.

"Uh, hey guys... There's someone in here." Luna stood at the bars of the cell, staring inside. In the dim light, they were just able to make out a head and a pair of curled up arms and legs.

"Are they even alive?" Attila asked, peering at the person as best as he could. From where Darkflare was, he could see that they had shoulder-length, platinum-silvery hair, but it was hard to tell whether the person in question was male or female.

"Only one way to find out."

There were no bodies left to search, but Darkflare looked to where the third Marked One had initially gone off to. His eyes were drawn to a solitary key hanging from a hook on the wall. He hurried to it and brought it back to open the cell. The key fit perfectly, and the door opened with a light *chunk* sound.

"Kind of spacious." Darkflare cocked an eyebrow as he walked in. "Well, for a prison cell that is. You could fit a couple people in here."

"Must be someone important." Attila nodded to the sleeping one with his chin. "Think about it. Only one in a big cell with three guards attending them."

"Not to mention the only living thing on this floor," Luna added, as her eyes darted around cautiously.

"Well, he or she is still breathing. And if I'm not mistaken... I believe our mystery person is a he." Darkflare cautiously approached the slumbering person and stared for a moment. He turned to Kenji, remembering what he had said on the previous floor. "What about him, Kenji? If not worth saving, is he at least worth talking to?"

Kenji stared at the man for a few more moments before nodding. "It seems the Marked Ones have followed our system, to a degree. We used to keep anyone we didn't want to mix in with the vagabonds on this floor. Anyone we captured of significant notoriety we usually kept up here to question. You'd be surprised how much more willing people are to talk when threatened with being sent below to be locked up with their inferiors that they've mistreated." He grinned, somewhat darkly, and then gestured to the sleeping fellow. "He has no bruises, no wounds. He looks like he's been treated well. The Marked Ones are keeping him here for a reason. So, yes, he is at least worth questioning. Salvation depends on his answers though."

"Then let us get some answers."

Darkflare detached the longsword's scabbard from its position at his hip and prodded the man rather softly, like a child poking a resting animal. At first, there were no signs of stirring from his slumbering, which caused Luna to chortle at Darkflare's failed attempt. He exhaled frustratedly out his nose before trying a second time. Quite a bit more force was put behind the prod so that it visibly shook the lifeless body in the bed. This time, there was a noise that sounded like an interrupted snore, followed by a spasm of movement. Slowly sitting up, the man blinked his lavender, slightly narrow-slitted eyes open several times; there was no mistaking the color of his eyes that contrasted the darkness so vividly.

"Huh, what...? Is it already that time again? Alright, alright, I'm-... Hey now, you all don't look like the other guards," spoke the man with a somewhat bored, yet sarcastic tone to his voice. Darkflare assumed they could be around the same age due to the man's smooth facial features and lazy attitude. The prisoner grinned and itched his head as he sat up straight.

"That's because we're not guards," Kenji flashed his smirk toward the prisoner. "What are you in here for?"

"Oh, you're not? Huh, that's interesting. " The man lay back down. "Night now."

"H-Hey!" Darkflare had his scabbard ready to prod again, but the man opened one eye to stare at him. "We may not be guards, but we would appreciate it if you could provide us with some answers."

The man stared for another moment before sighing and sitting up. It looked like he would fall asleep again, but he shrugged his shoulders. "Sure. I can do that. Then you'll set me free?"

Darkflare put his hands on his hips, trying his best to seem in command of the situation. "That depends on what you tell us."

The man, as if sensing Darkflare's bravado, smiled slightly and then crossed his legs. "Alright. Let's talk."

"What are you doing here? Why are you the only one on this floor?"

"I follow wherever the wind takes me," the man said with a wink. "I've wandered across this land, looking for good drink and adventure... but I've also been known to help those in need. My last trip was to Pheeq, and I got a little too... daring."

"Whose pockets did you try to steal from?" Attila growled from behind.

"The king's sister." The man rolled his eyes, but then he startled forward. "I-I mean, I didn't steal from her! You have to understand that there was a very pretty young lady, and she and her siblings were begging for food. I gave them the last of my coin, but then I was broke, and well... I figured she could do without a few gold."

Attila growled again from behind Darkflare, ready to leap forward, but Kenji grabbed his arm and shook his head. Darkflare was hesitant, but once Attila had calmed, he cleared his throat. "There was an incident in Ceballe. Some people were kidnapped, and we were told they were brought here."

Luna leaned in and whispered to Darkflare. "Do you think they decided to go easy on him, and that's why they separated him?"

"Well, no." The man grinned. "They probably separated me because I fought back and nearly got away. I was able to knock out twenty guards in my escape from Pheeq." He held up one finger. "But the twenty-first! He's the lucky guy that tripped me."

"So you're a thief," Attila said with a shake of his head.

"No, no. Like I said, I'm a *wanderer* and I help those in need. I'm sure you understand," he said, waving an open hand at Darkflare. "You're here to save those people you mentioned, aren't you? Why else would you be in this spot of Pale with these demons?"

The irony was not lost on Darkflare. "Yes, we are here to save them. The people kidnapped are mostly of noble standings. Nearly all of them have no formal combat training."

"Wait," the man said, looking behind the group. "Are there just four of you? If there are nobles being held here, where are the rulers and why haven't they stormed the walls?"

"We're not sure. They probably went back to Pheeq to figure things out. We're the only ones to know that the prisoners are here, and we only learned that by barely escaping death."

"Well, coming here might have been a worse decision for you. Those things that run this place aren't just ordinary mercenaries. They keep telling me to give myself to darkness."

"So it's true," Darkflare murmured, shaking his head and turning to look at the others. "This place really is a breeding ground for the Marked Ones. They must take in anyone the kingdoms sentence and then use them as new hosts."

"Well, they certainly have a score of initiates to choose from below." Luna thrust her hand out to point down before turning back to the prisoner. "But those poor souls look like they're on death's door. It doesn't look like they've tortured you at all."

The man shrugged. "They've tried. Through my journeys, I've trained against countless opponents who knew a variety of fighting styles. While I've never seen anything like these things before, I knocked around the first few that attempted to assault me. That seemed to send a warning."

The man stood and stretched. Darkflare looked him over; he was a bit shorter than himself, but his lithe frame had muscle. He rolled his arm in a circle, stretching, and then fixed Darkflare with a smirk.

"To get to your noble prisoners, you're surely going to have to fight more of those creatures. And if that's the case, you're going to need all the help you can get. Let me go with you."

Attila scoffed, narrowing his eyes at the man. "Why? So you can pilfer from us when our backs are turned?"

"Woah," the man recoiled slightly, looking at Attila with obvious hurt in his eyes. "You may have found me behind these bars, but I'm a damn good swordsman. Just because a guy gets tripped and caught once, in the capital of all places, does not make him a criminal."

"Did they take your weapon?" Darkflare exited the cell and looked around the rest of the room.

"Yeah, they put everything into a crate over there. Kept it in eyesight to try and tempt me. If I joined them, I'd have it all back, they kept saying."

Darkflare's eyes followed the man's finger toward a wide trunk that sat in the corner of the dimly lit area; it definitely resembled a weapon crate. There was no lock, so he threw open the lid; on top was a silken white cloak.

"Allow me, please."

The man had emerged from his chamber and took Darkflare's place at the casket. He took the black shirt off and threw it to the side, and underneath the white cloak, he withdrew a black cuirass. He slipped into the armor, his arms easily sliding past the pauldrons, and he reached back into the chest. He put on two black gloves with armored forearms, as well as two long armored boots. Once properly geared, he withdrew the long cloak; it kissed the floor and came away without any dirt or grime. It looked brand new without the slightest sign of wear or use against the pure white. The cloak fastened around the neck and allowed the man to push it back behind him to still show the armor.

"This cloak is very special. I've had it for several years now and it's protected me from every weather condition. It was enchanted with astrelite magic to make it resilient to any climate; extreme heat, blinding blizzards, hailing rain. Whatever the condition, I can withstand it. And these..."

The man bent back over the casket and fetched out three beautiful weapons that contrasted his simple attire. The first sword sat in a royal blue scabbard that was trimmed in gold lining. Darkflare was impressed and found that he couldn't take his eyes off of the design. The man went to place it on his waist, but he stopped.

"Eh, forgot they took my belt too." The prisoner fished back into the casket to reveal what seemed like two belts, but they turned out to be one interlaced as he hooked it onto his hips. Armor hung down on both sides, snugly protecting his thighs, and a small cloth tasset hung from the front. Now that he had regained his clothing, Darkflare found he did look a lot more like a swordsman than a vagabond. The man put the fancy scabbard on the left side of his waist, attached it to his belt, and then patted it lightly. "This sword is called the Hyperion."

He reached back into the chest again, and this time, he withdrew two more swords, these ones more resembling Kenji's curved blade. One rested in a black sheath that had red trim to it, and as the prisoner checked the blade, Darkflare noticed the dark crimson metal. The third weapon was covered by a white scabbard that was trimmed in silver color. It was the least ornamented, but the designs on the weapon suggested that it was blessed by something holy. To finish, the man crossed both swords over his back, allowing the handles to poke over from the top of the cloak.

"The Muramasa and the Heaven's Cloud. You can never have enough blades." The man winked.

Indeed, fully equipped, the man seemed like he was more than just a thief. Anyone could wield a weapon, and it was entirely possible he could have plundered the blades, but it was the way that he handled the tools - checking the steel, notching the weapons without hesitation - as well as the way the short man stood straight without being weighted down by three swords which caused Darkflare to believe his claim of skill.

"The name is Roy Kinders, by the way. I don't think we've been properly introduced."

"Name's Kenji." Darkflare's guardian towered almost a whole foot over the newcomer, as he flashed the crooked smirk of his.

"I'm Luna," chirped the archer, still keeping some distance between she and Roy.

"… Attila," called the sullen voice from the back of the group. His hesitancy was pungent, and Darkflare thought he sensed a bit of jealousy in his voice - probably over Roy's weaponry.

"And I'm Darkflare."

"If I didn't know better, I would say you either had two heads," Roy pointed to where Oboro was peeking around Darkflare's shoulder, "or there is a wyvern attached to your back."

"Ah," Darkflare chuckled. "This is Oboro. Figured I was missing someone."

The wyvern cooed after Darkflare spoke, as if adding in his own greeting.

"Right. So how about it? This is who I am," Roy said, spreading his hands out to the sides. "I like strong alcohol, conversing at length with women, and wandering the world to find those that I can help, but I know my way around the battlefield better than most. I can move and I can dance my blade under the guard of any opponent. If you don't believe me, point me in the direction of those – what did you call them? Marked Ones? Or just believe me and let me help. Or, don't. And just let me go."

Roy ended his speech with a shrug and a wink, and Darkflare turned toward the others.

"Well, if there are no objections, we could probably use another blade on our side."

"And I do owe you all for busting me out," Roy said with a wider grin.

"Right," Darkflare put his hand out. "You'll help us get the prisoners out, and then you're free to do whatever you want."

"Thanks. First time in a while that I've been properly introduced to people. It feels nice." Roy beamed a smile as he shook Darkflare's hand, and then he stepped back and rubbed his own hands together. "Alright! So where are we headed?"

"Up. We didn't find anything on the first floor, and like we said, you're the only one on this one."

"Speaking of which, we should probably go," Attila motioned. "We don't want any other bandits checking in and finding their allies no longer here."

Kenji nodded. "There's another stairwell at the end of the hallway that will take us up to the third floor, and then onward to the roof."

"Right then. Only one way, and that's up," Darkflare said with a jerk of his thumb.

The three nodded in agreement and then moved to follow Attila. Darkflare waited for them all to leave before facing the main torch that illuminated the room. He placed his hand out toward it and used his runic powers to once again extinguish the flame. The harder it was to track them, all the better.

Chapter VIII

Darkflare caught back up with the others as they proceeded down the hallway at an even pace. There was an eerie sense of tranquility on this floor, knowing they were alone here. Not having to creep and crawl their way along the passageway made finding the stairs all that much easier. They passed rows of dead ends and empty cells, but their destination waited at the end of the straight path.

As they entered the stairwell, the torchlight illuminated their facial expressions enough to convey the emotions they kept silent. None of them seemed too worried or concerned from what Darkflare could make out, but they each had their own look of seriousness. This had been the most dire situation Darkflare had been in; he assumed the same could be said for Luna, but he wasn't sure about the other three. Before yesterday, he would have thought the same about Attila, but now he wasn't sure anymore what he knew about his friend.

When Darkflare began to hear noises once more, he felt a cold shudder pass through his body. Kenji motioned for them to stop, and Darkflare saw that they were coming close to an archway that must have led to the third floor. Kenji noiselessly ascended, hugging the wall as he crept forward. The swell of noise came from within that room, and Kenji cautiously peered in. His head kept slowly moving until it froze. Bounding across to the other side of the doorway, Kenji peeked back in and froze once more. Now several feet away from the others, he made symbols with his hands to try to communicate.

"What's he saying?" Luna hissed at Darkflare, confused by the gestures.

"Either he's telling me that the third floor's guarded and that there are two sentries in front of the doorway, or he's trying to tell me about a sorceress taking over a garden." Luna stared blankly at Darkflare as he rubbed his chin in confusion. "I'm pretty sure it's the first though. Whichever, we're going to have to not make any noise."

Darkflare turned to Attila and no words needed to be said, just a nod. Attila zipped up the stairs to join Kenji, but he was there for only a brief moment. Attila mouthed something to Kenji that Darkflare could not make out and then proceeded up more of the stairs.

"Where's he going?" Roy whispered as Luna continued up to Kenji as well.

"I don't know. Perhaps to make sure there's no one waiting for us at the top?" Darkflare responded, and as soon as Luna had cleared the doorway, he motioned for Roy to go, who ascended just as silently as his predecessors. Darkflare was the last and readied himself.

"Hey, you!" The deep voice came from inside the doorway. Darkflare felt all of his muscles tighten up, and he pressed his back against the wall as hard as he could, wishing he could blend in with the dark bricks. "Yeah, you! Calm it down or I'll send you down to first floor duty!"

There was a muffled curse back at the man, and Darkflare felt his body sag. He hadn't been noticed.

He waited another minute or so and then hurried up to the others. As he passed the doorway, he dared a look inside and sincerely wished he had not. All of the guards that they had expected to see throughout the prison were all amassed inside through that doorway, eating, drinking, and celebrating – probably due to the chaos they caused at Ceballe. There were a few profane symbols that Darkflare didn't recognize, drawn in deep red around the room. That sent a more violent chill through him than the return of the noise.

They continued up, in search of Attila. Kenji had not mentioned anything, nor did the others dare open their mouths to ask just yet. They had made it up in one piece, but how would they make it back down? The enemies on the roof might signal the alarm; there were going to be so many more people to sneak back down, what if one of them got hurt... Darkflare tried to repress the thoughts for the time being and concentrated on the task still at hand.

Attila was seated at the top of the stairwell, toying meticulously at wiping his sword clean. Slumped in the corner of the wall were the remains of two guards that disappeared in smoke and shadow as the group approached.

"Clean, quiet kills. Good job," smirked Kenji, placing his hand on Attila's shoulder as he stood up. Even standing a step below him, Kenji was taller than Attila, which Darkflare found to be slightly comical.

"Is there anything more to you, or is that your whole deal?" Luna waved her hand at Attila with a disapproving look. "You brood and kill, never smile. Only talk when you want to say something sarcastic or pessimistic. What makes you so different from these demons?"

Attila did not say anything back. He responded by sheathing his sword and moving for Kenji to pass toward the door. Luna rolled her eyes, and Darkflare looked at Roy, who shrugged slightly.

"Can't say I disagree. That's all I've seen, too."

Darkflare's gaze swung to Attila, but he was following Kenji. He wanted to speak up to say something to defend the man, but in the short time he had known Luna, and the even shorter time he knew Roy, he felt that he could get every honest answer out of either of them before he got one from Attila. He led the other two behind Kenji's trail, but he couldn't help but wonder; what *did* he know about Attila?

Kenji gently creaked open the metal door, revealing that the sun outside had faded further. Dusk was almost upon them, and the orange red tint of the light seared Darkflare's eyes for a moment, nearly blinding him. Once his eyes adjusted, he heard Kenji curse under his breath before peering out the crack in the open doorway.

"Found them," Kenji muttered to his comrades beside him after a moment.

"What are we looking at?" Roy remarked, climbing next to Kenji to get a better view. "Any particular damsels, and do they look like they're distressed?" When Luna scoffed and Kenji gave him a strange look, he shrugged. "I can be hopeful, can't I?"

"Lots of Marked Ones. It looks like they have materials to set up some sort of altar – probably for their sick 'conversion'. It seems like there are a lot of them there to watch, rather than actually do anything. There are only a few armed. The prisoners are being held in a container that seems to have a padlock on it."

"What sort of weapons?" Attila's voice spoke up from the back, to which Kenji shot him an inquisitive glance. "Well, if there are bowmen, we're going to have a slightly harder time than if the Marked Ones all had melee weapons."

Kenji nodded, looking back outside. "A few look like they're carrying bows. Going to have to keep our eyes on them, move fast, and take them out as soon as we can."

After a few moments of silence, Roy cleared his throat.

"I'd like to offer myself as a distraction. Both because I'm appreciative of your help, and so I can prove that these swords are not just for show. Let me go out there and cause some mayhem to keep them focused on me while the rest of you free the prisoners."

"What, and let you have all of the fun?" Kenji grinned, cracking his knuckles. "I'll go with you. If you can live up to your words, you and I might just be able to keep them at bay long enough."

"Are you both sure about this?" Darkflare looked back and forth at the two of them. "That sounds... highly dangerous."

"Eh," Roy shrugged, looking out the door. "I owe these guys a bit of payback for thinking they could keep me locked up in here and… convert me, or whatever."

"I like the odds." Kenji grinned darkly. "Just be quick about getting them inside, Darkflare."

"Thank you. Both of you."

"I should be fighting too," Attila said, shaking his head.

"You will be," Kenji jerked a thumb toward the Marked Ones. "You're going to be keeping the ones that get by us off of Darkflare and the nobles. We won't be able to distract all of them."

"Okay. I'll try and keep my sights on the archers," Luna added in, her chipper voice a light in the gloomy shadows. "I'll make sure to keep the pressure on them."

Kenji nodded one more time. "Are we ready?"

As a dead silence filled the small walkway, Darkflare noticed that each person had clenched the handle of their weapon, ready for combat. Numerous thoughts raced through his head before he answered Kenji, but he had to save the innocents and make it back alive. Grasping the handle of his longsword, he looked Kenji in the eyes and nodded.

"Let's do this."

* * * * *

Kenji threw open the metal door with one arm, causing the sound of it impacting the wall to echo aloud atop the roof. The Marked Ones turned as one in the direction of the clamor. Kenji ran out into the fading amber sunlight, Izayoi in hand, and plunged it deep into the first guard he reached.

Roy ran out onto the roof behind Kenji and leapt ahead of the dragoon, into a trio of incoming attackers, and stood his ground with the Hyperion. Even Kenji looked impressed by Roy's skill as he parried attack after attack from the oncoming swings. Watching the two men fight with such confidence and skill made Darkflare feel invigorated with a renewed sense of confidence in his own abilities.

After a few moments of watching the distraction, Darkflare figured that they had stalled long enough and ran out into the dusk-light with his longsword tightly within his grasp. Attila and Luna emerged right behind him, weapons drawn, as Oboro fluttered on above. Darkflare raced across the wide open rooftop toward the metal cage in the corner. The adrenaline began to pump so much throughout him that he cut down the first guard that ran at him with a single swipe of his sword; this time, there was no second thought in his action. Attila, to his right, made sure to make quick work of a Marked One that charged screaming. On Darkflare's left, Luna stopped to take aim at the archers across the way, loosing an arrow at the first to notch their bow.

Darkflare felt an incoming arrow whiz by his face, nearly nicking his cheek, but when he turned to gaze at who shot it, the Marked One fell with a return projectile sticking out of their throat. Darkflare waved a thanks back to Luna, but as she ran to keep up with him, she shouted something, pointing forward.

Darkflare's head swung back around to see a Marked One charging at him. Further away, Attila was caught between two other demons, trying to push them back and find an opening. Darkflare just ducked under the swing of an axe, thrusting up with his sword as he passed. The foe's arm disintegrated in a splash of black blood, but the other arm came around to club Darkflare in the back.

He rolled to the ground, forcing himself onto his back to face his opponent, but as it stalked over to him, an arrow hit the pale-skinned creature in the back of the neck. As it turned, another found its mark in its cheek, and then a third in the forehead, putting it down. Luna held her hand out to Darkflare as she approached, and she helped him back to his feet.

"I told you that you'd need an archer," Luna nodded.

"I owe you several times now. Thank you," Darkflare said to her as they continued running toward the prisoners. Attila was not far behind, having dealt with his duo.

"Oh, don't worry," Luna stopped again to loose another shot toward the remaining archers. "I'm keeping count!"

Darkflare kept running, and from the corner of his eye, he could see Roy and Kenji standing their ground and fighting off numerous attackers at once. Attila and Luna were on his heels and kept any others from closing in on his sides. As the trio reached the cell, the people inside rose together and pleaded with gaping mouths and wide eyes. Darkflare noticed the two calmest people that did not mob the bars and figured they must be Queen Faïne's right hand, Knight Commander Barrayos, as well as King Valesti's sister, Princess Aiyell Valesti. As the prisoners were huddled to the cell's bars with outstretched arms, Darkflare shook his head, grasping the longsword in both hands.

"Everyone back away! Pull back your arms!"

All of the royals instantly recoiled once he raised his sword. Darkflare swung his weapon down with both arms, but the lock simply rattled. He swung at the chain again and again, until finally the lock clattered to the ground.

The moment they were free, the gate swung wide open and the prisoners went mad; they pushed and shoved their way through, forcing their way out of their cage. Barrayos held Aiyell close, trying to protect her; Darkflare noticed the knight's chivalry and could not help but feel great respect. The dark-skinned man, with brown hair pulled into a ponytail, stepped out of the container and made sure the lean, fair girl with long, pig-tailed blonde hair was close behind him. He stood slightly taller than Darkflare, and his emerald eyes glared at him, piercing in their intensity.

"Who are you and how did you know we were here?" Barrayos's pose was defiant without the slightest bit of hesitation.

"What?" Darkflare stammered, trying to back away from the approaching knight. "Now's hardly the time for questions, Knight Commander! My name is Darkflare Omni, and we're here to rescue you all. So please, follow me and let us escape!" He quickly turned to his comrades. "Attila, cover the rear. Luna, make sure to target any incoming foes. Everyone else, follow me!"

"I do not know who you are, Omni, but you have my thanks for our freedom." Barrayos stared warily at Darkflare as he followed. "And you are indeed right about the lack of time. If this is some ploy-..."

"You have my honor, for what it's worth to you, that this is no ploy," Darkflare called quickly over his shoulder.

That seemed to satisfy the knight, yet he still hung back, guarding Princess Valesti.

As Darkflare picked up speed to get ahead of the crowd, he glanced at Kenji. He met his gaze with a nod and began to pull back while finishing off what was left of the Marked Ones. Roy caught the hint as well, ducking and weaving with grace through his opponent's attacks, finding weak spots to finish them off. His precision wielding the Hyperion matched Kenji's own style with the Izayoi as he ducked and spun, his cloak hovering just behind him and out of reach of his opponent, and then striking in quick with the blade's tip. It only took moments to finish off his demons in a swirl of shadow, and he turned and ran to catch up with the others.

They regrouped at the door and Darkflare was the first to step in, but he swore loudly as he stumbled back out, almost causing the prisoners to trample him.

"What?" Roy pushed his way through, coming up behind him.

"We've got incoming trouble!" Darkflare called, feeling his fingers grip his longsword tighter than he would have liked.

As Roy peered inside, he noticed what Darkflare had seen – the mass of enemies that had been blissfully unaware of their presence on the third floor were beginning to make their charge up the stairs. Roy turned to Darkflare and grinned, still clutching the Hyperion.

"If you've got any last minute tricks up your sleeves, now would be the best time to utilize them."

"Actually... I do."

Darkflare stared down at the third floor doorway that the Marked Ones emerged from. Something needed to be done to stem the tide. Darkflare brought both of his hands to his side and cupped them together wide enough that it could fit a large apple. Closing his eyes, he focused as he channeled his strength into the center of his palms. As if pulling energy from the very fabric of the air around him, he could feel small particles of heat fill the space in his hands.

Darkflare took a step forward. Upon doing so, he opened his eyes, thrust his hands out, and pulled back the tips of his fingers from one another. Like a blazing comet from the heavens above, the ball of fire soared out from Darkflare's palms and spiraled down the staircase.

Guards that had been escalating the steps, shouting in anger with raised weapons, suddenly took on expressions of surprise as the ball of flame flew toward them. The smarter Marked Ones dove to the ground, avoiding any contact with the spell. Some, despite their Sairephir-granted power, were not quick enough to avoid the mystical ball as it burned them with heat so intense that they burst to smoke before they became ash. The sphere of flame bounced on until it collided with the third floor doorframe in an explosion of brick, cinders, and a showering drip of fire.

Darkflare braced himself on the nearby wall, panting heavily, but he wanted to jump with joy. He figured it would take quite some time before they could manage to unseal the doorway; enough time that they would be long gone from Kailos.

Roy stuck his bottom lip out just slightly and arched his eyebrows up in a mix of satisfaction and impression.

"A little flashier than I had in mind, but that will do." Roy looked at Darkflare's chest and grinned. "And would that glow there happen to be a rune?"

The mention of the symbol gave Darkflare pause and his brows furrowed. "How…"

"Talk later, look alive," Kenji interrupted, pushing his way through the nobles to reach his comrades.

Darkflare and Roy both repositioned themselves in defensive stances as they realized what Kenji had meant. At the bottom of the stairwell, the remaining guards on their side of the barrier had begun to stir. After they got to their feet, they charged up the stairs once again, almost more bloodthirsty and ruthless than before.

Leaping from the railing of the balcony, Roy landed at the tail end, sandwiching the ten or so bandits in between he on the far end, and Kenji and Darkflare above. Rallying his longsword beside his guardian, Darkflare was ready to defend the nobles. Both men met the oncoming two attackers with a loud clash of blades that resonated down the winding stairwell. They could hear the identical sound of colliding weapons further below as Roy battled at the opposite end. Darkflare let the adrenaline do the work for him as the heat of the battle took prevalence over his mind.

Using the stairs to his advantage, he shoved hard in a weapon deadlock, which forced his attacker to lose his balance. As he wobbled one-legged on the plank beneath Darkflare, the young man plunged his sword deep into the mark on his opponent's neck. This not only took out the first attacker, but the one pressing in so close behind him. Darkflare could tell that a third attacker was coming up, and he had just enough time to withdraw his sword from the vanishing duo to block the attack. Kenji's curved sword came in and cut the foe down, sending them spiraling over the staircase. Smoke and shadow swirled around the dragoons with each defeated demon as the duo pushed their way forward.

The stairwell was barely two feet wide, but the Marked Ones could manage to fit two on a stair while a third and fourth fought to get in as well; Kenji and Darkflare fought side by side, but it was little comfort. While it had looked like a small stairwell before, as Luna, Attila, and the nobles crowded in behind them, it now seemed even smaller. With every kill that the trio had landed on their way to clearing the stairs, the royal prisoners inched further down toward their protectors while Attila and Luna held up the back. Once they were all the way inside, Attila cursed loudly.

"What's wrong?!" Darkflare called, not taking his eyes off of his opponent.

"No way to seal the damn door!" Attila called back.

"Figure something out," Darkflare called as he finished his fight.

As Darkflare struck down the last of the Marked Ones on the stairwell, Kenji went to swing again, and it was a good thing that his attack was met by another sword just as strong as his. Realizing that on the other end of the attack was Roy, Kenji let go of the deadlock and sighed heavily.

"Glad you know how to hold your own."

"Yeah, you're not the only one," Roy remarked. "I saw that blade and nearly soiled myself."

"Darkflare!" Hearing his name, he swiveled his head to glance back up the stairwell. It was Luna that the voice belonged to. "Attila's right, there's no way to lock the door back here! We've held them off, but there's more out there!"

"Understood. Keep an eye out back there and we'll make haste forward!"

Darkflare nodded at Kenji and Roy, and both took off ahead of the group; if there were any more Marked Ones ahead, he could trust them to dispose of them while he aided in guarding the nobles. They were so close.

As Darkflare hustled down to the second floor, Barrayos was alongside him, and Darkflare could already tell that he came equipped with another question.

"I need answers. Where are the kingdoms' leaders? Is Queen Ragwelv safe?"

Darkflare shook his head, wishing he had more information to give.

"I don't know, honestly. We hadn't any time to talk with them and explain the situation. One of the, uh, 'bandits' accidentally informed us that they were bringing people here, and so we had two options: set out to save you on our own, or take some unneeded and wasteful time to track the leaders down and tell them. We didn't want to think what might have happened if we tarried any longer." Darkflare shuddered, remembering the grotesque symbols. "The leaders left Ceballe right after the attack, and I think they might have gone to Pheeq with King Corsius. But that's all I know."

Barrayos nodded, keeping an eye on Princess Valesti to make sure she was safe behind him. "Yes, I think I speak for all of us by saying we appreciate the speedy rescue. It just took me by surprise that someone like you came to our rescue and not any familiar colors of the armies. Forgive me for being... wary, due to that." He lowered his voice and leaned in a bit closer. "Are these foes truly the demonic Marked Ones? And are you truly one of the warriors of legend? Are you a... a dragoon?"

Darkflare shot Barrayos a wary look out of the corner of his eye, but then after a moment of silence, he nodded. "Yes and... yes. I can control the element of fire. How exactly do you know of the dragoons?"

"By the gods," Barrayos let out a gasp. "I can't believe it, but your magic and the glow of your chest are proof! My father, Mokiwana rest his soul, was the Knight Commander of Syvail before it fell. His name was Mavezjean Ronseph. Some of my earliest memories are of him regaling me with tales of fighting these demons and dealing with a group of dragoons led by a man named Cal... Kales..."

"Calistron Omni." Darkflare tried to hide the shock from his voice.

"Yes." Barrayos's eyes widened as he hurried to walk beside Darkflare. "So that means...!"

"He was my father," Darkflare nodded proudly, smiling sadly at Barrayos. "I know what it feels like to lose family, and you have my deepest condolences."

"And you mine, friend. When this is all over, I implore you to visit Peralor. Queen Faïne Ragwelv would welcome you and your allies most graciously. You would honor her much as you have done me to be in the presence of one of such legend."

Darkflare felt his cheeks redden and his breath catch at the mention of Peralor and the queen. "I-I... I'm hardly legendary. It's just a-a title..."

Before Darkflare could say any more, he heard the clash of weaponry and clicked his tongue in anger. At that point, they had just entered the second floor's hallway, and it sounded as if Roy and Kenji had run into some trouble further ahead.

"They must have ran into the guards from the first floor!"

Motioning for the others to stay, Darkflare ran ahead with his longsword once again to join his allies in their fight. As he got closer, he began to hear screams that amplified with each step he took. At first, he figured the tortured screams were coming from the prisoners below, but he realized the cries were coming from the hallway. As he reached Roy and Kenji, he opened his mouth to say something, but his eyes were drawn down in horror to the stairs.

Mangled corpses of the Marked Ones lay scattered on the stairs, their screams turning to gargled moans of pain. Upon closer examination, Darkflare realized that they were burning, but the flames that scorched their flesh were not ordinary ones of fire affinity. They were black flames, void of all life or energy. They sucked the skin right off the bones of the demons and crushed any life from the vessels. As the moans faded away, Kenji let his open palm fall. He took a deep breath in through his nostrils, inhaling deeply.

"Purging these abominations... It always revitalizes my determination to stay alive."

A sick smile parted his lips as he continued downward. Darkflare felt a chill wrap its icy tendrils around his spine as he watched the man in the white overcoat continue downward with his blade in hand, not even daunted by the stench his chaos had caused. Darkflare braced himself on the wall, fighting the urge to retch. The smell of the burning dead was overwhelming, but it did not last long before the bodies faded into smoke and the smell vanished with them - but it was long enough for Darkflare to know that stench would haunt his dreams.

"You alright?"

Roy stepped closer to him, and Darkflare waved off a helping hand.

"I'm... I'm fine. Just need," Darkflare shook his head violently. "Just need another minute."

Roy stood there for another moment. "Alright. Let me go catch up to him before he burns the place down."

Darkflare heard Roy leave, but his eyes remained focused on where the Marked Ones had burned. He didn't know how long he had been there, frozen, staring at the dark splotches when something touched his shoulder. He swung around with his sword, and Luna jumped back.

"Woah! Be careful!"

"L-Luna? I'm sorry, I..."

"Attila and I handled the last of them back there, but... are you alright?" She stared at him with a look of concern, but he forced his eyes shut and shook his head. When he opened them, he nodded confidently to her.

"I'm alright. Just a little... lightheaded. They might be demons, but I'm new to this whole fighting to kill thing."

"As am I," she said, exhaling deeply. "But what choice do we have when it comes to protecting the living?"

"You're right," Darkflare tried to smile at her as they led the nobles down the stairs. "Are you holding up alright?"

"I'm fine. I'll be better when we get out of here."

Out of there. Darkflare hadn't given any thought as to what would come next; and upon hearing the ringing of colliding blades once more, he realized that the thought would have to wait longer yet.

He followed in Roy and Kenji's path on the bottom floor, breaking into a bit of a run once he was sure the others could follow his pace. The sound of fighting felt like it was everywhere, and Darkflare, having lost where his allies were, stopped at one of the many crossroads. Emerging from the right path were two armed guards, and Darkflare's longsword was at the ready in an instant.

He met with them, parrying the sword of one and kicking the other in the chest before he could swing. As the second demon fell over with the wind knocked out of him, Darkflare engaged in a deadlock with the first snarling foe. They clashed swords over and over with one another, trying to get the upper hand, but neither could. Finally, Darkflare's attacker withdrew a dagger from his side with his offhand. As the two collided once again, the attacker raised the dagger. Before the man could close in, Darkflare dropped his left hand, held it open at waist height, and concentrated as much power as quickly as he could. The ball of flame jumped from his palm, but not before the dagger pierced his left shoulder. Darkflare dropped to one knee from the pain, and the man was sent flying through the air, only stopping when a wall impeded him with a sickening crunch.

The other Marked One was upon Darkflare in an instant. He raised his sword, thankful his dominant shoulder had not been wounded, and struggled from keeping the blade from descending on him. Spittle formed in the ragged beard of his opponent, and the eyes were blood red as the pale face drooped closer toward him. Suddenly, the expression slacked, and Darkflare was able to press the sword off of him as the body fell.

Oboro fluttered down from the air and started cooing softly at Darkflare. Luna had come up with a smirk, but it faded when she saw the dagger and Oboro. "What happened?!"

Darkflare gritted his teeth and yanked the blade out. Stars dotted his vision, but thankfully it had not gone in too deep. "Bastard pulled this out." He threw the blade to the ground and Oboro hissed at it. "I'll be alright."

"Hold still."

Luna managed to yank cloth from the tabard of the Marked One before the body vanished. She exposed Darkflare's shoulder and wiped the blood with the cleaner piece of cloth, before wrapping it with another.

"Thanks," Darkflare said, standing once more. Luna's smile was the kindest he had seen from her, barring the first time she saw Oboro.

"You're welcome."

"Nice shot," Darkflare said, looking down at the bow. His eyes widened when he saw just how worn it was. There were bindings across the body that showed how it had been repaired several times.

"Darkflare!" Roy shot back from a corner in front of them. He and Kenji must have carved their way deep toward the entrance. "The Marked Ones ahead have been taken care of. Let's get going now before any others decide they'd like to dance!"

Darkflare nodded and waved the group he led forward. He was starting to understand how a cattle herder must have felt. Following his ally, Darkflare rounded the corner and around another until he could see the deep orange glow of the setting dusk straight ahead. Kenji stood waiting at the doorframe with his Izayoi in hand. They were so close, but something caused Darkflare to whirl around.

"Attila!" He heard steel clash once again, but it was from behind. He whirled around, and past the crowd of nobles, he saw his friend. As he moved to help, Roy's white cloak blurred past him.

"Leave this to me. I still have a score to settle."

Darkflare hesitated as he watched Roy go, but another voice called for his attention.

"Darkflare, hurry up!" Kenji was calling him this time. He stole one last glance at the fighting that took place behind them before urging himself onward. He knew that Roy and Attila could buy them the time that they needed, but it just felt so wrong running from them.

Darkflare shook his head and hurried onward. As they reached Kenji, he threw his arm out to the right, motioning at a caravan with a spacious interior; it could easily fit the entire group.

"One of the transport wagons, I'm assuming. We can use it to get them out of here."

"And what? Leave Roy and Attila at the hands of the Marked Ones? I can't do that." Darkflare turned to face the knight from Beauldyn. "Barrayos, I'm sorry, but we can lead you no further. Can I ask you to take them to Pheeq?"

"Leave it to me. You take care of your allies." Barrayos turned to address the nobles, still huddling around him in fear. "Everyone, into the wagon! We'll set out for Pheeq, where we will be safe with King Corsius's protection."

Aiyell Valesti was the second to last to enter the vehicle. She looked back toward the nightmarish keep, and then to Darkflare. "Your name is Darkflare, I believe? Tell me... What is the name of that man with the white cloak?"

"His name is Roy Kinders," Darkflare answered, quirking an inquisitive eyebrow. He prayed that Roy had not tried to steal from her before. "May I ask why, Princess?"

"Roy... Thank him for me. And thank all of you for your valiant efforts. I shall remember what you did here today." She bowed deeply before stepping into the wagon. "Thank you for saving all of our lives."

As Barrayos went to grab the reins, he motioned a salute that was foreign to Darkflare – it must have been the style that they used in the east.

"Thank you, Darkflare. We will meet again, someday. I have faith in that."

Darkflare raised his arm horizontally to his chest, returning Barrayos's salute with the one that was more widely used in the south.

"Thank you, Barrayos. Please, make sure you tell King Corsius about what you saw. Tell him to raze the prison to the ground if he must. He must come back and deal with the demons here."

"I will. I promise you that." Barrayos gave one look back to make sure the passengers were ready. "Take care, Darkflare."

"And to you!"

The horses took off, carrying the cart across the bridge and out of sight. Before Darkflare could even turn his attention back to the prison, Attila and Roy came strolling up beside him.

"Ah, damn. Look's like we missed the sending off party," Roy clicked his tongue and snapped his fingers.

"That's all of them. For now," Attila said with his sword still drawn, slightly favoring his ankle.

"Well, those were definitely some of the most challenging adversaries I've faced!" Roy said as he sifted a hand through his thick platinum hair.

"We have to get away from here." Darkflare motioned for the road, wincing as his shoulder hurt.

Darkflare stared at the ruins of Syvail from their campfire at the edge of the forest. He finally had a moment to breathe, now that they had put some distance from Kailos and the Marked Ones. The location to camp was less than ideal; he had initially wanted to go back to Crescentia, but the thought of leading those demons there convinced him otherwise.

They sat in a circle, Attila to his right, then Roy and Kenji across the fire, Luna to his left, and Oboro curled up at his feet. No one had said much since they left the prison. Darkflare decided he would be the first.

"Thank you, all of you. You all risked your lives with nothing to show for it. This," Darkflare put his hand on his chest where his rune was, "is all new to me. But I know that what we did here was right. But it is the first step in something much bigger."

"What do you plan to do next?" Luna asked, her eyes unflinching from the fire.

"This was not their main base. This was only a breeding ground for them. One of who knows how many others. We've seen firsthand how one-minded these things are. There must be someone organizing them, giving them orders. I plan on trying to find any rumors that may point me in the right direction."

"And you two?" She motioned to Attila and Kenji.

"I plan on traveling with Darkflare to teach him more about his rune," Kenji said. "He's going to need all the help he can get."

"Ditto," Attila replied, staring back toward Kailos. "I wish to hone my might any way possible. This path is clear to me."

"What's next for you two?" Darkflare gestured to Luna and Roy. "You both have no obligation to stay with us. What will you do now?"

"Well, I for one would like to continue traveling with you," Roy sat back, bracing himself on his palms behind him. "I wouldn't mind wandering with a purpose – a noble one at that. Saving the world from demons has a nice appeal to it. Plenty of things - and people - to see on a journey like that!"

Luna smiled as she looked at the others. "As dangerous as all that was, and even though I don't really understand this talk of dragoons, and runes, and Marked Ones, it was nice to be part of something, doing good. I've tried many ways to help people, but none of them ever felt... right. Being here, helping you all, saving those nobles from a horde of demons? It felt like something out of a fairy tale. I think this is what I've been searching for - like how I thought fate put me on the right path." Attila groaned at that, but Luna ignored him and continued speaking. "If the battle at Kailos showed us anything, it's that you need an archer to cover the distance against your foes!"

Darkflare felt the smile widen on his own face. "Thank you, both of you. I can't offer you anything in return, just yet. Only my friendship. Like Kenji said, we're going to need all the help we can get, and I know that you both are skilled fighters."

He looked down at his longsword, seeing the gashes in the metal; then to Attila's greatsword that seemed in no better shape; and then to Luna's stitched together bow.

"If only we had better weapons to wield that skill with."

"You know, I know of a man that can help us," Kenji said with a yawn and a stretch. "Tomorrow, let's head northwest. I'll explain more in the morning and answer any questions you might have, Luna."

"I'll take first watch," Darkflare stood, stretching his own legs. Oboro raised his head as his master stirred.

"How's your arm?" Roy asked, patting his Hyperion. "I can take watch if you need the rest."

"I'll manage. Thank you though."

Darkflare said goodnight to his allies as he put the fire out and leaned against a tree to gaze once more on the ruins of Syvail. Hope coursed through him that he never felt before. He was elated at their success in saving so many innocent people, meeting and being respected by both Princess Aiyell and Barrayos, and the fact that he was living out a life that was bigger than anything he had ever dreamed.

He snorted and shook his head, a smile plastered on his face that he couldn't shake off. He wasn't a knight, but he didn't want to be anymore. He was something better.

He was a dragoon.

Chapter IX

"So, you're telling me that Darkflare is a *king?*" Luna was still taken aback by the whole concept of dragoons. Most of the morning, Kenji had been giving her a history lesson similar to the one he had given Darkflare.

"I-It's only a title!" Darkflare waved the word away. "I'm in no way royalty of any sort!"

"Regardless, you can really hold your own in a fight – much better than most novices." Roy pat Darkflare lightly on the shoulder and then whistled through his teeth. "What I saw at Kailos was impressive, from all three of you. But there are areas of your techniques that could be polished. I'd like to pass along some unique fighting styles and skills that I've learned through my journeys. That is, if I'm not intruding too much in your department, Kenji."

"Feel free. I'm a bit more blunt in my fighting style than flashy." The veteran dragoon chuckled. "I can teach magic and history while you show them combat. I like that balance."

"There's nothing I'd enjoy more than being able to keep up with you two, but," Darkflare withdrew the longsword and held it up for them to see, "the next fight might be this weapon's last. It's falling apart, and I don't have the gold to buy a proper weapon to take its place."

"Not to worry." Kenji's mouth twitched momentarily into the predatorial smirk. "I figured that would be the case. That's why we're going mountain climbing."

"Is forging weaponry the next test Darkflare has ahead of him?" Attila was staring off, refusing to meet their gazes. Whether the added ice in his tone was because he was still forced to be cautious of his leg or he was bitter over not having the power of a rune, Darkflare was unsure.

"It's something along those lines," Kenji responded with a shrug.

"Wait a minute," Roy said as he looked at Kenji's sheath and narrowed his eyes. "Where did you obtain that katana?"

"The place we're heading to now. There's a man by the name of Gilgamesh, famous for his smithing ability in creating beautiful and extremely durable weaponry and armor. The kind of arms that legends are based off of. I'm assuming that's where you obtained your weapons, Roy?"

"Actually... yes." Roy looked at Kenji incredulously. "One of my swords. When I first set out on my journey, I had heard rumors of this legendary crafter who would reward others with rare relics for passing his test. I had to try, and the Hyperion and my cloak are proof that I succeeded. The other two swords are from elsewhere, but I did return to ol' Gilgy, and he did bless them with wards of protection for me. Nice guy."

"He's a master craftsman." Kenji patted his katana thoughtfully. "I can never trust another blade that isn't made by him after witnessing the durability of the Izayoi firsthand. Hopefully he will be interested in testing the resolve of these three."

"Wait, you mean me too?" Luna asked, her eyes wide.

"Of course. I did hear you correctly when you said you wished to continue on with us, correct?"

"You did, but... I'm no dragoon."

"So? Neither is Attila." Kenji flipped his thumb dismissively at the man who had been mostly silent as a shadow. "You don't have to be able to control magic to succeed in Gilgamesh's test."

"Well," Luna looked at her weapon and sighed lightly, "I could use a new bow. This one is close to firing its last arrow."

"Yeah, I noticed that." Darkflare glanced at the bow as well. "I'm really surprised it hasn't fallen apart yet, to be honest with you."

"It has broken a few times," Luna said with a shrug. "I've just gotten used to repairing it time and time again."

Attila turned to finally face Kenji. "If it's for a new blade, I'm up for the challenge."

Kenji met his gaze with a big grin. "I'd be surprised if you weren't. You put up quite a fight back in the prison and really surprised me at times."

Attila nodded, but he said no more. Attila really surprised Darkflare too, for several reasons...

They walked on for a few more minutes before Darkflare broke the silence.

"So where does this Gilgamesh guy live?" He looked around as their progress halted. The open plains of nature had disappeared and replacing them was a steep slope made out of rock and grassy knoll. They were at the base of a mountain that seemed to stretch into the heavens above. Darkflare tried to get a glimpse of the peak, but it was impossible from where they stood. After a pause, Darkflare quirked an eyebrow at Kenji's direction, having realized that he was making no attempt to go around. "He lives somewhere on this mountain?"

"Yep."

"Are... we going to have to climb to the top?"

"Eventually." Kenji swung his arm around Darkflare's shoulder, patting him lightly while flashing his smirk. Kenji began to lead the way up the cliff of the mountain, leaving Darkflare watching for a moment, shaking his head in disbelief.

* * * * *

They walked along at a pace that Darkflare found comfortable. At first, breathing in the fresh air, warmed by the inviting sun rays, he found his mind calming; but it was short lived, as his thoughts quickly went down darker paths. Were they wasting time, climbing this mountain, while the Marked Ones roamed the lands, looking to induct others into their ranks? The more rational side of thought reminded him that he could not keep fighting demons with a blade on the border of breaking; they *needed* to meet this man and see his trial through if they were going to protect the kingdoms.

No matter how dangerous.

He forced himself to focus on the task at hand, looking down at the dirt and gravel trail, and then back up to his allies. Kenji and Roy led in the front, ignoring the occasional turns off the main path; Luna and Attila walked as much alongside Darkflare as they could, the latter dropped behind when the path narrowed; and Oboro flew beside his master, swooping through the open air ahead and then behind them.

It was amazing how calming and serene the mountain climb was, compared to everything that had happened since the fight in Ceballe. There was no sign of Marked Ones or aggressive wildlife anywhere in sight. The occasional small creature would scurry away at the sound of their footsteps, but nothing dangerous impeded their path.

"Didn't you say there was a trial or something up here, Kenji?" There was hesitation in Luna's voice as she stared at the scenery.

"Not here, but up higher." Kenji replied, twirling one of his hands in the sky.

"Then I guess the rest of this mountain isn't as... tranquil?"

"That's correct. When Gilgamesh made his home here, he cleared out the dangerous elements to make it easier for travelers. Not all his visitors come for the trial. He has many contracts with people from all over the four kingdoms."

"Up there, past where he lives?" Roy jerked a thumb upward. "Whole different world."

There was a few moments' pause, as if Luna had regretted asking, until Attila cut the silence.

"Sounds like fun."

Darkflare wasn't sure if it was sarcasm or honesty from the stoic man who now stared up at the sky, but he couldn't help but smile. "While I'm up for whatever the challenge may be to get weapons like these two have, I'm not sure yet if I'd consider it 'fun'. Finding old men that each tell a part of a story, searching for the rare materials we would need for this Gilgamesh to craft our weapons, or testing our abilities with a duel all sound like ideas of fun; a mountain which very few come back from, does not."

"Agreed," Luna said, craning her head forward just slightly. "And I'm sure you two aren't going to tell us what this challenge is going to be like?"

"Ah, but that would be cheating!" Roy beamed a smile back at them.

"You'll see soon enough," Kenji said, inclining his head forward.

* * * * *

A little more than an hour had passed since they started climbing when Kenji turned off the main trail and then slowed to a stop. Darkflare's eyes widened at the massive doorframe carved right into the mountain. Windows were patterned on both sides of the door in perfect positions to let in bountiful rays of the sun's light. Kenji continued toward the entrance, motioning for the others to follow.

Darkflare was anxious to meet such a legendary craftsman, finding himself absently fiddling with the Drachenfaith. Kenji approached the entrance but didn't knock; he pushed the huge oak door open and stepped in. Darkflare was hesitant to follow, but the allure of the inside only took a moment to coerce him.

He stepped into a room that was so large, it seemed to be three put together; it was not separated by walls, but he could tell where one section ended and the next began. He had to stop himself when he realized that it was not made out of rock, but wood! The floors, the walls, it was all wood!

"This is incredible," Darkflare murmured, eyes wide, as he walked toward the kitchen area on his left. Fancy apparatuses sat in a row alongside the wall – a stove to cook meals, a sink to wash utensils and plates, and a large icebox to store food. It was a very modern crystal-powered kitchen, despite the fact that the mountain was miles away from any civilization. "Not that I would expect any less from the way you both have made him out."

Ahead of them in the main hall was a long cherry oak table with matching chairs sat all around, as if guests frequently visited in multitude.

"This room is stunning!" Looking across the hall, Luna stood in the middle of a large crimson floor rug with white swirls throughout. Its colors were illuminated by the fireplace behind it, crackling and dancing to several large, empty recliners that had been draped with cloths that matched the design of the sophisticated carpet.

There were also two areas that lay in mystery beyond what they could see. The first of which was further behind the oak table and up a spiral wooden staircase that poked out of the ceiling. Darkflare knew he should not have been, but he was amazed there was a second floor to Gilgamesh's house. He began to wonder if the entirety of the house *was* the inside of the mountain.

The second was guarded by two large suits of armor that bore a crest in the center that was foreign to Darkflare. They stood on both sides of a door similar to the one out front; this also had the same crest as the armor carved in the center and was cracked open just slightly. From the depths of the darkness, Darkflare faintly heard the sound of colliding metal. It was not the familiar sound of combat, but it was instead the methodical beat of a hammer. Roy stepped forward, clearing his throat.

"Oh, dearie me!" He called toward the door in a high-pitched voice. "What is a beautiful maiden to do, here, alone in this big house?!"

"Do you practice that voice often?" Luna shook her head, pinching the bridge of her nose.

"Not bad," Attila shrugged.

"Well, I-..." Roy cleared his throat, his voice returning to its original octave. "I hope he remembers me, or this may get a touch awkward."

The house filled with an eerie hush; the hammering had stopped, and they stood waiting for the man that Kenji and Roy had made out to be superhuman. Darkflare, Luna, and Attila had shared their different ideas of what the man might look like on the climb up; Darkflare thought he was an older man with one eye and missing an arm he had lost in combat, Luna wished for a handsome young man whose face she could dream of whenever she gazed at her new bow, and Attila thought he would be slightly older and graying on top despite his years of retained muscle.

Each of them was completely wrong. The man that emerged from the doorway was slightly taller than Kenji, his head almost skimming the ceiling. He had extremely striking features; a pointed nose, a sharp chin, a beard that went from ear to ear, and silver hair that flowed down his back. He glared at each of the intruders with confused aggravation. Darkflare, out of instinct, thought to go for his sword but second guessed himself when he beheld the strapping muscles. The monster of a man noticed Darkflare's hand move, and it caused his expression to brighten into a warmer grin.

"No need to draw your steel, boy. People don't usually just barge in here, disturbing my work; but seeing your company, I'm not surprised." Gilgamesh turned toward Kenji and Roy and beamed an even bigger smile. "Well, well… the Izayoi and the Hyperion. Never would have thought that you two would have ended up traveling together." Gilgamesh waved a dismissive hand at Roy. "I suppose that girlish voice was yours?"

"Guilty," Roy said with a bow, sweeping his cloak out to the side.

"Well, it threw me off, I'll give you that! Now, what brings you here? Need something patched up? A different kind of weapon, perhaps?"

"No, no," Kenji began. "Alas, it's been too long since our last meeting, but I can assure you the Izayoi has worked wonders for me. Our purpose here today is that we've brought new warriors that wish to test themselves. And it is this one," he jerked a thumb toward Darkflare, "that has brought us all together."

Gilgamesh looked up and down at Darkflare. He was still a frightening man, even smiling. His thick eyebrows were arched at such an angle that it always seemed as if he was fuming. It also did not help that his crimson and black gi was cut in a 'v'-like shape from his neck down, exposing his muscular chest and forearms. His baggy crimson pants helped to hide his burly legs, but Darkflare did not need to see them to know the man was all muscle.

"And your name, my boy?"

Gathering his senses, Darkflare forced himself to stand taller. "Darkflare Omni."

Upon hearing the name, Gilgamesh's expression became serious. Darkflare slowly glanced at Kenji, fearing he had done something wrong.

"Omni… No, you couldn't be… Calistron's boy?"

"Yes," Darkflare nodded rather solemnly. "Calistron and Sylphe were my parents."

"Are you a dragoon as well?"

"Yes," Darkflare hesitated for a moment. He had considered himself pretty well-learned, even though he had never known what a dragoon was before yesterday. It was slightly off-putting that everyone he was meeting already had some level of understanding of the word. "I am the bearer of the Rune of Courage."

"Holy Mokiwana," Gilgamesh hushed under his breath before he turned to Kenji and Roy with a nod. "The son of Calistron and Sylphe is also a dragoon. And if you're with him, Kenji, I assume that bad things are brewing if he's here for a weapon. As for the other two," Gilgamesh focused his attention on Attila and Luna. "Dragoons as well?"

Attila did not answer, but Luna shook her head, still obviously in awe by his presence. "N-No. We aren't as fortunate – we're just normal humans. My name is Luna Iylvein."

"... Attila Laise. I'm no dragoon, but I seek to become stronger."

Gilgamesh turned away, nodding several times to himself. The three looked back and forth at each other, as if unifying their confusion.

"So!" Gilgamesh boomed and whirled back around so fast that he startled all of them, including Kenji and Roy. "You three seek unique, powerful weapons, the like of which you'll never see in any market stall? No wonder; look at those scraps of junk you currently wield!" He walked over to Darkflare's side and put his hand out. The young man drew his sword and held it out for Gilgamesh, who let out a repulsed groan. Darkflare quickly sheathed the sword, feeling color rise to his face. "Not fit for anything besides being toothpicks! If you agree to undertake my test, your reward will be weaponry stronger and better crafted than you could ever dream of."

"We agree," Darkflare responded as his allies nodded. "We're ready to do what it takes, Gilgamesh."

"Good," the burly man responded, forming a smile that ended up looking rather sadistic. "Your quest is simple. Climb to the top of the mountain. There, you will find your reward."

"That's all?" Darkflare looked to the others, but their faces were impassive. "Is there something you wish us to bring back as proof?"

"No. Just you getting there will be proof." There was a hard look to Gilgamesh's face that Darkflare didn't like. "It should be no problem for the son of Calistron Omni."

"Right. Then we shall set out right away. Time is of the essence."

Darkflare held Gilgamesh's gaze for a moment longer and then turned to leave. He got so far as to the door before something told him to turn around. Attila and Luna had followed, but Roy and Kenji remained where they stood. Gilgamesh's grin grew even wider.

"Ah, I forgot to mention. These two stay here. They've already completed my quest. You three must go with just each other and lacking of my weaponry."

"That hardly seems fair," Luna said, putting her hands on her hips. "We barely got out of Kailos in one piece, and we probably wouldn't have at all, if it weren't for those two. Darkflare, is your shoulder even fully healed?"

"It's either that or nothing at all." Gilgamesh crossed his trunk-like arms over his chest. "Besides, they did not have any aid undertaking their tests. Make your choice."

Darkflare looked at her and nodded rather slowly. "I'll be alright. It wasn't my dominant arm. We can still do this, but you don't have to go if you don't want to. You owe us nothing."

"No, I… I don't want to pass up an opportunity like this." She glanced at Kenji's curved sword and the one Roy had wielded during the last battle. "It's like you said last night: if we can all wield weapons like that, we can stop the Marked Ones. We can make a difference. I'm going with you."

"We'll be fine," Attila said dismissively as he walked out of the door.

"Oboro, you stay with them as well, alright?" The small wyvern whined and hissed at his master's words, but it obediently flew off his back. Kenji patted Oboro lightly on the head as he flew over.

"They'll be okay, Oboro. Nothing to worry about!" The wyvern cooed sadly to Kenji in response, hesitant to sit next to him.

Darkflare and Luna exchanged looks again before they headed outside after Attila.

* * * * *

"I didn't doubt Kenji or Roy, but this… is a bit extreme," Luna said, one hand in her blonde hair, the other on her hip.

Darkflare stood beside her with a lack of words. The land had changed completely from the path before. The trail had all but vanished, and in its place, the land was dismal and rotten - almost the same sickening landscape as Syvail. Trees that had lost all life hung sullen and limp, huge slabs of fallen rock and debris were strewn all over, and bones of dead creatures lined what was left of the trail. Darkflare could not help but worry about what forms of life lay in wait for them as they scaled. The only one of the three that did not seem to mind the change was the same person who had not been fazed by very much at all since the start of the journey – Attila.

"Standing around here isn't going to get us anywhere. They prepared us for this. So what if the landscape's different? We just need to keep our wits about us, and we'll be fine. Remember, Darkflare, it used to be just you and I. There never used to be a Kenji or a Roy."

"You're right, Attila." Darkflare nodded, taking a few steps forward. "We can do this. This is all just still so strange for me. We always imagined ourselves on adventures like this, but to actually *be here*, on a quest for new weapons, me being able to cast magic… It all still feels like a dream."

"One very crazy, demented dream," Luna said, staring out at the decayed trees. "And while it might have been you two boys prancing around at your tournaments, remember that I'm here now. Don't be afraid to count on me when you need my help."

"No thanks," Attila said, continuing past them.

Luna scoffed, folding her arms across her chest, but Darkflare shook his head as he watched Attila go.

"Don't mind him. He's as stubborn as they get. He'll warm up to you, I hope. Eventually," Darkflare said, turning to face Luna. "But thank you. You have been a great aid so far. I'll continue to rely on that aim of yours."

Following Attila, the trio braved the rocky terrain to walk, what they could only presume to be, the barely noticeable path upward. While the layout of the mountain range was fairly linear, the turn offs could easily have been mistaken for the main path, and Darkflare worried that it could lead them into some dangerous situations. Upon reaching a crossroad in which the paths seemed to lead in the same direction, Darkflare stopped to ponder the situation.

"Two identical paths…"

"Yeah, but why is one *above* the other?" Luna stood beside Darkflare, examining the choice as well. The left path was higher elevated, hugging the face of the mountain, while the right path had curved a little below it, almost hidden. Beyond that, they both seemed to come back together several feet ahead of them.

Hearing a slight crackling, Darkflare's head spun to the left path. Small rocks had begun trickling down the side of the mountain, but they soon escalated to larger clumps of stone. Darkflare's eyes widened when he realized a shadow had descended over them. He threw his arm out at his side, his hand pointing.

"Go! Take the right path!"

At first, the small clumps of rocks drizzled onto the left path until there was no more room to cover. Then they overflowed over the side, missing the other path, and down to the abyss below. As they rushed to get to safer ground, several boulders rolled and took over the space where they had just been standing; they had cheated death once again.

Darkflare let out a loud sigh of relief as the sound of silence enveloped the area.

"Well, that was clo-..." He froze; he heard that crackling noise once again, but this time it was closer. Turning around to face his allies, he stared into their worried expressions. His gaze shot down, and the ground underneath him was beginning to crack and spread. Without hesitating another moment, Darkflare started running back toward the other two, but it was too late. The ground snatched his footing out from under him, giving in to the weight of gravity. Before he began to fall, Darkflare outstretched his arms and leapt, attempting to grab anything before he sank into the abyss below. His hands latched onto the edge and he hung for dear life as the gravel underneath his fingertips began to crumble.

His thoughts raced as he fought to pull himself up. He kicked the wall vigorously, trying to find footing, but it was hopeless. Just as Darkflare felt the ground giving way, he felt a pair of hands wrap tightly around his own. When he looked up, his gaze met a focused Attila as he tried to pull his friend back up.

"You're not going on me this early! Climb, dammit!"

Finally able to find a foothold, Darkflare was able to climb back up. Attila let go once Darkflare was standing, but that didn't last long. Darkflare fell onto his rear and stared up at the sky above as he panted heavily. Luna slunk back against the wall and plopped down beside Darkflare.

"That... was really close." Darkflare tried to calm his thoughts and breathe. His life had almost ended, had it not been for his friends. He cursed his rune; he would never have even come to Gilgamesh's mountain if it were not for that blasted magical thing. What good had it done him as he clung to the edge of life? He shook his head as best as he could and slowly rose to his feet.

"Rune of Courage... King of Dragoons... These weapons better be worth this journey."

Attila was leaning against the wall, supporting his weight with his arm. "You alright?"

"Yeah," Darkflare breathed, sitting up. "Shoulder is a bit pained after that, though. You? How's your ankle holding up?"

"I'm good."

Attila looked completely unfazed as he responded, but his foot tapped impatiently. Darkflare turned toward Luna, who seemed to be shaking slightly.

"Luna?"

"I'm fine." The warmth wavered in her voice, but it was still there.

"Good," Darkflare exhaled deeply and stood up straight. "That's one scare, but whatever else is on this mountain is not about to get any more over us. We know for sure now that there are things up here that are going to oppose us. Let's keep our guard up."

Placing his hands on his hips, still catching his breath, Darkflare looked over the hole that had been made.

"Thanks... Both of you. I appreciate it."

Attila nodded without looking up from the ground. Luna shook her head and stood up as well.

"You know, in the short time I've known you, I've saved your life an awful amount of times."

Darkflare looked toward Luna, a wide smile on her face, and she winked at him. He smiled back.

"Alright, so when all this is over, I owe you greatly. Don't forget that."

"I won't, but what are we going to do about this hole?"

"Well," Darkflare began to ponder again, looking around at every little detail. His eyes kept being drawn toward the freshly made chasm and the ground on the other side. "We could try to jump it. It's not really that big of a gap. We have to just hope that was the only part that was going to crumble."

Luna teetered to the edge of the cliff to join Darkflare's analysis. "I guess. What other choice do we have?"

Darkflare was about to answer when he noticed Attila had begun to back up. He was also judging the distance between the gap and the other side, but unlike the other two, he acted. After a few moments of standing and observing, Attila took off running to the edge. A wide-eyed Darkflare could do nothing but stand there and watch as Attila went speeding by. Just as he reached the end of his runway, he leapt through the air and landed on the other side on one knee. He slowly stood to dust himself off before turning to the others.

"No challenge."

"You're a real show off, you know?" Luna put her hands on her hips. "Who are you even showing off *for*? It's not for me, and I really doubt it's for him!"

As Luna pointed to Darkflare, he shrugged. "Well, if he can do it..."

He backed up, measuring the gap, and Luna turned to face him. Darkflare ran forward and leapt across the chasm, landing gracefully on both feet on the other side. He grinned back at Luna, waving his arm forward.

"If I fall, Darkflare..."

"You won't fall, I promise!"

"You will be owing me from the afterlife – I swear it!"

She sighed and measured the gap as well. Luna ran forward, her bow clutched tight to her chest as she jumped. Darkflare and Attila each caught an arm and steadied her. Darkflare patted her lightly on the back once Luna was balanced.

"Nothing like a little death defying leap to let you know you really are alive, eh?"

She let loose a satisfied chuckle and shook her head once more.

They continued on the path very cautiously. As they walked, the trio made sure to keep an eye not only on the path ahead, but also the ground beneath their soles. The road rose from the dip it had made, once again forming with the left path that had been blocked by the landslide. Darkflare paused, examining the pile of rubble and boulders that had previously impeded their path.

"What's wrong?" Attila asked, joining Darkflare in staring at the roadblock.

"There was no reason for this all to have just conveniently fallen in our way. There had to be something that triggered the slide from above."

"What could have done it though?" Luna inquired, trying to look at the above cliff. They were not too far from the top of the ridge now, but it was still impossible to see.

"Something we probably want to be prepared for," Darkflare turned back to the path once more with his allies in tow.

It was not a long climb up to the source of the rockfall; from where they were, they circled around for a few more minutes and then came up a slope. Reaching the apex, Darkflare was forced to freeze once more; this time he wrapped his hand around the handle of his longsword. Without turning his head, Darkflare peered over the landscape, his eyes bounding from here to there trying to grasp the entire area. What had caused him to remain motionless was another noise he had heard; something bestial was stirring around them.

Darkflare had lived close enough to the wilderness for enough years to know the difference between a naturally made noise and one that was created by a creature. Attila must have heard it too because his sword had already been withdrawn and readied in both hands. When Luna saw her allies ready themselves, she slipped a fresh arrow from her quiver.

Hissssss...

There it was again! Darkflare located the source this time. Off to the side behind one of the large boulders.

Hisssss! Hissssss!

Two more cries. This time off to the right, in the center of a hurdle of dead tree stumps. He and Attila exchanged looks of readiness, but they did not have another moment to spare. Leaping out at them from various spots of cover unwound five long creatures. As they uncoiled themselves, Darkflare found out that they were no ordinary snakes. They spanned at least five to six feet in length and raised their bodies at last four feet off the ground. Their spread hoods and venomous fangs made them a terrifying sight as they flew through the air. Preparing for the incoming attacks, the three each tried to dodge instead of parrying. Darkflare and Luna leapt closer to the wall of the mountain, while Attila took the more dangerous route and evaded as best as he could toward the edge. After all five missed their prey, they slithered along the ground, trying to regroup.

"What in the Pale are those?!" Luna pressed her back against the wall, fingering the string of her bow as she nocked an arrow.

"Snakes," Darkflare muttered as he kept his eyes on the aggressors that slithered back their way. "Really... really... big snakes."

Darkflare watched and waited as one crawled in his direction. It leapt at him, and this time, Darkflare was able to bring the longsword forward as he sidestepped the attack. Not only did he manage to dodge the incoming open mouth, but he also managed to cut down the middle of the snake, bringing the blade up and through the back of the hood as he moved away. The lifeless body of the creature slunk to the ground, its whole upper half of the head tore right off as if its detachment was natural.

Perhaps if it had happened in a different time or place, Darkflare might have been able to feel proud of the blow he had dealt, but just as he had finished the kill, another snake dove toward him with open jaws. He managed to evade the bulk of the attack by rolling out of the way, but he could not dodge all of it. Just as he landed on his feet once more, the tail of the beast came up with a thunderous whiplash toward his chest. Darkflare clawed the air in an attempt to stay on his feet, but it was of no use. He hit the ground hard on his back and his opponent had ample time to turn back around. Hovering over Darkflare's body, the snake hissed loudly, opening its mouth wide and revealing sharp fangs that were coated in either blood or venom; Darkflare was not about to find out which.

The snake shut its mouth just as quickly as it opened it, its yellow eyes reduced to slits as its hood flared. It whirled around, allowing Darkflare to see. Luna moved a little bit further up the cliff and had the arrow she was playing with fly right into the back of the snake's head. Unfortunately, it was not a killing shot, and the snake moved even more aggressively from the pain it must have been in.

As it slithered off in Luna's direction, Darkflare grasped his longsword in both hands and sat up. Just before the snake could get away, he dove with the sword's blade pointing down, penetrating the tail. The snake twitched with anger and pain as it found out that it could not move forward any more, it could only writhe in pain.

Jumping back to his feet, Darkflare withdrew the sword and stabbed it down several more times into the body of the snake. It lay helplessly, trashing and turning as it gasped its last breaths of life. When it finally lay still, Darkflare turned to Luna and nodded in order to thank her. They both moved to join Attila, who seemed to be enjoying the disadvantage he was at.

As the first one dove at Attila, he did not even blink. Instead, he flashed a smile. He met the beast with the flat side of his greatsword, slamming the blade hard into the side of the creature's head. As the once coiled body went limp, Attila sidestepped the snake as it tumbled off the cliff.

The second one slithered along the ground toward Attila, and he decided to meet it head on. Just before the two forces collided, Attila leapt into the air. The snake looked up for its airborne foe, and Attila plunged the greatsword down through the head and into the neck of the creature, decimating it before it even had a chance to bare its multi-layered fangs. Attila stood up and pressed a finger to his face, feeling that some of the snake's blood had splattered onto his cheekbones. He shook his head back, forcing his hair out of his eyes, and streaked his face with the blood of the snake as he tried to wipe it off.

There was still one more snake to deal with, and Attila seemed too distracted to remember it. Darkflare thrust his left hand out and focused as the creature slithered its way toward his stoic friend. It didn't take nearly as long as before to conjure the ball of flames as energy drew into his fingertips and balled in the center of his palm. Pushing forward, the fire blasted away from him and exploded with tremendous force against the snake, knocking it past Attila. His friend watched as the creature thrashed while it burned, and when it lay still, he turned a nod to Darkflare.

Once the three regrouped, they looked each other over, making sure no one had gotten bitten by the poisonous fangs.

"We found the source of the landslide." Darkflare said, sheathing his sword once more.

"How? And what were those *snakes?*" Luna shuddered as she mentioned the last word. "Ugh, of all things, why did we have to find snakes? Tiny ones are gross enough."

Attila pointed over to a section of jagged stumps. "See those? Those didn't just die. They were crushed. It takes quite a great deal of force to snap a tree that thick, Pale, any tree. But those did not just rot."

"Right," Darkflare nodded. "And I can tell you, by the tail blow I took, that they have a lot of strength in their slithering bodies. It's a good thing we didn't get coiled up by one of them."

"So they crushed the rocks and rolled them down the cliff?" Luna's eyes widened greatly as she spoke, looking from the stumps to the side of the mountain.

"That's got to be it. They're a *lot* stronger than normal snakes… Mutated over time, I suppose. They must be of the kobraikan species."

"The what?"

"Kobraikan are a snake-like species that have evolved and grown vicious over the passing decades. They have a variety of characteristics and colors. I've only seen a few in my life, and those were much smaller than these."

"How do you know so much?"

"I've read a lot. I have an unquenchable thirst for knowledge, you could say."

To this, Attila nodded. "He's the reader, and I'm the doer. He likes to find things out by reading them. I'll find them out the hard way, even if it means tearing things apart. Books aren't my thing."

Luna shrugged. "Balance in everything, I suppose."

"He just doesn't care for the finer things in life," Darkflare grinned at the man who rolled his eyes. "We need to continue on. Dusk will fall soon, and we need somewhere safe to stay for the night."

* * * * *

The summit looked to be another few hours climb, but that much more was asking a lot of their minds and bodies. They had been walking for the better part of the past few days; from the vast outstretch of plains that they had crossed from Ceballe to Kailos, to Gilgamesh's serene base that seemed too good to be true, to now the dreary climb of the mountain. The sky shone dimly with an amber color that reflected across the side of the mountain, and they knew it was only a matter of time until dusk completely took over.

As they came to a path that turned off the main road, Darkflare stopped, one hand rose to stroke his chin.

"We could try in there," Darkflare pointed toward a cave that sat at the end of the path, and he bit his lower lip. "We'd be better off clearing out anything in there now before it gets dark."

"Might as well," Attila muttered, moving forward to investigate.

Approaching the cave, they cautiously began to look around. Luna and Darkflare kept their eyes toward the sides to make sure that no more snakes appeared to surprise them, while Attila's hand hovered anxiously for an opportunity to withdraw his steel. They stopped once more when they reached the mouth of the darkness. It took Darkflare a moment to realize that they were waiting on him, and more importantly, his rune. He stepped forward, pausing for a moment to listen; but there was no noise from within. Taking that as his invitation to act, Darkflare cupped his right hand by his side, allowing a small spark of fire to ignite. He was just enough in the doorway for the fire to illuminate the roof, and Darkflare felt his heart drop when it did.

"Down! NOW!" Darkflare screamed as he fumbled for any other words, but it was too late. Before he could even finish his outburst, a swarm of angry winged creatures exploded from above. He fell to his knees, shielding the small ball of fire energy as best as he could as the bats flew by his head. Luna stood slightly confused as Darkflare spoke, but Attila pulled her down the moment he saw the winged creatures take flight.

Darkflare stood back up in complete disbelief once they had all flown out. There had to have been at least a hundred of the creatures. An uncontrollable laugh escaped his lips.

"Looks like we won't have to worry about cave clearing now!"

"Thank you, Attila." Luna eyed the dark-haired man cautiously. "Is it safe to say that we're all on the same page now?"

Attila grunted as he walked away from her. She smiled at Darkflare and lowered her voice to a whisper. "I'm growing on him, just you watch!"

Darkflare's grin widened, and he turned to follow Attila.

"Small cave." Attila looked around as they entered the hollow. The wall went on no further than fifteen or twenty feet; the ball of fire lit up the entire space.

"Well, I guess this works in our favor," Darkflare shrugged. "No more bats, small enough that we can tell nothing else is in here with us, and the fire will keep us warm."

Attila placed a small kindling of deadwood he had been gathering along the way down in the middle of the cave. Darkflare nodded his thanks as he placed the magic flame to rest in the center.

The trio plopped down around the fire as the sky outside transitioned to a purplish black. They sat wordlessly, simply staring deep into the core of the flame that burned brightly in front of them. Darkflare broke the silence by letting out a slight chuckle, shaking his head. Luna and Attila simultaneously turned to face him as he drooped his head back between his shoulders, eyes shut.

"What?" Luna asked.

"It's just funny how fate works."

"Oh, here we go again," Attila grumbled.

Darkflare brought his head forward to glare at Attila, but he didn't say anything. He wanted to call him out for keeping secrets, for feeling like he barely knew the real him, but he kept his mouth shut. He always knew Attila had secrets, and it was wrong of him to hold a grudge or pretend that Attila hadn't always given him his all, standing by his side.

He turned to stare at the blaze he created, smiling sadly.

"It's just hard to still grasp the fact that I've inherited this title of Dragoon King, control over the element of fire, and this phenomenal destiny. I always wanted to be a knight, but this... This is something entirely overwhelming. Magical powers, running around sacred ruins, saving the nobility, fighting an army of demons... It's a lot to just plop into someone's lap in – what – two days?" Darkflare sighed, clenching his fists. "As enchanting as all of this is, are we – am I – really ready?"

"What do you want?" Darkflare could feel Attila's cold stare. "Do you want to just give up and go back to Crescentia until you figure this all out?"

"No." Darkflare's eyes darted quickly from the flame to Attila's face. The sad smile vanished and he drew his brows down. "No, of course not. This fate, this rune, is mine; and I may be overwhelmed by it all, but I have accepted the responsibility. It's what my father would have wanted." Darkflare paused for a moment, shifting uncomfortably as his gaze returned to the fire. "It's what I want."

Another moment passed in silence as Darkflare worked up the courage to continue.

"I don't know what lies in wait for us, but I'll stand strong against it all. My parents died fighting against that Graymahl Vulorst person. They gave their lives to protect this world. For their sacrifice, I can't let myself just give in to the weight of my responsibilities. Ever since my powers first activated, I've felt the flames flowing through my veins. At first it was only a slight tickle, but with every battle, it grows more and more intense. It will take time to become attuned with my powers, and the world is not just going to stop in the meantime. The four kingdoms need a protector that can go beyond the boundary lines etched out by proclamations, and if that someone's me, I'll gladly rise to the challenge."

Luna smiled, staring into the fire herself. "Facing your fears and standing up against the unknown to protect those that cannot is a noble calling. It's what made me want to travel with you to Kailos in the first place – that passion you have to protect the innocent, I knew I was in good company or I would have walked right out of those ruins. Whether you feel yourself ready for the challenge or not, you have people supporting you."

"I shouldn't need to say it, but I will." Attila had turned to his blade, whetting the sharp side whilst wiping off some splattered blood he had missed prior. "You know I will always stand alongside you. How it's always been, how it always will be. And, Luna," Attila paused, not moving his eyes from his blade. "You seem alright. I wouldn't mind someone else helping me to watch out for him."

Her eyes widened, and she stared at Darkflare with a look of victory. Then she turned back to Attila with a serious expression. "Thank you. Though dark and broody on the outside, you really have a caring heart under there, don't you?"

"Watch it," he said, not looking up again.

"I appreciate it... Both of you." Darkflare's attention turned back to the flame, watching it wave vividly back and forth, then fall still, only to repeat the process over again. It was not much for entertainment, but it captivated their attention nonetheless.

Luna opened her mouth to let a yawn escape as she stretched her arms behind her.

"I don't think it's that late, but my body feels so heavy."

"You're worn out. We all are." Attila sheathed his blade, placed it on the ground behind him, and then laid his head down on it. "It's about time we got some rest."

"I'll take first watch," Darkflare said, forcing a smile.

Both of his allies mumbled their thanks, and Darkflare nodded, but he continued to stare at the flame for a few moments as the other two prepared for sleep. He couldn't help but think about his parents; it was almost like he could see them in the center of the flame. There was Calistron with his long but thinning brown hair and bushy beard, and there was Sylphe with her thick mane of poofy blonde hair. He could see their brown and jade eyes respectively staring back at him.

Darkflare hoped they were watching over him. What did they think of the man he had become? If they could speak, what advice would they give their dragoon-in-training son? He wanted to tell them not to worry, that he would always protect the innocent and fight for those he cared about – just like they did.

He stared away for a moment and unconsciously clenched his fist as he thought about the legacy that his parents had left behind. Now was the time to start his own, and Darkflare felt confident about the allies that stood with him.

Darkflare turned and leaned against the cave wall, feeling odd without the added weight of Oboro, and stared out into the encroaching night.

Chapter X

The dawn's light penetrated and illuminated the cave as the sun ascended. Darkflare could feel the brightness behind his closed eyelids, but he struggled to keep them shut as long as possible. After a few minutes, Darkflare finally gave in to the sun's demands and forced himself to sit up. He did not remember being so tired the night before, but perhaps all of the walking finally caught up with him. Luna followed his groggy awakening shortly after, Attila standing and ready having been the last on guard.

"Morning," Darkflare muttered, standing to stretch.

"Shall we be off?" Attila said, barely looking their way.

"Ugh, no time for morning tea, I suppose?" When Luna's eyes fully opened, she moaned before standing. "Ah, I had the most pleasant dream that I was in a bed somewhere comfy, safe, and not on a mountain."

The trio set out for their final ascent up the mountain once Luna dragged herself up and ready. Darkflare figured they would reach the summit by noon, if no other distractions presented themselves. After the bats and the snakes, the group made sure they were on their guards for anything else that could be sneaking up along the treacherous trail of the mountain, despite the overhanging tiredness that lingered in each of their minds.

"So, Attila. I've heard a little bit about Darkflare's family, but what about yours? Parents, siblings, pets, anything?" Luna poked Attila lightly in the shoulder as she asked him.

Darkflare glared at her, shaking his head quickly. Attila had been staring out over the edge of the cliff, and it was obvious that he had no intention of answering her.

"What? Okay, bad subject. Understood." She cocked an eyebrow at Darkflare, as if looking for more clarification.

"What about you, Luna?" Darkflare smiled, trying to quickly change the subject. "Where are you from? How about your family?"

"Oh, I'm from Echlow. It's a small farming town in the northwestern area of the kingdom."

"Ah, yes. I can just barely picture where it is on a map, but I do believe it's past Pheeq?"

"Way past Pheeq. It's very close to the border of Verankner."

"Wow! That's some distance from Syvail. What in the Pale are you doing on the other side of D'sylum?"

"Well," Luna let an exasperated sigh out, playing with a lock of her blonde hair on the side of her head. "It's a long story, but the gist of it is that I more or less ran away from home. I wanted to explore and see more of the world, and my parents did not like that idea. So I left against their wishes. I had heard about the fighter's tournament in some of the towns I stopped to rest at along the way."

"Ah, I see. How did you become so good at archery then?"

"I learned how to use a bow when I was very young. Mostly for sport, you know, the sort you see at Ceballe's games like hit a moving Ravenshade peach – which, I've never understood, by the way. They might be black on the outside, but they're extremely juicy and sweet! But I've always had good coordination. Mostly. You saw how my arrow struck a glancing blow on that snake."

"Still caused it a fair amount of pain, from its expression! I meant to ask you, did you find anything interesting at Syvail?"

"No, I barely began to search when everything happened. If there was treasure, I didn't find any."

"Eh." Darkflare scratched at the back of his head, squinting up at the blinding ball of light in the sky. "I doubt there's anything of note in there. I would think that they would have removed anything of value or that represented national pride to D'sylum before they sealed it."

"Calling it a sacred place is just a cover story," Attila interrupted, still as calm as ever as he gazed at the scenery down below, unvexed by the nauseating distance. "I think Corsius is trying to conceal something he doesn't want the rest of the world to know is there."

"Like what?"

Attila shrugged, falling silent once again.

"Look!" Luna's eyes widened and a smile beamed across her face as she pointed ahead of them. Darkflare casted his eyes at what she was so excited about and soon shared a similar expression – they had finally reached the summit, and it was not what any of them expected to find. It was neither cold enough nor high enough of a mountain for there to be a snow-kissed peak. Instead, they found themselves at a small lakeside. A crystal blue pond of water sat motionless, devoid of any aquatic activity, taking up most of the mountaintop. Surrounding the edges of the cliff were large pine trees; the first touch of blossoming nature that the trio had seen since the bottom.

Darkflare looked around the oasis, as if expecting for the others to come springing out of nowhere to congratulate them for passing Gilgamesh's test.

"This… This is it? That was Gilgamesh's oh-so-scary test that many failed at conquering?"

"It's kind of anti-climactic, but what are we supposed to do? He said getting here would be proof we accomplished his test." Luna looked around for anything that stood out.

"Wait," Attila raised a hand to the side of his head. Both Luna and Darkflare turned to look at him as he closed his eyes. "Do you hear that? That rumbling?"

Darkflare's eyes darted back and forth as he looked over the landscape. Everything seemed perfectly normal; the fully furnished trees with growing grass surrounding them, a pool of water that seemed-…

A pool of water that suddenly had an ominous black shadow in the dark depths below. Darkflare's eyes widened at the rising shape as he grasped the handle of his longsword.

"I-In the water! There's something there!"

Attila withdrew his sword, grasping it with both hands. "About that anti-climactic finish…"

All three of the warriors flinched back defensively as geysers of water shot up from the serene sapphire surface. Eight thick orange tentacles towered over them more than twice Darkflare's height and waved crazily as several suction cups on the undersides of each sucked at the air.

The eight limbs formed a circle around a bulbous scaly skull. The beast's twin slits of eyes darted back and forth at the three warriors. As it thrashed about in the water, its jaw hung right below the surface, opening to inhale the cooling liquid and then gnashing shut, colliding its several rows of spiked teeth together. Waving its tentacles back and forth and clamping its ferocious spiked jaw, Darkflare had never seen anything more terrifying.

"Kraken," he muttered, frozen in fear, his heart pounding. They could head back down the mountain, but for what? To hide in a cave? *This* was the real test. They needed to fight, and they needed to win! But the question was how? The kraken was massive!

"Darkflare!" It was Luna's voice. He turned to face her, his thoughts sundered. "Use your rune! Go dragoon, or whatever it is that you do!"

He nodded but hesitated from drawing in any energy. It was the obvious thing to give them an advantage, but did he have enough control or stamina to be able to smite the kraken with his magic?

He had to try.

Stabbing his sword into the ground, Darkflare cupped his hands together in front of his chest, gathering as much fire energy as he could summon from the Rune of Courage. The familiar technique caused a small ball of fire to form in the center of his hands, quickly expanding. Once he had collected enough power, Darkflare thrust his hands forward, separating his fingertips from one another while keeping the base of his palms locked. The ball of fire leapt forward from Darkflare's palms, hurdling straight toward the kraken. Stars dotted his vision and he had to steady himself, but if his body could manage the strain, Darkflare hoped it would only take two or three fireballs of that power to submerge the beast once more.

Darkflare thought wrong. The kraken didn't flinch as the burst of energy exploded against the side of its face. The flames scattered all around it, the embers trying to burn their way deep through the kraken's scales, but they failed in their attempts. The fire attack seemed to only enrage the beast more, which unleashed a loud roar from its jaws half submerged in the water, and its eyes fell upon Darkflare.

"Not good!" Darkflare withdrew his sword from the ground, readying himself once more into a defensive stance. "It had no effect! How is that possible?!"

"Think about it! It's a creature of the water!" Attila raised a hand to point at the kraken's head, its watery scales noticeably glistening in the sun's reflection. "We have to find a weak spot!"

Darkflare swore under his breath and watched as one of the forward tentacles started to rise and sway. The sky above his head darkened as a large shadow descended upon them. Darkflare barely had time to move and dove into a roll to the left, which allowed him to narrowly dodge the incoming attack. One of the kraken's tentacles slammed against the ground where Darkflare was, causing gravel and debris to scatter like dust from the impact. Once he scrambled back to his feet, Darkflare realized that his allies had gone in the other direction; the kraken thankfully had not killed them, but it had managed to divide them, making organizing a battle strategy more difficult.

The kraken repeated its previous actions by roaring and raising four more of its tentacles high in the air. Two tentacles crashed down toward Attila and Luna, but Darkflare was not able to witness the results. One of the tentacles plummeted down upon his position; Darkflare rolled to the left and again managed to evade a close encounter with death. But that only accounted for one of the tentacles.

Darkflare's attention remained fixed upon the second scaly appendage as it danced wildly out of the water. His plan was to wait until it dropped and then he'd make his move to rejoin his allies, but the kraken was taking too much time to act. He could feel the sweat in his palm that was clenched tight against the grip of his sword; he did not want to act too hastily, because if he made one ill-fated move, it would all be over. He tried to steal a glance toward his allies, but instead he witnessed the first tentacle that he had dodged stir toward him. He could only stare helplessly as he was too slow to avoid the tentacle hitting him with full force in the chest.

Darkflare's arms flung out and up, and the grip he had on his longsword loosened as, in that instance, he could no longer feel his hands. His arms flailed, trying to grasp anything he could to keep himself from falling off the cliff, until he slammed viciously into a tree trunk. He fell to the ground, letting out a cry of pain, and he wasn't sure if the sound he was hearing was his back breaking or the bark splintering.

He forced himself on his hands and knees, fighting through the pain, and shook his head to clear the hundreds of bright stars that dotted his sight. He reached for his longsword, only to see it finally coming back down from being thrown, plummeting down the side of the mountain.

"You've got to be *kidding* me," Darkflare's voice went shrill from a mix of anger, fear, and exhaustion; and in that moment, he forgot about his enemy. "This can't get any damn worse!"

Darkflare had enough time to finish his sentence before he realized that he was beginning to slide back toward the pool of water. Whipping his head around, he realized the tips of one of the tentacles had wrapped around his legs, pulling him to the kraken. Darkflare thrashed and kicked with all of his might, trying to free himself, but it was no use. The beast slithered its grasp around his torso, raising him up above its head. Looking down at the monster below, Darkflare stopped trying to struggle; it was no use. If he broke free now, he would plummet right into the mouth of the kraken.

"What the Pale have I done...?"

* * * * *

"No, Darkflare!" Luna drew her bow, but seeing Darkflare raised into the air, she dropped her aim. She flung her arms out at her sides as she turned to stare at Attila. "What do we do?!"

Attila showed an expression that Luna thought was impossible from him - fear - as he witnessed the bestial strength of the kraken. Exhaling deeply, he closed his eyes and clenched his left fist.

"I will not let Darkflare get eaten by some ugly fish."

"Then *do* something!" Luna's voice was shrill with panic.

Her eyes were drawn to Attila's clenched fist. She swore she saw the air around his hand contort and swirl across his knuckles. She became less concerned about Darkflare and more for Attila's sake as he shook with what she thought could only be rage.

"Attila...?"

His eyes snapped open, as if he had been suddenly disturbed from the deepest of nightmares. Luna flinched from his icy stare as he clenched his greatsword with both hands. She knew it was not her that he was focused upon, but she still trembled, knowing the brutality he was capable of.

"I'm going to distract the kraken and try to get it to focus on me. Wait for an opportunity to shoot it in the eye. Do not disappoint me."

"W-What?! What if I miss? What if my bow snaps? What if you get grabbed by it too?!"

Attila began to move toward the kraken, only stopping once to answer her. "I know you have good aim. Make sure you hit it."

Luna swallowed hard as she watched Attila run off. She took a deep breath and brought herself to focus. They were depending on her. She placed any worries she might have to back of her mind as best she could before she moved away to seek a better position to snipe the aquatic beast.

* * * * *

Attila closed the distance to his target, and as he came to a stop, raised his sword diagonal with his chest. He felt a burning *rage* inside of him. He caught the attention of the kraken and it paused, dangling Darkflare away from its mouth. Seeing the new prey, it roared and threw another of its waving tentacles toward the ground. As the tree trunk of a limb descended on Attila, he rolled out of the way, standing back on his feet in one fluid motion.

The kraken had yet to drag its arm backward, and Attila wasted no time to think. He leapt into the air with sword raised over his head, and with a great swing of both his arms, pointed it down at the tentacle below him. His blade plunged deep into the flesh of the appendage, and Attila continued to force it down until he buried the blade to the crossguard. The kraken flailed its pinned limb and raged within the water, almost shaking the raven-haired warrior off. Attila held his greatsword with both hands, again feeling *rage* pulse through him, and he viciously severed the tentacle off from the kraken's body.

Attila quickly glanced up at Darkflare; he was still there, but he was looking pale, probably from being held upside down and rocked back and forth so violently. But at least he was still alive.

Attila leapt off the huge slab of a tentacle, regaining a battle stance once more. He needed to clear the other limb to give Luna a clear shot at its face. The kraken faced the stalwart warrior once more, water spewing in anger from its many-toothed maw. The sea-beast roared with ground-trembling ferocity, but Attila made sure his facial expression was a blank state, not giving his monstrous enemy any clue of what he was thinking.

Watching as the second tentacle came tumbling down in his direction, Attila remained perfectly still; he made no immediate movements in either direction. Instead, he plastered his face with a sinister smile. As calm as ever, he waited until his moment of opportunity came and then held his sword at his right side with both hands. Bending at the knees, he leapt into the air – much higher than he should have been able to, he realized. It distracted him for the merest of moments, but not enough to take his eyes away from his opponent. As he was about to collide with the massive, meaty arm of the kraken, he swept his greatsword with both hands up and over from his right side across his left shoulder.

With that one swift motion, Attila had propelled himself just enough to swing at the beast and move out of the way of the impending doom; and as the tentacle hit the ground, it was not connected to anything. As he nimbly touched down, he pushed a lock of his long black hair out of his eyes. He froze as he stared at his hand. The air distorted around it in spiral-like currents.

* * * * *

Luna could scarcely believe what she was seeing. She had witnessed Attila fight at Kailos, and even with the snakes below, but his ferocity against the giant beast was frightening.

The kraken expanded its eyes as wide as it could as it thrashed and whirled in a frenzy within the pool of water. She looked to Attila, and he whipped his head to her, his eyes flaring with intensity.

"Now!"

As she fingered the string of her bow, preparing for the attack, her hands shook wildly. She took several deep breaths. This was just like any other target she had ever hit. She needed to focus, take aim, and fire.

She inhaled deeply, fitted the arrow to the bow, and pulled the string back. Staring at the wide-open target that lay in front of her, she measured the distance and pulled the string back ever so slightly more. Something did not feel right though; the bow seemed to warp tighter than ever, as if she was pulling on it too hard. She knew what it was, felt it too many times before, but it didn't matter. She needed to shoot.

Luna exhaled her held breath, letting go of her fear as she let go of the string. The arrow flew true, but the bow snapped in half with a strange musical noise; the string split, the bend warped, and the notch crumbled.

"Oh no…" She groaned, biting her lip and staring at the remains of her bow on the ground. There was no salvaging it this time.

* * * * *

The arrow penetrated the kraken's eye with a spurt of blood. The monster unleashed a deafening roar that even made Attila wince as it threw its remaining arms out at its sides, seemingly gripping the ground for support. Attila's eyes widened as he watched the grip around Darkflare release. He thrust out an arm, as if willing his hand to grab the plummeting body.

And then Darkflare stopped.

Attila couldn't believe what he was seeing, and it seemed neither could Darkflare, as he stood wide-eyed on a solid current of air! Attila lowered his arm, slowly, and the stream drifted to the ground. Darkflare leapt off, and Attila stared at his hand. Had he…?

"Attila!" Darkflare's voice cut through. "You've got to finish it!"

Any satisfaction that he might have felt in saving his friend soon dispersed as he looked at Luna. Her bow lay in pieces at her feet, and he had witnessed Darkflare's sword fly away.

He was the only one left with a weapon, against one angry six-armed kraken. The odds were against him.

Just the way he liked it.

Attila felt a blood-lusting grin form as he rushed toward the water's edge. The kraken was distracted, still fighting with the fact that it had one eye; Attila was going to make sure that he finished the beast off for the trouble it had put them through. He leapt atop one of the tentacles that was still linked to the kraken's body and used it as a bridge to get closer to the creature, rushing across it until it began to slink into the water below.

Attila bent his knees and leapt high – again, higher than he should have been able to! This time, his flight sent him forward toward the head of the kraken that sat gurgling in pain. Time seemed to slow down as Attila reached back with the greatsword in one hand. He felt something crawling across his left shoulder, and the strange sensation spread across his back to the other side, until the air around his body seemed to hum and pulse with energy. Using the blade like a javelin, he threw the sword at the beast; and as the weapon released from his hands, it flew straight ahead, a coil of wind encased it and propelled it forward.

It was amazing watching the greatsword fly faster than a bird, impact through the kraken and out the other side, quicker than any ichor could spout, and then shatter into pieces. The beast's cries were instantly silenced.

He realized he had been standing in midair through the whole experience. Attila looked down – he was standing on one of those air currents that had saved Darkflare.

But it only lasted a moment.

He felt the wind rush through his hair and the world spun around him. One moment his body had felt light like a feather, and then the next, a great heaviness descended upon him and drained him of his energy. He didn't have the will to fight the closing of his eyes as he was enveloped by darkness and cold water.

* * * * *

Darkflare couldn't believe what he was seeing! Was Attila really controlling the air? Using his sword in such a brutal manner was fitting of the 'new' Attila he was coming to terms with, but after the attack, Darkflare knew something wasn't right. The wind that had been conjured was now raging out of control, creating a swirling vortex in the center of the water, sucking everything in the lake down. Darkflare watched horror-struck as Attila collapsed, the current of air he stood on vanished, and his body plummeted into the center of the whirlpool.

"No!" Darkflare and Luna ran up to the water's edge. They were helpless as they watched Attila and the kraken begin to swirl down in the briny darkness. The arms of the kraken, draped on the land, followed the body as they were pulled below.

Luna let out a sharp scream of pain as she was knocked off her feet, but her cries were silenced almost immediately as she plummeted deep under water. The arm she had been standing by was *not* severed; it dragged her down with it.

"Luna!" Darkflare tried to dive for her hand, but he just missed her fingertips as he slid along the ground, almost falling in. "Dammit all! Dammit all to The Pale!"

His mind raced as he tried to think of something to do to help, but his thoughts were so scattered that he couldn't focus. Shaking his head, Darkflare closed his eyes and made a choice. He dove headfirst into the whirlpool, leaving his fate in the hands of Odin.

All around Darkflare swirled in a blurry mess the moment he went underwater. He felt powerless to do anything; all Darkflare could do as he was hurled along with the current was helplessly flail his limbs. His eyes strained hard to make out the shapes of his allies; all he could see was the blurry outline of the kraken's body ahead of where he was forced to go.

Darkflare had the sick realization that he was nowhere near a source of air.

Clawing his arms in the water as best as he could, he tried to swim back up, but it was no use. The vortex's swirling pull had a grip around the body of the warrior and was not letting go.

Slowly the oxygen drained from Darkflare's lungs and left him straining for air impossible to attain. He felt the blurry vision begin to fade from his eyesight, turning the water into an encompassing blanket of darkness that swept over and entangled him.

* * * * *

Drip... Drip... Drip...

Exhaustion held Darkflare's eyelids shut, but his mind spun as it started to reawaken. What had happened?

Where was he?

What hour of the day was it?

Were the last few days some vivid dream of his wild imagination?

Drip...

Was it raining?

Darkflare finally managed to blink his eyes open as a droplet of water slid down the side of his head. Where was he? How long had he been unconscious?

Drip...

Darkflare shot his arm up over his head to block the dripping. After a few moments, he rolled over onto his back, to where he thought he'd be safe.

Drip...

His eyes narrowed in frustration as another water droplet fell onto his nose. Darkflare let out an aggravated sigh and forced himself to sit up with a grunt. Things were starting to come back to him now. The mountain, the climb, the kraken...

The kraken. He remembered the fight and just how close he had come to being eaten. Yet he was still alive, somehow. Well, that took care of what happened - but his brow furrowed as Darkflare surveyed his surroundings, trying to figure out where he was. The torches set along the walls showed he was in a cave of some sort, but nothing else stood out to make it identifiable. Several feet away, the remains of the kraken lay partly sprawled out, partly curled in a ball. Darkflare had to rub his eyes after blinking a few times to be sure that he had seen something correctly on the ceiling above the kraken's body. It was indeed a man-made mechanical type of cover. It must have been the drainage system for the water; it was certainly wide enough for them and the kraken to fit through.

Darkflare was slow to rise to his feet, still baffled about the whole situation that had just happened, and aching terribly. He rubbed his injured, sore shoulder. When this was all over, he needed a good few days of rest. Once he was able to get his balance, he realized that there was another aquatic sound; the soft gurgling of flowing water was coming from the other side of him. He turned to look and found a stream that probably recycled the water from above. He stared down to look at the reflection that the torchlight displayed. His face seemed no worse for wear, but his armor was another story. Darkflare placed his hand on his chest, just now realizing how damaged his leather armor had become from the battle.

A shuffling brought him back to the moment. Sprawled out on either side of him were his two comrades who just began to stir. Darkflare rushed over to help Luna, who was coughing vehemently; and Attila sat up with a jolt, almost as if he had just woken up from a troubled sleep. She let out a soft groan as she strained to look at Darkflare.

"Please explain to me what in the world just happened?"

"You passed the test." The three spun toward the voice; Gilgamesh led Kenji, Roy, and Oboro across a walkway that was further ahead of them. Gilgamesh stopped and narrowed his eyes at them. "Mind you, the victors usually come back down the mountain the same way they went up, but there's a first time for everything, I suppose."

Oboro flew into his master's loving arms, licking his face and nuzzling his head into Darkflare's shoulder as they reunited.

"I'm okay, my friend. Glad to see you too." He turned his attention to the other three. "The kraken – that was the test, I hope?"

"All of it was. As adventurers, you'll face opposition like the mountain on a regular basis. But yes, the kraken was the final part of the test." Gilgamesh let a rather small, saddened smile part his lips. "I think that might have been my oldest kraken yet, too. Luckily for me, this time of year is mating time for them."

The group stared at Gilgamesh, slightly confused. When he noticed all of their eyes fixed upon him, he shook his head and cleared his throat.

"Err, right. Sorry. Anyway... I'm sure you're all wondering about Attila's blustery display – and before you ask how I know about it, I built everything on this mountain. I know what goes on and I see everything. So, allow me to rid all doubt from your minds... Attila is indeed a dragoon."

The attention instantly shifted to the black-haired man as his eyes widened in disbelief. Attila's mouth opened as he stared in confusion and rubbed his shoulder lightly, but it took a few moments for him to actually produce any words.

"Me?"

The outline of the rune throbbed on Attila's shoulder a mystic orange glow as they spoke of it. Roy rubbed his chin deep in thought as he stepped forward, looking it over.

"From what Gilgamesh told us happened, it's obvious what magic you have mastery over. You can control the element of wind. But the rune-..."

"Rage." Attila shook his head as he said the word, looking around at the others as if he hadn't said it. "I… I think it's the Rune of Rage. Just like Darkflare heard the word 'courage,' 'rage' was the one word that kept whispering from some voice."

Kenji stepped forward, glancing at the shoulder mark that was throbbing dully off of Attila. "I see. The runes are reacting to Darkflare's. They're obeying the call of their king."

"What do you mean?" Darkflare placed his hand on his chest; his rune also began to glow a dim red color, resonating with Attila and Kenji's.

"The King's Rune, as the Rune of Courage is sometimes called, has the ability to awaken runes that are dormant in other people. Attila's seemed to react to the King of Dragoons being in trouble and knowing that its wielder wanted to help. Very interesting."

"So, I'm the fourth one, huh?" Attila looked at his hands as the wind swirled around them.

"Fourth…?" Kenji looked at Luna, slightly confused. "Did something happen to you up there too?"

"Not me." Luna was still sitting down and shook her head tiredly.

Darkflare's eyes widened as he looked at Roy's right hand that had been hidden within his cloak. As he pulled it out, there was a symbol on his palm, resonating a soft lavender color that mimicked his eyes. "Roy?"

"Ah, yeah," Roy grinned sheepishly, scratching the back of his head. "You see, I kind of… called forth some magic to help us against the Marked Ones when I went back in to help Attila at Kailos. That's how he knows about that."

"I should have figured by your skills." Kenji's eyes narrowed as he looked at Roy with a very sly look. "I had a hunch prior, but I wasn't positive. You kept your rune hidden well."

"Yep. My Rune of Wit allows me to harness the power of ice magic." Roy held out his hand for the others to look at the star-like shape that had illuminated on his palm. "I was going to wait for the right opportunity to tell you guys. It's a long story."

"That's remarkable," Luna walked over, staring at each of their symbols in turn. "You can all really control magic. That's amazing. And if that's the case, then, maybe… Maybe someday, I…?"

"In due time, you might be able to as well, Luna. Let's talk about this later," Gilgamesh cut in, his arms held across his chest. "We still have an important matter to attend to here."

Gilgamesh gestured with one of his muscular arms toward Luna, Darkflare, and Attila.

"I have replacements for the weapons you lost that'll work far better than those rusted pieces of junk ever could have." He turned to walk back the way he had come, waving his burly arm. "Come, follow me. We have a ways to go."

* * * * *

The endless torches that illuminated the tunnel did nothing for Darkflare's sense of direction. The path curved and snaked so many times that they could have been retracing their steps for countless minutes and he wouldn't have been able to tell! He had been inspecting the walls, looking for any signs or indications of where they were, when he almost tripped down a sharp incline. He caught himself before he stumbled into the burly Gilgamesh, but the added weight from Oboro nearly toppled him head over heels. This was definitely a new path.

"So, Gil," Roy called from the back, "that's three more victorious trial-goers. Just what does that bring the total up to now?"

"The number is low. My reputation is for being a weaponsmith, but not many know of the quality of these sort of weapons I can craft. There have been those adventurers who have asked, yet when they see whichever pet I've chosen to be their opponent... Well, many scurry back down the mountain rather than test their might! That's why you don't see too many people running around with unique weapons designed by yours truly. I have molds that allow me to replicate a great number of blades for an army or to outfit a merchant's number of bodyguards, as well as for the regular person to buy – but it all comes at a price. I save my most elaborate designs for those that have earned them."

"Well, you can add me to the list of non-magical beings that have slain a kraken!" The exhaustion was still in Luna's voice, but their victory managed to bring some of the chipperness back.

"Well, yes... But I hate to point out that you *did* have the help of two dragoons though." Darkflare chuckled lightly as Luna tutted playfully at him.

"Yes, yes - minor details we need not concern ourselves with!"

"You never know." Attila's arms were crossed over his chest, his voice raised a bit higher than normal, as if still in shock, staring at his knuckle.

"Anything is possible!" Darkflare turned to look behind him. "Right, Kenji?"

"Sure." Kenji shrugged from the back of the group, barely meeting his gaze. The dismissive tone of his voice didn't sit well with Darkflare, and he was sure Luna had felt it too by the way she looked away, her smile fading.

Gilgamesh stopped and put his hands on his hips as he grinned wide. The corridor that he was eyeing off to the side seemed to stretch on endlessly.

"Here we are! Darkflare, first room on the right; Attila and Luna, first and second on the left."

Darkflare exchanged nods with both of his allies, including a nervous but excited grin with Luna. They entered the long hallway, which was noticeably different with its cobblestone path and ornate brick walls, and Darkflare approached the door that Gilgamesh indicated. He found his heart racing with anticipation as he grabbed the handle of the door hesitantly, and it pulled open with a soft creak. Darkflare turned back once more to look at his comrades.

"See you in a few moments, I suppose."

"Here's hoping the reward was worth the risk," Luna said as she stepped into the room, shutting the door behind her.

"Just as long as I get a new sword, I'll be fine." Attila didn't look back as he stepped inside and left Darkflare standing alone.

Left with just Oboro clinging to his shoulder, Darkflare swallowed the nervousness from his excitement. Still holding one hand on the handle of the door, he finally looked into the chamber, his eyes wide. A golden altar sat at the very rear of the room and was illuminated by torchlight from either side. Darkflare felt as if his feet were moving on their own as he slowly crept forward, the door creaking shut behind him. With each step closer, Darkflare felt the air escape from his lungs, as if the kraken had grasped his body once more; but this time was not out of pain but rather awe. Oboro could only coo lightly, his bulbous black eyes absorbing the same sight as his master. He slowly reached his hand out, and the treasure that lay before Darkflare's extended fingertips was more than he could ever dream of possessing.

Oboro leapt from his back to unhinder his master, and Darkflare tore the ragged leather from his body, discarding it into the corner of the room. He reached for his new armor, but his fingers delicately paused over the cape that Gilgamesh draped over it. A design of a dragon with bowed head and shielding wings was sown into the material; vertically down the middle of the dragon was a sword that pierced through an orb of light. Carefully throwing it over the back of the armor, he prepared to dress himself in the most elegant of battle riches.

$$* * * * *$$

The tapping of Gilgamesh's sandal echoed impatiently as the tall man stared down the hallway impassively. Roy's eyebrow twitched as the sound finally broke his calm. He exhaled slowly through his nose before he spoke.

"Are you, uh, okay there, Gil?"

"I'm just hoping I picked the right weapons and armor. I think what I chose should match their individual personalities and fighting styles, but I just can't wait to see what they think!"

Kenji chuckled; he was leaning with his back against the wall, staring at the ground. "They're probably too overcome with the fact that they actually have real weapons and armor and not flimsy training blades. I know I was at first."

A drawn out creak echoed down the hall from one of the doors. Each of the three turned their heads toward the corridor, waiting to see which one of the three would emerge first. The figure was lean and short, and the blonde hair revealed it to be Luna.

The torchlight illuminated her brilliant beaming smile, and she spun around for the other three to get a full look. Roy's eyes were immediately drawn to the green of her attire. She wore a jade breastplate with an armguard that extended from her right pauldron, with a hood attached to the back. Her leggings were of the same green and seemed to flow for easy movements. Roy nodded in approval; perfect colors to blend in an archer to their natural hunting environment.

Luna's hand dropped to her waist to fix the yellow sash she wore as a belt. It extended on her right side, forming a long cloth that she smoothed out. She finished spinning on her brown leather-booted heel, and as if she suddenly remembered something, she brought her left leather-gloved hand up to her neck. The necklace she was wearing was a pendant of a winged cross with a turquoise jewel in the center; it didn't seem to be crafted by Gilgamesh, but with the current attire she wore, it shone more prominently.

"Well? How do I look?" Her pearly white teeth twinkled in the torchlight, and she had a sing-songy quality to her voice.

"You look great. What do you think of the bow?" Kenji indicated with his chin the weapon she had clenched in her gloved right hand.

"This bow is… magnificent!"

Luna stretched her arm out in front of her, gazing at the weapon as if it was a small child. She held the bow by a brown leather handle that combined the two long turquoise limbs that looked much sturdier than her last bow. Roy noted the handle must have also been where she would notch an arrow from the quiver on her back. Looking at the weapon more closely, Roy could see the design was a bit more intricate.

"Hey, uh, Gil. Humor me here, what kind of weapon is that?"

"It's a bow, but yes, you've got a keen eye on you, Roy. Luna, there should be a twist lock around the area that you're holding. Go ahead and turn it."

Luna nodded, doing what she was told, and the grip folded up to reveal twin blades hidden on top of one another. The bow separated from the middle and became two short swords that she grasped by the turquoise handles, all the while tethered together by the bow string.

"This… is awesome!" She gaped at Gilgamesh. "I've never seen such a weapon before!"

"The Elyria. Just recently christened, too. It's part bow, part tethered swords; a new design I had been tinkering with. An archer's greatest weakness is if their enemy gets too close - but with this, the tide can be turned to allow yourself to not be drawn in and left defenseless! Treat it well, Luna, and it shall protect you in return." Gilgamesh still had his arms crossed over his chest, admiring his own handiwork as he approved of how both the weapon and armor looked on Luna. Roy himself felt slightly jealous of such a unique weapon. He had considered asking the big guy to make him a new blade, but he couldn't justify where to carry it in addition to the three other swords weighing him down.

"Oh, I will. This thing is so neat!" She placed the blades back on top of one another and twisted the lock back in place to bring the weapon back to its bow form. "I won't have to worry about this breaking apart, and I have a weapon stronger than my old dagger to use at close range!"

"Aye, she's a blessed weapon; I enchant all of my work with magic. It would take strength from the Rune Gods themselves to break anything I've made. Might just take some time to get used to it. It's a bit more weighted than your last bow."

"What do you think, Roy?" Luna was still beaming as she took in the feel of her new gear. "You're awfully quiet!"

Roy considered telling her the truth, that she was a pretty girl whose features were only accented in her new attire and that he was jealous of her unique weapon. But that would not do. Instead he turned to her, looked her up and down, and nodded with a shrug.

"That's all you have to say?" She cocked an eyebrow, her smile faltering.

He smiled and shook his head. No, that would not do either. He needed trust. He needed... friends. So he'd meet her halfway. "It truly fits you. The green plays well with the blue in your eyes. Bows aren't really my thing, but that is one beautiful weapon. You've earned it."

"Oh!" Her cheeks reddened a bit, seemingly from surprise, but her smile quickly beamed once more. "Thank you! I don't know what I expected you to say, but I appreciate your words."

She turned toward the other dragoon, and Roy noticed that some of her smile faded again. "Well, Kenji? I might not be a dragoon, but is this sufficient enough to still be counted upon?"

The older dragoon stared at her a moment, and Roy felt concerned about the lack of answer. He had felt the tension before when the possibility of Luna being a dragoon had been dismissed. Roy wasn't sure why Kenji had reacted that way, but he was impressed by Luna's tenacity in the face of the older man's challenge.

Another creaking door diffused the situation immediately. This time, Luna joined in staring as they waited for the next person to emerge.

The next shadowy figure to stroll into the light was the longhaired slayer of the kraken, Attila. His figure looked even more menacing than before as they bore witness to his new armor cast in the shades of white and black.

His frame seemed even more hulking than usual due to the white-trimmed, black pauldrons covering his shoulders. They must have been connected to a breastplate of some sort, but Roy couldn't see past the black tabard, the white trim of which went straight down the width of his neck to just above his ankles. Keeping it in place was a black leather belt with a silver buckle tied tightly to Attila's waist.

The weight of his enlarged shoulderwear helped to make Attila seem almost as bulky as Kenji or Gilgamesh, but from his waist down, he was not nearly as armored. He wore baggy black leggings, somewhat similar in design to Luna's, and Roy noticed almost an excessive amount of leather buckles on his black boots. He was not sure if they had any purpose besides decoration, but from the smug look on the warrior's face, it was evident he was pleased.

In his black gloved left hand, he held the handle of a blade stained completely blood-red. Resting over his shoulder, the blade definitely seemed longer and thicker than the former greatsword. He raised his left hand to push the black strands of hair out of his face, and Roy noticed it was bare; instead of a glove, he only wore a black metal forearm guard.

Attila stood under the light and stared right at Gilgamesh.

"I like it."

Gilgamesh held up one thumb. "Good fit indeed."

"What do you call this gorgeous reaper?"

"The Crater Buster – aptly named for a weapon of its size and power, wouldn't you say?"

Attila brought the blade down from his shoulders to gaze it over, rocking it slowly in his arms, and nodded toward the master smith. His eyebrows furrowed as he stared at something. Roy looked the blade over and saw it was wrapped maybe seven times in leathery bandages close to the hilt. Attila's head shot up toward Gilgamesh.

"These are...?"

"Ah, yes. The wrappings are from a far away village in the far north called Balmoria. They've been blessed by the highest ranking priests there and are supposed to cleanse the sword despite all of the bloodshed it is expected to inflict." Gilgamesh paused, noticing Attila's eager look. "Are you familiar with the region?"

Attila remained silent, gazing at his sword, as the third and final door creaked open. All heads craned once again toward the direction of the noise, now anxiously awaiting the emergence of Darkflare. The clinking of metal footsteps preceded the spikey-haired hero, closely followed by his winged companion.

* * * * *

Darkflare looked down the corridor and saw them all staring at him expectantly. Oboro, flying beside him, cooed Darkflare on to continue moving. He tried to walk as normally as possible, but he felt very unaccustomed to his new attire. The heavy cerulean armor that he now wore felt very bulky, despite the fact that it conformed perfectly to his body. The raised neck guard in the back also felt strange, despite the fact that it didn't hinder his movements, as he tilted his head back and rolled his shoulders in his bulky pauldrons. He couldn't help but feel dignified as he glanced back and saw the long black cape that fluttered just above the floor behind him.

As he walked, he looked down at the cerulean greaves that were taller than any boots he had previously owned. The poleyns crowned the footwear of the same royal blue as his body piece. His right hand absently felt for the new blue obi that held up his black leggings, and he straightened out the cloth tasset that now draped down his front.

Darkflare stopped under the light of the torch. He raised one of his near elbow length, cobalt-colored gauntlets to center the Drachenfaith pendant so it could be seen more clearly. The other hand reached at his side for his weapon. The scabbard was beyond beautiful – it had to have been made with the richest black oak and then detailed with the finest gold paint.

He withdrew the longsword and held the blade out in front of him so that he could see the aura of confidence his face shone with. His eyes took in the golden handle and guard of the sword and then slowly moved up the blade. The blade spanned nearly four and a half feet long, and it was as if the metal that it was made from was dyed in the richest blue that Gilgamesh could find to compliment his armor. Swinging the sword to his side, Darkflare absorbed the awestruck and amazed expressions of the others.

"The Lionheart. I've been waiting to find one worthy enough to wield that sword, and I believe that you can live up to the namesake of that weapon, King of Dragoons," Gilgamesh said, and Darkflare could have swore that he saw a tear welling up in the old man's eyes.

"I couldn't ask for anything better. Gilgamesh... Thank you. Not only for the armor and weaponry, but also for accepting us to perform your trial. It not only showed that I haven't fully grasped my magic as a dragoon yet, but it also strengthened the teamwork between Luna, Attila, and I, proving what we're capable of when we work together." Darkflare sheathed his sword and smiled at the smith. He stood straight and calmed his features into seriousness. "We needed this. Thank you."

"Heh. Truly spoken like a leader, Darkflare."

Darkflare was taken aback by Gilgamesh's comment. He had considered Kenji to be the unofficial leader of the group; he knew much more than Darkflare did and was many times more experienced in combat. He felt his face flush with color and hoped that Kenji did not think anything of the comment, but his guardian's face remained expressionless.

"I have to say that you five look like the epitome of true warriors in the armor I've smithed, and I hope you can entrust your lives to the weapons I've blessed. I know Roy and Kenji have gotten much use out of theirs, and now you three can actually stand a chance keeping up with them!" Gilgamesh guffawed and then inclined his head toward the path. "Let's return to my house. I'll fix us up some supper and you all can get a good night's rest; I'm assuming you'll have a long journey ahead of you from here."

As Gilgamesh led on once again, Darkflare lagged behind slightly, still getting used to the heavier armor. After being accustomed to the lightweight leather for so long, wearing a heavy breastplate with pauldrons and a cape was like going from one extreme to the other. He was not about to complain though; the new armor and the Lionheart sword were better blessings than he could have ever hoped for. Weapons and armor as capable-looking as these would have taken him a lifetime to afford.

"This is unbelievable," Darkflare said to Attila, a wide grin lighting up his face; but he felt it fade, thinking back on Ceballe. "How do you think Rai would have reacted?"

Attila turned and put a hand on Darkflare's shoulder as they kept walking. "He would be proud."

Darkflare smiled sadly and fell lost to his thoughts, unaware how long they had been walking uphill by the time that Gilgamesh stopped again. He realized that the surroundings suddenly became a familiar wooden color as he stepped onto floorboards.

"What? Where are we?"

Gilgamesh simply grinned and pushed open the door in front of him to reveal that they were back in his living room. The door that Gilgamesh had originally emerged from was where they were standing currently.

"That's certainly convenient!" Luna threw her arms in the air and walked through the door, collapsing into one of the chairs in front of the fire. "Thank you for the armor, thank you for the weapon, thank you for the shortcut," she nuzzled in and rested her head on one of the arms of the plush seat, "and thank you for the rest."

Gilgamesh let out a ground-shaking guffaw as he wandered over to his kitchen. Even wearing his new armor, Darkflare still couldn't help but feel extremely nervous around the giant of a man.

"Go on! The rest of you sit down and rest while I get dinner cooking!"

* * * * *

Whether it was that he had worked up a massive appetite from his latest near-death experience or that his taste buds were still spoiled from the buffet of food from Ceballe, Darkflare found dinner quite enjoyable. He was amazed at the unique flavors in each of the numerous dishes that Gilgamesh offered them. At first, Darkflare thought it odd, seeing the man preparing dinner in so modern of a kitchen out in the middle of the mountains; but the aroma of spices quickly shoved that thought out of his mind.

After an evening of pleasant small talk and delightful dining, Gilgamesh showed them to their beds up the spiral staircase. However, sleep was the last thing Darkflare had wanted at that moment. Even though lying down for a few hours would have done his body good, he was far too deep-rooted in his thinking to just doze off to sleep. Instead, he waved them along, saying he'd catch up, and then headed out the front door.

The moonlight illuminated the greenery around Gilgamesh's house, casting its beam on the flowers and low grass. Hearing the droll buzzing of insects and the few soft cries of the mountain's natural inhabitants was more peaceful than Darkflare had thought. It reminded him a lot of Crescentia and helped to ease some of the worry clouding his mind.

He sat on the edge of the cliff closest to the house, gazing out at the cover of dusk that encroached upon the land, and he couldn't help but think about Rai... and then about his parents.

Now that he had a moment of peace to himself, he was able to recall the memories of his youth with clarity - as much as, he assumed, most people could recall from that age. Whatever block his rune and his parents' wishes placed on his past had completely dissipated. A sad smile spread across his face as he remembered running through the town and around the fields with Terra and Meredia; he remembered his father's proud smile, one hand on his hip; he remembered his mother's warm embrace, holding her children in a tight hug; and he remembered Kenji watching over them, the mischievous smirk still present even all those years ago. And yet, even in his memories, Kenji looked almost the same, if there were any changes at all.

Strange as that last detail was, he shook his head, focusing his thoughts. He had to carry on the legacy his parents left. He was determined to create a better world - not only for his parents, but to prevent another life like Rai's from being taken, and to honor all those that lost their lives in Crescentia.

The only one to follow him out, Oboro, was curled up in a ball beside his master, his eyes shut tightly and his body frame heaving up and down. Darkflare turned to the small wyvern and rubbed his head softly between the ear frills. Oboro opened his large black eyes to stare up at his master, cooing softly in amusement at the attention.

"Oboro, my friend, I still can't believe that we're here, in this moment. It's crazy. I guess I've finally come to terms with having magic at my very fingertips, but I must wonder about the road ahead. The path before us is unclear, but the road seems rocky. I can only hope that our journey will take us to see the entirety of the four kingdoms, visiting all the various places we've dreamed of, and helping as many people as we can. Together, with this group beside us... Tomorrow just seems brighter than ever before."

"I'm glad you feel that way."

The voice made Darkflare jump, and he swung his head to the side just in time to see Gilgamesh sit down next to him. He patted Oboro lightly on the head, seemingly oblivious to Darkflare's startle.

"I'm glad I have some time to speak with just you. There's... something that's been worrying me as of late. Even though I've already spoken with Kenji and Roy about it while you three were up on the mountain, I feel it best to make you aware as well."

Darkflare's attention faded from the serene night. The foreboding tone sat uneasily with him as he carefully regarded the master crafter. "Yes, of course. What's wrong?"

"You see," Gilgamesh cleared his throat, his eyes focused on the sky like Darkflare had been, "the others told me about the attack at Ceballe. I had heard rumors about bandits becoming unruly lately, but organized gatherings have been unheard of since your parents quelled their last leader. The resurgence of the Marked Ones is... worrying."

There was a pause as Darkflare tried to absorb what Gilgamesh was getting at.

"It also worries me that Odin activated the Rune of Courage when he did, even if it saved your life. There's always a reason for the King's Rune to awaken, and as you saw, now Attila's rune has become active as well. That's two new dragoons – that at least I know of – traveling together, in the last twenty-some odd years. Your rune calls to others for a reason. It brought you both Roy and Kenji, who had theirs awaken during the last time there was a Dragoon of Courage – even though I'm not really sure on the specifics of when and how Roy came to be a dragoon." Gilgamesh sighed and shook his head, glancing briefly at the young man. "The Marked Ones' resurgence and your rune activating are signs of something bigger afoot in the universe."

Darkflare let another moment of silence hang in the air before nodding slowly.

"So do you think there is a greater evil pulling the strings behind the bandits? That Odin, or whatever, can see the bigger picture and wanted me to harness my power of fire magic and embrace my destiny before the world falls to ruin?"

"Something like that. I can't give any concrete answers." Gilgamesh waved his hand dismissively. "I'm telling you all of this and why I'm worried because you need to be careful. Your rune grants you a great deal of power, and if it is not kept in check… it might lead to some very dark situations."

"What do you mean 'dark situations'?"

Gilgamesh shook his head again, his lips pursed as if he was deeply considering his next words. "There is a fine line between relying on your power to aid you and letting that desire become an overwhelming force. Just keep your magic – and your emotions – in check. Never gamble too much on your rune. Always remember why you fight, what your purpose is."

Darkflare nodded, staring back out at the night's sky. What darkness? Of course he knew why he fought. Surely, Gilgamesh didn't think that he would use his weapons to become some sort of evil entity like that Graymahl person?

"You'll be fine. You've got a good group with you. Kenji and Roy will make great mentors, lending you their knowledge and advice. Luna and Attila are also off to a good start as far as warriors go. Your group will be able to triumph over whatever villainy stands in your way."

"Gilgamesh, do you… Do you think this all has something to do with Graymahl Vulorst?"

"I… What?"

Darkflare could hardly believe he had startled the burly man, and he turned to look at him.

"Well, he wasn't destroyed completely, was he? His power was sealed in an extremely powerful crystal of sorts, right? What if he managed to be revived and he's the one behind the bandit attacks?"

"I strongly doubt that." Gilgamesh's voice, as quiet as he was speaking, was filled with ice. Darkflare instantly regretted broaching the subject and had a hard time keeping the crafter's gaze. "Your father made sure to seal Graymahl's soul far away from this mortal realm. The Marked Ones heeded his call, but he is not and will not be the only person to ever control dark magic. No, I fear this might be some new threat."

Darkflare nodded a few times, slowly turning his head to look back out at the night.

"I just think it's ironic." Gilgamesh raised an eyebrow, waiting for Darkflare to continue. "Such great power we wield to do good, only for it to activate when an even greater evil threatens our existence. I had thought we were going to be living in a time of true peace, thanks to the efforts of my parents, but I guess the attack on Ceballe shattered that illusion."

Gilgamesh smiled and pat Darkflare lightly on the back.

"You still have much to learn about this world. Not everything in books and tales are quite true. As long as I've lived, I can safely say that I've never witnessed a thing such as true peace. While there is good in the world, there will always be evil. Emotions such as jealousy, lust, anger, and fear will always lead the mortal mind down twisted paths. There might be times of relative peace, but dark hearts will ensure that it is never permanent."

"But just because you've never seen it does not mean that it cannot exist." Darkflare steeled his nerves and forced himself to lock eyes with Gilgamesh, who sat back, arms crossed. "It is my goal, as lofty as it may be, but I dream of a world where people can live in peace, a world where people can focus on caring for the needs of their brethren, a world where those of kind hearts can stand up to the dark hearts and claim victory. If I am to be named this King of Dragoons, I will use this title, for all that it's worth, to ensure that my dream *can* become a reality for everyone to embrace."

Gilgamesh tilted his chin up at Darkflare, staring down his nose at him, his lips drawn back as if impressed. He nodded slowly.

"To do so, you must first take up your blade to smite any that would stand in the way of such ambitious dreams. It will be a long journey, and you are going to have to make difficult choices along the way.

The world, in its current state, cannot be changed in a day to become the one which you seek. You might have to decide who is more important to protect - your friends or your dream of a world of peace? And if it comes down to it, could you sacrifice everything if it meant attaining your goal?"

Darkflare bit his lip, but he kept his eyes locked with the man next to him. "I could answer you yes, right now, but what good would that do? I won't know until I'm in that moment, where I have to make those decisions. But right now, right here, I'm telling you that I will do anything it takes to protect as many innocent people as I can."

A wide grin spread across Gilgamesh's face. He stood up, which caused Darkflare to rise to his feet and Oboro to startle awake.

"Good. Very good indeed. I'll tell you one last time though; keep that in mind no matter what you do, never lose sight of why you fight or who you fight for. Don't *ever* let rage consume you, and you must *always* be in control of your rune. If you keep those things in mind, there's not a single soul – not even Graymahl Vulorst – that could combat the strength that you have in your heart."

Looking up at the night's sky one last time, Gilgamesh turned and walked away. He paused after taking a few steps.

"Oh, and Darkflare. Get some sleep. I can assure you the world won't fall to darkness in a few hours. I've been around long enough to know that."

Watching the large man walk away, Darkflare allowed a smile to crack through his stony expression. Before he could even make a motion to Oboro, the wyvern knew it was time for bed and prepared to leap on his master's back.

"First thing in the morning we set out again. And I think, truly," Darkflare patted the sword on his hip and smiled down at the armor he was wearing, "this will feel like the real start of our journey."

Chapter XI

"Aunquil, Aunquil… Aunquil?" Luna repeated the town name as they walked the path. There was a collective sigh of relief as the peak of the mountain grew more distant and the lush green spread around them once more. "That *is* where we're going, correct? I've said it so many times that it sounds strange now!"

"Yes, that's where Gilgamesh directed us to investigate," Kenji said as he led the way beside Darkflare; the flaps of his coat swayed lightly behind him as the wind picked up. "Some of the latest rumors from traders was of increased 'bandit' activity in the northeast of the kingdom, close to the border with Beauldyn."

"Thank the stars for Gilgamesh's web of connections," Luna said with a smile.

Darkflare regretted not getting more sleep when the wind tugged at his cape and he swayed with it. While the heavier armor did not bother him much yesterday, probably due to all of the adrenaline, today it was a very unaccustomed weight. They had left with the rising sun to get a head start on the path before them, and since setting out, Darkflare could only think about his conversation with Gilgamesh. Why had he stressed so heavily that Darkflare be in control of his rune and emotions? Did he really think that Darkflare was capable of becoming so enraged that he'd smother the world in flames? Or was there some darker secret to these runes that he was unaware of?

"Everything alright?" Kenji's question pierced Darkflare's thoughts, dragging him back to the moment.

"He's worrying, as usual." Attila crossed his arms over his chest as he stared blankly at the path ahead.

"Speak your mind!" Roy said enthusiastically from the rear, his arms secluded within his large, white cloak. "Provide us with some entertaining conversation for the road!"

"It's nothing! Nothing entertaining, at least. I tend to get lost in my thoughts from time to time." He smiled back at the others; he could see the tiredness in Luna's face, almost a hint of it behind Attila's dark gaze, but Kenji and Roy were in good spirits. "Aunquil is another merchant town, isn't it?"

"Yep." Kenji nodded beside him. "It's nowhere near as big as Ceballe, but its primary purpose is to allow travelers between the two kingdoms a place to buy and trade. Gilgamesh said that the once friendly and welcoming atmosphere has soured and turned hostile. Aunquil is one of the towns on his trade route, and he's seen the attitude of the people grow wearier over a short time."

"And King Corsius's hasn't sent anyone to investigate?"

At the mention of the king, Luna uttered some noise under her breath that sounded like a mix of a scoff and a growl. Darkflare looked at her, but she refused to meet his gaze, scowling off in the distance.

"Hmm." Roy glanced at Luna out of the corner of his eye; he must have heard her too. He stopped and looked over their surroundings. "Kenji, let's rest here for a bit. I think it would do us all some good."

Kenji turned to look, and Darkflare did as well. They had been walking under the outskirts of a forest, and where they stood was thickly shaded. Kenji nodded, almost reluctantly, motioning for the others to go and take a rest.

"Aunquil isn't too much farther, but since we're more than halfway there, I guess a rest wouldn't hurt our pace."

Darkflare sat down on the grass, leaning back against a tree once Oboro fluttered down to curl up beside him. "Does Gilgamesh come to Aunquil if he needs to restock on supplies?"

Roy dropped down next to Darkflare and shook his head, his long bangs of platinum swaying on his forehead. "No. From what he's told me, everything he needs he can harvest from the mountain. He'd surely only buy from Aunquil if he's in a pinch for something that perhaps Beauldyn would have more naturally than D'sylum. Gilgamesh is one of the main suppliers of armories throughout the world, so I suppose going to Aunquil to send his latest shipments out to the east is easier than making Queen Ragwelv's knights come all the way south. If he needs something delivered, I'm sure they do it right away. I doubt they would want to see someone of his size and reputation angered."

Darkflare chuckled and turned to glance over the landscape. It was a tranquil area that they had come upon, and there was not a soul on the path in either direction. Darkflare found that second detail strange, but he attributed it to whatever trouble the area had been having. Kenji was seated a few feet away, his legs crossed, his sleeves rolled up, and his eyes shut.

"Even when you're resting, you're not really at ease, are you?" Darkflare asked with a sarcastic smile.

"Me?" Kenji's face remained expressionless. "Meditating keeps the mind and body sharp. It helps me to focus and prepare for the coming battles."

"Something you should take note of, Darkflare." Attila shot a comment out as he leaned with his back against a tree close to Kenji.

Darkflare rolled his eyes and changed the focus of his attention. Luna was seated on Darkflare's other side, her head in her right hand and the other wrapped dew-stained blades of grass around her fingers. Her mood seemed to have soured ever since the mention of King Corsius.

"Hey," Darkflare said the words softly as he lightly nudged Luna's knee. She looked up at him slowly, and he could tell there was a sadness within her blue eyes that he had not beheld from her before. "Everything alright?"

"Yes." She inhaled deeply and let out a large sigh, turning to play with the grass again. "My brother is a soldier in the D'sylum army. My father used to be."

"Oh?" Roy leaned forward and raised his eyebrows at her. "Military family, huh? Color me intrigued in this story."

She glanced at Roy hesitantly before turning back to fiddling with the grass.

"My father, Dhaunt, is a retired soldier. Not out of choice. He was extremely loyal and dedicated for many years in our *beloved* king's service. One thing that's not appreciated in King Corsius's army? Compassion. It's as if it's expected that every person to serve in his army is supposed to be a bloodthirsty, ruthless, stone cold killer," she nearly spat the last few words, shaking her head. "My father never got any praise or recognition that he deserved; the promotions and the medals always went to Corsius's most outspoken and brash patrons. When he married my mother, he was only given leave for the day of the wedding, and the same for the days that my brother and I were born."

Darkflare noticed the building anger in her face as she constantly tried to school her features to calm.

"Darrow is the older of the two of us. Knowing Corsius's policies and wanting to better our education, my father used one of the very few perks of being in the army to send one of us to school outside of the nation. Darrow went to military school here in Pheeq, while I was fortunate enough to spend my learning years in Tiresek."

"Tiresek?" Darkflare quirked an eyebrow. "The capital of the Verankner region? Isn't that pretty far away? Why not one of the schools in D'sylum?"

"Well, since there has been peace for so many years between the four kingdoms, the good relations allow for children to attend schools across the borders. Pheeq and Iysumus have good military schools, but it's no secret that Tiresek and Beauldyn have some of the best libraries in the world."

"That makes sense," he nodded. "I can understand that whatever the schools here have to offer pale before the knowledge in those libraries."

"Right, but mind you, my father being in the army was what allowed me to learn how to use a bow when I was so young. Darrow helped train me before he went off to Pheeq, and before I went to Tiresek."

"Well, that's one thing to thank King Corsius for, right?" Darkflare tried a smile to cheer her up, but she held his gaze, ice in her own.

"No. I have *my father* to thank for that." She paused, collecting herself. "Sorry. I know you didn't mean anything by that. I just despise that man so much. My father ended up getting injured in a training drill due to how relentless Corsius trains his soldiers; it's all he focuses on. My father took his eyes off his opponent for a half a second and they cut open his leg – with a real blade, not a training blade. The chirurgeons managed to heal his wound with magic, but he was dismissed right after. The other man claimed my father *wanted* him to use a real blade, that he had been drinking and attacked him. When my father came home, he was a changed man. He still had his love for us and my mother, but he was... hollow."

"I'm so sorry." Darkflare furrowed his eyebrows, staring at her as she played with the grass. "I... had no idea what military life was like. I'm sure the pain your father felt emotionally was far worse than anything physically. I could not even imagine what that must have been like."

Luna shrugged. "He served his king and country for many years, selflessly, expecting nothing in return. And then someone looking to make a name for themselves stepped on my father's career like it was nothing. And they believed him because he was young and spouted off lies. My father was so shocked, he could barely defend himself. After all his years, they barely listened to what he had to say."

Luna balled her fist around the clump of grass she was playing with, ripping a few strands out of the ground.

"I came home right away, but they pulled Darrow up from schooling and told him he would take my father's place immediately. We corresponded back and forth, and I tried my best to make sure he knew father was alright. Darrow swore he'd never let that happen to him."

Darkflare stared at Luna for a few more moments until she finally looked up at him. Her eyes looked watery, but she chuckled a little bit and shook her head, staring out across the field.

"I haven't seen Darrow since before he left for school. Since everything happened, I got a letter once and a while, but as the months dragged on, they had become much rarer. My mother does most of the work around the farm anymore. Father helps as best as he can, but mother has told me that he gets this far off, spacey look in his eyes and can barely continue after some time. He talks about wanting to enlist as a town guard, somewhere where they would need an added sword arm, but mother has forbidden him. He's not the man he once was, but he won't accept that."

Darkflare stared at her for a moment, putting the pieces together. "Luna, why did you come to Ceballe again? Why did you leave your parents?"

She chuckled. "It seems stupid to say out loud, but I guess you could say revenge? I heard the leaders were going to be at the tournament, and I wanted to see the man that made the decision that took everything from my father in person. After the attack, and the Marked Ones, I didn't want to go home. I love my parents dearly, but I couldn't stand to see the void in my father, to hear the bickering of my parents whether he would return to a fighting job or not, and so I tried to go anywhere but the direction of home."

Darkflare did not say anything, but he put his hand on her forearm, reassuringly. Roy nodded, leaning back once more against the tree trunk.

"You have my condolences. But at least you and I have something to relate to now. My father was in the Purcillian army. I know how unfair military life can be." Darkflare and Luna looked toward Roy, but he stood up and clapped his hand together. "But that's a story for another time, perhaps. We should probably get going, wouldn't you say, Kenji?"

The elder dragoon rose in one motion, his chilling eyes opening to look at Roy. "Indeed. Back on the path to Aunquil."

As Luna and Darkflare stood, she turned to him with a smile. "Thank you for listening and being so sincere."

Before he could answer, his eyes were drawn to Attila. He was still against the tree, but his poise seemed tenser than usual, and his expression – he looked angry? Brooding was usual, but angry was not.

That was when Darkflare noticed the blade held against his throat.

He withdrew the Lionheart, and Luna must have noticed his concern, because she too turned with bow drawn. Kenji and Roy whirled around and their own weapons were out in a flash. As they crept closer to Darkflare and Luna, a voice called out.

"Don't! The tan one here dies if anyone moves closer."

The voice sounded feminine, but Darkflare couldn't be sure. He glanced to Kenji, but the man's face was concentrated as he gazed at the blade. Darkflare swung his head back to Attila and the attacker, and he felt his teeth grind.

"Who are you? What do you want?"

"I want to know about the marks."

Darkflare and Luna exchanged confused looks, and Darkflare shook his head. "Marks? What are you talking about?"

"I saw the marks on the blue-haired guy's wrists! I need to know what I've been hired to kill!"

Kenji shook his head, rolling down the jacket sleeves. "Who hired you?"

"Your days of terrorizing Aunquil are over! And I'll start with this one if you don't tell me about the marks!"

"Wait, wait, wait!" Darkflare held a hand up, as if the assailant could see. "I think there's been a misunderstanding. We've never been to Aunquil, but we *are* going there to help! If you've been hired by the town, then please, come out and talk to us."

The voice was silent for a moment. "The marks – what are they? I was told the people who are threatening Aunquil have marks on their necks. Why are yours on your wrist?"

"The symbols that they're referring to," Kenji stepped one foot forward, "are the brandings of demons. These you saw on my wrist refer to the magic that I can conjure. My friends here," he gestured to Roy, Attila, and Darkflare, "they all have marks like mine. One on his palm, one on his shoulder, one on his chest. They can control magic too."

"And her? Why can't she?"

Darkflare saw Luna blush as she looked away. "It's not that simple. Some of us are gifted and some aren't. Watch."

Darkflare held his hand out and materialized a ball of fire faster than he thought he was able to. He held it up toward the none-too-comfortable Attila, as if his attacker could see through him.

There was a pause, but then she brought the blade down and shoved Attila forward. He stumbled toward the group, whipping the Crater Buster out in a frenzy, air contorting around the blade. Kenji grabbed him by the arm and stopped him from charging forward. Darkflare rolled his wrist and the flame vanished.

The assailant stepped forward, wearing armor that was almost pitch as night, the color of black outlined with dark blue and purple accents. The figure pulled back the hood and mouth covering to shake out her long brown tresses. There was a look of pleading in her hazel eyes as she looked at all of them, and then she pulled away the hood from her neck.

"If the demons have marks on their necks, then what is this? What is this symbol? Am I... Am I a demon too?"

Darkflare's eyes widened as there was in fact a symbol on her neck – but it was not the seal of one who had sold their soul to Sairephir. The blue shape resembled a water droplet, and then below it were two lines that resembled rippling water. Darkflare's breath caught in his throat as he looked at Kenji, who equally seemed surprised.

"What? What is it? Am I a demon? I can't be!"

"No," Kenji exhaled deeply. "You appear to be one of us... You appear to be a dragoon."

"Wh-what is that?" she stammered, still keeping her blade, which Darkflare could now see was a sai, in the other hand held in defense. "How do I even know I can trust what you say?"

"Listen," Roy stepped forward, eying Attila cautiously as Kenji stood before him. "We-..."

"I said stay back!" She jumped back, throwing something at Roy. The star whistled past his face, and Darkflare's eyes widened when he saw the cut it left. It took Roy a moment to react, but he put his hand up to his face, surprised.

"That was a throwing star," he murmured to himself before looking back to the woman. "What is a ninja doing being recruited as a mercenary?"

She looked at them like a caged animal, her gaze darting back and forth, and then she threw something at the ground, covering them in smoke. Darkflare coughed and tried to get out of the haze. Attila, standing by him, swung his arms in an arc, sending out a gust of wind that cleared the area; but the ninja was gone.

"What the Pale was that?!" Luna exclaimed, looking through the trees, as if the ninja were above them. "What do we unpack first? That she's a ninja? A dragoon? A ninja dragoon hunting Marked Ones?!"

"Where did she go?!" Attila growled, hurrying through the trees to look for her.

"Attila, enough." Kenji's voice was cold, his expression dark. "You can't handle a trained ninja, no matter what Gilgamesh gave you. We need her on our side if she is a dragoon."

Attila finally relented, punching the tree she had pressed him against as he passed.

"She was hired by Aunquil, right?" Darkflare looked at the others. "Then we have to hurry. I'm sure that's where she's headed. We need to tell them the truth before they assume *we're* Marked Ones like she did!"

* * * * *

Their pace had quickened, and Darkflare could feel the tension between them all. He didn't even dare to ask Attila how he was doing.

"How do we know how many other dragoons exist in this world?" Luna said, shaking her head.

"We don't," Kenji's voice had gotten surly, and he had not said much as well. "That's why we have to try and find as many of them as we can."

Roy brushed the cut on his cheek once more. "That's a very precarious place for a rune. I can see why she's scared if she's been hired to kill people with symbols on their necks. But what's equally frightening is a new dragoon who is unsure how to use their magic. That can have some very bad effects."

Darkflare thought about if Kenji had not been there to explain things; what if his magic surged out of control and flames from his rune ran wild through a town, all the while him not knowing how to control his magic? He shuddered to think about the lives that would be lost.

"That's got to be it," Roy inclined his head toward a city's gate that came into sight. The entrance was open wide, exposing the one to two story buildings within.

"Hopefully we got here in time," Darkflare murmured, resisting the urge to sprint forward.

"Don't get too excited. Something's not right," Kenji said as they approached the outskirts of the town.

Darkflare narrowed his eyes, squinting in to see what Kenji was worried about. From what he could make out, there were two groups of people standing around the center of the town, and they seemed at odds with one another. The members of one of the groups were clad in, what seemed to Darkflare, scraps of armor.

"Marked Ones." The word was followed by the metallic scratch of Attila withdrawing the Crater Buster.

Following his lead, the others withdrew their weapons without hesitation. The two groups were paying no heed to the warriors that were standing at the outskirts, but Darkflare figured it was better to be cautious. There were alleyways on both sides of the street, allowing the group to split into two and still get a good view of what was taking place.

Darkflare stepped out of the gate, leaning against the wall as Oboro hovered beside him. "Alleyways on either side of the main street. They both look to come out at the same place."

"Right," Kenji nodded. "Take Luna and Roy to the left. Attila will come with me to the right. Meet together in the middle."

They exchanged nods of agreement and set off. Darkflare led his duo, Oboro flying low beside him, down the cobbled street. He kept peering up at the windows of the brick buildings surrounding them, but no heads popped out to spot them. All attention seemed to be in the middle of the town. He finally stopped at the agreed intersection and watched as Kenji did the same across the street.

The other group was most likely townsfolk, and there was one individual that stood out from the others. The leader looked to be an older man who was dressed in slightly more refined and less rustic clothes than the others.

"We're sick of it!" the man exclaimed, holding his ground with anger so fierce toward the 'bandits' that stood in front of him, that his complexion was almost as red as Darkflare's flowing bandana. "We will not allow you to soil our town's name any longer! Because of all of the raiding and the hostility and the taxes, you ruffians have made this place almost into a ghost town. We're standing up for ourselves now and saying we won't tolerate any more of your unbearable tyranny! Leave here, at once!"

The scruffy group rang out in laughter, and the leader stepped forward to grab the elder by his shirt collar.

"This town falls under the jurisdiction of the bandit king. All taxes go to him and not the false king in Pheeq. What do you think you can do against our might? We know of your attempt to hire mercenaries – we even allowed that to happen – and where are they all? None dare to stand against us."

The Marked One turned the elder around for the rest of the villagers to get a look at his face as he struggled from being held in the air.

"Behold this pathetic man that thinks he can do what is 'just' for his people. You know not what you stand against when you impede our will."

"I've had enough of this."

Darkflare grinded the words through clenched teeth as he stood up and walked out of his cover. The tail of his cape waved behind him as he took several vigorous strides forward. He felt the heat from his anger rise in his face as he stared at the man who was marked by Sairephir. Oboro flew out alongside his master, which in turn sparked Kenji to leap from the alleyway right after. The other three warriors assembled to flank behind the duo. The sound of their footsteps caused members of both groups to glance over at the newcomers marching toward them. With the sun shining brilliantly off their new armor, Darkflare felt confident that they looked impressive.

One of the bandits nudged the leader to get his attention. The man glared at the warriors, not releasing his hold on the civilian. "Be you mercenaries or adventurers, stand down and leave this town. This is not your fight. This issue is between the town of Anquil and the King of Bandits, Thalland Faleenwar."

"Thalland!" Kenji said with shock, holding an arm out in front of Darkflare. "Thalland is behind all of this?!"

"Thalland Faleenwar has given us a purpose, a mission. If you are to interrupt his business, you do so at your own peril."

Darkflare gave Kenji a wary look; his guardian seemed frozen. He pushed past Kenji's arm, taking another step forward.

"If you want a fight, then challenge someone with a weapon. Let the man go."

The bandit grinned darkly, turning his attention back to Darkflare.

"As you wish."

The Marked One set the elder down, and as his feet touched the ground, he tried to run to safety; but the bandit was quicker. A sword swung out and cut a diagonal swath in the old man's back, sending him spiraling face first down at the dragoons' feet.

Darkflare's eyes widened and he swooped down to his knees to try to aid him, but Luna was quicker. She cradled the older man in her arms and villagers ran forward, handing whatever cloth they had for her to stop the bleeding. She looked up at Darkflare with conviction in her eyes.

"Take care of them. I'll try to keep him alive as long as I can!"

Darkflare nodded; he stood up in front of Luna and swung his sword horizontally in warning as the Marked Ones closed in on his group. Townspeople fled in a panic, away and into their houses to hide. And that was when they revealed their true selves; flesh paled gray, eyes burned red, and the hideous mark of Sairephir shone true on the demons' necks.

"You'll pay for shedding the blood of innocents."

"Blood is blood," the demon answered in a bizarre harmony of the voice before and something much more sinister. "Yours will be the next to flow on these streets."

The leader raised his arm, and the other Marked Ones rushed upon the warriors with battle cries and screams of fury. By a quick assessment, Darkflare thought there were thirty-five; they had numbers, but he remained resolute. He honed in on the first enemy that came toward him and braced himself for the attack.

The man swung in with both arms, and Darkflare managed to duck and weave past him. The next came rushing in at him, and Darkflare brought his sword up to parry. Hearing the first coming around again, Darkflare spun around to the back of his foe; the first's blade slashed down through the second adversary. Darkflare swung his sword up, knocking his opponent's guard high, and the Lionheart moved with a strength and fury Darkflare never possessed, back down to slice through the chest of the demon.

Darkflare had a moment to breathe and witnessed their leader standing resolute in the back, screaming orders and insults at the other Marked Ones. Darkflare placed his hopes in the hands of his own allies to take out the lesser demons while he surged through the crowd and toward that foe.

He had faith that they would not disappoint.

* * * * *

Attila met his first opponent halfway. Holding his sword low at his waist, he ducked under the vertical slice of his foe and continued on until he shoulder tackled the demon back and into others. Aided by distorting the air around his body for quicker movements, he tore his way through the wave of attackers until he stood in the middle of their group. Taking advantage of their confusion, he raised his shoulders up, bringing with him the full weight of his Crater Buster. With several quick flails of his sword, he managed to sever the right arm off of one of the demons, cut a clean slice through the chest of a second, and pierce the neck of a third. The three bodies fell together, black blood coalescing before the bodies vanished.

While the initial rush kept his opponents off guard, he realized now that he was surrounded. The danger was riveting; he felt truly alive as he stared his own mortality in the face. One of his adversaries ran screaming at Attila with a raised sword. Before it came within swinging range of the dragoon, a torrent of water overtook it and several others, spilling them into the town wall with great force.

Attila whipped around and saw the ninja standing several feet behind him, hiding in the shadows with her hood pulled down over her face. She waved her hand to the side and a wave of water materialized and crushed down on the other enemies around Attila, washing them away.

"You!"

"Consider this my apology for attacking you! Also, behind you!"

He turned, and another demon was on him. His sword would not be quick enough; he raised his metal arm guard to deflect the attack. A little lower and that would have been his hand, gone. He cursed himself and brought the sword up to cleave through the chest of the Marked One.

Attila turned back, ready to charge the ninja, but she was gone. He screamed a curse as he threw himself back into the next Marked One that came his way.

* * * * *

Kenji gritted his teeth as he swung to parry the third Marked One that converged upon him. They had assaulted him so fiercely that he couldn't find the right opportunity to attack back. A fourth was drawing in close, but a sword curved in and sliced the creature in the back.

Roy ran past the downed foe, not giving him a second glance, before he twirled in and sliced the sword arm from one of Kenji's attackers. It disappeared in a whirl of smoke, and the demon reared on Roy. Kenji ducked out to the right and swung down in a large arc, dispatching the other two demons.

He looked back to see Roy, one of his swords in either hand, ducking and jumping away on the defensive as two other demons sparred with him.

"Oh, come on," the platinum haired warrior groaned as he jumped around, effort forming in his tone. "If you're going to try to entertain me, at least put a little more effort into your attacks! You guys couldn't hit the broad side of a dragon!"

Kenji went to swing at Roy's opponents, but the man turned and ran down an alley. "Roy, wait!"

"I got this!"

Another demon came at Kenji, forcing him to leave Roy to his now three attackers. He parried with the Izayoi in one hand and grabbed one of the Kukri Knives from his waist with the other. He plunged the smaller blade into the demon's marked neck, hearing it howl in pain, and then finished it off with a swing from his katana.

He sheathed the dagger and turned back to Roy. He was coming up toward a wall, and with nowhere else to run, he looked trapped. Roy wheeled around with the Hyperion, splicing the air in front of him, splitting the space that it moved through, and caused a sonic boom-like effect to happen. From the arc of his swing, a crescent-shaped wave of energy ripped forward and passed through the Marked Ones as if nothing happened.

They all stopped moving, as if the energy wave had frozen them in place. Roy hurried past them, letting the back of his cloak flutter in the air behind him as he raised his right hand in the air. Bringing his thumb and middle fingers together, he snapped. From the waist up, the demons' torsos slipped off of the lower halves of their bodies. The crescent of energy had split them all clean in half horizontally; it had just taken a few moments for the results to become visible. It was not until the tops hit the ground that they vanished in shadow.

Roy hurried back next to Kenji, holding the Hyperion in one hand and the Muramasa in the other. Kenji raised an eyebrow, looking to where the demons had fallen.

"Impressive technique."

"Oh, I'm sure you have plenty up your sleeves."

Kenji looked back as the demons regrouped, screaming guttural noises as they moved in. He thought about Roy's words as the other man leapt into the fray with both swords.

"Actually, good point. I do."

His first target had a purple rag wrapped around his head, with an orange tattoo that crawled down the side of his face, past the red eyes, and into his frizzled black beard. The dragoon waited until his foe thrust his sword; the movement his muscles made, demon or not, easy to read. After sidestepping the blow, Kenji reached forward and grabbed the man's extended arm, stepped behind him, and twisted it tight around his back. Kenji heard the cry of another foe coming in behind him and subsequently whirled around to face it. The sword pierced the demonic body Kenji held before him, causing the flailing Marked One to burst away.

The second demon bore its fanged maw at Kenji; his response was baring his own vicious smile. He felt the magic within him growing stronger as he witnessed four more demons who were rushing toward them, soon to fall at the hands of the Izayoi.

As the first two went to swing at Kenji, he cartwheeled forward in between the sword swipes, kicking both of his aggressors in the face. They cried out, clutching their faces, and Kenji stood up and turned back toward them on the ground. He held the great katana down by his waist and bent his knees just slightly, putting his weight onto his back foot.

One of the remaining two rushed at him, swinging its sword around in a frenzy as it closed the distance. The expert dragoon waited until the foe got within reach and raised his sword to parry the blade. The force of the swing, as Kenji brought it up with both hands, combined with the weight of the katana caused the lesser-quality sword to shatter into pieces and rain shards down. Several fragments from the broken blade impaled the foe, and he faded to smoke before falling to the ground.

Kenji tilted his head to witness the last creature turn toward Roy, whose back was turned. Kenji felt no remorse as he relaxed his defensive stance, which allowed him to regain his balance on both feet, and he proceeded to outstretch his free arm. With the palm open and facing the demon, Kenji kept the thumb, index finger, and middle fingers all straight, while he closed the other two. He blinked his eyes and a ball of blackness launched from the tips of his fingers. The orb sizzled through the air with great speed and then exploded on the demon, causing a frenzied scream that was laced with terrible agony. It rolled on the ground as the black flames ate away at the gray flesh. Kenji knew that his dark blast not only injected his foe in a world of physical agony, but it plagued the mind. In this case, he was sure the Marked One was seeing the weight of its choices, maybe even a life that it had left behind and forsaken.

One of the demons he had kicked had risen, and Kenji turned just in time to deflect the attack; or so he thought. He saw the rip in his sleeve before the wound registered. It was deep, but the slice of his coat aggravated him more than anything. The demon took sick pleasure in the sight, but Kenji switched hands and still managed to cleave a bigger wound in the demon's chest.

"I have been so careful with this coat, and now it'll need stitching. Shame." Kenji drove the Izayoi through the creature's neck, exploding it in shadow before it could react.

The last of the demons rose, and Kenji's anger had gotten the better of him. He raised his foot to walk forward, and in an instant, Kenji had appeared past the foe. Once the blade slid into its sheath, the demon's head rolled clean off the shoulders and the whole thing vanished.

Kenji approached Roy, having finished off his own demons, and the latter, out of breath, gave a thumbs up.

"That was impressive." Roy pointed to Kenji's jacket. "You alright?"

"Oh, this?" Kenji held up his arm. "Demon got lucky and sliced my coat."

Roy stared at it for a moment. "Incredible luck they didn't get you. That would have really bled."

Kenji nodded, looking once to the arm. There was no cut or blood. "Let's get back to the others."

* * * * *

Darkflare clashed blades with the lead Marked One as soon as he was within swinging range. He did not have to worry about Oboro getting in the way; he had stayed behind to protect Luna. It was solely him and this Palespawn, locked as they pressed on each other's blade. The cruel, sadistic smile the creature had on his face sickened Darkflare. How could any creature, demonic or not, get such enjoyment from slaughtering the innocent?

Darkflare pulled away from the deadlock, slipping back slightly into a defensive position as he waited for the perfect moment to strike. The demon lunged, Darkflare could see it in the way its body and arms contorted, and he was ready to parry the attack. As sword clashed with sword once again, Darkflare braced himself. The two exchanged a series of parries: one on the offensive and the other one the defense, then they would reverse. Each took their time trying to find the other's weak spot. The Marked One seemed to be putting its full effort into each swing, trying to break Darkflare's defense and concentration, and Darkflare feared it might work soon.

The demon finally forced Darkflare back a few steps and retreated a bit itself, putting several feet between it and the cobalt-clad warrior. Darkflare caught himself as he stumbled back, his sword back up at the ready. A mix of ire and craze swept over the enemy's face as it flung its arms out to his side.

"Did you honestly think you could challenge the warriors of Sairephir and leave with your life?!"

With a quick flick of its wrist, the demon pulled something out from a satchel attached to his belt and flung it at the dragoon. Darkflare dropped to one knee and threw his hand up in front of him. The Rune of Courage swooned to life, allowing him to project a small heatwave of fire from his open palm at the flying object.

His rune had protected him once again - the thrown object was a bomb of some sort, and Darkflare saw the Marked One bring its arms up to cover its face as the projectile exploded not far from it. He took the unexpected opportunity and surged forward as a cloud of smoke hung low. The demon had only had a brief second to defend itself as Darkflare came rushing in with the Lionheart. His foe's one line of defense crumbled as Darkflare's longsword broke through and shattered the opposing sword.

The demon was lucky enough to only take a few scrapes and cuts as it fell backward. It struggled to get to its feet, growling low and fierce, but Darkflare thrust the sword forward so that the tip rested on the flesh of the creature's gray nose.

"Enough," Darkflare forced as much confidence as he could into his voice as he stared down at the snarling creature. "You threaten those that are weaker than you, and then when a greater foe steps forth to challenge you, you cannot even win with the dirtiest of tricks. I hadn't planned on using my runic powers, but you forced my hand."

Darkflare hesitated. His next move was either stupid enough to work, or it would get him killed.

"Get up. Use whatever powers you have to conceal yourself as a human bandit once more. Tell your bandit leader that the King of Dragoons has returned, and he has come to make whoever's responsible for the damages that he inflicted both here and at Ceballe pay for his crimes. This town shall be under free rule once more. If he has any problems, tell him I await his challenge."

The demon's snarl faded and a strange smile crept onto its face. In a moment, its skin looked living once more and its eyes returned to a dark green. The Marked One stood, brushing its leathers off, and walked away without a second glance back.

Darkflare sheathed the Lionheart with a shake of his head, and he turned to look around. The silence was frightening.

"D-Darkflare!"

It was Luna. He ran toward where he had last left her, in the center of the town, and prayed that she and Oboro were alright. He hoped they hadn't missed one of the demons…

Luna was nowhere to be seen at first, but Darkflare noticed the crowd of townspeople gathered tightly together. He pushed his way through, finding her in the center with a panicked look. Her hands seemed to be pinned to the body of the elder, who was coated in a silver aura that made him seem ghost-like as he lay on the ground. A look of pain wrinkled his face, but he did not move at all. Her head whipped up and her eyes locked on Darkflare's.

"I-I don't know what's going on! I don't know how to stop this!"

Darkflare dropped to his knees and placed his hand on the chest of the elder. The strange glow was unexpectedly warm, and not just physically, but emotionally and spiritually as well. When he touched it, positive memories from his past seemed to replay over in his mind, and he found that he could not help but smile. In the warmth of the glow, it felt as if he were truly happy, without a care in the world.

The light began to fade, and Darkflare recoiled his hand; the feelings had also faded, and he returned to the real world again. He felt stupid, being the only one to have a smile on his face, and tried to shake off the embarrassment with a stern look. The townspeople didn't seem to notice; they were murmuring and gasping over something else. When he turned to look, he couldn't believe what he was seeing. As if by some miracle, the village elder slowly sat up and started coughing vehemently.

"You wanted a rune, there you go." Kenji had slipped through the crowd with the others right behind him. "You have one that has bestowed you with natural control of healing magic."

Darkflare and Luna both looked down at her leg. A demure white crescent lay pulsating in beautiful silver light – it *was* a rune. Their eyes met once more, as if she was going to say something to Darkflare, but she turned pale and her eyes rolled. He had to quickly catch her as she passed out.

"Hold on, I'm coming," Roy was quick to move to Darkflare's side. "You okay, you got her?"

"Yeah, I'm fine, but we need to get her somewhere to rest." Darkflare did his best to hold Luna in both arms, but he relented a bit when Roy swooped down to help. She was almost as pale as her rune and her expression was slightly pained. He focused his attention on Kenji. "She'll be alright, correct? This is just from her rune activating?"

"Yes, she will be fine. Her rune takes a lot of power to use – even more so than any of ours, as it drains from her own energy to heal others. She's a… Well, she's basically a living, breathing miracle. Best way I can describe it."

"Please," the village elder said in a rather hoarse voice as he stood to his feet. "Please. You must stay here for the night and rest. It is the least we can do to offer you our thanks. You have brought me back from near-death and have rid those monsters from our town. We are more in debt to you warriors than I could possibly ever fit into words."

Darkflare glanced at Kenji, who simply shrugged.

"And you," the village elder looked past the dragoons, and Darkflare's eyes widened when he saw the woman from before. "You must be one of the mercenaries we hired."

She nodded. "Yes, Tessy Suisei. My apologies for being late, but I had to make sure these warriors were not the Marked Ones you wrote of in your letter."

Attila scowled, putting his hand on his blade, but Darkflare shot him a look that forced him to relent.

"But it seems like your problem is over – and *I* am ready to get paid!" The ninja named Tessy put her hands on her hips and grinned widely. "I'll even settle for slightly less than you wrote for, seeing as I showed up late. But then there's the added fee for not mentioning that there were going to be other warriors here, and…"

Tessy seemed to add and subtract various things in her head, counting them on her fingers, muttering to herself. The elder stared at her in disbelief. Darkflare couldn't help but share in his shock at her priorities. "Err, yes. Once things settle down, I promise you shall receive your payment." He turned back to Darkflare and the others. "As I was saying, please, stay here and rest."

"Thank you, sir. It's probably for the best we do, to make sure that no more Marked Ones return."

"No, no. Thank *you*. Maybe now our town can finally restore some honor to its name. If what I heard is true… Are you really a… a dragoon?"

"Yes. My name is Darkflare Omni and," he paused, contemplating explaining his newfound title, but he thought better of it. "And these are my friends; Attila, Kenji, Roy, my wyvern is Oboro, and the young woman is Luna."

"Oh, blessed are we to be honored with the presence of such great warriors! It truly was fate that you came here to our town." That earned an eye roll and a hushed sigh from Attila. "The gods have answered my prayers! My name is Roper Nikita and I am the elder of this village. Please, come with me right away."

Darkflare turned once more to face his allies and shifted Luna's weight. The concentration and energy needed for him to conjure a small fireball wasn't as taxing as it had been, but the exhaustion from using magic was still fresh in his mind. He looked at her and smiled sadly.

"I'm going to take Luna to rest. Can I count on you all to help the people here clean up? Someone should check the town for any other Marked Ones, as well."

"I'll stay and help!" Tessy tilted her head sideways slightly and grinned. "Who knows who might throw some gold my way for saving them?"

Attila watched Tessy walk off, and he sneered. "I'll watch her."

Kenji put his hands in his pockets and shrugged. "I'll do the perimeter, see if anything's hanging around."

"Okay," Darkflare turned to Roy, nodding. "Let's go."

"I'll match my strides to yours."

As they walked to catch up with Roper, they received a mixed reaction from the townspeople that had now come back out from hiding. Some of them gawked and stared at Darkflare and Roy as they carried Luna, whispering rather loudly things about dragoons and magic, while others grinned far too nervously. Darkflare tried to ignore all of the stares, but every once and a while, he could not help but notice another person gawking at the armored man and the company he had with him. Oboro could sense Darkflare's uneasiness and hissed every now and then at the closer residents that pointed and murmured. Darkflare tried to imagine how he would feel in their situation. It was not too long ago that he was blissfully unaware about all of this.

"Ignore them," Roy whispered to Darkflare, unflinching from the path ahead.

"Wh-What?" Darkflare arched his brow down in mock confusion.

"I can see you catching one of their glances every so often. They'll continue to stare, but just ignore them. This is one of the reasons why I rarely show my magic, why I hid it from you all, too. Here on out, we're going to be getting a lot of this sort of reception, more than likely."

"Should we try to reassure them? Try to talk to them and tell them we're here to help?"

"It doesn't matter what you say; they're scared. I tried to dress plain when I first came to D'sylum so I wouldn't stand out; you can't get any blander than black and white, and the cloak usually covered my armor. People stared and whispered still because I carried swords. They wanted to know why a warrior would dress so plain and not wear armor of any kind. I tried to mind my own business and stay out of focus. It never helped. Everywhere I went, everywhere I looked, people always had something to say. People fear what they don't understand, and they try to rationalize it by ridiculing it. So I just stopped caring about what others think. I'll drink when I want, wear what I want, and act however I feel comfortable acting – even if it's usually in their best interest and they don't realize it."

Darkflare nodded at the sage advice, trying his best to ignore the gawking that made him feel like every stare burned a deep scar into the back of his neck. Sure, he had been gaped at before at tournaments and the like, but now that he was a dragoon, it felt different. People were not staring at him because he saved them or he was providing them wonderful entertainment – they stared because he was different, as Roy said. He felt like an animal or beast of some sort, anything except like the hero that he should have felt like. To try to clear his mind, he looked around at the surroundings of the town, trying to take in the details to help him relax.

The town was widespread to accommodate the population density that it had. It was nowhere near as populated as Ceballe, but it was almost as immense, if not more, by the way the buildings were spread out. There was a great deal of empty space throughout the town, which in turn allowed more walking space. Aunquil was made for passing by as much as it was for trade, but the residents seemed to lead pleasant lives. Darkflare figured they were all either merchants or farmers of some sort; they lived in quaint houses that were generally two stories at most and not too wide.

The town had a main focal point in the form of a large fountain, right near where they had first noticed the bandits and townspeople fighting. It was an elegant stone design that shot up water in spouts at different intervals. Now that the chaos was over, people had gathered around it, talking in loud whispers as they watched him go.

They knew which house belonged to the elder the moment they had laid eyes upon it. Both dragoons exchanged impressed glances as they approached the largest house in the area; it was as wide as about two or three of the other residences, and the design was a bit more intricate.

Roper was waiting outside of the doorstep and let them in very excitedly.

"Come in, come in, please! Feel free to make yourselves at home. What's mine is yours, my friends. Let me show you where the lady may rest."

As they stepped inside, they were greeted by a cool breeze overhead. There were fans in every room rotating lightly and propelling air around the house. The dragoons followed the man into a side room from the entrance where he motioned at a small bed for Luna to rest in. The duo carefully set her down, and then Darkflare pulled a blanket up and over her.

They returned to the sitting room, and the man motioned for them to sit. Oboro curled up in a ball at Darkflare's feet as he and Roy took chairs in the center of the area.

"Take this time to relax. May I offer you anything? Something to eat – or maybe some tea?"

"Ah, thank you, but sit with us." Roy smiled coyly, bowed his head, and spread his hands. "Surely your *daughter* can attend to the tea. Where would she be?"

"Uh… I don't have a…"

"Tea is fine, thank you." Darkflare gave Roy a sharp look, to which his ally looked hurt, opened his mouth, and shrugged as if he had not the slightest idea what Darkflare was getting at.

The old man smiled rather confused at first, but soon he disappeared behind a wooden door, leaving the dragoons to themselves. Roy settled in more comfortably to his chair and shrugged again, his smile widening.

"Listen, I'm allowed to wish that I'll meet my dream woman after doing a good deed just once."

"That's great and all, but don't do anything stupid that could tarnish the good name of dragoons. Roper seems to genuinely be thankful for what we did here today."

"Me? Do anything stupid? I'm not Attila, you know."

Darkflare's eyebrows went up and he looked to the side. "You have a point."

They sat there for a few more moments; Darkflare leaned his head back and closed his eyes, trying to calm his body. The sound of the front door clicking open caused both Roy and Darkflare to crane their heads to see who it was. The man with the blue ponytail looked around as he stopped in the entranceway. Kenji finally saw where they were and smiled, making his way toward them.

"Nice place."

Right behind him, the ninja – Tessy, was it? - casually sauntered in, and Attila stared daggers behind her. The two dragoons pulled up chairs to sit beside Darkflare and Roy, while Tessy sat a bit more aloof from the group where she could see them all.

"Where's the elder?" Kenji said, raising an eyebrow.

Darkflare pointed a thumb toward the wooden door. "Making tea."

"And Luna?"

"In the other room, sleeping."

"Good. She's going to need to rest for a little while. We probably shouldn't move anywhere until morning, for her sake."

Darkflare eyed Tessy cautiously, and she glared back at him. "So do you believe us now? That we're not the enemy?"

"Sort of. You're not my enemy right now, no. But they had marks. And you have marks. And I have a mark. So doesn't that make us all Marked Ones? How are they different from us?"

"Well," Darkflare looked toward Kenji, but he waved his ward on. "You've seen what the Marked Ones look like. They're demons, in every sense of the word. They've sold their souls for power, but we've been chosen by deities to wield their magic."

"She uses water," Attila said, keeping his eyes fixed on her.

"I do," she returned the glare and then looked back to Darkflare. "I got this mark when I was younger, after saving my mother from a mugger, but I never knew what it meant. All I knew was that my mother told me to keep it hidden – from everyone."

"So then you're not a new dragoon." Darkflare shrugged. "You've had your powers for years. How did you learn how to conjure the water?"

It was Tessy's turn to shrug. "I dunno. It just... came to me. The path to being a ninja involves a lot of patience and mental fortitude, so

I used my training to harness the magic when no one else was around. I would hear the crashing of waves nowhere near the ocean. I could hear myself submerging underwater when I was walking on land. I knew the water was calling, telling me of its *tranquility*, so I trained myself to harness its strength.

"And then," she paused, tapping her chin with her knuckles. "Then the barkeep at my usual tavern told me he'd received a letter that Aunquil was looking for help dealing with strange people with symbols on their necks. I knew this was my chance to find out what this *thing* meant." She paused again and then slammed her hands down on the arms of her chair, causing Darkflare to rear back. "But why am I 'chosen'? I didn't ask for any god's help. I've lived my life fine without knowing I was this, this…"

"Dragoon," Roy finished for her.

"Whatever!" She exhaled in frustration, crossing her arms and leaning back in the chair. "Whatever."

"We don't choose to get picked or not," Kenji shrugged. "We answer the call of those in need. Those that lust for power end up as Marked Ones. Those that are reluctant are the ones usually chosen. That's how it goes."

"Wait, wait," Roy leaned forward. "Is this why you were so dismissive over Luna?"

Kenji eyed them carefully. "We needed her help, dragoon or not. I didn't want her to get too focused on it and fall into the path of becoming a Marked One. I knew that if she was meant to be a dragoon, her rune would answer the king's call eventually."

"So there it is, Tessy." Darkflare shrugged. "We're all dragoons. You're one of us. And even though we don't know you very well, and you any of us, you've been chosen for a greater destiny. What you do with that information is your choice."

She stared up at the ceiling, pouting, when Roper came back through the doorway carrying a long plate. His gleeful smile underneath his stubby mustache made it seem as if he had a caterpillar crawling on his upper lip.

"Ah, I'm glad the rest of you found your way here. I brought enough cups for everyone."

After passing out tea to all five of his assembled guests, Roper pulled up a chair of his own to sit down. Clearly sensing he walked in on an uncomfortable moment, the man nervously cleared his throat.

"Ah, this silence is unbearable. Let us talk. You must tell me what brings a talented group such as yourselves to our quaint little town. I am extremely appreciative that you all showed up, but it's not every day we see skilled warriors come through here; usually only traders or travelers come to pass by. Because of that, I apologize for any... glares or gestures that you might have already received. The only armed people they've seen for quite some time have been those bandits."

"That's quite alright," Darkflare said, placing his own saucer down gently on his knee. "Your situation is what brought us here. We heard rumors that bandit activity had increased." Darkflare glanced around at his allies before focusing back on Roper. "It all ties in with a grander plot than just trying to take over towns. I'm just thankful we arrived when we did."

The images of the prisoners of Kailos becoming thralls of the Marked Ones flashed in Darkflare's head as he thought of the fate Aunquil was saved from. The village elder nodded to himself, rocking back and forth slowly.

"I see, I see. Yes, we know lots about those Mokiwana-forsaken ruffians. They started plaguing our town only within the past few months, but that's long enough to sully our name as a welcome rest stop. They just came in one day, talking about their bandit king, Thalland..."

Darkflare furrowed his brow and turned to look at Kenji. His guardian had reacted strangely to that name before, and now he looked rather contemplative, ignoring his ward.

"Thalland..." Roy cupped his chin, painting a rather inquisitive look on his face. "Didn't one of them mention something about a Thalland?"

"Yes, Thalland Faleenwar – the greedy oaf is the leader of those heinous bandits – demons – whatever!" The old man looked as if he was about to faint by the way that he had worked himself up, his face flush red and veins popping on the side. He exhaled deeply and tried to calm himself down "There I go again... Getting so agitated over those stupid barbarians..."

"Thalland Faleenwar," Kenji finally spoke, shaking his head with his eyes shut. "I remember him very clearly. He was a notorious bandit back before Graymahl's wake. I fought him years back with Calistron and Sylphe. His skills were impressive, for a bandit, but he was no true warrior. It's true though, that he was vicious enough even then to unite many downtrodden to his cause. During our last fight with him, Sylphe took one of his eyes out with an arrow. We had thought that would be the end of his group; the remaining bandits either scattered or lay dead. Guess we were wrong."

The old man frowned, causing his forehead to wrinkle heavily.

"Yes, it's been about, what, roughly twenty years since the terrible destruction of Syvail? What a terrible tragedy." Roper took a long sip of his tea. "Thalland appeared here with a bunch of his men, claiming ownership over the town. We disputed with him and were ready to fight for our land, but it was obvious that we were outmatched. The first thing he did was put forth a tax over all products that went in and out. It was bearable, until his 'bandits' started hanging around our shops and stalls, causing mischief and mayhem. They drove countless people out and scared nearly any travelers away. He was destroying his own profits by letting them stay here, but still blamed it on us. It came to the point where he wouldn't let those that lived here leave, and he stationed men to watch anyone going in or out. It was starting to become too much; we were starting to lose more money than we could make. I gave letters to those that managed to leave, in it saying that we needed mercenaries. I had received answers from several people, including Tessy, here, but she was the only one to actually arrive."

"What about the military?" Darkflare shook his head incredulously. "I can't imagine that King Corsius would let such a travesty go on for so long. Where have the D'sylum soldiers been?"

"Heh. That's the strange part. The king stationed men here several times to check on the situation, but someone must have tipped Thalland off each time. He, nor his crooks, showed any of the times that we had soldiers here. Every time, the military men thought we were just mocking the army and wasting their time. After a while, they simply stopped sending help, saying that we were wasting their time. The king's court wrote that they needed their soldiers training and patrolling instead of taking leisure trips out to the other side of the country."

"What about the other kingdoms?" Attila's voice was laced with disgust. "Peralor did not send help?"

"I'm sure Queen Ragwelv would have, if she were able to."

"Territorial dispute." The sage Kenji nodded to Attila. "King Corsius might take it as an act of war if Beauldyn soldiers were being harbored in a D'sylum town, bandits or not. He would have immediately accused Queen Ragwelv of plotting an invasion."

Roper nodded once more.

"It was a good thing you all showed up when you did. I would not have had another day to seek help had you not."

"Think nothing of it." Darkflare smiled warmly. "I'm even more confident in my gamble now. Thalland will hopefully show his face to us, now that he knows we're aware of his presence."

"That's a good point." Roy leaned back in his chair again, staring deep into his cup of tea as if he was talking to the liquid instead of the others. "But we need to find out where their base is. If Thalland has been here personally, it can't be far. I doubt he'd have come if he had to travel a distance." He finally looked up at Roper. "Does anyone in Aunquil know where the bandit hideout is?"

"Eh… That, we're not quite sure of. No one in the village has ever been brave enough to follow Thalland's men. We figure somewhere in the eastern mountains, but only because that's the direction they leave in. The only problem is that there's nothing there. It's a gorge that connects D'sylum and Beauldyn; and the eastern kingdom has had no reports of bandits from what travelers have told me."

"So basically," Attila interrupted the elder, "the situation is this: we have a brazen bandit on our hands who somehow commands an army of demons, and he tried to prove his might by kidnapping and trying to turn some of the world's top royalties. Is he a Marked One, as well?"

"If he is, he's stayed quiet for so many years." Kenji's arms were crossed and his eyes opened as he muttered toward the ceiling. "Like I said, I thought he was dead. But why make two large shows of force at major trading cities? If Kailos was a breeding ground for Marked Ones, was this all just a distraction to keep us from seeing something else?"

Darkflare turned to look out the window. The town had grown quiet, and dusk settled on the world outside. Getting up, he stretched his arms and rolled his neck.

"Whatever the case may be, it's getting late. We shouldn't really go exploring in the dark, and Luna wouldn't like us just up and leaving her."

"True enough," Kenji rose to his feet as well.

"Allow me to show you to your rooms," Roper nodded, having some difficulty standing.

"Ah, that won't be necessary for me." Tessy stood, walked over to Roper, and held out her hand. "I'll be taking my payment and leaving, thank you. You can all have fun taking out the bandit guy and following your destiny and what not. I'd rather keep making money and looking for treasure!"

Kenji let out a sigh of disgust, and Roper nodded as he dug into a pouch at his waist. Tessy watched him struggle and then shook her head, sighing of her own. "Never mind. This hasn't been worth my time, anyway. I'll come back to collect the fee once Aunquil has gotten back on its feet."

She sauntered over to the door and left. Darkflare, unsure what else to do, got up. "I'll find mine later. Thank you, Roper, and excuse me."

He made for the door, Oboro up and fluttering alongside him. He closed it cautiously behind them and jogged to catch up with Tessy. She stopped and turned around, cocking an eyebrow with a sultry smile.

"If you're here to pay me for the old man, I'm afraid to tell you he owes me quite the sum of gold."

"You don't feel a connection to any of this? You don't want to work with us to stop Thalland? Save the world from demons?"

"Everything comes at a price, dear, and my skills cost quite the penny! You're adorable, really, but I'm moving on to my next job! I don't work for free!"

Darkflare put his arms out to his sides and dropped them, watching as she walked off. "Just promise me you'll think about it. Saving the innocent should be payment enough!"

She turned back to him with a wink and a wave and then continued on into the night.

Darkflare sighed with exhaustion as he walked back up and sat down on the front steps. There were various lights on from streets and houses that illuminated the area around him drearily, as well as the silver glow of the moon; but for the most part, the town was engulfed in shadows. Oboro rested again at Darkflare's feet as the young man stared off into the night's sky.

The power that Sairephir's mark granted must have been remarkably dark to make Kenji as worried as he seemed. But what if Thalland wasn't marked? What if it was someone else posing as him to strike fear in the minds of those that knew Thalland?

He looked down as his gauntleted fingers played with the Drachenfaith, twirling it in between one digit to the next.

Perhaps there was more to the past than Kenji was letting on; perhaps he was holding information back from Darkflare. He wasn't surprised as he considered this. There was probably a lot that Kenji wasn't telling him. There were still plenty of questions that Darkflare had that were unanswered, now that his memories had returned.

Hearing the door slowly creak open behind him, Darkflare awaited for the looming presence of Attila or Kenji to hover beside him, but he was surprised to find someone different. Darkflare could tell out of the corner of his eye that it was Roy by the contrast of his silver hair and white cloak against the shade of night. He didn't say anything as he sat down next to Darkflare and stared with him up into the darkness.

"It's a nice night. You'd hardly believe an attack had happened here earlier," Roy spoke, his voice as calm as the night's sky.

Darkflare nodded, staring up at the star-speckled blackness. "After all we've been through in the past few days, a night like this is a nice change of pace. Helps me to relax and think."

"Sounds contradictory, if you ask me."

"Hmm?" Darkflare turned to Roy. There was a sly smile forming at the corner of the other man's lips.

"It doesn't take a know-it-all like Kenji to understand you. I know you aren't the least bit relaxed when you're thinking. You're usually worrying or stressing yourself out over something you have no control over. You need to let go of thinking for a little while and actually relax, or sleep for that matter."

"Eh... Whatever." Darkflare waved his hand up at Roy.

There was silence as they glanced up at the moon together. It was slightly awkward for Darkflare; even though they got along fine, he did not really know Roy as a person too much. They had saved him from Kailos, but other than that, he had just been a traveling companion.

"So," Roy broke in, "regretting at all letting me out of that cell?"

Darkflare was startled by Roy's bluntness. "No. Not at all. What would make you ask that?"

Roy let a smile part his lips as he pushed off the porch and walked back to lean against the house.

"My attitude and views on the world tend to push people away. While my noble antics have nearly ended me up in jail more times than I can remember, they're just that, antics. I'd like to think I could get a woman to fall in love with me, but truth be told, Darkflare? I don't remember the last time I took a lover."

"Their choice, or yours?"

"Neither!" Roy laughed. "When I get drunk, my comments get the better of me and ward off all company! Before I met all of you, I was a warrior who had all of this runic power, yet no cause to fight for, no allies to fight with, and nothing to pledge my blade to. I was lonely, and I let my antics get the best of me, hoping this random woman would fall in love with me when we barely shared words. I regretted it at first, thinking how stupid it was, finally getting me caught; but if I hadn't gone out of my way to give her the coin, I wouldn't have met you."

Darkflare looked at Roy and smiled. "You're very passionate about what you do, I have to give you credit for that. It's one of the first things I picked up about you. The way you handle yourself, the way you treat your gear, the way you get into your stories, the commitment you put into every action. I don't know you very well, Roy, but I can appreciate who you are. I believe you have a noble heart, similar to my own. I'm going to go out on a limb and say we might just be kindred spirits, you and I."

Roy nodded, narrowing his cat-like eyes slightly. He looked back to the house once and then smiled mischievously at Darkflare.

"You know… Now seems like a good time to show you a useful technique that Kenji might not even know. He's a skilled warrior, but we've been trained differently. As I'm sure you've seen, my fighting style is a bit more flashy, a bit more akin to your tournament fighting."

Darkflare's eyes widened. "I'd be grateful for anything you have to teach me."

Roy stood up and walked over to a pile of firewood that lay at the bottom of the stairs. He set one up vertically, a little taller than his waist, in the middle of the road. He backed up, putting several feet between the log and himself. Darkflare watched vigilantly from his front row seat.

"Watch carefully," Roy called, withdrawing his Hyperion from the sheath at his side. "Blink and you might just miss it."

Roy twirled the Hyperion around in his right hand several times before holding the blade still. He pulled the blade down to his side horizontally, the tip pointing out and away from him. Grasping the weapon with both of his hands, Roy bent his knees slightly to assume a fighting stance.

Roy pushed off the ground with his right foot and dashed toward his target. Despite the short distance he stood from the log, he moved faster than Darkflare anticipated. Just as Roy got within swinging reach of the target, his movement came to a halt, and he whipped the sword horizontally with both of his arms in a full one-hundred-and-eighty degree swing from side to side.

It was indeed almost missed, but Darkflare jumped up when he saw the wave of energy sear from the blade and go through the log. Roy approached the firewood and poked it, causing the top half to fall clean off.

His jaw draped open in shock, Darkflare ran over to the wood and picked up the two pieces, examining just how fine the slice was; there were no splinters or slivers. It was as if the two had never been one in the first place!

Roy sheathed his weapon and set up another piece of firewood. When Darkflare finally turned, Roy motioned for him to stand where he had been.

"Your turn."

As Darkflare walked over, his eyes remained fixated on the new plank, as if trying to mimic the technique in his mind before he performed it.

"Concentrate. Focus your strength and effort into the blade of your Lionheart. I know you have what it takes to perform this technique; you just need to believe in yourself and your powers. Mimic exactly what I did, placing everything into the swing. Use the speed as a momentum to power your slice up even more. Try not to focus on getting into range as much as actually swinging your sword and emitting the power. If the sword makes contact, the energy will disperse. Think you're ready to give it a go?"

Darkflare bobbed his head up and down rather slowly as he did not want to interrupt his line of sight. It seemed simple enough; run in, swing, fire forth energy, finish. Darkflare pulled the Lionheart from the sheath at his side with a soft, metallic swishing noise as the dark blue sword was exposed in the moonlight. He held the blade crossed over his side like Roy had done before him.

He ran at the firewood, his mind focusing on swinging the blade and creating the sonic boom, but he tripped over his target and fell forward. He braced himself as he hit the ground and felt the heat in his face. Roy smirked and shook his head as Darkflare picked himself up.

"Too much focus. Gotta still be aware of where the thing is."

Darkflare nodded once, got back into position, and closed his eyes.

Concentrate. Focus.

Darkflare closed his eyes and tried to focus as he bent his right knee. His left hand grasped the handle tightly aside his right as he felt the fierce fire tingle and lap at his fingertips. Darkflare could feel the power from the Rune of Courage flowing through his entire body from head to toe.

Pressing off the ground with his right foot, Darkflare took to a running start again as he shot his eyes wide open. His auburn eyes honed in on his target as Darkflare ran forward. This time, he would not fail.

As he came within inches of the wooden stump, the Lionheart crossed Darkflare's whole body frame from left to right. Darkflare's left hand lost its grip, forcing the swing to move more wild than he wished. Darkflare had seen it though; he had seen the crescent energy from where his blade had sliced, causing time and space to distort and cut straight on through the wood.

An aura of confidence swept over Darkflare as he swung the Lionheart over his shoulder and faced Roy.

"I did it! I saw the energy shoot from the blade! That was amazing!"

Roy looked amused, but in a different sense than how Darkflare was. With his right hand on his chin, he inspected the wooden block, knocking the top half off of it.

"What would you call your work, Darkflare?"

"I would have to say that the second time I did it flawlessly."

"And I would have to call it sloppy."

Darkflare's sudden excitement faded, his body frame heaved in disappointment, and he stared at the wooden log. "What do you mean 'sloppy'?"

Roy waved his hand over the top of the stump.

"See the incision? The blade was moved off slightly from the horizontal angle, leaving a slight diagonal mark to your slice. That's fine and all, but I wanted it to be perfectly horizontal like mine was. Emitting a diagonal wave of energy distorts the power balance and makes one side stronger than the other, as opposed to the even power that is achieved from a horizontal slice. You're too new to the technique to pull off a diagonal slice with equal power."

"Is that it?"

"No. The way you cut the wood, because of how distorted the slice was, and partly because you're new at the technique, left the cut somewhat splintered as you can see. That's from various spikes in the wave's power, which we'll have to work on making a universal force."

"Right, right." Darkflare nodded, looking at the stump from all angles. "Okay, I see what you mean."

Roy picked up half of the wood block, pointing to the splinters. "This is what will make the difference between winning and losing a fight. If you do not have your skills honed and you go in unprepared, you'll find yourself slipping, and your enemy will exploit that."

"You're right. So when is the next time we'll practice?"

Roy smiled. "I'm not quite sure. Next chance we get to take a rest, if you want to train, just let me know. I've got more than just this technique. This is the first step."

Roy turned to walk away, but he stopped and lowered his head, not turning to look back at Darkflare.

"Hey. Thanks, by the way."

"Thanks...? Why are you thanking me? I should be the one thanking you for the advice and the training."

"Heh, thanks for being the first person in a long time that I can truly call a friend."

Darkflare smiled once more as Roy disappeared back into Roper's house. Thinking about the future scared him, but in that moment, thinking about the new allies — maybe even friends — that he had gained over the past few days, he felt at peace.

* * * * *

Night had fallen, and the world was encased in darkness once more. Just because it was evening did not mean it was time for all that inhabited Caelestis to sleep. One particular person was busy stuffing his face on the most succulent and juicy spiced meats that D'sylum had to offer. The bulky man choose to eat the meat as undercooked as possible, and it showed by the fresh blood that spewed each time he sunk his teeth into flesh. While gorging on the scrumptious delicacies, the swine of a man chased the food down with the most vintage of wines that money could buy — or that could be pillaged. The hulking brute was not only tall, but gluttonous in his weight; so much so that his silky blue pants barely stayed on his waist, exposing his hairy gut as he sat several inches back from the table.

Scraps of food that did not quite make his vigorously chomping mouth cascaded down into the scraggly gray mess of a beard that stretched off of his chin. It acted as a net to keep food from his silken mauve-colored long-sleeved shirt and the elegantly designed crimson vest that adorned it. The patch-eyed man's beard seemed to catch any drool or slobber besides food particles that dropped from his voracious eating habits. He knew he was a vicious sight to behold as he scarfed down what would be considered a week's worth of food for an entire household of people.

A whining creak echoed throughout the brightly torched dining hall and caused the man with the black bandana around his head to look up, his long gray ponytail in the back dangling as he suddenly turned. Swallowing hard, he stopped eating to address the intruder.

"Who dares interrupt my dining? All know this is a sacred time! State your reasons quickly!"

The frame of the man who ran in seemed like an ant beside the gluttonous sloth. He kneeled down swiftly beside the chair in an attempt to make amends for interrupting his leader's nightly feasting. The obese man looked down at him with a mighty snarl, the food particles still clinging to his matted beard of gray as he snorted.

"Forgive me, your lordship. I return from Aunquil with grave news."

It took the glutton a few moments to recall where he had sent this grunt, but the mentioning of Aunquil and the fresh wounds caught his attention.

"What, the merchant town? What of it – what happened? Speak!"

"There was an uprising in the town today."

"WHAT?!"

Thalland Faleenwar rose from his seat, standing nearly seven feet tall. As he rose, his imposing gut almost smacked the whelp before him in the face. Seeing the hairy horror, the man leapt to his feet and crossed his arms over his chest into a saluting stance that mimicked the Mark of Sairephir.

"Don't you dare tell me that you let a bunch of old, decrepit, pathetic merchants beat the ever-loving piss out of you!"

Thalland punctured each word with a jabbing index finger at the demon's chest, causing him to wince with each poke.

"No, My Lord!"

"Then what the Pale happened?! Where did those wounds come from?!"

"A group of warriors appeared that we've never seen before. They banished all our men back to The Pale." The Marked One's eyes remained fixed on Thalland's, but they wavered as if trying to break free. "Their leader told me to return to you and offer a challenge."

"A challenge?! GWA! HAW HAW HAW!"

Thalland Faleenwar shook the gilded halls of his dining room with his laugh, causing the gold on his table and walls to tremble, and the man in front of him darted his eyes with unease.

"Does the fool not know who I am?! I am Thalland Faleenwar! I am the greatest bandit to ever roam these lands. I've traveled all across the continent plundering and pillaging, raising the greatest army that anyone has ever laid eyes upon! I am richer than the richest merchant that pompously skips down the streets of Ceballe. I have more power and influence in the south than Corsius has in his pinky! Women line up to my throne room just to get a glimpse at the marvelous wonder that is my body." At this, Thalland flexed his arm, and most of the flab turned to a grotesque mound of muscle. He slammed his hand down on the table and then spread his arms out with a malicious smile. "I *am* the greatest man to ever live, and if this fool thinks that he has what it takes to challenge me, then I welcome the death of the inglorious bastard! No mortal has ever surpassed the prowess and skills that I have in combat. I've wrestled bears with my hands tied behind my back, blindfolded. I've tackled the sea's worst kraken with simply a sailboat and oar, but I live to tell the tale. I'll take this fool on barehanded, stripped of my armor, and show the world once again why I am the King of Bandits! He and his army of... How many were there?"

"Six, Lord."

"He and his army of six are not-... SIX?!" Thalland's face reverted to a look of anger as he reared on his subject again. "*Six*?! How the Pale did you get wiped out by an army of *six*?! Pale, that's not even an army! That's a damn squad! Not even a squad! A... A... A group? Yes, a meager *group* took out your men! Were they six monstrous ogres with bone-crushing strength?! For Pale's damn sake, you have the powers of the devil Sairephir himself!"

"That is the grave part, My Lord," The man swallowed hard, as if what he was about to say would be his last words. "They were dragoons."

"Poppycock bull spit! There are no such things as dragoons anymore. Graymahl Vulorst destroyed the last of them years ago. Fools running around claiming to be such things of the past will be crushed underneath my ambition!" Thalland picked up his goblet and started inhaling the liquor again.

"No disrespect, My Lord, but I witnessed it with my own eyes. I watched them cast magic."

The bandit leader paused from his drink to speak, a sneer on his face. "Did this man tell you his name?"

"He said it was Darkflare Omni."

Thalland grabbed the demon by the collar of his leathers with his free hand, pulling him up directly off the ground and into his face.

"What did you say? That name. Did you say…Omni?!"

The overbearing stench of Thalland's breath, combined with the fact that the man was already being choked off the ground, made him gasp frantically for air, unable to answer the King of Bandits. Thalland threw the Marked One across the floor. Free from his king's grasp, the peon panted for a few moments. As soon as he could, he leapt once more to his feet, saluting again.

Thalland stroked his gray beard, and in the process, removed any particles of food that remained. He sucked the morsels off of each finger, one at a time, as he stared pensively into the fireplace that roared behind his velvet and gold chair, as if looking to the embers for more answers than his grunt could have delivered. The devilish grin that stretched from one corner of his face to the other was illuminated rather sinisterly by the crackling flames.

"An Omni, eh?" His voice was soft and pensive, speaking to no one in particular. "Even better. This makes things all the more interesting. Perhaps a son of Calistron lived through Graymahl's rampage after all."

Thalland whirled around once more. This time, in his meaty right hand was a large broadsword that he impaled deeply into the Marked One's throat before he could react. The man gasped for air, raising his hand to his lord, but Thalland met the frame of his body with a hard kick from his curled, red slipper. His ogre-like foot sent the man reeling backward across the floor, sickeningly disconnected from the sword's embrace.

Thalland sat down once again, drinking deeply from his glass of wine as the body vanished in smoke. The sword clattered on the ground at Thalland's side, drenched in black fluid. He swirled the amber liquor around, narrowing his brow deep in thought.

"An Omni… Could it really be? If so, I have a big surprise for the Omni boy. He couldn't have popped up at a better time. I've been waiting for someone to take notice of what I've done of late, and if he's come to Aunquil, then he already has. I didn't want to believe that myste-rious sodding bastard when he told me about him before, but the civies couldn't have taken out the demons I sent. This was an opportunity I'm glad I didn't waste. I'll bide my time for now and prepare the defenses. This Darkflare Omni will fall. I'll make sure of that myself."

The glass of wine that Thalland had been holding with his left hand shattered into pieces around his plate from his grip. As the combination of wine and blood trickled down his palm and onto the table, he licked a few drops of the black liquid before flicking the shards of glass away from his now cold delicacy.

"No one can stop me from ruling this land. Not even *if* he is an Omni."

Chapter XII

Luna slowly opened her azure eyes, trying to focus on her hazy surroundings. Moments from her past rushed upon her and caused her to breathe deeply, as if emerging breathless from a deep lake. The last things to come to her were a memory of her parents and then of the people she had met the past few days. All of the memories surrounded her with a blanket of emotions, making her feel safe. She felt warm and smiled despite herself. The rush of memories and emotions made her feel *loved*.

The stinging sensation in her right ankle made her instinctively drop her hand down to caress the skin. She examined the mark that was inscribed there; a sort of crescent moon shape with spiked tongues in the middle. Could this be...?

Her eyes widened and she gasped. Was this a rune? Had she now one of her own?!

Luna shook herself from the shock to look around the room. Where was she? She remembered the walk to Aunquil, but after that, things were a bit hazy... There was a battle, someone had died, but she had brought them back to life with the power of her rune. Were they still in Aunquil? Had they moved on and taken Luna with them – or worse – did they leave her somewhere?

Slightly agitated at the thought, Luna swung her legs around the side of the bed and stood as best as she could. It was strange at first, her legs were rather wobbly and she still felt lightheaded, but she managed to catch her balance. The Elyria and her quiver of arrows rested beside the bed, and she threw them on her back and walked out of the room. She could hear voices, low, as if trying to conceal their volume in a nearby room, but nonetheless she could pick out the various tones of her comrades. A sigh of relief parted her dainty lips as she smiled. She was thankful that Darkflare knew better than to abandon her.

* * * * *

Darkflare, Oboro, and their three allies all turned their heads toward Luna as she stood in the doorway. She placed one hand on the wooden frame, stabilizing herself as she rubbed her eyes and face with the other hand.

"Please tell me someone's saved me some tea?"

"Luna!" Darkflare leapt up and walked over to help her into the room, but she raised a hand and walked in herself. "Are you okay?"

"I feel fine, thank you for the concern. I'm a little tired, but other than that, yesterday's just a little hazy. I know I have this... this mark on my ankle. Does that mean that I'm a dragoon?"

"Yes." Kenji leaned forward, letting both of his arms rest on his knees. "You saved that old man, Roper. Brought him back from the brink of death. Your rune has the affinity of life magic. Such an amazing gift of magic comes with a taxing cost on your own body. Nothing permanent, but it will leave you feeling much more drained than the rest of us when we conjure magic."

"Oh... I have that kind of... power?" Luna stammered then suddenly remembered the flash images of her past. "I-I think it's called the Rune of... Love. I keep hearing it in my head." She shook her head and smiled widely. "I can't believe that, it's amazing!"

"Right, and Luna," Kenji cleared his throat, sitting up straight. "I'm sorry for how I acted before. I just didn't want to give you false hope."

"I appreciate that," Luna replied coolly. "No hard feelings then. Where is, uh, Roper, was it?"

"Out." Attila's cool voice eased into the conversation from a corner of the room. He leaned against the wall with his arms crossed, staring at the floorboards. "I went for a walk this morning and saw him leaving. Probably has a lot to do to calm his people."

"I see. Good to see you're as dreary as ever, friend." She winked at him, but he rolled his eyes in response. "So what happens next? Do we know where the Marked Ones are?"

"That's what we're discussing now," Darkflare said as he sighed. "No one in Aunquil knows where their base is. We didn't have the opportunity to follow them, nor did we just want to go looking without you."

"I'm flattered that you'd wait for me, thank you." She smiled as she sat down. "That still doesn't make us even, you realize?"

Darkflare was about to answer, but something called his attention to the large front window. A crowd had gathered, and if Darkflare hadn't known better, he would have thought he was watching Luna's rune activation scene from yesterday play out again.

"There are a lot of people out in the street."

"Want to check what's going on?" Roy said, rising to his feet.

"Probably should." Darkflare nodded, standing and stretching. "We want to try to keep the peace with the townspeople, and if there's a problem, we should try to help resolve it."

Oboro had been sitting in his usual spot by Darkflare's feet and had leapt up to follow his master the second he felt the weight shift. One by one, they stood and followed Darkflare out the door.

The sunlight descended upon them, blanketing the group in a layer of warmth and blinding light. Blinking away the pinpricks of stars, Darkflare walked toward the group of people; he managed to count at least thirty. They were drawn by the sound of loud sobbing that echoed through the street, above the throng of chatter. The furthest two townspeople from the group were talking, looking at each other sideways, and just so happened to catch a glimpse of the dragoons approaching.

A mix of terror and awe showed on their faces as they turned to murmur to their neighbors. The attention slowly shifted from the crying person in the center of the group to the approaching warriors. The townspeople parted a straight path for Darkflare, revealing the source of the cries as a woman who looked to be in her early thirties, if he had to guess. She sat on the corner of the street with her face in her hands, sobbing endlessly. Another person, presumably her husband, had his arm around her shoulder, trying to comfort her. As Darkflare approached, the man leapt up and backed away from the woman.

Seeing the frightened man's reaction, Darkflare held up his hands in peace and knelt down beside the woman. He could hear vague words in between her sobs that resembled something about a son; her baby son. Empathy assuaged Darkflare's face as his eyebrows arched upward and he tried his best to look as calming as he could.

"Excuse me, madam…"

The woman took her hands away from her face, sniffling as she struggled to open her eyes. Once she saw the person that was kneeling in front of her, horror struck her face as she began to shake. The fear diffused to anger as she balled her hands into fists and shoved Darkflare away, leaping to her feet and recoiling toward her husband. Darkflare fell back on his rear, not even bothering to try to catch himself. He was too taken aback by the reaction. Sure, the people seemed terrified of him, but none looked at him with such anger as this woman had. Confusion etched his brows into a strained look as he stood to his feet, gazing toward his comrades, then to the woman.

"So much for trying to keep the peace," Attila murmured, shaking his head.

Her sobbing had overtaken her voice once again as she stretched out an arm toward Darkflare. Once her sobs stopped choking what she strained to say, Darkflare could just barely understand her.

"You…! It's… It's all your fault! My son! My precious baby! M-M-My only… my only son! He's gone and it's your fault!"

Darkflare was even more befuddled with what the woman said than when she had not spoken at all. He crossed his arms over his chest, craning his head slightly to further illustrate his confusion, while still trying to seem calm and welcoming.

"I'm sorry, but…"

"My son! Oh, my only son!"

"Madam…"

"Lost and gone! He's surely dead!"

"…Please…"

"I just wanted him to live normally and go to school! What did he want? To fight monsters and be a hero!"

Darkflare sighed, listening to her cries about her son some more. Glancing back at his allies again, they either shrugged or shook their heads, unsure of what to do either.

"And it's your fault that he's gone!" The woman extended her arm again to point at Darkflare while still sobbing a river of salty waters.

"Listen, please, madam. What exactly happened to him?"

"My son ran away this morning and hasn't come back. And who's to blame? Why you, you ruthless, bloodthirsty, animals! It's your fault he's gone!"

"I'm not quite sure I understand what you mean. We've been at Elder Roper's residence all night, madam…"

"See? It's not their fault…" The husband had finally spoken. He seemed like a rather timid man, and his voice was more high-pitched than Darkflare expected it to be, reminding him of a mouse. "Everything is fine. It's all going to be alrig-…"

The man's head turned from a devastating slap that even made Kenji wince in pain.

"*No!* It's *not* going to be alright! My son is missing! This is your fault! You dragoons! Had you not stayed here, everything would have been fine!"

Darkflare took a deep breath and exhaled. "I understand, I'm sorry. Truly. How can we help? When did he go missing?"

"This morning," the woman had broken into sobbing again, as if the thought of the memory was too painful to deal with. "He went looking for the bandits, saying he was going to chase them down once and for all!"

"We'll find your son," Luna approached and kneeled down next to the woman. "There, there. He can't have gone far. We'll find him."

"You have our word," Darkflare nodded.

She latched onto the husband again, sobbing fiercely. He turned to the dragoons and mouthed a 'thank you'.

* * * * *

"I don't get why it's on us to find this child," Attila said, rolling his eyes.

"Because it's the right thing to do," Luna chided, pointing her finger at him as they walked the trail out of town. "Besides, if he really did follow the Marked Ones, he might bring us straight to them."

"Or maybe we're going on a wild goose chase, distracting us from our main goal."

"Always the optimist." She glared at Attila, who refused to meet her gaze, and then she turned to Darkflare, who shrugged.

"Luna's right. It's the right thing to do. And that's why we're here."

"Right," Luna hesitated. "But, do you think Aunquil is going to be safe? What if the Marked Ones return?"

"They are likely to come through this way, in which case, Aunquil should be alright. But we should prepare for anything."

As they traveled on, Darkflare tried to remember the layout of his maps. Aunquil was founded in the middle of a path between D'sylum and Beauldyn as one of the main crossroads of the two nations. The area between the two nations was surrounded by high cliffs and arid lands, the peaks of the rock formations able to be seen even before they first entered Aunquil.

Darkflare led the group to a stop as the path into the chasm split in two. The right path ascended several feet into the air creating a bridge of sorts, while the left trail sloped downward against the base of the cavern's walls. He couldn't see past the winding walls, but he assumed that the walkways had to reform at the other end. Darkflare figured they would need to cover both, and the quickest way was to split up.

"Alright," Darkflare said as he stroked his chin lightly and considered the best way to proceed. "We're going to have to split into two groups to search the area more thoroughly. If we're lucky, we'll also find some clues on the Marked Ones."

"Right." Kenji nodded, looking over the landscape that lay ahead of them. "Well, I think it's been proven that you, Attila, and Luna work well together; why don't I take Roy with me?"

Darkflare turned to face the others and shrugged.

"That okay with everyone?"

"Perfect," Attila walked forward to stand beside Darkflare.

"Ugh, if I must," Luna walked forward to elbow Darkflare lightly. "Just kidding! Works for me."

Roy nodded and stepped forward to stand with Kenji. "Wherever I'm needed, I'll follow."

"Right," Darkflare turned to Kenji and motioned toward the lower path. "You two take the left route and we'll go above. If you find anything, give some sort of sign. Otherwise, we'll meet back up at the end."

"Gotcha." Kenji flashed his suave smirk and turned to walk the path with Roy. Darkflare nodded to Luna, Attila, and the flying Oboro.

"Let's get going."

* * * * *

Darkflare had worrisome flashbacks from Gilgamesh's mountain as the trail sloped upward. It wasn't as high as the trial's trail, but they were still several feet in the air. The first stretch of land acted as a bridge connecting two broader areas; the first piece of earth that they walked up and then a cliff further away. Because the bridge was so high up, the bottom had actually been tunneled out, allowing those of the lower path to cross underneath.

The path narrowed a little more than Darkflare liked, and one glance back at Luna showed she was particularly uncomfortable.

"Are you alright?"

Her eyes nervously swung to Darkflare's direction, and she gave him a very forced smile.

"Me? I'm fine. Perfectly. So, uh, does this place have a name or anything?"

"It's come to be called Twinfold Gorge, due to the two intertwining paths."

"Ah. Well, as glad as I am that we have Kenji with us, I feel more at ease asking you these things."

"Thank his books," Attila said rather disdainfully.

"Ah, yeah," Luna nodded and tapped the side of her head. "I remember you saying that. You're the reader and Attila's the doer."

"Yeah," Darkflare added rather sheepishly. "I love useless information, what can I say? I'm a seeker of knowledge; I like to be well-versed in a multitude of subjects and know what I'm talking about, rather than just assume."

"And I would rather find out firsthand," Attila grinned rather slyly, as if taking a shot at Darkflare.

"Yes, you, who assumes all the time, and usually makes a jerk out of himself," Darkflare shot a glare toward Attila, who cast it off as if it were nothing.

"So I'm assuming neither of you have been here before?" Luna seemed unfazed by their bickering.

"No, we've never had a chance to go this far from home. Always polishing our techniques or training for the next big tournament." Darkflare looked around as he spoke, taking in the various carvings and ridges in the rock walls. "It's barren, but it's still got its own charm and beauty – it is something different than what I'm used to."

Luna nodded, looking around as well. Twinfold Gorge lay in between two grandiose mountains that seemed to try to kiss the sky, enfolding the valley they were walking in with very little sunlight. The valley itself led in and out of small caverns in the walls, as well as through the tiny passages that lay within the heart of the gorge. The landforms surrounding the area seemed to have a reddish-brown tint to them and colored the passageway in its aura. The lighting made Darkflare feel like dusk was about to fall, when it was really still mid-morning.

"I never knew the world had so much to offer," Luna said rather dreamily as she brushed her hand across the rock wall. "Sights like this make me want to see everything the world has to offer. Everything, everywhere, is so much different than the last place. Even those that seem similar have the biggest differences in their details. It just all amazes me so."

"Yeah, I agree. Reading about a place and seeing pictures helps to know what you're looking at, but actually going out and experiencing it," Darkflare paused, as if seeping in the glory of actually being out of Crescentia and on the road. "It's a whole new, wondrous feeling."

"Whatever. It's just rocks." Attila shrugged, as if their surroundings meant nothing to him.

Darkflare and Luna both sighed.

Just as they were about to cross the middle of the bridge, Darkflare looked down at the other group passing underneath them.

* * * * *

"Man," Roy narrowed his eyes as he looked around, as if trying to look for the smallest, most minute detail in the cavern as they passed underneath and through it, "I don't see anything out of place that even hints at a Marked One. You'd think bloodthirsty demons would leave some sort of trail."

Kenji snorted, nodding. "I agree with you, but they're more intelligent than they may seem. Vicious, brutal, and utterly sadistic, but they seem to share this strange hive mind when together."

"I just hope the kid is okay. At that age, it's not safe to wander away anywhere. It would be horrible if the Marked Ones got to him."

"The Marked Ones have to be expunged by any means." Kenji's voice had turned to ice, and Roy turned to meet his gaze. There was a hardness there, lurking just under his neutral expression. He had sensed it in their conversation when Darkflare wasn't around, but it was plain here, talking about the demons. "The only reason I'm even going along with this farce of a romp is because if the child has actually followed the Marked Ones, we must find out where they are – and utterly destroy them."

"Heh." Roy turned back to examining the walls, finding himself a little uncomfortable with the zeal of his comrade and what must have happened to make him so committed to the Marked Ones' destruction. "So Kenji, is it that you control the void magic, or does that power feed off of a void within you?"

Kenji simply shrugged as they entered another cavern in the wall.

* * * * *

"You know, if I squint really hard," Luna put her hand up to shield her eyes from the sun, as if it could help her see, "I think I can just make out the spires of Peralor."

"What? There's no way." Darkflare tried to mimic her, but what he could see past the gorge's outline was a hazy mess at best.

"Right there? You don't see that tall blur?"

"You're imagining things," Attila said, joining in the squinting.

"Alright, perhaps I am," she relented with a sigh. She had regained most of her cheer and color once they got on the other side of the bridge. "But if this business with the Marked Ones takes us into the Kingdom of Beauldyn, do you think we could visit the capitol, if only just to see the crystalline palace?"

Darkflare whistled through his teeth, thinking of the drawn pictures from his books.

"Peralor's palace. Every piece of art I've seen of it looks absolutely resplendent. I read a history book once that I picked up from one of the merchants in Ceballe that talked about how they managed to form the materials into the castle, dating back generations before Queen Ragwelv." Darkflare paused, trying to hide the glee from his face. "I also have read they have one of the best libraries in the world. I would love to page through the volumes of information stored there. *After* we deal with the Marked Ones, of course."

"Right, but we're holding you to that." Luna walked over to where Oboro flew beside them and put her hand out for him to nuzzle his head in. "Isn't that right, Oboro? You'd love to fly through the wide open fields of Beauldyn, wouldn't you?"

"Traitor," Darkflare muttered under his breath. The wyvern gave him a sheepish glance, moving to him and nuzzling his shoulder.

The path led them through several more caverns and winding passageways. The calm was almost worrisome; no signs of the child, no bizarre symbols of the Marked Ones, and only the very rare dashing away of startled scaly inhabitants. The two groups passed each other several times, exchanging looks to signify their lack of findings.

When they reached the other end of Twinfold Gorge, Attila let out a sigh and crossed his arms over his chest. Kenji and Roy appeared around the corner from the left path, and the latter shrugged apologetically.

Darkflare bit his bottom lip and feared the worst might have happened to the child, but the sound of laughter caught his attention. They all turned to look at a pair that emerged from one of the side paths. The black and purple garb of the ninja, Tessy, nearly choked him with surprise.

"I thought you didn't do jobs for free?"

"See, Jonathan? I told you the other dragoons would be coming this way." There was a tenseness behind Tessy's smile when she turned to Darkflare that worried him; there was a seriousness in her eyes that had not been there before.

"It's you, it's you! It's really you!" The boy was jumping with excitement as he looked at the warriors.

Darkflare couldn't help but smile, despite his worry. He nodded and then kneeled down to the boy. "I'm glad you're safe. Is everything alright?"

His gaze was focused on the boy, but the question was aimed at Tessy. She gave him a single nod. So it wasn't the boy that had concerned her.

"I'm okay, but sir, sir! I think I found where those bad guys live!"

"Did you show Miss Tessy here?"

"Yeah! She said she'd play with me until you got here!"

Darkflare's eyes flashed to Tessy for a moment, concern still on her face, and then he looked back at the boy. "Jonathan, that was a real brave thing you did, and you've helped us a great deal. But you must understand, if something happened to you, your mother would have been so terribly upset – even more than she is right now. And that should be the most important thing to you."

The boy, who couldn't have been any older than nine years old, bowed his head. "I'm sorry. I-I didn't even think about mom. I wrote her a note, and I, and I…"

"It's alright," Darkflare said, patting Jonathan on the arm. "I need you to listen to me though. You know how to get home, right? Back to Aunquil?"

Jonathan nodded.

"Alright, we'll take it from here, but you need to return to your parents and show them you're okay. And promise never to run off on them again, understood?"

"I promise! Thank you, sir! You guys really are heroes!"

As Jonathan ran by, Roy put his hand out for a high-five. Darkflare stood up and faced Tessy.

"So why are you really here?"

"Really, to help him. There's a strong magical presence here that could have killed him."

She stalked back up the trail, and Darkflare motioned for the others as he followed. The path opened up to a wide, well-lit room, but it was a dead end. The only thing of note was a large boulder merged into the wall at the far side. Darkflare cocked an eyebrow as he looked at Tessy. She looked at him incredulously.

"Don't you feel it? Don't you sense the energy pulsating here?"

He looked at the others, but they seemed just as confused. "Kenji, is 'feeling' energy a skill that comes with being a dragoon? Because I'm not feeling anything."

"No," the guardian said, shaking his head. "I've never had any power of the sort."

"What do you mean?" Her brows furrowed and a hand dropped to one of her sais. "How do you not feel it? It's so thick. I thought you said I was a dragoon? If I'm a dragoon, why can't you feel it?!"

Darkflare heard Attila reaching for his sword and put an arm out to stop him. Luna stepped forward.

"Tessy, you need to calm down. We're just trying to figure out what's going on. We're not going to hurt you."

"Uh, we might not," Darkflare turned to see Roy pointing at the other end of the cave. "But that thing might just."

When he looked back, he nearly jumped. The boulder had two yellow eyes staring out from dark depth within it. The ground rumbled and the boulder began to move. It stood on two stony legs, while two giant rocks spun in to form the creature's arms. The rumbling stopped, and the monster, which Darkflare realized with horror was some sort of golem, stood and glared at them.

Darkflare was frozen, unsure if he should try speaking to the golem or draw his sword and take advantage of an opening. The yellow orbs narrowed, and for some reason he couldn't say, Darkflare felt like it was in anger. He turned to the others, slowly.

"Run," he said softly, just under his breath. When the others didn't move, his eyes widened and he screamed it this time. "Run!"

The golem let out an ear-piercing shriek so deafening that Darkflare was afraid his eardrums would pop. Stones started falling around him, and he barreled out behind Kenji. He saw Oboro in the lead, soaring out and dodging falling rocks; he counted the other five heads before him and didn't look back.

They ran until they passed through the narrow passageway and back into the more open area. Darkflare fumbled for his longsword as he motioned for Oboro to go up, onto the higher paths, to wait.

"What the Pale was that thing?!" Luna cried, her bow out and an arrow aimed. All of them had their weapons readied, standing poised to strike.

Darkflare opened his mouth to answer, but the ground shook ferociously again, and he put his arms up to protect himself from another shower of stones. He heard Attila and Roy groan before nearly having the wind knocked out from a large stone bouncing off his chest. He realized, with great thankfulness, that if he had been still wearing the leather, he would have been out. The golem burst out from a wall in the mountain, its arms extended at its sides, and it stalked toward Darkflare.

"Darkflare, back up." It was Kenji, his voice harsh and cold. "That damn thing will not hesitate to destroy you; get back here!"

Darkflare tried to back up slowly, but the enraged monster swung down its outstretched arms toward him. He leapt backward just in enough time to avoid the impact, but as the massive fists hit the ground, Darkflare nearly fell over from the vibration. The force that the boulders of fists created formed two craters, which Darkflare could only guess was not even a fraction of the creature's true power.

"How the Pale did they get something like this?!" Darkflare frantically retreated to where his comrades stood, finally able to withdraw his longsword.

"Beats the Pale out of me," Kenji said, standing next to his ward, "but ready yourself. Here it comes again."

The golem readjusted its body frame to stand straight up, and its eyes focused in on its tightly grouped foes. The rock-beast latched its lanky stone digits into the mountain and, just as if he were picking a pebble off the ground, it ripped free a large boulder.

"Go! Go!" Darkflare turned to see Roy pushing Tessy and Attila in different directions, and he noticed the gash down his forearm the rock must have ripped. "Separate!"

Darkflare, along with Luna and Kenji, ran in different directions before the golem managed to get the massive rock over its head, and he prayed their retreat would confuse the creature. He turned back just enough to see the boulder smash into the ground where they had been, too late. The golem shrieked again, and with ground-trembling footsteps, it began to ferociously search around for its prey.

Darkflare ran until he reached the upper paths once more. He didn't feel safe. Nothing about this situation felt safe as he held tight to the cliff and stared down at the beast stalking below; all the while his heartbeat echoed in his ears. On this crazy journey over the past few days, he somehow had come to term with demons; he had accepted the fact that he could use magic and was heir to this legendary title; but staring face to face with the natural earth, given life in a hulking, monstrous shape, was terrifying.

There was a blur out of the corner of his eyes, and he watched, astonished, as Kenji darted out from one of the caves below. He held the Izayoi low with both hands as he ran at the beast from behind.

"Back to The Pale with you!" Kenji swore as he arced the blade up at the golem.

Darkflare expected to see a clean slice tear through the back of the beast, or at the bare minimum, the sword should have cleaved a chunk of the rock-face off of it. His jaw hung open when the blade did not even cut into the exterior of the bouldering brute. The sword chipped against the stony body, but that was it.

The golem swung around with its massive arms, one massive fist collided with Kenji's body, and at that moment, it did not matter how strong he was or how many battles he had seen – he was still made out of flesh and bone. He was sent flying several feet with a sickening crack and crashed into one of the walls of the twin cliffs with an impact that put a severe dent into the mountain face. The Izayoi slipped from his grip and dropped against the ground with some clamor.

Darkflare leapt up in both fear and anguish as he watched his combat-savvy guardian manipulated as if he were a child's toy. Unsure of what else to do, Darkflare measured the distance and prayed Odin was watching. He leapt down, aiming straight for what he assumed was the head of the monster, and he scrambled to find something to hold on to. The golem came to a complete halt when it realized something was on top of it.

Now on the head of the bewildered rock monster, Darkflare was not sure what he had planned on doing. He had made it pause, but that was not going to be enough. Twirling his sword around with his right hand, he attempted to plunge the Lionheart down into the creature with all of his strength, but the effect was identical to what happened to Kenji. The blade poked the rocks to no effect, despite the blessings that Gilgamesh put upon it. Darkflare had to steady himself after the first stab, as the bounce almost tumbled him off. He tried again and again, hopelessly stabbing into the creature's cranium.

Darkflare knew it was only a matter of time before the golem fought back, but by the time that he had seen the monstrous arm coming up to brush him off, all he could do was bring his right arm up to shield himself from the mighty mountain. The force of the blow was nothing like Darkflare had ever felt before, and his body reacted by going numb, barely holding on to the blade in his hand. There was a gap in his memory from the time the golem hit him to realizing he was soaring through the air. Something in his mind told him when he hit the ground and started rolling, even though he couldn't feel it. He finally felt his right hand empty. Even through his new armor's layered protection, his body still felt the brunt of the blow and it hurt – bad.

Darkflare lay coughing for a few minutes. His body shook and he felt sick once he *could* feel again.

He stretched out his hand in search of the Lionheart as he tried to regain focus on the situation. His hearing returned just in time to react to the thunderous pounding of the golem's feet as it lurched closer upon his position. Darkflare braced for an impact, unable and incapable of trying to dodge another attack, but it never struck. He rolled over and noticed this time it was Attila swinging away at the creature, but it didn't look like he was trying to damage it. For once, the brazen, boldly spirited combatant was trying to lure his foe away instead of fighting a head-on assault.

"Kenji, Darkflare! You both need to get up and get out of the way!"

Attila was trying his best to keep the rock beast's attention on himself, dodging the attacks with the power of his wind rune aiding his speed and defending everything it threw at him. It was only a matter of moments before Tessy and Roy joined him, each swinging away at the beast from different angles.

"I got your back!" Roy nimbly danced in to prod at the golem with both his Hyperion and the Heaven's Cloud, backing off before the foe could react. "Don't get caught up in its attacks!"

"I don't need help!" Attila called back.

"Then keep moving!" Tessy was relentless with her sais as she dove in from another angle. "This thing will smash you into the ground!"

Between the three of them, it seemed the golem was having a hard time picking a target to focus on. It was obvious that their attacks were doing nothing to damage the beast, but Darkflare was thankful they were keeping its attention away from him.

"Darkflare!" Luna fell to her knees in front of him as she helped him to a seated position. She held one hand over him and a pained look crossed her face; Darkflare felt some of his own pain alleviate and sat up straighter. "Are you okay? Careful, it looked like that really hurt."

"Thank you. I'm fine now," he responded, still trying to uncloud his head. The blow was a lot stronger than he was expecting; but then again, he was hit by a creature that stood at least twenty-five feet tall, made out of mountains, and filled with rage. He found the Lionheart near him and picked it up once more. "I need to get back in there."

"You need to wait! You're going to get yourself killed!"

"I can't just let them fight without me!" He turned on her, his anger flaring. "They're the ones that are going to end up dead."

"You'll have to think of a different strategy! Going at it head on isn't going to work!"

Darkflare opened his mouth to respond, but he was nearly forced to his feet by what he saw. The golem had withdrawn its arms, only to fling them outward again. As if they had detached from its body, the appendages whirled around in a circle while the golem stood still, expelling the three dragoons away from its sides. Attila was the first to be hit and was sent flying far down into the path below. Roy managed to dodge the first and brought the Heaven's Cloud up to defend against the other. He was not hit as hard as Attila, but he was sent skidding back against the ground. Tessy had managed to backflip and slink away before the golem could even touch her. The monster began to stomp over to the only visible target.

"Well, that's great." Roy spat on the ground, bringing his swords up again in a cross. "Before you splatter me into the ground, I want you to know that your mother is nothing more than an oversized pebble, and your father was probably manure!"

The golem raised its arm over its head, but before it could act, it dropped them at its side and let out a blood-curdling roar of pain. A black, swirling ball of energy cracked full force into the back of the monster, exploding with such impact that it almost toppled the beast over onto its face. The initial shock of the unexpected attack forced Roy to jump back, probably afraid he was going to be squished. Darkflare could see the visible charred stain on the golem where the magic had eaten away at stone as it whirled around and back up in one motion.

Kenji was on his feet, using the Izayoi in his left hand for support and holding his right arm outstretched from the void blast he had sent at it. A wide smirk laced his face, as if taunting the beast.

The golem raged once more and seemed ready to charge, but it paused. It turned toward Darkflare and Luna instead. Darkflare's eyes widened as he watched the golem change direction and charge faster than before at him.

"Darkflare! *Move!*" Kenji screamed. "Use your rune! Don't just sit there!"

Darkflare looked at a terrified Luna, and he realized he had to do something to save them both. Leaping to his feet, he impaled the Lionheart into the ground in front of him and cursed the lingering pain. Cupping both of his hands in front of his chest, he channeled as much power as the Rune of Courage would allow him to. He figured he did not even have a full minute to cast the spell; the beast was coming quickly, quaking the ground with every terrifying footstep it made.

Before the golem could raise either arm to attack the duo of dragoons, Darkflare thrust both of his arms outward, the crease in between his cupped palms pointed directly at the creature's black hole of a face. The golem came sliding to a stop as the flame surged forth into it. The magical fire exploded into the dark hole that was its face, scorching and burning at whatever lay underneath the bed of rocks. It flailed its boulder arms around madly, roaring in agony as the fire billowed away at its front.

"Luna, to your feet," Darkflare recovered his weapon and put an arm around her to pull her up. "We have to go!"

Before they could put any distance between them, the flailing arm of the golem collided into a towering pillar next to the duo and smashed it with momentous impact. The crazed monster ran in the opposite direction, away from Darkflare and Luna, and back toward Roy. In the wake of its frenzied assault, the slab descended directly down in their direction. Forced to make a split decision, there was not enough time to try and dodge. Letting go of Luna and leaping up into the air, he swung the Lionheart upward with as much power he could muster, connecting directly with the midpoint of the slab. Cleanly as Darkflare rose in the air, the blade cut through the middle, forcing the two ends to fall in different directions and away from where Luna stood.

When he landed, Luna put a steadying hand on his arm, helping him to stand.

"That's one for me," Darkflare said breathlessly.

"Yes, we'll tally the count later!"

Though tired, Darkflare forced himself to continue back toward the group, and his eyes went wide as he watched Roy channel his powers for the first time.

"Smoke rising from the void in the back and flames flickering from the front. It looks like a little bit of ice should help even things out." Holding his left palm up in front of his face, Roy curled the fingers inward and smiled as frost began to delicately kiss the tops of each of his fingertips.

A small ball of ice, no bigger than a dewapple during the ripest of harvest time, flew from Roy's fingertips as he threw his hand out, causing small pieces of frost to line the otherwise barren, rocky floor. Upon making impact with the flailing golem, the ball of ice expanded like a blooming flower across its body. At first, the eyes and face of the creature crystallized, then the icicles spread toward the extremities, until they wrapped around the back, leaving the golem frozen in place.

The silence that followed was even more frightening than before, and Darkflare shivered. The only sound was the crackling and popping of the ice as it continued to hold tight against the once raging beast.

"Well, that will at least hold the thing in place for a few hundred years," Roy said with a grin.

"Hold that thought," Darkflare said, and Roy looked at him. They both turned their attention upward.

Somehow, in the flurry of the magic blasts, Attila had made his way to the upper path; and now that the creature was fully frozen, he leapt from his spot, raising his Crater Buster overhead. A tunnel of air formed itself at the tip of Attila's sword and sharpened to a point that extended out several feet. Right before he hit the ground, he swung the sword down in a mighty arc, and the pointed air current cut straight through the ice, severing the target clean in two. As the air blade dissipated, small bursts tore the ice sculpture apart, scattering the golem into tiny pieces across the gorge.

Pleased with his work, Attila let a grim smile cross his face as he sheathed his sword over his back. Roy stood with his mouth agape, wanting to say something but instead palmed his face. With nothing of the golem left, the four dragoons gathered around Kenji as he recomposed himself. Tessy and Oboro had reappeared sometime during the magic attacks and now stood with Kenji. The wyvern rejoined Darkflare with a nuzzle of his snout and hovered beside his master once more. Roy's arms were crossed over his chest, and he tapped his foot angrily as Attila approached.

"You know… We could have kept him there and let some other unsuspecting group of warriors deal with him in a couple centuries the same way we did, but *no*! You just had to go and completely demolish my frozen work of art."

"Heh," Attila flashed a rare smile at Roy. "It made me mad. I'm feeling much better now."

"And here I thought I was the violent one," Kenji said with a playful look on his face.

Darkflare approached Kenji and looked him up and down, struggling to keep the anger from his face.

"How badly hurt are you? No – you know what, what the Pale got into you that made you think you were untouchable? You yourself said to me that it wouldn't hesitate to kill! Shouldn't you, the all-knowing one, have heeded your own advice?"

"And *here* I thought I was the guardian." He flashed Darkflare an obstinate smile and sheathed the Izayoi, standing of his own free will. "I'm fine, I promise you. It just took me by surprise. Haven't ever fought one of those before. I recognized the beast and heard the tales of its defense, but it's been quite some time since coming up against something my blade couldn't cleave with one slice."

"Well, whatever." He was surprised Kenji showed no obvious sign of injury. Darkflare shook his head and looked to the others. The cut on Roy's arm didn't look too deep. Attila looked in worse condition. There was a wound streaming blood on the side of his head, as well as two on his left arm, and he noticed the limp returning. "Luna, are you okay? Do you think you can use your magic on Attila?"

"I'm fine," he said, staring at them with narrowed eyes.

"I'm alright, but once I heal him I'll need a few minutes to gather myself before I'm ready to continue on."

She walked over to the dark-haired man, and he shied away from her touch. Luna put her hands on her hips and gave Attila an annoyed look before he finally relented and sat down. While Luna worked, Darkflare turned to Tessy.

"Thanks for your help. Attila might have gotten hurt a lot worse if it weren't for you."

"Don't mention it," she said, flipping a curl of hair over her shoulder. "I'll just take it out of my cut."

"Your... cut?" Darkflare cocked an eyebrow at her.

"Of whatever we find at the Marked Ones' fortress, of course. They used to be bandits, right? So what do you think they did with all of their gold and treasures? You get me there, and I'll take whatever Roper owed me and my cut of the remainder."

Darkflare hesitated, but he realized it might be the only way to convince Tessy to work with them. "Fine."

"Hey, if we're talking about cuts," Roy cleared his throat as he stepped in. "I'd like to discuss my pay."

"We'll discuss that after we take care of the Marked Ones," he said, shooting Roy a pointed look.

"Oh, alright. But I'm holding you to that."

"That's two promises!" Luna called from where she was now resting. "I'm counting!"

"Hey, guys," Kenji called from the narrow path. "You might want to come see this."

"Go on," Luna waved. "I'll be right along."

Roy, Tessy, and Attila followed Darkflare as he cautiously walked through the destruction that the golem wrought. The path was wide enough now for them all to walk on, and the cave it had been sheltered in looked larger now that it wasn't there. Then Darkflare noticed the hole.

"You think it leads to their fortress?"

"It's got to." Kenji put his hands on his hips. "Why else have a sleeping golem here?"

Darkflare walked up to the opening and looked in; the passageway continued on for some time. The others came up and Roy whistled through his teeth.

"Well, I'll be. I guess the golem acted as a guard to let the Marked Ones come and go. Not many could take on a creature like that and live if they stumbled upon it – we barely managed to. No telling what else they have at their disposal."

"Then I'm sure that first bellowing scream was an alarm," Attila said as he assumed his usual solemn stance with arms crossed once more. "I'm sure it was loud enough to hear on the other side of wherever this leads."

"Well, only one way to find out," Luna said, walking up to rejoin the group.

"Right. Everyone be on your guard. If they did hear the scream, they're going to know something woke the golem. If we're lucky, they'll just think it killed us." Darkflare nodded toward the path they had just come from. "No turning back now."

Chapter XIII

The six dragoons crept down the secret path, and even though Darkflare was prepared to illuminate the way, there was surprisingly no need. Beyond the first veil of darkness, the rest of the tunnel was lit, albeit dimly, by torches on both sides of the hall. As far down as the dragoons could see in the ambient light, not only was the linear stretch of tunnel that they walked spacious enough for three of them to walk side by side, but the sea of torches never seemed to come to an end.

"What sort of cultist hallway did we stumble upon?" Darkflare muttered, looking around.

There were various designs carved into the lilac-colored stone walls. The etchings were morbid and foreboding, ranging from depicting decapitations with large pointed weapons, to cannibalistic feastings of humans eating their brethren alongside wolves, to men being assaulted by a wall of arrows, to a number of other gory and gruesome visages of death. Despite the pang of terror that dragged its icy tendrils down Darkflare's spine, he could not turn his gaze away. The symbol of Sairephir interspersed in these drawings made it so there was no doubt that these carvings were demonic.

Darkflare stopped short. After having looked at the walls for quite some time, he noticed something different about where they were about to pass in front of.

"What's wrong?" Kenji asked, noticing that Darkflare was studying the carvings rather intently.

"Look... Look at this. This one is very different from the others."

Kenji raised an eyebrow as he bent in to take a closer look at what Darkflare was examining. The crude design on the wall was that of a 'man' grinning with what appeared to be a bow and arrow in his hands. Opposed to the other carvings of archers, this one was turned toward the onlookers while the others were faced sideways. There was also a hole in the wall where the arrow was supposed to be in the bow. Kenji looked back and forth from Darkflare to the design and must have known what he was thinking.

"A trap?"

"It'd be too simple for them to just make this a straight path without obstacles. Besides, that would also explain why these depictions are so… gruesome. I guess they're supposed to represent the fact that no living creature should walk this hall."

"Thalland was always clever, but this seems above even his thinking."

"There's an easy way to handle this," Roy said as he stepped up to stand beside his allies. "Both of you back up, please."

They obeyed as Roy stood solely behind the sights of the design on the wall. Holding out his hand in front of him, his palm glowed light blue as the air around it froze and materialized into icicles. He brought his hand back slightly, balling it into a fist and then thrust it forward, causing shards of ice to fall when he opened his palm.

The particles scattered across the ground until a few of the brick tiles began to sink. A mechanical grinding could be heard throughout the cave as the group braced themselves for whatever was about to happen. In a diagonal stream, four slits opened ahead of them in the wall and arrows shot out from one side of the cavern wall to the other. When they finished, the tiles repositioned themselves. Tessy walked over to one of the arrows and looked at it rather inquisitively. Kenji soon followed and bent to pick one up, but she smacked his hand away.

"Don't. They're poisonous. Not just the tips either; the whole shaft of the arrow has been coated in venom."

Luna bent down beside them to get a better look.

"Yes, these arrows look poorly made, but I can definitely see the coating on them. I don't really know anything about poisons, but they're probably designed with the intent that when the shafts break, they splash the target. Deceitful little things."

Kenji put his hands in his pockets, his face beaming with pride. "Well, it seems I'm out of my element on this one. It seems we all have our areas of expertise."

"It should be safe to move on now." Roy nodded to Darkflare.

"Right," Darkflare said. The dragoons converged around him once more, and Oboro hovered beside his head. "We need to keep an eye on the walls. We nearly missed that one, and who knows what other traps they have. The exit doesn't seem too far, but we can't let that distract us from the dangers at hand."

Their walking pace had slowed down drastically as they carefully tiptoed forward, paying attention to every symbol and detail from the walls to the floor and ceiling. A bead of sweat dripped down from underneath his bandana, trickling down his neck and underneath his armor. It was not out of heat, even though it was fairly warm in the tunnel, but it was more out of the stress of the dynamic situation. He could sense it in the others too, since conversation had halted. The only sounds that reverberated through the tunnel were their unorganized patterns of inhaling and exhaling, their armor and boots clanking with every step they took, and the beating of Oboro's wings.

The demonic carvings on the walls never ceased. Because of how closely he had to look at the details of each one, it wasn't like he could blur them out in his mind. He had to painstakingly analyze every morbid creation. He started thinking it was all part of the Marked Ones' trap; a mental torture in addition to the threat of a physical one.

His thoughts were cut short as he heard the grinding of stone slab once more. He and Kenji had been walking along the sides of the wall while the others had been in the middle of the path; and without any visible warning, the floor dropped open like window shudders under Luna. She yelped and grabbed the ledge behind her with both hands as she dangled over the black pit below.

"No!" Darkflare screamed out the word. He and Kenji could do nothing to help from the side they were standing on, but the others had not crossed over yet.

Attila, Tessy, and Roy had been stunned for a moment, unsure of what had happened. Attila and Roy fell to their knees, reaching for Luna's arms as she dangled on the edge. Tessy dropped to her knees, ready to brace the other two.

"I-I'm slipping!" Luna frantically called, trying to scramble up the edge. "I can't find a foothold!"

"We got you, don't worry," Roy tried to calm her as he and Attila pulled her up. "It's alright, we're here."

Luna sat there for a moment, heavily breathing, refusing to look toward the pit. Finally, she rested her head up against the wall.

"Thank you," she uttered breathlessly. "Any longer and well… I-I don't want to think about it."

Darkflare walked to the edge and peered down cautiously. He could not see much, but far below were the jagged tips of spikes. He gulped and pulled himself back. It was better Luna didn't know.

Tessy rose to look at Darkflare and Kenji, and she shrugged.

"Well, now what?"

"Jump." Kenji shrugged his shoulders back, as if the answer had been blatantly obvious.

"Jump? Are you kidding me?" Luna's eyes shot open and she glared at Kenji. "Do you really think we can make the gap?"

"Well," Darkflare mused, rubbing his chin lightly. "I really don't see any other way for you guys to get over here. We'll catch you as you jump; it's not too far. We did it on the mountain, and you can do it again, Luna. I have faith in you."

She got to her feet, stared over at the pit, and visibly shivered. "If you say so."

Darkflare craned his head to face the small wyvern on his back.

"Oboro, do me a favor; go check ahead and see if it's clear on the other side. The less downtime we have, the better."

The wyvern hissed lightly in his master's ear and then pushed off, flying toward the light at the end of the tunnel. As the sound of his flapping wings faded, Darkflare nodded to the others.

"Attila, get over here so you can help Oboro."

Attila shrugged and took a few steps backward. The metal of his armor clanked methodically as he ran to where Luna nearly met her doom. He leapt over the gap, landing with a thud, without any help from Darkflare or Kenji.

"Too simple."

"Good, then get moving." Darkflare rolled his eyes at Attila's sarcastic grin. He swore for years that Attila's overconfidence would be his downfall.

"My turn then."

Roy took several steps backward to ready himself. His run was slightly more graceful than Attila's but just as effortless. The other two stabilized him as he landed, and even though it was not needed, he nodded his thanks before following the path to meet up with Attila and Oboro.

Tessy looked at Luna and gave her a hesitant smile. "You alright?"

She waved her on but refused to meet Tessy's gaze. "Yeah, I'll be fine. You go on ahead."

Luna hadn't finished talking when Tessy was already jumping across. She sauntered past Darkflare and Kenji without needing a word; she continued on to the others.

Darkflare looked back at Luna. She still hadn't moved. "Luna? You alright?"

"Yep. Yes. I'm coming." She sighed and readied herself. She shook her head to clear her thoughts and began to run. She reached the edge and closed her eyes as she threw herself to the other side. When she landed, she nearly dropped to her knees, but Darkflare and Kenji had a tight grip on her arms and pulled her to a standing position.

"Thanks," she said, not daring to look back. "One more obstacle we've cleared."

"Yeah," Darkflare nodded, hoping she was alright. "Let's catch up with the others. Hopefully we'll be in the clear for a little bit."

* * * * *

Roy, Tessy, and Attila stood at the mouth of the tunnel's exit with Oboro hovering midair by Attila. Once the other three had joined them, Oboro swooped to his partner's side once more. Darkflare nuzzled the wyvern's head with his right palm before turning to look at his surroundings. All around them were rocky, pointed cliffs; no greenery or life could be seen anywhere. Only one thought came to his mind, and Roy spoke it before he could.

"Anyone have an idea where we are?"

"Somewhere deeper in the mountains," Kenji said, looking around puzzled. "I haven't ever been back here. I never even knew that this path existed."

There was only one way to go, and so they continued onward. The road curved and dipped several times, but there were no turn offs to misguide the group. The path they walked was tucked far away from sight, due to the mountain walls that rose high on both sides, concealing them deep within. The only way anyone would know such a trail existed would be if they were to fly overhead or go the way that the group had, through the golem's resting spot.

Darkflare felt his worries slip along with his guard. The atmosphere was more calming now that they were back to fresh air instead of being trapped inside the tomb-like tunnel. Still, he could not help but feel a little anxious. If they were indeed heading toward the Marked Ones' fortress, they were sure to start seeing the demons sooner rather than later, and the serenity would be gone once again.

"You know," Roy broke the silence. He stopped, cupping his hand to the side of his head, as if trying to hear something far off. "If I didn't know better, I'd swear there's water somewhere around us."

Darkflare stopped as well and tried to pick up on the noise Roy had heard. It was faint, but he could hear the sound of rushing water ahead of them.

"That's definitely water."

"It's close." Tessy nodded. Her hazel eyes jolted all over the place, as if trying to pick out the source. Without warning, she began to bolt ahead of the group. "I can feel the energy vividly!"

"Tessy, wait!" Darkflare and the others ran after her, but he still did not understand how she could 'feel the energy.' He figured that since she controlled the power of water she knew where the source was, but it did not explain her comment about the golem earlier. The sound got louder and louder as they chased after the ninja, and at the rate Tessy was moving, Darkflare was worried that the next bend might send them over the edge of a waterfall.

As they turned a corner, they all had to stop themselves from crashing into the person ahead of them. Tessy had halted abruptly, and Darkflare was about to chastise her, but the sight caused him to fall silent. The path had come to an end, and the mountain was spliced again in two. Starting several miles out to their left was a towering waterfall, something that Darkflare had never witnessed and was surprised to see in the mountains. He watched in awe as the water rushed on below, cascading against rocks and flowing down to the stream loudly in the tall canyon walls.

Darkflare approached the only way across, a bridge made of wooden planks that was supported by many hundred strings of rope, and he shook the sides rather roughly, testing its endurance. It did not seem like a trap; it truly seemed like the only way forward.

"You guys have fun. I'll just, uh… wait here." Luna slinked back from the group, trembling slightly. "Moral support. Yup, that's what I'll do to help from here. You guys go get 'em!"

"What?" Darkflare turned around with an incredulous look on his face. "Don't tell me this has you scared. After all we've been through – sneaking through a prison, fighting a giant kraken, bringing someone back from near death, and battling a living rock – height will be your biggest nemesis?"

"Uh, yeah, about that…"

Kenji rolled his eyes and shook his head. "We're going to need you in case any of us get wounded. You have to get over this fear and just cross the bridge."

"If it makes you feel better, I can always carry you in my arms." Roy said as he shrugged.

"Excuse me?" Tessy snarled. "Are you trying to get handsy?"

"Hey, hey! I was joking to cheer her up! She's not my type!" To that, Roy received a sharp look, this time from Luna. "That's not a bad thing! You're a pretty girl, yes, I'll admit it. But I didn't think you *wanted* me to start hitting on you!"

"No, but thank you for the compliment anyway!" she said with a grin.

"Ah, and see! It's already helped your mood. That's the attitude we need you in!"

Darkflare smiled too as the wind brushed by them, swaying his cape behind. His eyes widened and his smile broadened.

"I have an idea. Why don't you hold on to my cape as we cross so you don't feel like you're on your own? You said you wanted to get out and see the world; well this is a part of that. There's no other way across."

Luna looked around at her allies rather nervously and then exhaled deeply. A look of begrudging anxiety overwhelmed her face.

"Fine. You're right. I need to face this head on. If you'd be so kind as to turn around?" Darkflare smiled and handed her the end of the cloth. She rubbed it in her gloved hands, tugging slightly on his back. "Wow, very silky – actually I think it *is* silk!"

"I wish I could agree with you, but being behind me all the time, I haven't ever gotten the opportunity to examine it." Darkflare rubbed his exposed arm on the material and was shocked. "It *is* silk! Impressive!"

The others had already begun to walk across the bridge, and Darkflare made sure to take slow, methodical steps to cater to Luna. Oboro turned his head and stared at the frightened girl as they approached the bridge, as if also trying to help encourage her. Luna took her first step on the planks and seized up when it rocked back and forth, creaking under her footstep.

"Okay... I can do this," she muttered to herself.

Darkflare tried to think of something to get her mind off of the situation. He looked back at the waterfall.

"Hey, Luna, look to the left."

After a few feet onto the bridge, they passed the edge of the gorge that had been otherwise blocking their view of its entirety. Luna smiled as she stared at the wonder that lay before them.

"It really is so beautiful. I've never actually seen a waterfall before."

"I've seen pictures, but again. Doesn't really compare to the real thing. Look at the walls of the canyon; the light from the sun reflecting on the water paints a really pretty scene."

"Yeah! It almost makes me forget about what we're about to step into." She fell silent for a moment. "Almost."

Brandon Rospond

Darkflare nodded. What they were about to step into... He took a moment to consider the severity of the situation. The closer to the center of the demonic activity they came, the more they put their lives in danger. He hadn't even considered what was going to happen when they found this Thalland person. If he really was the one behind the Marked Ones' activity, which all signs seemed to point to, what were they going to do? What was the purpose for all of this unneeded bloodshed he had orchestrated?

What was the purpose of killing Angelus Despil?

No, this would come down to a battle of blood to prevent him from killing any more innocents or oppressing anyone else. Marked One or not, whoever was responsible for this madness had to be stopped.

"You okay?"

"What?" Darkflare looked over his shoulder. "Oh, yeah. Just thinking about the weather is all."

They both looked up at the sky. The clouds had transformed from a white fluffiness to a murky black patch. It was still off in the distance, but by the way they were moving, it would only be a matter of time before the darkness descended upon the group.

"Wow," Luna said. "It looks like it's going to downpour any minute."

"And I can't decide whether that's a good or bad thing."

"What do you mean?" Luna was looking up at the sky, as Darkflare craned his head, and he was glad the smalltalk was working.

"Well, if it rains, it's obviously going to put a damper on our movement, no pun intended. But then again, it might make sneaking in easier. Maybe the darkness will obscure our movements better, or maybe they just won't expect a rain assault."

"Ah, well then, maybe things will work out in our favor for once."

"Now that is asking for too much," Darkflare smirked, his voice laden with sarcasm.

They were just about to the other side. He could not believe that talking about the weather was enough to keep her mind from her fears. He stole another glance at her looking up at the sky and realized that she probably had not gotten to talk to many people since coming back from Tiresek. Another similarity. It was comforting for both of them.

Darkflare stepped off of the wooden bridge and onto solid ground again. Once Luna stepped firm, she held her breath and looked

- 237 -

down. Seeing that she was off the bridge, she exhaled a sigh and dropped Darkflare's cape.

"You alright now?" Darkflare asked, turning to face her.

"Yeah," she met his gaze with a real and radiant smile. "Much better."

"Right. Well then, let's catch up with the others."

Darkflare had begun to take a few steps with Oboro leaping off to fly once more.

"Hey, Darkflare..."

He came to a quick stop, whirling around. Luna turned around to look back at the rope bridge. He raised an eyebrow at her in confusion.

"Yes?"

She turned back to him with confidence on her face.

"I know it may have seemed silly, but... thanks. I appreciate it. And thank you for not making fun of me."

Darkflare returned the smile with one of his own, nodding sincerely. "Anytime. Anything I can do to help, just let me know. That's what friends are for, after all."

"Friends," she said with a nod. "I like the ring of that!"

Their allies had only been a little bit farther ahead of the bridge. The path remained straightforward, but it started to arch upward, forcing the already weary adventurers to take heavier footsteps as they climbed.

"Ugh, who built this road?" Roy complained. "If Thalland's as big as Roper says, I can't see him walking this thing very often."

"Probably another diversion tactic." Tessy spoke as if the incline made no difference to her.

"Do demons even feel like we do?" Attila mused, looking at how worn and beat the path was. "They don't have their humanity, after all."

"True." Roy nodded. "It's just tiring after walking for... How long now? Almost the whole day on a straight path, being flung around by a giant rock-thing, avoiding traps, and now climbing uphill. I'm going to need a nap before we storm the castle."

Roy yawned and stretched his arms in the air to mockingly emphasize his point.

Kenji, in the lead, raised a hand to command silence. The other dragoons stopped; no one moved while they waited for him to say something. Darkflare felt his hand twitching nervously around the handle of the Lionheart.

"We're here," Kenji whispered back to the others. "Cling to the side of the mountain and follow me."

Kenji cautiously walked over to the rock wall and clung tight as he crept to a set of three stone archways. Darkflare wanted to get a better look inward but instead listened to his guardian and led the others in behind him. Kenji knelt beside the base of the stone pillar farthest to the right as he warily poked his head out to get a better look.

"Welcome to Narvile…"

"Narvile?" Darkflare echoed the foreign word, confused.

Kenji pointed toward a wooden sign that was rocking back and forth in the breeze beneath the middle archway. The word 'Narvile' was carved into it very poorly, but Darkflare could just barely make out the letters.

"What's the situation like?"

"Take a look for yourself," Kenji shifted over. "Just be careful not to be seen."

Darkflare crawled over to where Kenji had been and waited a moment before peeping his head around the stone pillar. Security appeared to be stricter than Kailos, as the guards performed tight patrols around the area. Darkflare easily spotted four Marked Ones making their rounds; their paling skin made him shiver. There was one going around the perimeter of the fortress, two going up and down through the middle, and one seemed to be scanning the alleyways. Who knew how many more were lurking further than they could see?

The fort was better constructed than Darkflare had imagined. The streets were lined for miles with intricately designed and patterned two-story buildings. Most of them had to be barracks, but they were fancier than most of the homes in Ceballe's residential district! It was obvious that Thalland had put all of the gold he pillaged to use. The streets in between the barracks were broad, but none were as wide as the path through the middle of the town, which was a suicide route for the dragoons.

A looming pyramid-like structure caught his eye, and he wasn't sure how he nearly missed the monstrosity at the other end of Narvile. It stood out and up above the other architectural designs, as if representing the pinnacle and the heart of the stronghold.

"I'm assuming the giant golden building in the back is his?"

"One can only assume so," Kenji replied, keeping his voice low.

"So, what's the plan?" Darkflare recoiled his head as he and Kenji turned to look at Luna. "How are we getting in?"

"How do you think?" Kenji raised an eyebrow at her, as if she had asked for an obvious answer.

Attila smirked grimly and cracked his knuckles. "I like where this is going."

"Sorry." Kenji shook his head to dismiss Attila's happy thoughts. "I didn't mean it like that. I meant that we can't just go up and ask them to lend us safe passage through to their leader. We're going to have to sneak in."

Attila let the smile vanish and crossed his arms once more, visibly saddened by the decision.

"Probably for the best," Roy whispered, doing his best to look around the pillar as well. "Who knows what other traps that they might have in store or if there are any other golems looming around?"

"There are more."

Darkflare turned to look at Tessy. She had a far-off look in her eyes as she stared up at the bleak, gray clouds, as if trying to hone in on their magical presence.

"There is more than one here. I'm not sure how many, but the magic is thicker than in the gorge, which means there are more than just one of them."

Kenji narrowed his eyes into a cold stare, keeping them locked on her for a prolonged few moments. When no further elaboration was given, he shook his head. "We need to sneak in there quickly and quietly, especially if there are golems. Once the next guard passes by, we'll try to rush across toward the gap between the first set of barracks on the right and on through the alley until we get to the keep."

The group gave a unanimous nod. It was the safest route and the one that made the most sense. Darkflare knew if they were seen, this whole journey would be for naught. If Thalland was alerted to their presence, who knew what sort of army the "bandit king" had to throw at them; after all, they were in the heart of one of the Marked Ones' fortresses.

After a few moments, Kenji very slowly peered out beyond the stone pillar to check on the sentry's position. Darkflare, very cautiously, followed his lead. The patrolman was just crossing the middle of the town and would pass around the corner of the farthest left barrack in a few seconds. As for the ones in the middle, they were of no concern if they made a quick breakaway for the right. Kenji kept his eye fixated on the man's position, watching and waiting like a snake, poised to strike.

Darkflare felt his arms and legs stiffen as he anxiously anticipated the moment to make a dash across the courtyard. The waiting seemed to make time go by even slower. If Darkflare wasn't watching him, he would have sworn the demon had stopped to sniff the fresh mountain air and pick some wild flowers before continuing on its route.

Kenji's hand raised and his body flexed. The sentry was turning, and Darkflare readied. A moment later, Kenji ran like lightning out into the open, and that was all Darkflare needed. He had not even thought about it; his legs simply took off running on their own, as if spurred on by an uncontrollable impulse.

Darkflare did his best to keep the armor from clanking under his swift movements, but it was rather difficult. The distance between the stone pillars and the closest alleyway was at least thirty to forty feet that they were running in clear sight, but they could make it without being seen, before the next guard came, if they hustled fast enough. Darkflare did not bother to turn back to check if his comrades were following; he could at least hear the light beating of Oboro's wings as the wyvern followed behind. The shade of the alleyway was so close, but it felt like the distance stretched infinitely.

Kenji slowed down as he reached the side of the barrack wall; Darkflare was right on his heels and skidded into cover. He made sure to move in enough for the others to be fully out of sight as they came in one after the other. He was not breathing loudly, but he felt his heart pounding and took a few steadied breaths to calm down. Roy was the last one in and cautiously watched their flank, making sure they had not been spotted. Now that they were hidden once again, Darkflare sighed and hoped to have a moment's reprieve.

"Not good," Attila murmured, causing Darkflare to look around.

They could not have possibly seen it from the entrance of the town, but it turned out that all four sides of the barracks had doorways. If they remained in one spot for too long, it would only be a matter of time before a Marked One left the building and spotted them. They needed to keep moving.

Darkflare took the initiative to lead the way this time, as he seemed to notice the danger before Kenji had. Sneaking over to the edge of the building, he careened his head out to the left. The next set of barracks would only take a few seconds to run across, but he wanted to be safe. The two middle guards were nowhere to be seen, but a different, unaccounted for guard was patrolling the corridor on the left side of the barracks. Darkflare slunk back into cover before he was spotted.

"We need to hurry." Darkflare turned quickly to the others, filling his voice with as much steel as he could. "There's a guard across the way that's patrolling the barracks on the left. We need to get across before he circles around to us."

The others nodded, except for Kenji. Darkflare noticed the wide grin that swept across the face of his guardian, but he didn't have the time to dwell on it. It almost seemed like Kenji *wanted* him to lead.

Darkflare peered around the corner once more and was relieved to see the sentry was looking the opposite way. Darkflare pushed off from his position and dashed across the street to the next corridor. Oboro and the other dragoons swarmed behind him in one shadowed blur, sharing in Darkflare's newfound drive. It was only a few seconds that they had been exposed, but if someone had caught even the slightest glimpse of any of their noticeable features - Kenji's white jacket, the winged Oboro, Roy's silver hair, the green or blue of Luna and Darkflare's attires - it would not have mattered how quick the others were.

Two down; but how many more to go? His mind drifted to think of what would happen once they reached Thalland, and so many more thoughts and questions danced around in Darkflare's head as he crept up to the next corner.

It was all because of the dreams; because of Graymahl Vulorst. That was why he was so determined. He needed to find out if Thalland had some connection between the Marked Ones, the master of the Runes of Torment, and his dreams.

"*Darkflare!*" The whisper hissed out behind him, stopping him in his tracks, and forcing him to turn around. He looked back at Tessy and her hand was on her head, as if suffering from a massive headache. "It's here…"

His heart dropped as he saw the mass of rocks piled against the wall of the barracks on their right hand side. He instinctively reached for the handle of the Lionheart, even though his brain screamed at him that it would be of no use.

The rocks began to resonate and move, shaking the ground, and coming to life. Darkflare was too paralyzed with fear to do anything as he watched the golem begin to form itself into a standing position, like they had seen earlier. It began to take a more physical shape with arms, legs, and two glowing eyes deep within the cavity of its chest.

"Darkflare, move." Kenji's voice was imperative, but Darkflare could not budge to take his eyes off of the creature that towered over the dragoons. Darkflare knew what was coming next and withdrew the Lionheart to point with it to the door of the barracks to the left.

"Go, quick!"

"What?!" Luna cried out, staring at him incredulously.

"Trust me, and *go!*"

The golem raised its right arm and then swung it around in a circular motion toward Darkflare. He had been ready for the attack, but there was not much room to maneuver. As the massive fist of rock came arching around to him, he tucked his body weight low and rolled down the length of the building. He was able to dodge the crushing impact, but not without slamming his body against the wall.

The result of the attack left a devastating hole in the barrack on their right, and having missed its target, the golem shrieked the same high-pitched whine that the last had done, clearly in an effort to alert the Marked Ones.

Roy and Attila helped Darkflare to his feet as Kenji swung the door of the other barrack open, leading Tessy, Oboro, and Luna inside.

"Are you okay?" Darkflare could barely hear Roy's voice in the midst of the panic as he hurried to help him stand.

"Yeah," he lied as the pain surged across his back, "let's get out of here!"

Darkflare hurried the other two into the building the others went in, leaving the golem to shriek in a fit of rage alone.

Sirens began to echo throughout the fortress as the worst thing that could have happened, happened, for the six warriors and their winged companion. Darkflare knew they only had moments before the golem would give them chase, but before they could discuss what to do, the Marked Ones in the building they had intruded on noticed them.

"Uh oh," Tessy gaped at the enemies that began to approach with drawn weapons. In a heartbeat, she donned her ninja hood once again. "So much for stealth."

"Looks like we get to do it your way after all, Attila," Kenji growled under a rather dark expression, readying the Izayoi.

"Just the way I like it," Attila said, drawing his own sword. "The odds stacked against us."

Because the room was so small, Kenji and Attila together rushed the center and attacked in wide swings to keep their opponents on the defensive.

Darkflare managed three steps toward them before another impact behind them nearly knocked him off his feet. The golem's fist exploded through the wall and peppered the dragoons with debris.

Luna steadied Darkflare as he almost toppled over her, but before either could say anything to the other, Roy ran to them. He skidded to a stop beside them and threw his hand out hard toward the rock beast, and with it, a wintry white orb flew from his palm. The ball of diamonds collided with the golem's outstretched arm, freezing it up to the elbow, which caused the golem to shriek once again. The creature went into a raged frenzy, thrashing about madly as it tried to unfreeze its limb.

"Now, before it regains focus!"

The trio wasted no time in letting the golem thaw and fled to their allies. Kenji and Attila had just finished their combat and led the others through the northern exit. Once Darkflare was beside Kenji again, he could see why. The dining hall lay directly northwest of where they were, and the dragoons could see a force of Marked Ones gathered around there.

"They're rallying," Kenji muttered under gritted teeth.

"I can sense more golems," Tessy added, rather worried as she hugged her twin sais against her chest.

"Then we need to stay out of the open and get indoors again," Darkflare said as he ran across the street to the next barrack. The Marked Ones could not spot them from inside, and the golem had still been too distracted to pay attention. Once the others had all entered, Attila shut the door behind them.

"Sounds like they're all cleared out of this one," Darkflare said as he listened carefully for footsteps.

"Can we do anything about the doors?" Luna asked, frantically beginning to look around.

"There," Kenji pointed to the corner of the room where four large metal bars were propped. "We can barricade the doorframes with those. It won't stop the golem, but it'll keep the others out."

Kenji, Luna, Darkflare, and Attila each grabbed one of the metal slabs and brought them over to the doors, sliding them in snugly to the latches that they belonged to.

The six humans gathered in the center of the room once more and exchanged worried looks. Darkflare's mind raced with what they could do, but everything he thought of seemed hopeless at this point. Even if they were dragoons, half of them were still too inexperienced to tackle both a golem and a magnitude of Marked Ones and expect to win. He heard the clawing of paws and looked toward where Oboro was perched on a stairwell, looking inquisitively back at his master.

"How many levels do these places have?"

"Your guess is as good as mine," Kenji responded and shrugged.

Attila, being the closest to the stairs, craned his head back to look up.

"One more floor up and then seems to lead to the roof."

Darkflare's eyes widened as he snapped his fingers.

"The roof - thank you, Oboro! These buildings are closer together than the ones we were dealing with when we first came into Narvile. I'm sure we could leap across a few to get us closer."

"And what about the Marked Ones?" Roy asked, cautiously looking outside the window.

"Get their attention."

"What?!" Roy exclaimed as he turned back.

"If they think we're still in here, they won't be looking above."

"Brilliant," Kenji smiled. "They'll be busy fiddling with the doors until the golems can open them, and by that time, we're already gone."

"Yeah, but we need to act fast."

Hearing Darkflare's plan, Roy opened the window ever so slightly.

"Hey, armorilla brains! Yoohoo! It's us - you know, the dragoons! We're in the barrack over here!"

There was an awkward pause for a moment, but Roy's shout did exactly what Darkflare hoped it would do. He heard a chorus of angry snarls followed by the Marked Ones pressing up against the doors and shaking them vigorously. At first, the warriors were not so sure the metal bars were going to hold up and braced themselves for the enemies to come thrashing through. After realizing that they were momentarily safe, Darkflare nodded to the others.

"To the roof."

Oboro leapt up to follow his master as Darkflare bounded the spiral metal steps, taking two at a time. He threw open the steel door at the top, expecting to be greeted with the familiar glare of light, but the sun was gone; the clouds had all but devoured the sky as thunder bellowed.

Darkflare walked across the rooftop and was overjoyed to see that the buildings were indeed close enough to each other that they could vault them with ease – even Luna and Attila, what with her fear and his tender ankle, shouldn't have a problem. They just needed to hurry before the other golems had been called to awaken. Without giving it another thought, Darkflare took off running, letting adrenaline do the thinking, and once he reached the edge of the rooftop, he leapt and crossed effortlessly.

One by one, the other dragoons leapt across behind him. Oboro hovered between buildings and was ready to help them across if need be, but he flew back to Darkflare's side when they reached the fourth building. Darkflare looked around at their surroundings once they were back together.

"If we get down to the bottom again and run through the alleys, we should be safe; we just need to stay to the right as much as we can."

The wailing from several creatures rang out throughout the mountaintop as Darkflare finished speaking. They all knew the cries well enough by now; the other golems had awoken. Darkflare took a deep breath to calm his anxiety and then kicked open the door, and together, they descended the steps.

The dragoons rushed out the back of the barrack and continued on in silence; they were spurred on by their ambition and drive to succeed. Darkflare led them through the alleyways, running as fast as he could; he completely lost track of where he was going. Left, right, right, left, straight, right, left... The turns just all seemed to blend together as he was forced to keep running. He could hear the destruction of the barrack they had blockaded as the golems forced their way in. They had enough trouble dealing with just one golem... What would they do if they had to face several at once?

Making one final right turn, Darkflare came to a short stop. Luna grabbed his back, almost collided into him because of how suddenly he halted.

"What?" she said, nearly panting. "What are we stopping for?"

"We're here."

The others stood beside the King of Dragoons as they looked at what he was staring at. In front of them lay an ascension of red brick stairs that led up to the golden pyramid-like palace that they could only assume belonged to Thalland Faleenwar.

"We're here," Luna repeated, swallowing hard.

Darkflare looked back to make sure that the Marked Ones were still distracted with the remains of the locked barrack. It would only hold their interest for a few minutes more.

It was now or never.

Chapter XIV

Darkflare's footsteps mirrored his pulsing heartbeat as he ran with the others up the flights of brick stairs, hurried by the sound of destruction behind them. His resolve was as strong as the tightened grip around the Lionheart. There was no way but forward.

He paused as he reached the top; the entrance to the palace was wide open. There were no doors, nothing hindered their progress forward. Darkflare was worried that perhaps there were Marked Ones inside, expecting them and luring them into a trap. Within those few moments of pause, he also noticed just how grandiose the palace was up close. Thalland had gone out of his way to make sure that this building stood out above the others with its golden columns and illustrious carvings. They crept in to the brightly lit hall and looked cautiously around for any surprises or traps that might be waiting for them.

"Be on your guard."

Kenji's warning was unnecessary, as all six warriors already had their weapons drawn. Oboro was ready as well, as he bore his teeth in a snarl, hovering beside his master. The silence, broken only by their movements, made Darkflare's anxiety spike, but he smiled inwardly. The dream he and Attila once shared about becoming knights felt like a fleeting fantasy; standing inside of the building that housed one of the biggest villains of their time, one that had even fought with his parents, was something he never imagined he would be doing.

The inside was just as grandiose as Darkflare was expecting it to be, and there was another flight of stairs to ascend. This one's steps were thinner and made of a finer material that shined under the light; marble was the first guess Darkflare had as to the component. The passage at the top of the stairs was closed off by two large red doors with many golden buttons lining the face.

Thalland had to be beyond that door.

"There they are!" A voice interlaced with the two tones of a Marked One called out, echoed by a cacophony of snarls.

There were more enemies than Darkflare could count; they came from the two hallways on either side of the red door, as well as two at the base of the stairs.

"Here they come!" Darkflare took a quick steadying breath; as long as the golems did not make an appearance in this fight, they still had a chance. "Attila and Kenji, take the halls down here. Luna and Tessy, try to get that doorway shut any way you can – Oboro, help them out! Roy, with me to the top; you take right and I'll take the left."

"Right!" The group called out in unison. Darkflare and Roy wasted no time in fighting their way up the marble staircase as Kenji and Attila disappeared just as quickly underneath them. The Marked Ones surged with such a frenzy, undaunted when the dragoons separated to take them on.

Darkflare had picked Roy for a reason, as the duo bounded up the stairs, ducking and spinning past the jagged blades of the Marked Ones who attempted to meet them halfway. He saw Roy parry the swings he could not dodge, both swords working as if they were an extension of his arms, and Darkflare tried his best to emulate him. He felt a blade whoosh too close to his head, and his free hand snapped out in reflex to knock the attacker back.

The duo stood proud at the top of the stairs, the advantage of the high ground now in their favor as they stared down at their opponents.

"Show them no mercy!" Roy called as he held both blades across his body.

Darkflare gritted his teeth and tightened his hold on the Lionheart as the Marched Ones lunged forward again. Heat tingled in his fingertips and fire licked its way up his blade. He would avenge the fallen.

* * * * *

Luna searched the frame of the doorway to somehow find a means of closing it. She could not help but keep stealing glances back toward the others; the sooner they found a way to protect their flank, the sooner she could get back in the fight. Tessy did not seem to have much better luck on the far side, and Oboro scanned high above what they could see.

"There's got to be some way to barricade this opening." Luna smoothed her hands against the wall in hopes of finding a hidden panel. "Hopefully you find something up there, Oboro. After all the traps that we went through, they wouldn't be so careless as to just not set up some form of self-defense."

"Like a switch?" Tessy called to her.

"Yeah! Or a handle, or a button combination, or, or… something! I don't know. But there's got to be *something*! What kind of a castle doesn't have a way to seal its main entrance?"

"You said a handle?"

"Yes, maybe!" Luna called as she started slamming her hand on certain pieces of stone that were textured different. "Thalland was one of the smarter bandits, right? He must have figured the army would find him someday, and..."

Before she could finish rambling, Luna was startled back. A giant metal shutter noisily clattered down and sealed the open doorframe. Luna whipped her head toward Tessy, who had her hand precariously on a lever in a hidden stone.

"I think I found the handle," she said with a big grin.

"Good going!" Luna yelled excitedly, swinging the Elyria forward and notching an arrow in one fluid motion. She took aim at the mob on the stairs and fired at one of the Marked Ones as it was about to swing on Darkflare. It poofed in a crackle of shadow; that was another one he owed her.

The back of the group of Marked Ones turned and finally noticed Luna and Tessy. Luna drew her bow back to fire another shot, but three small pointed objects flew from the side and punctured the throats of the demons, slaying them instantly. Tessy ran from beside Luna, leapt into the fray, and drove her sais into the side of two more Marked Ones' heads.

Oboro came down and cooed by Luna.

"You might be better off up in the air!" She loosed another arrow at a Marked One turning to Tessy. When it did not slay the creature, she shot another, and then another, until it finally fell and disappeared.

* * * * *

Even though they were at opposite ends of the hallway, Attila tried to keep track of how many Marked Ones Kenji defeated. He had noticed the fervor that Kenji worked up whenever he dealt with the demons, and it gave Attila the perfect challenge of trying to keep up with him. He was trying not to tap into the power of wind to propel him forward. If he drained his stamina too soon, it wouldn't matter how many demons he took down.

He swung his blade around in wide swaths; it succeeded in keeping his foes at bay, and he took advantage of that by keeping the intensity up and forcing them on the defensive. Some of the Marked Ones failed to evade the massive blade and found themselves felled by it.

Attila groaned as something stabbed at his armor; it deflected most of the damage, but it still startled him. He swung an elbow to fight back, but the Marked One leapt back and away. Attila heaved the Crater Buster up to keep the foe back, but the blade that struck him this time pierced the same spot the first had, and it had found skin.

Attila nearly fell to one knee, but he fought back, swinging back around once more. Before he knew it, *he* was the one on the defense, struggling to keep the attacks of the three, now four, Marked Ones back. He fought through the pain, but it was not making it easy to move the heavy weapon.

When he thought the end would close in at any moment, a bolt of black seized two of the enemies, causing the third to turn. Kenji came up and sliced that one down the chest with a clean cut. Attila took advantage and shoulder tackled the last one, creating an opening for his blade that felled it.

He heard footsteps and raised his blade, his face snarling ravenously, but Kenji held a hand up as he approached.

"What are you doing? You can't be so reckless!"

"I'm fine," Attila grunted, looking toward the next wave of enemies.

"You need to get healed by Luna. Why did you think you could keep up-…"

"I'm *fine!*" Attila roared as he rushed at the oncoming foes. He jumped into the air and slammed his blade down in the middle of the group. He felt the surge of a storm brewing within, and as the Crater Buster pierced the ground with a thunderous rumble, he felt a trickle on his shoulder that caused the wind around him to whip feverishly. The demons were thrown back with such intense pressure that they vanished to smoke as soon as they impacted the wall.

Attila almost fell to one knee, but Kenji grabbed his arm to support him.

"You're a damn fool."

"Maybe," Attila said with a weak grin, "but those last few put my numbers over yours."

* * * * *

Darkflare and Roy fought vigorously against the Marked Ones, the high ground helping them to keep their opponents at bay, but they forced their way to equal footing quicker than Darkflare would have liked.

Parrying another attack that came too close with a chime of clashing steel, Darkflare found himself nearly back to back with Roy. He kept having to move his blade quicker to parry, making it near impossible to find an opening to strike back.

"Roy!" Darkflare called over his shoulder. "We have to turn the tide!"

"Switch off!"

"What?!" Darkflare almost fell backward from defending against the latest blow. The demon on the other side was foaming at the mouth, his fangs draped in spittle.

"Light my side up and I'll cool yours down! Got it?!"

"A-Alright!"

Darkflare prayed that Roy's gamble would pay off as he deadlocked with his opponent. Sure that he would not flinch, Darkflare kicked with as much force as he could, sending his opponent stumbling backward. In unison, both dragoons stabbed their weapons into the tile. Darkflare dropped to one knee and cupped his hands tightly together, following it up by swinging to face the opposite direction. As Darkflare turned to Roy's group, his ally did the exact mirror of his movement, but he stood instead of kneeling.

Darkflare threw his hands forward, and a small ruby sphere of light burst forth from his clenched palms, looking as if he threw a ripe, red dewapple at his foes. Upon impacting the chest of the first demon it touched, it was as if the small red orb changed shapes from a distinct sphere to a shapeless bubble that ruptured after prickling against a sharp blade of grass. The sphere of crimson caused a sea of flames to explode and wash over the upper floor of the balcony, reducing the Marked Ones to smoldering ash as it burned them back to The Pale.

Roy's ball of ice had a similar destructive effect as it exploded on the left side. The small sapphire orb froze the side of the hallway and everything that stood on the ground upon impact. As if the harshest winter's breeze from Purcille had swept in through the doorway, the ball of ice molded the demons and the floor tile into one. The diamond-freeze covered all on Roy's side and made it look as if the floor had belonged to a master sculptor who had just finished carving models out of a reflective cerulean jewel.

Darkflare and Roy exchanged exasperated looks.

"Well done!" Roy roared as he recovered his sword and then patted Darkflare enthusiastically on the shoulder. "That was perfectly executed!"

"Thanks," Darkflare said, his voice weak as he grabbed a handrail to steady himself. "That's the most power I've used. I feel a bit lightheaded."

Realizing that the rest of the hall had fallen silent, Darkflare leaned over the railing as he waited for the others. Attila limped up the stairs with a look that mingled fury with some strange satisfaction. Luna's hands were still glowing with magic, presumably just having healed Attila, and she led Kenji and Tessy behind her. Oboro returned to his usual place by his master's side with smoke trailing from his nostrils.

"Is everyone okay?"

"Mostly," Kenji shot Attila an annoyed look. "As long as no one else gets cocky, we should be fine. And you?"

"We're good," Darkflare eyed Roy, who gave a nod. He then turned, inhaling one more deep breath, and looked at the red door. "Thalland."

He walked forward and let his fingers trace the feel of the gold buttons; designs that had been crafted from blood money, built on fortunes pillaged from honest people.

No more.

Darkflare shoved the doors open, and at the opposite end of the room filled entirely with gold from floor to ceiling, wall to wall, was an obese man sat on a gilded throne. The black-armored fighter impatiently tapped his foot, rattling the rusted chains and grotesque spikes across the breastplate. One hand held a massive battle-axe that stood on the ground by its double-sided head. Darkflare followed the long, disgusting gray beard up to a snarling face; a black eyepatch over one eye and a look of disgust in the other.

"Well, well," the man bellowed out in a growling, deep voice. "Took you long enough to get here. I didn't think a few sniveling bandits would be much effort for someone proclaiming to have the last name of Omni. You *are* the son of those self-righteous ashes that were once Calistron and Sylphe, aren't ya?"

Darkflare gritted his teeth, and he felt like he couldn't be holding the Lionheart any tighter than in that moment. He felt Luna's hand on his shoulder to restrain him, likely knowing his urge to dive sword-first at the fat oaf.

"Oh? Touched a soft spot did I?"

"Don't you *dare* insult my parents! You have no right to speak ill of anyone! You, who summons demons from the depths of The Pale to do his bidding!"

The snarl turned into a devious smile on Thalland's face. "Demons? Yeah, I guess that's one word for them. But I'll tell ya, I've never been to The Pale before!" Thalland craned his neck, exposing the symbol that made Darkflare's stomach drop. He feared it would come down to this, but he had hoped otherwise. "We prefer the term, 'Marked Ones.' If only your parents were here so I could see the look on their faces, but – oh, right. They're *dead*."

Darkflare fought to keep the sword from trembling in his hand, the rage threatened to consume all rational thought. "I swear that I will send you to meet the devil that you so worship – for my parents and all that your accursed Marked Ones have slain!"

"Ah, I think not. As much fun as it would be to mount your head over my throne, I have more pressing matters to attend to."

Thalland struggled to rise, but once on his feet, he swung the axe over his shoulder and snapped his fingers, causing shapes to materialize from the shadows. The beings that appeared behind him were clad in full suits of heavy armor and wielded more durable weapons than the other Marked Ones. There was no seeing the faces behind the helmets, and that gave them an even more sinister look.

"These men," Thalland gestured with a wide swing as he walked by them, "will make sure that this will be your final resting place, in my absence." He nodded to the armored figures and ran past a silken cloth behind his throne. "Toodles, lads!"

"Coward!" Darkflare cried, furiously cutting the air with his sword.

"We'll handle them!" Kenji stepped forward, as if to challenge the bodyguards. "Go and chase Thalland."

"Yeah, leave this to us." Roy rolled his neck in a circle and held the Hyperion and Muramasa low, ready to strike.

"Finally," Attila grinned wickedly, wielding the Crater Buster before him. "Some real competition. Bring it!"

"We'll show them what we dragoons can do!" Luna unfolded the Elyria and prepared her chained swords instead of the bow form.

"No one is standing between me and this loot room!" Tessy said, donning her hood with her sais at the ready.

Oboro growled, nudging his master onward.

After the unanimous decision to buy their ally some time, the dragoons rushed Thalland's bodyguards in an intense clash of steel. Attila and Kenji took on two each, while Tessy and Roy each took on their own. Luna stood removed and fought her own with some aerial aid from Oboro.

Darkflare ran through the melee, past a swing from one of the guards battling Attila, behind the throne, and through the passageway. Thalland might have had a head start, but it didn't take long for Darkflare to close the distance.

"*Thalland!* Get back here, you craven!"

Darkflare heard the bandit grunt. Thalland did not stop running as he stole a backward glance. "Tch, underestimated ya, kid. Oh well."

Thalland knocked over everything he passed to try and barricade the path, and Darkflare assumed the oaf had prepared the passage in case of this exact situation. He had to slink around empty bookcases, skirt around tables, and leap past chairs that were all conveniently placed. One barrel that was knocked over contained many small, silver, spiked balls that spread out as they rolled all over the floor. Having had experience bounding large gaps recently, Darkflare leapt over the hazardous floor, and his pace only slackened briefly.

Thalland continued to knock detailed busts of his own image, suits of elegantly royal plated armor, and whatever else he passed with no pause to his run. No matter what Thalland threw at Darkflare, he pressed forward. Thalland proved that he was one of the Marked Ones. He had to be stopped. Everything that happened, everyone that had died, it was all because of him. This is what Darkflare's rune was trying to prepare him for, and he felt it pulsing within him, he saw the red glow coming from his chest.

"I'm getting sick of you, boy!"

Thalland passed a table bearing an elaborately lit candlestick holder and spilled it with one shove. The candles fell onto the floor, igniting the silken tablecloth that tumbled on top of it in a wild trail of fire. Darkflare was not even fazed by the blaze that blew up right in front of his face; his Rune of Courage was burning into him brighter and stronger than ever yet. As he reached the flames, they parted around him, as if making way for the master of their element; not daring to scorch or burn his flesh.

Darkflare had to stop for a minute and make sure he was okay. He stood in shock as he realized he ran straight through the blaze. His eyes narrowed and he regained focus; Thalland.

The bandit king paused at the top of a stairwell that must have led to the roof. He seemed astonished that Darkflare had managed to still follow.

"You just don't give up, do ya?"

Darkflare wheeled around the staircase, haunting Thalland's tracks as he stalked him up and outside. There was nowhere left to flee – he had Thalland trapped. The Marked One hustled to the center of the roof and slowed to a stop, turning angrily to face the man in the blue armor that had been tracking him like a rabid hound. The ominous black clouds had engulfed the entire skyline while they had been inside, and the smell of rain was pungent. Thunder crackled in the distance.

"Do you really wanna do this, boy? Do you even know who you're about to tangle with? Do you know the pure *strength* that I possess?!"

"This is your last chance to come peacefully." Darkflare remained collected as he slowed his breathing. "It doesn't have to end like this."

Thalland's snarl faded as he burst out into laughter.

"GWA HA HAHAHAHAHA! Boy, I've crushed ants bigger than you with me small finger! Come peacefully? The only peace I know is the type that hides and takes sanctuary in the sound of death, destruction, and chaos! Tell me, why should that brat Nim, or that spoiled witch Faïne, get all the riches? What authority do they have? They know nothing! They haven't seen the horror of war the likes of me and me men have! Taking what we need and shedding blood of any that question us – that's the bandit's way of peace." Thalland's snarl returned after a scoff. His great axe was slung over his shoulder once more. "And that's what happened when I took the mark of the devil, Sairephir himself. I got more power than I could have ever hoped to have on me own. Now, tell me, boy," his voice distorted to take on that dual tone of the Marked Ones. "Do you really think you have what it takes to put me down?!"

"I'm no *boy*. My name is Darkflare Omni, and I am the King of Dragoons!" Darkflare swung his sword horizontally, as if to show that he was accepting Thalland's challenge. "I am the son of Calistron and Sylphe Omni - warriors that put you down once, and martyrs that sacrificed their lives to bring peace to this world; peace that you shattered. I refuse to let you keep bringing more Marked Ones into this world! You *will* answer for your crimes!"

Thalland smirked smugly, spinning his large war axe in front of him with both hands before commanding an offensive stance.

"Heh. Show me whatcha got, boy-king."

Like the bolt of lightning that rip-roared suddenly overhead, Darkflare charged at Thalland, letting out a cry of anger as his feet swiftly tore across the roof of the palace. The sinister clouds followed the bolt with a bellow of thunder as the Lionheart collided against the body of the war axe that Thalland raised to block. The collision of their weaponry sent heated sparks flying through the air as they entered a stalwart deadlock.

With their weapons pressed tightly against one another, Darkflare glared into Thalland's repulsive face and realized for the first time just how hideous and unsanitary the portly bandit was, noting chunks of food particles still left in his beard. Thalland forced the upper hand by using the strength within his larger body to push Darkflare off, sending the dragoon staggering backward.

Thalland was on him immediately; Darkflare barely had time to react when he saw the hefty axe being raised high in the air. He braced himself by thrusting his left foot hard against the ground, grasped the handle of the Lionheart with one hand, and rested the other end in the palm of his gauntlet. He raised the blessed sword over his head in an effort to deter the incoming intense force.

The momentum that the quickly falling axe had was stopped upon impacting the body of the Lionheart. Once again engaging in a standstill, Thalland looked ready to bring the fury of The Pale down upon Darkflare; his eye bloodshot red and spit flying from his mouth. Darkflare focused hard to remain standing, despite the weight of the weapon trying to push him down to the ground. Both men pressed against the other's blade with all of their might in an attempt to break each's will. Against all odds, Darkflare thought he was winning the test of strength as Thalland's weapon was beginning to recoil.

Darkflare was proven wrong once he felt a large, armored boot connect with his stomach. The air in his lungs was expelled without any time for him to guard the cheap shot. He stumbled back several feet more, trying to regain his wits.

The kick forced the winded Darkflare's world to shift completely out of focus for a few moments. He heard some sort of a whistle and saw a shape rushing toward him. He fumbled for his sword as he prepared to defend, and he realized that the shape was Thalland and the whistle was his mind distorting the bandit's cry of anger as he prepared to smite Darkflare. His sight was restored in just enough time to witness the blade of the axe coming in horizontally toward him at waist height. Darkflare, now conscious of his surroundings once more, managed to force enough strength in his body to throw himself backward in a rolling motion and out of the way of the slice.

Recoiling to a standing position once more, he felt adrenaline being pumped through his veins by the Rune of Courage and tightened the grip on the handle of his blade, focusing his strength. With nimble speed, he rushed at the Marked One and prepared himself for the next attack. Predictably, Thalland swung back around from the other side of his waist from recoil. Meeting the second swipe of the axe head on, Darkflare managed to deflect the attack with a ferocious blow of his own, knocking his opponent's blade downward. Darkflare rushed in for a lunge on Thalland's torso, but the elder bandit was quicker than he looked and managed to raise the body of his weapon to parry the Lionheart once more. Darkflare unremittingly plunged his blade at his foe, as if trying to break the shaft of the axe, but it was no use.

The echoing rhythm of blades crashing upon one another rang out as Darkflare tried hopelessly to destroy Thalland's means of resistance. He parried every swing that Darkflare made at him without a sign of relenting or releasing his guard. It was a foolish attempt, but Darkflare was beginning to get desperate.

The bigger man looked completely surprised. This had been the third time that Darkflare had caught him in a parrying battle, and his face showed that he could not bring himself to believe that the 'boy' possessed such power. After parrying what felt like the fiftieth swipe from the unrelenting youth, Thalland brought the body of the axe up in front of him to knock Darkflare off of his offensive stance and away from where he stood. Losing the strength test for the third time, Darkflare felt the grip he had on the Lionheart suddenly vanish as it was sent flying across the roof.

Darkflare cursed hard under his breath as he watched his sword fly from his fingertips, in what felt like an everlasting moment of the beautiful blade spiraling through the air naked of his grasp. He suddenly felt as helpless as a moth to the flame as he saw the look on Thalland's face shift to one of ruthless pleasure. Thalland swung his weapon in a rage of unhindered power, and all Darkflare could do was leap away from the violent swings of the war axe as the beast of a man charged him, his incessant attacks haunting Darkflare's footfalls. Thalland laughed remorselessly as he kept up the offense; with each swipe, he got closer and forced the unarmed Darkflare to the edge of the roof.

Darkflare could barely keep his eyes on the blade of the axe while watching the space between him and the ledge. He was just *barely* keeping away from death, and he could not keep dodging forever. It would only be a matter of time before Thalland either knocked him to the edge of the roof or caught him with the blade; either way, the outcome was not promising. He just needed to get to his sword – then he could at least parry Thalland into a test of strength once more and increase his odds of survival.

The only issue was that Thalland must have known this too, as he was keeping himself between the dragoon and his weapon. Darkflare went to leap backward once more but felt something catch him hard in the gut, hindering his movement altogether.

Thalland had managed to hook the broadside under a hitch in Darkflare's armor, which at least put an end to the catch and release. The corners of his lips curled menacingly into a smile once more as he flung the axe up and over his shoulder. Darkflare was flipped overhead with tremendous force from the weapon. Flying through the air, he was powerless to do anything. All he could do was watch as his footing disappeared from underneath him.

Darkflare braced just in time as he crashed with a sickening thud that echoed alongside the rattle and clang of his armor. Even with the padding and protection, the attack was more than he had been prepared for. The severity of the collision sent a shooting pain throughout his body and racked his bones. Blood; he could taste it in his mouth even though all around him had gone starry.

Darkflare's vision focused just as Thalland took several slow strides over to the fallen warrior, stood above him, and raised his axe overhead. A lightning bolt streaked across the dark skyline, followed by a resounding boom of thunder at the same time that the axe reached the apex of its ascension.

"None shall stand in our way. This world will be reborn anew, and those self-righteous as yourself will bow before our might! GWAHAHA-… Huh?!"

Thalland's guffawing laugh was cut short as he was sent flying back nearly the entire length of the rooftop and just about off the edge. It was as if the roles had suddenly been reversed, and this time, Thalland was the one caught by the axe and sent through the air. The devastating impact that sent the obese man flying like a toothpick was from no mortal weapon though. Darkflare was propped up by his elbow and his vision strained to watch it all. His hands were in that cupped, spell-casting formation, but his grasp was open instead of closed; smoke was emanating from his fingertips.

He had placed his life in the hands of the Rune of Courage like Kenji had taught him, and it had saved him when his sword could not.

"Sometimes… fighting is the only option," Darkflare pushed himself up from his elbows and leaned on one knee. His right hand supported his weight from falling over against the ground while the left one hugged his prone knee. A tinge of anger lined his face as he spit a mouthful of blood beside him. "If I don't fight for the people who can't, the peace that shapes our way of life, and to keep the memories of loved and cherished ones alive, who will? No, Thalland, I will never lay my weapon down and let scum like you destroy everything we hold dear!"

"Darkflare!"

Although he ached down to his core from Thalland's last attack, there was no mistaking Luna's voice. Two pairs of hands reached under his arms and helped him to his feet. Focusing his gaze, he noticed it was Luna and Roy who acted as support. Oboro hovered beside him, nudging his master lightly in an attempt to help regain his senses. Darkflare noticed that they were not the only ones to make it to the roof. Tessy, Kenji, and Attila stood beside him as well, each with their weapons drawn in a protective manner around their ally. Attila reached out his hand to Darkflare, to which the latter had to blink at a few times. It was almost like a role reversal of the first time they had met. Finally realizing why his friend had extended his hand, Darkflare gratefully seized the Lionheart from his grasp.

Luna held her hand against Darkflare's back and he felt the warm embrace of healing magic. "Are you okay?"

"I'm hurting, not going to lie."

"Argh." It took a few seconds, but Thalland struggled up and to his feet. "Alright ya… ya… What?!"

Thalland's jaw dropped when he noticed the five other warriors surrounding Darkflare. The fight had suddenly shifted against him, but despite that, he did not look defeated. Something in the way his face took on a maniacal cast told Darkflare that this fight had never been what Thalland had been focused on.

"So this is it then, huh? I've been waiting for this moment. I've got a real show in store for you dragoons. 'Specially you!"

Thalland raised a trembling hand to point at Kenji, all the while focusing a deranged smile across his face. Darkflare was not sure if it was from the fiery blast or the fact that he had been greatly outnumbered, but either way, Thalland had noticeably started to quiver.

Kenji narrowed his eyes and slightly turned his head, loosening his guard as he watched Thalland's deranged state.

"What are you going on about...?"

"You... You were with the Omnis years ago. I remember you. But that doesn't explain how you were able to get it."

There was something in Kenji's manner that broke, and Darkflare almost thought he seemed scared. "Get what?"

Thalland reached into a pocket on the side of his armor and revealed a small shard of crystal that shimmered a dark and eerie black – something Darkflare had never seen before. The only time he had even heard about something bearing the resemblance to it was when Kenji had explained the story of his parents' deaths.

Darkflare glanced over to look at Kenji and could hardly believe the expression on his face. Kenji's eyes bulged and he was shaking his head softly, as if trying to wake himself from a horrible nightmare; Kenji was truly frightened.

The story of his parents' deaths. Darkflare's eyes widened.

It was the dark matter.

"No... No, that can't be." Kenji's voice was low and cold in disbelief.

"It is – the crystal that bound my lord and master!"

"Liar! That shard disappeared after it sealed Graymahl and took the lives of Calistron and Sylphe!"

"Oh, really? I'm the liar?!" Thalland swung his free arm. "You're the one that hid the thing! You're the one that's swearin' up and down that it doesn't exist, but look! What do ya call this?"

Kenji remained silent but gritted his teeth in anger at the Marked One's words, glaring furiously at the crystal in his hand.

"Kenji...? You knew the dark matter still existed...?" Darkflare was in shock at what Thalland had said, but even more so that Kenji was not denying any of it.

"Ah, yes, *Kenji*, we found where you hid it. Pale, you led us straight to it! Burying it in Syvail, one of the first places to have been destroyed, was very clever, but not clever enough. When my spies spotted you headin' to Ceballe, we decided it was the perfect opportunity to stir up some trouble. Bring some more royalty to our ranks. Make you sweat. Make you really concerned over the shard. And then... you brought us right to it."

Kenji cursed low under his breath. "I... No! That's impossible!"

"Gwa ha haha! It doesn't matter anymore. We had been searching for this thing for so... so many years after our master was defeated." Thalland held the crystal up to his good eye and it looked like he was about to weep over it. "But now... Now the time is perfect. You led us to the dark matter. Now, behold its power."

"What are you talking about?" And that was when it hit Darkflare; that moment was when it all had come together. "You can't! You're not really going to...!"

"Aye, I am, Omni boy!" Thalland's one good eye lit up red with sickening, ruthless joy as it turned back to Darkflare. "I'm going to release me lord and master Graymahl Vulorst upon this world to wreak destruction once more! You think we Marked Ones were vile?! The world will learn to *tremble* before darkness once more! All will bend to the will of the dark master and suffer the same fate as those twenty years ago! GWA HA HAHA!"

Kenji broke into a run to try to stop Thalland. It was too late. Thalland threw the crystal at the ground, causing an explosion of darkness that enveloped the roof with purplish black smoke and forced Kenji to stop, retreating as he shielded his body with both arms raised before him. The shattered pieces of the crystal melted into darkness, leaving no trace of Thalland behind.

"Yes... This power... This darkness! The Runes of Torment have finally been released once more. O, Great Lord Graymahl, grant me one of your runes of power to dispose of these mortals for you! Give me the strength I so rightly deserve!"

"NO! You fool!"

Kenji struggled to regain his momentum, but there was naught he could do; they were too late. From the ominous black smoke, several ill-omened symbols vanished into the stormy skyline, expelled in different directions, as if seeking out their newest host form.

One remained.

Chapter XV

Thalland's shadow grew in the dark haze; his plea had been heard, and one of the Runes of Torment had begun to fester on the darkness in his heart. A monstrous roar boomed from the blazing shadows, and as the smoke cleared, a creature that could be described as anything but human loomed.

The laughter that bellowed was several octaves lower than Thalland's, with the duality the other Marked Ones shared in. The form that once belonged to the bandit leader Thalland Faleenwar had grown several feet in size, and his war axe oozed a dark crimson fluid that reeked of tarnished, stained blood. Darkflare felt his stomach rock with nausea as he gazed upon the most disturbing thing about the transformed Thalland. The spikes on his armor had multiplied tenfold, and certain ones around his neck and shoulders grew several feet out – above, in front, and behind him. And from the chains on his breastplate now hung skulls.

Thalland's eyepatch was gone, his pupil in his good eye disappeared, and the slots where his eyes should have been took on an olive-yellow coloring, standing out vehemently against the paler, almost blue, skin. The beard that was once saving scraps of food now held bones, peeking out from the even scragglier mess of gray. Pointed fangs shone through Thalland's sickening smile as he chuckled to himself.

"Kenji, w-what the Pale... What the Pale happened?!" It took Darkflare a few minutes to spit the words out; he was still fighting down the urge to vomit.

"He... He's bonded with one of the Runes of Torment." Kenji too was having problems forming his words as he stared at the horned diamond shape glowing on Thalland's stomach. "Why? After all we did to stop these runes from ever seeing the light of day again... Why have they been allowed to return?" Kenji snapped himself out of his reverie and turned to his allies. "We only have only option. We have to kill him."

Darkflare's eyes widened as he stared back at the hulking beast.

"Ah, great Polyphemos! God of the Rune of Gluttony!" The dark two-layered voice roared out across the roof of the pyramid as the sky boomed thunder and cracked lightning louder and stronger than before. "So this is what mastery over magic feels like. I can feel your power over rock and stone rushing through my veins; you have granted me your strength, and I thank you. I shall not let you down! I offer you a sacrifice of the blood of the dragoons!"

"I won't let you harm them!" Kenji's voice roared over the newly transformed Thalland's cry of thanks, and he rushed at him with the Izayoi held down low at his side.

As Kenji came up to attack, Thalland grinned once more. With surprising ease, he brushed the veteran dragoon away with a one handed smash from the side of his axe. Kenji was sent flying through the air with such astounding force that it seemed as if he was a toy that the creature had grown sick of playing with.

Darkflare could only stare as Kenji slammed hard into the concrete nearby. Luna and Tessy rushed to check on him while Roy, angered by the new foe's daunting strength, rushed in where his ally previously stood. Approaching the creature, there was a fury and might in Roy's swings that had not been seen prior as the Hyperion and the Muramasa viciously sliced through the air. Despite the impressive display of power, Thalland still managed to parry the attacks with one-handed ease. Roy was sent flying backward as well, but it was not by the body of the axe; instead the brute's massive arm smashed into him, effortlessly brushing him away.

Tessy appeared behind Thalland and relentlessly swung away with both sais, trying to cut her way through his armor. It seemed to not faze the Dragoon of Gluttony; he whirled around with the body of the axe and slammed the tainted weapon into Tessy. She spiraled through the air, and her body bounced against the ground, nearly rolling off the edge.

Before he had a chance to follow up his attacks on any of the three dragoons, an arrow struck into the back of Thalland's armor. Much like the previous attack, it did not seem to hurt or hinder him in the slightest; the arrow just sat there, remaining as another battle trophy among the bones. Turning around, he searched for the source of the attack; his olive-yellow slits for eyes fixated on Luna.

Raising his axe above his head, it appeared as if he was going to swing from several feet away, but the distance between the two proved not even he could reach that far. Instead, the air above his head distorted and quivered, as if something were about to burst from the very space around him. Tearing at the air, a slab of brown stone began to materialize, rapidly increasing in size as Thalland conjured it. It was as if the boulder had been called forth from the very void itself, as ground began to materialize where there was none and it expanded its mass as if it was an evolving organism. Once the size was large enough to smash through the entire side of a house, the axe he held above him descended, and the giant rock dove down toward the archer. Luna let out a yelp of fear as she ducked; she had nowhere to run, nowhere to escape.

A gust of wind pushed Attila through the air, piercing the giant rock in two with a cut so precise and accurate that there was no doubt who had destroyed it. Following the slice was a cone of flame – that had not come from Darkflare – to char the remains. The two flaming halves of slab fell to the rooftop on either side of Luna as she stood up, relieved but confused. Attila grunted as he stood on ground again, Oboro hovering beside him. Darkflare couldn't believe his eyes that Oboro had finally breathed flame! He didn't have time to revel in the feat as Attila turned to face him.

"This isn't working! His tainted power is stronger than anything we can throw at him!"

Darkflare looked around at his injured comrades, unsure of what to do.

What *could* they do? The monstrous creature before them revived Graymahl Vulorst's power; the supposed ultimate evil that his parents gave their lives to stop. To top it off, Darkflare cursed to himself, he had been given the same kind of power that the dragoons had, by one of Graymahl's Runes of Torment. Thalland had the power of ultimate darkness on his side and everyone had given everything they had, only to be thrown around like ragdolls.

"I..." Darkflare stammered, trying to find words. "We need to concentrate our attacks together! Separate, you're right, we're no match for the power he has, but we're six different dragoons! We each wield a different element, and combined, we have the power it takes to destroy him!"

Darkflare's hands were trembling, but he managed to slide the Lionheart back into its sheath. He needed to concentrate harder than ever to channel the full extent of his powers, even if it meant draining his own life force to do so. Darkflare began to conjure the power of the Rune of Courage into both hands, and he felt the familiar warmth of the magic swirl within his palms. Many thoughts tried to prod their way into his mind, but Darkflare forced himself to dispel all of them; he had to focus on uniting their attacks and keep his mind clear of everything if they were to succeed. This was the only thing he could think of that had a chance to work.

"GWA HA HAHA! It's of no use, you pathetic whelps!" Thalland's nightmarish tones screamed out. "Nothing and *no one* can destroy the power that I possess! I have been chosen by Graymahl Vulorst himself, blessed by the Rune God of Gluttony, Polyphemos! After I defeat you, I'll make sure the world knows that the dragoons are nothing but faded memories, stamped out of existence by *me!*"

Following his threat, it appeared Thalland was preparing another magical based attack. He raised the despoiled axe of his into the sky once more, but this time he focused more of his energy into the blood-stained weapon. As he concentrated, he began to glow rather menacingly, as if the newfound powers of darkness were taking over his actions instead of his own will. Darkflare had only seconds to try to outweigh Thalland's massive power, and he focused all of the strength that the Rune of Courage fed him into the core of his attack. As the overwhelming amount of energy surged through his body, Darkflare felt his heart beating faster and faster. The adrenaline and passion begin to lap around the beating fire that fueled his heart; the sensations were becoming so strong that Darkflare felt as if he were about to burst into flames.

Darkflare let all of the emotions he was feeling overwhelm him and focused them into his cupped palms. Fire began to resonate and surge as he watched Thalland concentrating energy of his own to unleash another blast of tainted earth element. Darkflare heard a cry of pain over all other noise and realized it was coming from himself; he had reached his threshold of control. Fearing that he would turn into the element he controlled if he did not unleash the power soon enough, Darkflare thrust his arms forward. An inferno of flames surged from his palms, as if the palace had been built upon a volcano and Darkflare forced it to erupt before their eyes, overflowing right toward the being that once was Thalland Faleenwar. The flames ruptured so fast and so fluidly, it mimicked a steady stream of destructive water, lapping its way down a lake or brook.

Thalland recoiled and placed his axe in front of him to defend against the tide of fire. The disruption in his conjuration caused him to lose focus on the stone. The war axe seemed to no longer be a weapon of destruction but instead a barrier against the magic.

"Nice try, Omni, but I told you – NOTHING can destroy me! Not even the power from Odin's Rune!"

Thalland opened his mouth as if to let one of his guffawing laughs follow his words, but he stopped after realizing that something else had begun to couple with the fire's power. From another angle, there was another element that had conjoined the stream of fire, forcing

Thalland to lose all thought he had on an attack. Darkflare looked toward Attila and noticed that his stalwart friend had focused the power of the storm's gusts overhead into his palms, firing off a stream of razor sharp blades of air into the current that soared from the tips of his fingers to aid the fire against Thalland. The two elements curled around each other at their target's barrier; the whipping blades of air sliced along the trail of flames as it desperately tried to tear through.

The sinister smile on Thalland's face vanished and was replaced by one of snarling seriousness as he still managed to defend himself against the coupled stream of energy.

"You may have the power of pure elements, but you're nowhere near as strong as I or the powers of darkness that I command!"

Now in control of the situation once more, having kept both elements at bay, Thalland looked poised to attack once more. Before he was able to even cast the stone, he was caught by another burst of energy from the other side of the fire. This time, the unified stream was joined by a wave of sub-zero, diamond-crystallized energy. The source of the third spiral of magic emanated from the frozen palms of the Dragoon of Wit, Roy, as he got to his feet once more. A trail of blood slithered out from underneath his platinum hair and down the side of his face, but there was still fight left in his body; a look of ferocity had overtaken Roy's otherwise pretty-boy features.

"Alone, we may be weaker than your powers of darkness, but you underestimate the strength of our unity!"

Thalland was about to retort to Roy's comment, but then another blast of energy exploded from another angle. This time, it was a surging typhoon of water that could have only been delivered by the Dragoon of Tranquility, Tessy. She was in slightly more visible pain as she had limped closer, also bleeding from the corner of her lip. Still, she, like Roy, had willed herself to join her allies when they needed her.

"No more innocent people will suffer at your hands! Back to the shadows with you, creature of darkness!"

Thalland's expression hardened once more as he gnashed his hideously yellow fangs out of anger.

"Fools!" He spat the words out, his temper having reached its limit fueled by the dark magic that overtook him. "I have untold power that you cannot even begin to fathom! Not even four of you can bring me to my knees!"

"Maybe five can!"

Thalland quickly shifted his gaze to try to find the source of the voice, but another element forced itself against him. The purplish black coil of void element thrust into the mix and added its strength to the unified stream.

"You may have sided with Graymahl, but you have no idea how to control the darkness that eats away at your soul. Now you'll feel what happens when a master of the void unleashes their fury!"

"Argh! This power…" Thalland winced as his axe pressed back against the streams of the five elements coming together. "I am one with the dark lord, Graymahl Vulorst – the true heir of darkness!"

The pressure and strength of the dragoons' elemental attacks was finally showing wear on Thalland's defensive stance. His right foot slid backward as he stumbled to brace himself once more. The multi-colored stream of energy ferociously clawed against the barrier that his war axe had initiated, striving to break through. They just needed something else to penetrate the barrier.

"Luna!" Darkflare hoarsely cried. His body was starting to feel weak from the strain of all of that magic he was producing. From the start, it was a battle of time, and Darkflare knew they had to finish the assault *now*. "Your arrows! Fire at him! We need to crack that barrier!"

Darkflare was unsure if her healing magic had any offensive capabilities, but the blonde archer did not hesitate; she must have heard the necessity and stress in Darkflare's words and raised her Elyria into position. Aiming right at the center of the elemental stream, Luna's eyes did not waver. Releasing the hold she had on the bow's string, she let an arrow fly. Darkflare lost sight of it as it was engulfed in the power stream, and he prayed it found its mark as it vanished from sight.

The axe and its barrier could not hold back the immensity of the runes' power anymore. While it had been enhanced by the dark magic, it was not blessed with unbreakable strength like the dragoons' weapons had been. The arrowhead's point, amplified by the magical stream, was the last piece of offense that the dragoons needed.

The stream of elements, spearheaded by Luna's enhanced arrow, splintered the axe shaft into pieces and left the head to hit the ground without any support. Having no barrier to stop the attack anymore, the arrow pierced through Thalland's thick armor and acted as a catalyst for the blaze of power to tear away his chained, spiked breastplate, which left his husky chest exposed. Smoke hissed from the obese mass of flesh as it remained motionless, stunned, and unarmed. The Rune of Gluttony sat evilly in the center of his stomach; it had burned deep into the skin, showing that Thalland had paid in flesh for his lust for power.

One by one, the streams ended. Attila, Roy, and Tessy collapsed, struggling to regain both their stamina and breath, leaving Darkflare, Luna, and Kenji the only ones standing. Darkflare could feel his body shaking and struggled to remain upright, but he needed to finish the fight. He could not feel his legs anymore; he just knew they were bringing him forward at great speeds, rushing him toward the darkness faster and faster with every step. His hand flew to the Lionheart, and it was back out in a flash. Thalland grasped what was left of the shattered war axe's head; he was badly injured but not quite dead.

"Submit... to the darkness, Darkflare! In the end, the darkness... it consumes all!"

"I'll *never* give in!"

Thalland tried to raise his arm to parry the Lionheart with the remains of the war axe, but his reflexes had slowed. Darkflare's unfettered speed, even at the peak of exhaustion, was more than he could have expected; his sword struck deep, piercing into the chest of the former bandit. As the sword found its mark, Darkflare panted heavily as he held the blade with both hands, staring into Thalland's eyeless sockets. The Marked One's black blood oozed from the wound. The bandit king looked down at the sword and gasped for words. Darkflare withdrew his weapon and stumbled backward until he fell onto his rear.

Thalland glared at Darkflare again, his face contorted with rage, but he made no effort to move; his hands didn't even rise to cover his wound. Instead, he clawed fiercely at the rune on his stomach, causing the skin there to bleed.

"Why...? Why, Master Graymahl...? Lord Sairephir...? Why was my reign... my reign of darkness... so... short lived...?"

Thalland's knees gave way, but he never reached the ground. The rune itself was eating away at his body and flesh, almost as if the darkness was devouring his mortality as a sacrifice for utilizing its overwhelming power. Instead of falling dead, he began to fade into a black cloud of smoke that lingered in his place for a few moments, before being lifted up into the sky and fading away entirely.

Darkflare sat up, trying to figure out what had just happened as the sunlight began to slowly peek in through the bleak clouds, slowly expelling the storm from the sky. So much had happened in such a short time that it still had not hit him that they had just destroyed a Dragoon of Torment – the Dragoon of Gluttony was dead.

Kenji was still standing perfectly fine. If he had been afflicted by the loss of stamina, he certainly was not showing it. He walked over to Darkflare and extended his hand to help his bewildered ally to his feet.

"What... just happened?"

Kenji met his gaze with a look of sullen seriousness. He sighed and then turned away to look at the sunlight coming through.

"The Runes of Torment, the runes that Graymahl created and what your parents gave their lives to seal, have been released once again upon the earth."

"Does that mean... Graymahl?"

"Possibly." There was no trace of Kenji's smile; only a hardened look of regret. "I honestly have no idea. Our top priority is going to be to destroy all of the released runes. If he's been revived, then he'll have less power with them out of the way. If he hasn't been, well... Perhaps we can prevent his resurrection. We've already destroyed one here today," Kenji paused and a slight smile returned, as if reflecting on what had happened, and then he chuckled. He looked at Darkflare and placed a hand on his shoulder. "You truly have Calistron's power and personality flowing through you."

"Maybe." It was Darkflare's turn to look at the sun that had begun to reveal itself from behind the clouds. "My father gave his life to protect this world – he gave his life to protect *me*. I can never repay him for that, but I can pick up where he left off. As the next King of Dragoons, I have to continue his fight. I have to make sure to defeat Graymahl and all of his Dragoons of Torment."

Kenji nodded. "You're right. But, Darkflare... There's just one thing you must understand." Kenji paused, as if picking and choosing his words very carefully. As he met Darkflare's gaze, his look was stern and his words extremely cold. "From here on, we're going to be exposed to a lot of evil powers. Whatever happens... You must never allow that darkness into your heart. Your rune in particular can be exploited due to its great powers. Thalland was right about one thing – darkness consumes all."

Was this what Gilgamesh was talking about? Was he worried about his rune being exploited, and that's why he had said what he did to Darkflare?

Darkflare turned and nodded once more. The two headed back toward their allies as they picked themselves up; despite their wounds and exhaustion, smiles were on each of their faces at their victory. Darkflare felt the sun at his back, shining warmly through the remains of the obscurity.

Chapter XVI

Darkflare was lost deep in thought as he leaned over the railing of his porch. Almost a week had passed since the death of Thalland Faleenwar, and while most of the Marked Ones' activity had diminished dramatically, the dragoons had not been fooled. Their enemies were still out there, building their numbers, and waiting for the next one they'd call 'master' to ascend. While they searched for the scattered remains of the Marked Ones' forces, the dragoons had a new quest ahead of them. The Runes of Torment spread in search of new hosts, and it was up to Darkflare and his allies to make sure those villains were dealt with. And that meant traveling across the four kingdoms in search of the darkness.

A smile parted his lips, breaking the seriousness of his thoughts. It crossed his mind how much things had changed over the past few weeks. He felt like he was an entirely different person from the last time he stood on this porch, the day before the tournament. Not only that, but he was not just a part of a trio anymore; for the first time in many many years, there was a group of people that now called Cresentia home. Darkflare had friends. And not only did he have them to protect now, but with Graymahl's darkness on the loose, he had the entire world to worry about as well. He was the King of Dragoons, and in time, once more people knew of the dragoons' purpose and good intentions, they would look to him and his allies to protect them.

"This is it," Darkflare muttered to himself as he looked down at the blue-scaled wyvern curled up by his feet. "This is the start of the grand adventure we always dreamed of."

Oboro poked his head up and cocked it sideways at Darkflare. He smiled and patted the wyvern on the head. Sure, the original dream of knighthood had ended, but the journey he went on in the past few days was more exciting and challenging than anything he'd planned in his head. He wasn't tied down to serving a single ruler or kingdom. Right now, they could go where they wanted, do what they wanted, and help out whoever they wanted to without having to worry about stupid ideals like politics.

Before becoming a dragoon, he had never traveled further than Ceballe. He always wanted to know what lay behind the gates of Syvail or what horrors were hidden within the daunting prison of Kailos. He had answers to those questions, but now new ones sprang up to take their places, and it made him want to see more of the world. And he could, with new friends he never imagined having.

"C'mon. Let's go see how the others are doing."

As Darkflare went to step off the porch, Oboro took to the air and followed right beside him. The other dragoons were sitting in the middle of Crescentia, talking among themselves. There was one thing that stood out as odd, yet truly comforting; they were all laughing and smiling. Even Attila had a smirk crawling across his face.

"I guess we're done for the day, eh?" Darkflare smiled as he approached the group.

"Yeah, I'd say so. We've gained a lot of progress in the past couple of days," Roy grinned back and scooted over to make some room for his ally. "We can afford to take some time to relax for a bit."

"Mhm," Kenji nodded, looking to the northern part of the town. "They don't need to be completed so soon; we can take the rest of the day to just relax."

They had been talking about Crescentia's newest couple of buildings. When they had returned from Narvile, it was decided that if Crescentia was to become their base of operations, they would have to set to work on forging several new buildings. They would each get their own houses, as well as Kenji and Roy would manage a building for training. They also decided to finish the inn that Darkflare and Attila had been working on, and there was the idea of adding a storage house for shared spoils. The framework for the buildings had already been laid out; they were well on their way.

"Oh man," Tessy moaned, nearly salivating at the mouth. "This would have been so much easier if we had just taken some of that gold and hired people..."

"You already got your owed cut," Attila replied in his icy cold tone. "That gold was not ours to take."

"Yeah, yeah" Tessy said, tossing the large pouch up in the air and catching it. "But now I'm all paid up to work with you guys!"

"I didn't think Roper was going to stop thanking us," Luna said with a light chuckle as she poked at the ground with an arrow. "Hopefully he sent a good word to that jerk, King Corsius."

"Yeah, but," Kenji said, nodding, and his tone grew a little more serious, "I really don't want King Corsius finding out about us or Crescentia just yet. The king might try to exploit us or this safe haven if he finds out where we are. We'll operate in the shadows and keep our distance from him. He can divvy up that gold; it's not our place to."

"You think he will?" Darkflare wanted to think positively of the ruler of D'sylum, but something nagged at the back of his mind. "That's a lot of gold to try and find who it rightfully belonged to. I mean, anyone can just go to the court and say, 'hey, bandits stole my entire fortune!' If I had to guess, I'd say he'd probably invest it back into the fortification of the land – especially using the bandits as an excuse to."

"Perhaps. But there are people that know the gold has resurfaced, and Thalland's demise will spread throughout D'sylum fast – even if the story of the Marked Ones gets covered up. I think he'll restore some to the people of Ceballe and Aunquil, even if just to save face."

They sat in silence for a few minutes more, letting the glory seep into their minds still of the bold accomplishment. While it had been a couple days removed, they all, even Kenji, took a couple minutes to reflect on the fight whenever it was brought up.

"Well," Tessy broke the silence, grinning rather brightly. "We've got everything all set pretty much, except for one thing."

"What's that?" Roy asked, suddenly getting very excited. "We're finally having that victory party? Excellent! I'll procure the wine and dancers!"

Luna and Tessy glared at him, and Roy put a hand up and shook his head.

"Alright, wine – no dancers. Got it!"

Darkflare shook his head and looked to Tessy.

"Go on. What do we need?"

"A name."

"A name?" Roy asked, sitting straighter. "Like… for our group?"

"Yep!"

"This is true," Attila mused. "All of the greatest groups have names… Something that we can connect with and others can identify us with."

"Yeah," Darkflare agreed, sitting back in thought. "People have to know what to call us – not that there are too many groups of dragoons, right?"

"It's got to have meaning, yet reflect on what and who we are," Roy rubbed his chin intelligently.

"Something simple, but not too short. Something a little elegant, but not over the top," Luna added.

"Something cool but still classy," Tessy said with a nod.

"Well," Darkflare stood up, taking turns looking at each of them as he spoke. "We're like… like a family now, right? No. Too cliché. We're more of a... a clan – we're a clan. A clan of the greatest warriors. Individually, each of us is a dragoon. You want to keep it simple, have a lot of meaning, and still seem cool? Then why don't we call ourselves... The Dragoon Clan?"

"The Dragoon Clan," Attila muttered the words with a large smile radiating his dark face.

"Good call, Mr. Leader."

Darkflare turned to look at Kenji with a wide-eyed look of sheer astonishment. He almost had to do a double-take on the words that came out of his guardian's mouth. Kenji was sitting back with his arms crossed, very relaxed.

"L-Leader? Kenji, I..."

"Who just came up with the name? Who was the one that took control of things at Narvile? Who was the one who defeated Thalland? Who was the one that thought of the idea *to* defeat Thalland? Who has united us together?"

"Yes!" Tessy jumped up to her feet and hopped up and down several times, thrilled over the thought. "You really should be the leader! I'd even give you a discount for my services!"

"It's obvious." Roy grinned, standing as well. "In everything you do, it's obvious you're ready to lead our motley group of warriors, and you know I'll support you with my all. We've got a lot of work to do, but I'm ready to follow you wherever you lead, Darkflare."

"The people will need to see someone they can trust." Luna stood as well, a wide smile on her face. "Someone with a bold and courageous heart who will make the right decisions. It's you – it's been you since the day I met you. Maybe it's your Rune of Courage giving you that bravery, but you're meant to lead. I'd be honored to call you my leader."

Attila was the next one to rise, standing in front of Darkflare with crossed arms.

"You know I've stood by you from the very first days of our childhood, my brother. If you're going to be a leader, it just means I'll have to strive harder to surpass your strength, so I can protect you better."

Kenji finally stood and slowly pulled the Izayoi from its sheath.

"Let's make it official. From this moment on, we shall be called The Dragoon Clan; the protectors of all people of Caelestis and the reaches beyond. We'll grow stronger with each passing day and each new experience so that we can continue to fulfill our mission: to destroy the Runes of Torment. We'll lend each other our complete unhindered strengths and follow our leader and friend, Darkflare Omni, until the end of our journey. It is up to us to always do what is best for the people."

Kenji raised his katana in the air in front of him, the tip pointing straight up to the open sky. One by one, the other dragoons drew their weapons, allowing the tips to touch Kenji's in agreement. Darkflare was the last one to bring his weapon in; he was lost absorbing the moment and realizing the bond that they had formed in such a short period of time. Assembling the Lionheart in with the other weapons, he smiled brightly.

Things were finally looking up. Darkflare had made another promise besides The Dragoon Clan's pact that day. Darkflare swore silently to himself that he would be the best leader that he could be and refused to let his allies' expectations down. He would avenge the fallen and never let another death like Rai's, or any of the others that perished in Ceballe, happen if he could save them. He welcomed both the arduous perils and the joyful happiness to challenge their futures. He was ready to take on every obstacle that hindered their path.

He was ready to lead The Dragoon Clan.

Epilogue

Meredia closed the book with a sigh. She had lost track of how many times she had read *The Modern History of D'sylum*, but it had nearly gotten to the point where she could recite the cover front to back. The book was outdated, but she could recall every leader up to the late King Edwin Quinn, the history of every major town (of course, with no mention of Crescentia), and every wild fruit and flower in the region.

She leaned back, resting her head of shoulder-length brown hair against the frame of her bed as she sat on the floor. Her eyes drifted over the books on the shelf. She had read them all, so many times. She looked at the drawing pad on the desk; she wasn't sure if there were any unused pieces of paper left. Beyond that, there wasn't much to do, locked in this tower. She stood up and looked out the large window of her room. The blue expanse stretched on endlessly, broken by clouds that were eye level with her. Even if she wanted to escape, the castle in which she was locked floated so high in the sky that she could not even see the ground below.

There was a knock at the door.

"Yes, brother."

The door opened, but she did not turn around. She already knew who it was. He was the only one that visited her.

"How are you today, sister?" the voice said. There was the slightest trace of warmth in the tone, all that was left of his caring heart. Just the thought saddened her. At least he still remembered her.

"Same as every day, brother. Immensely bored and trying to find a new way to whittle the hours beside reading, drawing, and sleeping. I tried creating a new song, but as my only critic, I'm not sure if I've actually made progress."

Her eyes still locked on the outside, she heard him approach her. She finally turned her head and looked at what he had in his outstretched hand. Her eyes widened and a smile spread across her face as she took the three new books joyfully.

"They're not much," the man said, his voice lower now, almost sorrowful, "but it was all I could procure on the latest scouting mission."

Scouting. The word made her smile drop, and she put the books down gingerly on the bed, her joy at new reading material suddenly slipping away.

"Did you... Did you have to..."

"No." The man had no emotion in his voice. "Not this time. I only have to order deaths if anyone gets in the way of our mission. We were met without any interruptions this time."

"Then how did you…?" She looked at him, and for the first time in a long time, there seemed to be a hint of emotion, almost sheepishness on the face of the man with long, wavy brown hair, his eyes wincing ever so slightly.

"I actually went into one of the human towns to procure them. I used some coins that the scouts had found from previous missions. We have no use for it otherwise. I wanted to make you… happy."

"Brother…"

Meredia put her arms around him, but he did not respond. He stood still as a board, almost at war with himself as she looked up into his brown eyes.

"Brother, have we not had enough of living here? Please…"

"Meredia, no." The voice was emotionless once more, any love there gone, despite the fact that he constantly took care of her and made sure she was happy. She knew that she only remained here, alive, because of her brother's demand. But the love he once spoke to her with was long since gone. He pushed away from her and looked her in the eyes, with that stern, cold gaze. Her attempt at pleading to his humanity had failed, again. "We are not having this conversation again, sister. This is our home. You are safe here."

"I am only safe here because you will it so! If she had her say, I would be disposed of."

"Enough." The man stepped away and turned to leave. He looked back at her one last time. "I will do all to protect you, dear sister, but I will not hear you speak a word against Sinscery."

He pulled the door silently shut and she turned to look at the books, shook her head, and then turned to look back out the window. Their other brother had to be out there, somewhere, still alive. Maybe he…

Maybe Darkflare could help pull their brother back from the enchantment that the astrelite creation, otherwise known as Sinscery, had placed upon him. Maybe Darkflare, wherever he was, could help save Terra.

Meredia sighed and looked to the books that Terra had brought. She sat down and grabbed the first one.

A History on Ceballe Tournaments…

I. Post Introduction

When writing a novel and envisioning not only a continent, but a world, on the scale of *The Dragoon Clan* series, there are a lot of names – kingdoms, towns, people, and even races; and most of them aren't used in everyday speech. While fantasy words such as "elves," "dwarves," and even "vampires" have become more common in today's fiction and television, and in some cases modernized and redefined with each iteration, there was a time when these were known to solely a niche audience. When Tolkien wrote Lord of the Rings, did he envision that Frodo and Bilbo would be the personification of the word "hobbit" more than half a century later – even that hobbit would be synonymous or even more common than the word "halfling"? Did George R. R. Martin think that a generation would start naming their children "Daenerys" after his tragic hero? When talking about wizards and vampires, it is necessary to clarify whether you mean Gandalf or Harry Potter, Edward Cullen or Dracula.

That said, I understand that the names I use for my characters are not the most traditional – in a medium that has been ever-expanding and growing since the epic of Gilgamesh, is there such a thing as "original" anymore? So to help assist in understanding pronunciation, and in case readers are as much seekers of information as I am, I decided to add appendices to list all of the characters (both major and minor), the runes and their gods, the locations visited, and the races encountered. With each book in the series that I write, I plan on updating these appendices so that they always stay current but do not give away any spoilers about the current novel.

I hope you enjoyed the first book in The Dragoon Clan series. This is but the first of many journeys for Darkflare and his allies as they travel across the world to combat the Runes of Torment.

~Brandon Rospond

II. Major Characters

Darkflare Omni (dahrk-flayr / ahm-nee)
Age: 22
Height: 5'8"
Weapon: Lionheart (longsword)
Darkflare is the second son of Calistron and Sylphe Omni. He knows that he is the last remaining member of his family, but what ended their lives prematurely remains a mystery to him. The only relic that he owns to link himself with them is a necklace that he inherited that he dubbed the Drachenfaith. He grew up teaching himself everything, alongside his friend, Attila, and his wyvern, Oboro. The trio lives off of wages that they earn in tournaments in Ceballc, as well as odd jobs they do to assist the townspeople. He enjoys honing his swordplay, understanding battle tactics, and helping those in need. Darkflare has also been known to be called a "seeker of knowledge," as he enjoys learning as much information as he can about anything and everything from texts.

Oboro (oh-bohr-oh)
Age: Wyvern.
Wingspan: About five feet.
Weapon: Claws, teeth, and elemental breaths.
Oboro is the closest thing that Darkflare has left to family. Darkflare's parents entrusted him with the care of a wyvern's egg when he was still a child. When it hatched, the young Darkflare poured all of his time into nurturing the baby, and the two developed a deep bond. Their friendship is beyond what humans create between one another, as Darkflare and Oboro are connected through their emotions and thoughts; Oboro empathizes with his master to show that he understands his words. Not just anyone can befriend a wyvern, and it is a testimony to Darkflare's pure heart that Oboro faithfully hovers by his master's side.

Attila Laise (uh-till-uh / lay-sss)
Age: 23
Height: 5'10"
Weapon: Crater Buster (greatsword)
Quietly arrogant and severely stubborn, Attila's loyalty has never been in question to Darkflare. Even though he refuses to talk about his past,

that has never stopped him from standing by his friend's side since he first wandered into the town of Crescentia. Even though Darkflare is his closest friend, he also considers him a rival, as Attila is always seeking to become stronger. He is not keen on letting other people into his life; he would rather be alone than work with a group.

Luna Renai Iylvein (loon-a / reh-nay / eel-vayn)
Age: 20
Height: 5'3"
Weapon: Elyria (bow that unfolds into tethered swords)
At an age where most girls were off pretending to be princesses and play with their dolls, Luna was practicing how to string a bow and loose an arrow, taught by her father and brother. Because of this, she was always getting into trouble as a child; more than her mother could keep up with most times. When she was seven years of age, her parents sent her off to school in Verankner. Because Dhaunt was in the D'sylum army, and there was peace between the four nations, he opted to send his daughter to the nation with better libraries than military. Verankner had the best scholars in the world, and because of her age, Luna attended her classes with the young prince, Nim Valesti. After her time in the west, Luna came home to help her parents around the farm, but she couldn't stand their constant bickering. She decided that she wanted to see more of the world, and despite her parents' opposition, she left anyway. She hadn't planned on going very far; originally the coast had seemed a nice idea. When she stopped at the inn in Kripillon to rest, she found out that King Corsius would be attending a grand tournament in Ceballe. Her mind made up, she decided to try and see in person the man that she despised, and she headed to Ceballe.

Kenji Morikuo (ken-jee / mohr-ee-coo-oh)
Age: Appears 34.
Height: 6'2"
Weapons: Izayoi (katana), Kukri Knives (daggers)
The journey alongside Darkflare was not Kenji's first adventure — it was actually alongside Darkflare's father, Calistron. He was with Calistron and Sylphe the day that Crescentia fell, and somehow, clung to life while all of his allies perished. Ever since that day, Kenji has used his second chance at life to watch over Darkflare without interfering in his growth. He made sure that he and Attila always had fresh food or coin so that they never would be lacking, but he chose to stay in the shadows until the

time when Darkflare's rune awoke. He is the most knowledgeable of the group, but there is something dark behind his grin that sends chills down his allies' spines. He takes the role of being a dragoon and expunging the Marked Ones very seriously.

Roy Kinders (roy / kin-durs)
Age: 25
Height: 5'1"
Weapons: Hyperion (longsword), Muramasa (katana), Heaven's Cloud (katana).
Despite being locked up in Kailos for pickpocketing when Darkflare and his allies first met Roy, he is a very noble person. Having wandered the land looking for a purpose, he enjoys helping out those in need – as well as the company of pretty women and good drink! Even though he dreams of meeting a woman that would see enough good in him to marry him, his passion is in mastering battle techniques. In his travels, he has fought countless enemies and now wishes to pass what he has learned onto Darkflare – who he sees as a kindred spirit.

Tessy Suisei (tess-ee / swee-say)
Age: 22
Height: 5'8"
Weapons: Kikoku and Tojaku (dual sais)
Very little to nothing is known about this ninja, except that she is quirky and sometimes paranoid, more worried about her pay than helping people. When she first encountered the group, she nearly fought them on the assumption that they were Marked Ones. She revealed she also had a rune and wanted to know what made them different from the demons. She ran from the group, only to rejoin their efforts two other times. Her conscience often wars with her greed, finding it hard to rationalize working for free.

III. Minor Characters

Calistron Omni (cal-eh-strawn / ahm-nee)
Age: Deceased
Height: 6'0"
Weapon: Honorbound and Glorydriven (sword and shield)
Being the father of Darkflare, leader of a group of dragoons, and founder of the safehaven known as Crescentia, Calistron is an icon that one would think they would find written in history books as an influential and powerful persona. However, that is not the case with this late hero. Calistron and his group kept themselves low-key and did not wish to openly display their runic powers, in fear of what the world might think. Some, but not many, knew of their exploits and respected what they did; this is what drew warriors to Crescentia when it was founded, away from the politics that were being played in the four kingdoms. When Graymahl attacked Crescentia, Calistron and Sylphe instinctively tried to save the house that they believed held their children, while their allies fought the dark lord and his minions. With the combined strength of their two runes, they were able to protect the house and land around it, but the rest of the Crescentia, and their allies, burned to cinders that day. With the last of their strength, Calistron and Sylphe trapped Graymahl's power within a crystal called the "dark matter" that was given to him by the astrelite leader, Nooremiil Phimtair, but it came at a high price. Both he and Sylphe's life energy were required to seal the dark lord's immense power. He died believing that his children had been saved, and placed his faith in their hands for the future.

Sylphe Omni (silf / ahm-nee)
Age: Deceased
Height: 5'9"
Weapon: Seraphii (winged lance)
Sylphe was Calistron's wife and second in command of their group. While her husband bore the Rune of Courage with command over fire, Sylphe bore the Rune of Hope, which gave her power over holy magic. After combining her rune with her husband's to seal their children out of Graymahl's reach, they were separated and she searched in vain for any of her remaining allies. She found neither, and was instead met face to face with Graymahl Vulorst. She fought him to no avail, and as he was

about to deliver the finishing blow, Calistron jumped in the way to save her. Husband and wife stood hand in hand as they sealed Graymahl in the dark matter. The power within the crystal was too strong for either she or Calistron to withstand, and they both knew that their sacrifices were needed to seal away Graymahl's monstrous power.

Gilgamesh (gil-guh-mesh)
Age: Unknown.
Height: 6'7"
A master craftsman and a giant man with a bigger personality, Gilgamesh lives on a mountain that he personally excavated to house his workshop. He offers a challenge to any wishing to have a relic personally forged by him, to which few have passed. Somehow, he manages to keep the technology in his house up to date, which can be attributed to payment for the armor and weaponry he forges for the nations. These mass-produced weapons are better quality than most smiths, but not as illustrious as he reserves for those who pass his quest.

King Lazelus Corsius (laz-eh-lus / cohr-see-us)
Age: 48
Height: 6'0"
Weapon: Vitriolsear (greatsword)
Ruler of D'sylum, the southern kingdom, he is considered the most militaristic leader. Most of the taxes go toward strengthening boundaries and walls within D'sylum, as well as better training the military. While there has not been a war for over twenty years, should something occur, the southern kingdom would be protected by its elite soldiers and fortified towns. He took over ruling the south when Syvail fell during Graymahl's wake. He had served on the council of the late Lord Edwin Quinn, and it had been decided that while he was shrewd, he was the most apt of the councilmen to rule D'sylum. The destruction of Syvail could also be attributed to why he strives so hard to boost his nation's military forces and cares not about problems of the individual man or the land.

King Xellmosk Urad (zell-mahsk / ooh-rad)
Age: 54
Height: 3'2"
Weapon: Fellcleave (double sided axe)
Ruler of Purcille, the northern kingdom, King Urad is of the dweller race and is the only non-human ruler of the four major kingdoms. He has a

hearty personality for being the ruler of a frozen tundra. When people think of notable dwellers, King Urad's name often is at the top of the list; with his stout beard and hearty personality, he makes up for his height with his large persona. Xellmosk acts as a neutral agent between the other three leaders; he helps to balance out Lazelus's stubborn military thinking against Faïne and Nim's beliefs that the people always come first. He has made sure the region of Purcille has thick walls to keep out the cold, since most of the northern kingdom is covered in snow and ice, but still does his best to put his peoples' needs as top priority. He is the oldest of the four rulers and is usually bundled up in heavy armor to combat the cold.

King Nim Valesti (nim / vuh-less-tee)
Age: 22
Height: 5'9"
Weapon: Ambásion (needlepoint sword)
Ruler of Verankner, the western kingdom, King Valesti is the newest in politics, and this causes him to put the needs of his people first at all times. Nim was very lucky due to the fact that he inherited a thriving kingdom from his father; the land of Verankner has always been maintained and blossoming with beauty, and the people fully support the Valesti family, almost blindly. King Valesti does whatever he can to make sure his people are taken care of, even if it means dipping into the kingdom's coffers. This has caused some strife within his council, but no one dares to contest the ruler most loved by his people.

Queen Faïne Ragwelv (fay-een / rag-well-vh)
Age: 36
Height: 5'8"
Weapon: Radiance Splicer (spear)
Ruler of Beauldyn, the eastern kingdom, she is sometimes referred to as "Faïne the Benevolent". Queen Ragwelv, much like King Valesti, is favored very strongly by the people in her kingdom. However, the young queen knows when other affairs should come before the needs of her people, and her kingdom has never been lacking – thus, even all on her council strongly favor her. Despite the fact that she is the only female ruler out of the four, she is undaunted in her resolve in protecting her people and her kingdom, not to mention that she is very outspoken and stalwart on policies when the leaders gather. While she does not wish to see the realm ever come to war again, she has openly challenged Lazelus

on several issues before, as their beliefs often put them at opposite ends of discussion.

Knight Commander Barrayos Ronseph (bah-ray-yos / rohn-seff)
Age: 30
Height: 5'10"
Weapon: Camiella's Tears (greatsword)
Commander of the army of Beauldyn, and Queen Ragwelv's right hand man. Not much is known about the knight commander's past, except that it had been rumored that he was a survivor of the destruction of Syvail as a child. How he wound up in Peralor is unknown, but ever since he could first wield a sword, he fought in the army and ascended the ranks with great determination. Faïne, having noticed his resolve, promoted him to her knight-commander upon becoming queen. Some questioned why she would appoint someone so young as the commander of her army, but his expertise with sword and drilling his troops silenced any opposition.

Princess Aiyell Valesti (eye-yell / vuh-less-tee)
Age: 19
Height: 5'6"
Aiyell is the younger sister of King Nim Valesti. The siblings are extremely close, and it has been said that she is the prince's confidant in all decisions made. She is gentle and wise, always suggesting ideas to her brother on how to help keep the people happy. She personally tends to the bountiful garden that blooms year-round in Tiresek.

Rai Despil (ry / deh-spil)
Age: 26
Height: 6'0"
The oldest child of the Despil family, Rai is renowned for his fighting skills and claiming victory in Ceballe's tournaments year after year. While his family did not need the money, he enjoyed being the center of attention and beating around weaker opponents. Upon meeting and befriending Darkflare and Attila, he stepped away from the tournament scene, realizing that they needed the money more than his family did.

Angelus Despil (an-gel-us / deh-spil)
Age: 24
Height: 5'8"

The middle child of the Despil family, Angelus is very mild-mannered and timid. He doesn't have much in the way of aspirations or goals; he's usually forgotten when compared to Angelus's fighting skills and Gloria's beauty. He is friendly with Darkflare, but the two rarely get a chance to talk. Rai has started training him with a sword so that way he'd have something to do with his life.

Gloria Despil (glor-eey-uh / deh-spil)
Age: 22
Height: 5'6"
The youngest child in the Despil family, Gloria is a beautiful girl, although she is modest about her looks. Despite suitors constantly trying to win her hand, she has eyes for only one man. She thoroughly enjoys seeing Darkflare and Attila when her family goes to Ceballe, and she always makes sure to spend as much time talking with Darkflare as he lets her.

Hal Despil (hal / deh-spil)
Age: 58
Height: 5'9"
Head of the Despil family, Hal is a successful farmer from Lylenac. He enjoys bringing his family to Ceballe to see the bustling city, as well as to escape the quiet of countryside life; not to mention seeing his children's friends, Darkflare and Attila. He always tries to help them out with either a spare bag of coin or a fresh meal.

Pearl Despil (purl / deh-spil)
Age: 60
Height: 5'5"
Mother of the Despil family, Pearl is used to enjoying the finer things in life. She's proud of her husband's hard work, as well as the great assets each of her children have. She enjoys walking around Ceballe, gossiping with her daughter Gloria about all the strange people – as well as pestering her with asking when she and Darkflare are going to become a couple.

Roper Nikita (row-purr / nih-key-ta)
Age: 72
Height: 5'8"
Being the elder of Aunquil, and thus the leader of the trading town, Roper is very knowledgeable on many subjects. This is proven by the fact

that he is one of the few people who knows what a dragoon is. He has led the town in prosperity and peace for over fifty years, until Thalland and his brigands came to the region.

Darrow Iylvein (dah-row / eel-vayn)
Age: 23
Height: 5'7"
He is the older brother of Luna. Darrow and Luna did not have much time to grow up alongside each other; she went to school in Verankner and he was sent to military school in Pheeq. When his father became injured, he was called up to take his place, and ever since, he has had little communication with his family.

Dhaunt Iylvein (daunt / eel-vayn)
Age: 62
Height: 5'10"
The wounded father of Luna and Darrow. Dhaunt is from Echlow and was part of the reserve guard of the Syvail army. The day that the capital fell, he was home and powerless to do anything to help the late Lord Edwin Quinn. When Lazelus took the throne, Dhaunt knew how political he was, but as he was looking to replace the main body of the army that perished at Syvail, Dhaunt jumped at a chance to step up. After years of servitude, he was constantly passed over, while the more brash and loudmouthed soldiers were chosen. One day, another soldier injured him and claimed it was Dhaunt's idea. Lazelus discharged him from his services and instead took Darrow as a replacement. He now lives out his days back in Echlow as a farmer with his wife, Larissa.

Larissa Iylvein (lah-riss-uh / eel-vayn)
Age: 57
Height: 5'3"
Mother of Luna and Darrow, and wife of Dhaunt, Larissa has tended the Iylvein farm in Echlow since she and Dhaunt were first married. She cares deeply for her family, and even though she encourages her children to do what they feel is best for them, she worried deeply when they both were sent off to different schools. She still does most of the work around the farm, even though Dhaunt has returned home, as he is often lost in his thoughts of regret.

King Edwin Quinn (ed-win / kwin)
Age: Deceased
Height: 6'1"
The late ruler of D'sylum, when the capital was in Syvail. He had been one of the few people that Calistron had informed that his group consisted of dragoons, and he had been known to fully support the group of warriors in any way possible. Graymahl heard of this, and outraged, decided that Syvail would be the first place to be destroyed in his rampage. Quinn was said to be a noble ruler, who many all over the four kingdoms respected and revered. His passing was said to be a great loss that all mourned.

King Skylar Farrow (sky-lur / fah-row)
Age: Deceased
Height: 6'0"
Weapon: Phoenix Pinion (sword)
A character that has been immortalized by history, but long since forgotten in daily conversation, Skylar was the original divider of the land into the four kingdoms and the leader of the historical Phoenix Knights. Skylar originally served under the ruling army of the nation, the Roveyn Army, until he learned of the corruption that the king had harnessed for his own. He thus broke away with a few trusted allies and they started their own army – the Phoenix Knights. Skylar and his soldiers set up their capital to be Syvail, which eventually turned into a thriving city. The Phoenix Knights, under a more righteous banner, called together the land's strongest warriors and eventually usurped control. Skylar believed that no one man should rule alone; he christened the southern land he would rule over as D'sylum, and divided the rest of the land into Verankner, Purcille, and Beauldyn.

IV. Villains

Graymahl Vulorst (gray-maul / vuh-lore-st)
Age: Immortal.
Height: 6'2"
Weapon: Woeborn Requiem (scythe)

At one time, he was the greatest evil the land had ever known, and one of the most competent magic wielders in history; though, he was not always that way. Graymahl was a researcher on magic and tried to understand how the astrelite race had such mastery over magic. Eventually, his research led him to unethical processes that would have had him had him thrown in jail, but he had managed to escape before the king's guards could arrest him. He roamed the land for some time, his mind poisoned by the darkness of knowledge he wished to attain, until he found an ally that allowed him to set up his laboratory; this man, Sahgan Durande, just so happened to be the enemy of Calistron and his group of dragoons. The dragoons slew Sahgan, yet left Graymahl alive, thinking him a broken man for having destroyed his life's work of experiments. Once Graymahl escaped, he wandered the land lost and confused; he now realized that the astrelites were not the only ones to have natural mastery over magic, but that these dragoons did too. He was disgusted by their self-proclaimed noble purpose of having destroyed his work, and he sought to get his own rune. During his wanderings, he went from town to town, committing the deadliest acts a man could do, keeping a piece of each crime with him.

He returned to the place where he encountered the dragoons – where he first bore witness to their magic. Casting together the items of his crimes, he called forth Hades, the God of Death and Destruction; the counterpoint to Mokiwana. Hades, having seen the items, granted him the Rune of Torment, Hades's own personal brand of strength and command over all magic. He created creatures of darkness to bestow the other runes upon and prepared to take his revenge upon the dragoons. As he marched toward the source of their energy, Graymahl passed the capital of D'sylum – Syvail. The army had assembled upon seeing the oncoming swarm of darkness and tried to stop them, but Graymahl obliterated the kingdom for being allies of the dragoons, leaving naught in its wake but scarred land and ruined buildings. He succeeded in doing the same in Crescentia; he killed all that lived there, but not without being sealed in the dark matter by Calistron and Sylphe, who also gave their lives.

In the current age, Graymahl's name is but a dark curse uttered to scare children. Many have started cults in his name and fight to attain the level of power that he once had, but none have succeeded in cultivating that much darkness in their own hearts.

Thalland Faleenwar (thal-land / fah-lean-war)
Age: 55
Height: 6'2"
Weapon: Gormandizor (great axe)
A bandit that was under Graymahl Vulorst's services when he was still a researcher. At the time, he had control over a number of bandit tribes, but not all of them. Graymahl hired him to slay any that might impede the work that he and Sahgan were doing. Calistron and his allies had started to become an important name on the lips of people across the continent, and Thalland thought he would put an end to their whisperings by claiming his head. He underestimated the dragoons' abilities, and to add insult to injury, Sylphe put an arrow through his eye during the fight. Thalland escaped with his life, but not his pride. He lost respect from many of the bandits he commanded and was forced into hiding. When it was said that Graymahl attained power of a god and had slain the dragoons, many remembered that Thalland had once worked directly with him, and it was at this time that he returned, now harnessing the power of a Marked One. He claimed that Graymahl entrusted him with the rest of his plans after he passed away and that they should worship the strength he was blessed with. The enemies of Calistron and the dragoons banded together and considered Thalland their leader for uniting them – the King of Bandits – a mocking of how Calistron styled himself the King of Dragoons.

The Marked Ones
When a person offers their soul to the powers of darkness, they are completely stripped of who and what they once were. Their new power is denoted with the mark of Sairephir, ruler of The Pale, on their neck. Without a soul, their skin grays to the point of near-blue; their eyes redden with their bloodlust; their teeth sharpen to carnivoric fangs; and their voice takes on a second layer, the voice of Sairephir himself

speaking through the host. They are granted minimal levels of magic, enough to conceal their marks and telltale properties to blend in with average mortals. When they die, there is no body left to wither away; the Marked One vanishes in a puff of fire, smoke, and shadow, being called to The Pale where they will suffer eternally.

V. Runes & Gods

The gods do not exist within the same realm of existence as the rest of the people in Vivacidy. Dreamscape, the realm in which Mokiwana resides over, harbors their existence and growth. Not all that live in Dreamscape are gods though; all inhabitants born there start off as spirits or lesser beings that help to make the realm prosper. It is those that are truly great that ascend to the title of god and harness the power to create runes; the dragoon thus almost represents a parallel in Vivacidy to the god in Dreamscape and acts as an avatar. All of the gods were born and attained their powers during a time when Hades's forces of darkness and Mokiwana's children of light were at war with each other. It should be noted that spirits in the realms outside of Vivacidy (The Pale and Dreamscape) cannot die, as there is no life; they can however experience such trauma that they cease to exist.

Rune of Courage (Odin)

When the Dreamscape was still young and Mokiwana's power was not quite as strong as it was to shield out Hades and his followers of darkness, the spirits of good and evil clashed quite often. Odin was one such warrior who stood brave in the face of all of Hades's dark creatures, even when odds were stacked against him. Due to his boundless courage, he rallied the troops of the Dreamscape to fight back and survive. During one such fight, Odin was surrounded by scores of members of the legion of darkness; they bled him and strung him up by his own weapon to die. When he was on the brink of nonexistence, Mokiwana harnessed the power of courage that he showed to the other spirits; and from that strength, she gave him his own rune – the master of fire and thus, the first elemental god.

Those that Odin bestows with the power of his rune are usually natural born leaders; those that are full of inner strength, even though they may lack it on the exterior. While they may not consciously have the courage that Odin judges worthy, he summons it from deep within them for the time when their rune will blossom. Because Odin was the first Rune God and his rune bestows much greater strength than the others, there is usually the risk that the dragoon might succumb to the darkness that Odin himself fought so hard against.

Rune of Rage (Zhangbu)

The town in Dreamscape that Zhangbu lived in was attacked by the creatures of evil, and its people were enslaved. He watched as his family, friends, and loved ones were tortured day and night, broken to the point of almost nonexistence. Finally, Zhangbu snapped and fought free from those that ensnared him. He was a skilled rider and had a prized red horse with a fiery mane. Calling it forth, the duo tore through the ranks of the enemy, and driven on by the rage that burned deep within, Zhangbu almost slaughtered the minions of darkness that subjugated his town, singlehandedly. They barely saw him as he flew through them on his steed, his blade whizzing through one and onto the next in an instant. Once Mokiwana was able to witness what the warrior had done, she bestowed upon him the Rune of Rage; to mimic the speed and tenacity he rode with, she granted him control over the power of wind.

Zhangbu does not normally grant his Rune to the timid; those that are brave and can fully transform the emotion of rage into power are the subjects of his choice.

Rune of Love (Evelina)

Evelina is the youngest of the Rune Gods, as she came into her power toward the end of the war between the forces of light and darkness. She was not a fighter, but an ordinary female spirit trying to live in the realm of Dreamscape and understand the different realms. Spirits feel emotions just like the beings that live in Vivacidy; love was no exception.

There were many men that fell in love with the beautiful woman, but she only had eyes for one. She felt very foolish around this man, and always thought to never be good enough to have him reciprocate the feelings she felt. Eventually, when she believed she was worth only the lowest of men, it was when the man she loved stepped forward and expressed his own feelings. Mokiwana, watching how the story unfolded and so impressed with the modesty of how beautiful of a spirit that she created dealt with her situation, bestowed upon her the Rune of Love to both heal the emotional wound of doubt she had obtained and so that she may heal others in the same way.

Evelina is able to look deep into the future of the dragoons that she picks to see the fate that awaits them. Usually, she picks those that will eventually be in need of the love that her rune can give, or those that must make momentous decisions involving their heart's calling somewhere down the line of their life. The rune can heal almost any ailment as well as allow the dragoon to perform some defensive magic.

Rune of Contempt (Poseidon)

How does one change their fate? Who they are, what their lineage has brought upon a people, how they feel and act? Poseidon pondered these questions for quite some time during the wars. He was a demon and thus, should hate the creatures of light and despise the realm of Dreamscape. Mokiwana heard the clouded judgments in the head of the demon before Hades could ever sink his claws deep enough into him. She met with the dark spirit and tried to answer his questions as honestly as she could; answers that might cause him to despise her even more caused him to only be open to the truth and despise what the darker spirits had done. Poseidon opted to leave The Pale and join Mokiwana in Dreamscape, in hopes that he could start his own group of dark spirits to live alongside the light. She granted him control over void magic; not quite the darkness that he had been used to, but magic that was closest attuned to it without tainting the soul.

Poseidon's chosen dragoons are usually those that must at some point deal with the contempt for things they cannot control; who they are, where they've come from, what they will become. His chosen are granted strength to face the same questions that he had to.

Rune of Wit (Odysseus)

Odysseus was more of a tactician than a warrior, but he built many great designs to help aid Mokiwana's forces against Hades's. He used his brain to outsmart those that would rely solely on brawn. Sure, there were many spirits on both sides that had a high level of intellect, but Odysseus's was so extreme, it was thought that he  could outplay Hades' forces before even they knew what their own plan of action was; he could see every outcome from every angle and chose to act before being acted upon. Due to this, Mokiwana bestowed upon him the Rune of Wit. When she asked him what element he wished to control, he replied with ice, "so that I can start making sculptures out of my enemies."

The dragoons blessed by the Rune of Wit usually have a high degree of intellect; they can feign stupidity at their whim and chose to enact sarcasm on things they are knowledgeable about when they wish to undermine their enemies (or maybe even their friends). They have been known to use battle plans to surprise their enemies, outthinking them ten moves in advance. They are not usually known as brutes, but finesse and grace are their fine points.

Rune of Tranquility (Lysistrata)

Much like how the story of Poseidon was a demon who wished to switch

to the side of light, there were stories of how the denizens of Dreamscape were corrupted by the whispers of Hades. Lysistrata's village was one of the groups of people that fell to the false whispers of the dark lord and began to question why they should continue to do as Mokiwana willed them to. Lysistrata, unhindered by Hades's promises, saw through the guise he had casted on her fellow townspeople and tried to talk them out of turning on the creator. At first, many did not heed her words, as she was a woman, and Hades convinced them that a man's word was far superior to that of a woman (ie, he to Mokiwana). Eventually, she convinced the women of the village to see how Hades was poisoning the minds of their husbands, and the wives forced their husbands to remember that they were a combined unit; man *and* woman, and that one is not more superior than the other. When all of the villagers were able to come back to their senses, Mokiwana visited the village and they prayed she forgive them. Knowing it was not of their conscious will, she did, and bestowed the Rune of Tranquility to Lysistrata for bringing her people back to peace; she chose water, as when it is still, there is no element more tranquil and serene.

Many of Lysistrata's dragoons are calm and relaxed; a beacon of tranquility. There have been those that are not, to which the rune focuses the tranquility that one may get perhaps in battle or in conjuring magic; it focuses on the stronger aspect of a person and aids them against inner strife so they may be at peace with themselves.

Rune of Gluttony (Polyphemos)

The urge for *more*: that is what keeps the glutton going on; whether it is for power, money, food, the glutton craves *more*. Polyphemos, one of Hades's trusted generals, was a brute of a man. He was constantly eating, continuously trying to gain more influence in darkness, and unendingly searching for ways to make himself stronger. The more he gave into the flow of darkness that inhabited The Pale, the stronger that Hades made him, and the less he could be redeemed. He did not care if he could never step foot freely in the Dreamscape, and he did not care how much pain the darkness inflicted upon him; his cravings drove him on. It was these desires that made him able to withstand more pain and evil than any being before, and why Hades bestowed upon him the Rune of Gluttony so that he may control a tainted version of stone elemental magic.

Polyphemos picks a host which can amplify his cravings in Vivacidy; one that does not care about slaughter and mayhem. The viler, fatter, and the more desires, the stronger their power from Polyphemos becomes.

Mokiwana (moh-kee-wah-na)

Where does life originate from? Where does the creator get created? Some answers lie outside the understanding of mortal minds. Mokiwana is known as the creator of Dreamscape, The Pale, and Vivacidy. She created pure life in Dreamscape, and The Pale was originally supposed to be a prison, until Hades began to create darkness there. Vivacidy was made to be neutral; a place

where mortals would thrive and make their own decisions. She oversees that life and time proceed, and sometimes she meddles in the affairs of the mortals to tip the scales in the favor of good. She has also been rumored to take an earthly appearance so that she may get to know how her people act toward one another. She is the Supreme Being and rules over the Rune Gods, even though she gives no rune herself.

Hades (hay-deez)

To balance out the good in Mokiwana, Hades has been her counterpart since the formation of the cosmos. He took up The Pale as his realm once it was decided that he and Mokiwana could not share the same dimension due to their contrast of good and evil. Who knows what drives on this sinister being besides the all-consuming need to destroy life? Much as Mokiwana creates, it is his job to destroy life. He sends forth his minions of darkness to extinguish all that Mokiwana has created, and he tries to tempt the people of Vivacidy to join in revelry for death. The final blow that ended the war with he and Mokiwana was thanks to the combined effort of her Rune Gods; they shattered his existence, causing his power to diminish greatly to the point where he now resides within a chamber in The Pale that Sairephir consults occasionally.

Sairephir (say-reh-fear)

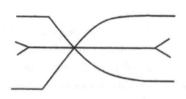

After the war between Hades and Mokiwana's forces was over, The Pale became what Mokiwana originally intended it to be – an impenetrable prison for those that had done immoral and evil things to suffer eternally, away from the good-hearted, benevolent people of Dreamscape. To fill the void that was left in the wake of Hades's destruction, Sairephir, Hades's greatest disciple, rose to take the throne as ruler of The Pale. While he did not have the power that Hades had to cross dimensions, he was the strongest being there. He made sure the demons remained up to strength, to someday battle Mokiwana again, and to construct The Pale into the way he saw fit for all of the demons to live in. He is also able to bestow marks on those in Vivacidy to symbolize his hold over them.

VI. Locations

Caelestis (kai-less-tis)
The main continent that the story takes place on. It is divided into four major kingdoms; D'sylum, Verankner, Beauldyn, and Purcille, but there are also minor kingdoms that fall outside their rule. The climate remains the same year round; the shining sun warms the land while the night brings the cool wind. Certain areas are known for their more severe weather conditions than others. The most notorious of these lies in the heart of Purcille, the northern kingdom, as it is known for being layered in thick snow.

D'sylum (duh-sy-lum)
The southern kingdom on the continent of Caelestis. Originally, the capital was the town of Syvail, but after its destruction at the hands of Graymahl Vulorst, King Lazelus Corsius moved it to Pheeq. One of the key factors of the kingdom is how most of its towns have heavily fortified walls around their borders. The peoples' needs are rarely heard, but they feel protected.

Pheeq (feek)
Population: High
Primary Function: Capital
Shadowed by the spires of the tall buildings, Pheeq is the capital of the south. King Lazelus Corsius and his family reside at the palace here, among many other of the higher ranking nobles of D'sylum. Some of the lower class live among the outskirts of the city, but for the most part, it is only home to those of the upper class. The army can be heard and seen constantly training, most times doing patrols around the city. Pheeq is home to the continent's best military school, as King Corsius has made sure that D'sylum has the strongest army to stand ready in case a threat such as Vulorst ever occurs again.

Crescentia (kreh-sent-cha)
Population: Deserted
Primary Function: Ruins
Once a safe haven to a handful of warriors, it has been reduced to consisting of two houses, the frame of an inn, and a graveyard that

harbors the remains of the ruins. Very few ever knew that the town existed, and to those that did, it remains nothing but a lost memory. Its residents are Darkflare, Attila, and Oboro. Crescentia is out of the way for any, if not all, travelers; it lies on the outskirts of D'sylum and the ocean washes upon the beach at the southern part of the town. That said, there is plenty of room to expand the town's borders, should such a need arise...

Syvail (si-vayl)
Population: None
Primary Function: Ruins/Former Capital.
Formerly the capital of D'sylum, Syvail lies locked away in ruins. Syvail had originally been christened capital of the south by Skylar Farrow, the leader of the fabled Phoenix Knights, as it was his hometown. The capital was built up and strengthened greatly over the years, but nothing could prepare the town for the destruction of darkness that Graymahl brought with him. There were few escapees; among them was rumored Barrayos Ronseph, who is currently the leader of the knights of Beauldyn. The area has since been sealed off, because it was considered a sacred graveyard that King Corsius did not wish to disturb – or perhaps he purposely left the ruins as is to remind people that war is inevitable.

Ceballe (se-ball)
Population: High
Primary Function: Trade
Home to the Merchant Guild, Ceballe is the trade capital of the south. Many merchants gather here from across the continent to have their wares protected by the guild and to sell their merchandise to whatever wandering eyes pass upon them. Besides trade, the town also has a residential area, as well as the continent's largest arena. Ceballe is home to many fighting tournaments that are hosted as both local events, and on rarer occasions, worldwide competitions.

Kailos Prison (ky-lohs)
Population: High (Imprisoned)
Primary Function: Prison
Long forgotten to most people, Kailos exists on an island off of the main continent in between Crescentia and Syvail. Once run by the people of Crescentia, it has since been taken over by bandits. Very few have ever gone in and come back out in one piece, and most that do are merchants

looking to sell the last of their goods.

Aunquil (on-qwil)
Population: Medium
Primary Function: Trade
Aunquil is one of the smaller trade cities throughout D'sylum. It is not as grand as Ceballe, but while it lacks the arena, it makes up for more foot space for travelers. Aunquil helps to serve as a town that those passing to and from Beauldyn and D'sylum can rest and trade in. It is headed by an elder by the name of Roper Nikita. It is also unique in the fact that just outside this area is where the land begins to change from fields of green to the arid mountains.

Twinfold Gorge
Population: Indigenous
Primary Function: Pathway
North of Aunquil, the gorge serves as a pathway that the traveler must go through to reach the eastern kingdom of Beauldyn. The only life forms that inhabit the pathway are indigenous creatures, as Aunquil serves as the closest populated town in D'sylum. It has several winding pathways that split in two directions; above the ground to make a bridge and below into the gorge's pit.

Narvile (nahr-vie-uhl)
Population: Low
Primary Function: Stronghold.
Not much is known to the average person about this hidden stronghold. To access it, one must go through a secret path tucked away in Twinfold Gorge. If they are successful in evading the traps that are set up, they will encounter a giant waterfall – possibly one of the few in D'sylum. It is after the rope bridge by this waterfall that one would find Narvile, the home of Thalland Faleenwar's bandits. It is a complete army stronghold with many high-lined barracks and golems that patrol and protect the alleyways. In the back of the area is a large pyramid-like structure that belongs to the bandit leader, Thalland Faleenwar.

Echlow (esh-low)
Population: Low
Primary Function: Farming

A small farming town in the southwestern area of D'sylum. It is not very populated, but the people there make a living off of the land. Because of this, a small wooden fence is all that makes up the town's borders, leaving it very exposed for the farmers to expand their crops and herds. This is contrary to the king's belief in strengthening town's borders, but the people protested that they needed open space to properly farm. One of the prominent families in the town is the Iylveins.

Verankner (ver-ank-nuhr)
The western kingdom on the continent of Caelestis. The capital is Tiresek. There are scattered towns throughout the region, which has led to spacious plains of grasslands throughout the pathways in between each. The people's morale soars high, as their leader, King Nim Valesti, is very kind to them in giving them anything that they could desire. There is no disparate land in the kingdom, as there is in D'sylum, but instead, the Valestis try to cultivate as much life in nature as they can.

Tiresek (tear-sek)
Population: High
Primary Function: Capital
The capital of Verankner and home to the Valesti royal family. The castle is elevated on top of a hill that has a winding slope that leads down to the rest of the town. Not just the upper class live here, but the royal family has made it affordable for the middle and even lower class members to afford property in the town. The castle has a library, and while it is nowhere near the magnitude of the one in Beauldyn, it still houses a plethora of information. Flowers and greenery are constantly blossoming year round, especially in the garden in the interior of the castle. Buildings are not spaced too closely together as in Pheeq, giving the town a more open, welcoming look to it.

Beauldyn (bee-yewl-dun)
The eastern kingdom on the continent of Caelestis. The capital is Peralor. This region is the most visually appealing, as there are many cliffs and natural formations, as well as the land is always a lush and verdant green; flowers are constantly in bloom across the nation. The morale of the people is arguably the highest out of the four nations, due to the fact that Queen Faïne Ragwelv has been said to be the kindest and most benevolent ruler of the four. The nation is not as well defended as D'sylum or Purcille, but they are also home to the famous pioneer in

skyshard technology, Lehnes Kearin.

Peralor (perra-lore)
Population: High
Primary Function: Capital
The capital of Bealudyn and home to Queen Faïne Ragwelv. The city of Peralor is said to be like none other; the castle is made out of crystal so shimmering and extravagant it is thought to be otherworldly, and the capital's library houses all written information ever to have been compiled. The design of the buildings and the layout of the roads reflect the regality of the capital, but there is also a seedy side that the lower-class has inhabited; Queen Ragwelv has permitted its existence to make it equally fair for all people in her kingdom, but she has soldiers constantly watch it to make sure no trouble arises.

Purcille (pur-sile)
The northern kingdom on the continent of Caelestis. The capital is Iysumus. This region shows some proof that perhaps at one time, millenniums ago, Caelestis may have been a part of a larger landmass. The landscape in the most northern part of Purcille, where Iysumus is located, is a frozen tundra of snow, due to how much higher elevated the land is there. Almost all of Purcille is higher than the other three kingdoms, and when one looks north from the other realms, they can usually see the mountains in the distance. At the baseline of the territory that borders on the other territories, the climate starts to get cooler, and the farther one goes north, the higher the land escalates and the colder it becomes. The people that live there, while usually bundled up in heavy layers, endure the cold as if it were nothing; it has been a part of their everyday lives for as long as they have known. The kingdom is heavily fortified, between the natural defenses of the land and the structures that their leader, King Xellmosk Urad, has established; and because of this, the king can focus on the needs of his people, keeping the morale usually high.

Iysumus (eye-sum-us)
Population: High
Primary Function: Capital
The capital of Purcille and home to the Urad family. It is located in the tip of the north and the heart of snowstorms. Because of all of the weather the capital has seen over the years, the buildings are almost

painted an icy blue from the ever-falling snow. The capital has no military academy or library, but their breweries are second to none on the continent! Xellmosk Urad prides himself on the fact that if Purcille was not inhabited by sentient beings, the tundra might become a home for indigenous and dangerous creatures. He also believes that his people are the toughest on the continent of Caelestis, due to how much cold they endure.

VII. Races

The continent of Caelestis is filled with a vast amount of different life forms. The human race is just one of the many that inhabit it; while they might be the most common form of people, they are far from being the only one. Primarily, there are two types of races that call the continent home. The "humanoid" races are bipedal and can speak and interact with one another. The human is the most ideal standard, with each race having their own differences that make them unique. The members of the "bestial" races tend to be quadrupeds, have wings to enable flight, for the most part cannot speak the same tongue as "humanoid" races, or they have a carnivorous appetite for blood that cannot be satiated.

HUMANOIDS:

Human

The most populated form of life on the continent of Caelestis. They have high enough intellect that they can form sentences and converse with one another, but that does not mean that they all share the same wisdom; there are some humans that are so unintelligent that they make wildlife seem smarter. They can learn to harness magic with intense training over countless years, and they have very strong emotional responses to everything that occurs to them. Their skin color consists of varying shades of pale-white, tan, beige, and black. Depending on their geographical location, their hair and eye colors can range wildly.

Astrelite

A race with advanced control over magic. While the humans evolved from a more primitive type of species, the astrelites' ancestors were beings of pure magic; the astrelites' control and conjuring of natural elements, brightly colored irises and hair, and synthetic wings are proof of that. They are paler in appearance than the human pigmentation, and their facial features and compositions are usually much more slender and regal. While they tend to remain concentrated in their home, the Vebustra Forest, located somewhere in the northwest part of Caelestis, many have left to live in mix with the humans; some even bearing children with humans to create hybrids. They tend not to react so quickly to their emotions as humans do, which sometimes makes them come off uncaring. They are the pioneers behind the crystal technology concept, and it is thanks to them that the land has evolved the way it has.

Dweller

A race of humanoids that do not generally stand any taller than four feet. At some point in this race's history, there was a split in where they called home; some stayed in the southern half of the continent, while others moved to the cold of the north. This has caused a schism in their culture and upbringing. Descendants of the northern dwellers tend to be stockier, with rugged features and thick beards; while those of the southern dwellers are almost always clean shaven – or have slight facial hair – with rounder more cherubic features. It is thanks to the northern dwellers that Purcille has such a complex underground system; and if one is looking for good mead, this race excels at making strong, hearty, and tasteful brews.

Leofer

A race that has feline heads, hands, and tails but speaks the tongue of humans. While the astrelites' ancestors were of magical origin, it is said that the leofers' were more bestial. They still maintain some elements of their ancestors – muzzles, whiskers, clawed hands, some have manes, and a terrifying roar – but they have integrated in humanoid society like any of the other races. Their appearances are a bit rarer, as rumor has it that they didn't originate on Caelestis but another continent completely. Most take to mercenary or bodyguard work, as their muscular bodies are made for combat. It is said they cannot be killed by age – only disease or combat.

Ocyalean

Creatures who appear human but resemble reptiles. They have scales on their cheeks, bodies, arms, legs, and tails. How many scales and where they are depends on the individual. They are also quite taller than humans and, arguably, more advanced in technology. They have claws for hands and feet and long tails. There are different sub groups of Ocyaleans, such as jungle, river, and sand; this determines what color their hair and scales are. Some lesser-intellect humans have a hard time telling male from female, as they lack breasts. They are a polygamous race, and it is said that their emperor has many wives – and even a husband.

Palli

A reptilian race, similar to the Ocyaleans; they are more dragon-like than the Ocyaleans lizard-like features. They are more conservative and wise; not to mention, unlike the Ocyaleans, monogamous. They see the Ocyaleans as inferior and do not get along when they encounter each other at a neutral location, such as Ceballe.

Dragoon

An ancient, selective title thought to be only a myth. Anyone of any race can be a dragoon, as long as they have been marked by a rune. It is the possession of this rune that would set a dragoon apart from, for example, being simply a human. This rune is a sign that the person has been marked by a Rune God to be their physical manifestation and avatar in the realm of Vivacidy. Each dragoon is given mastery over that god's element.

The Rune Gods did not develop the name of their avatars' race. When Odin first bestowed his rune, the human asked what his newfound race should be called; to which, Odin said that he would leave it in his chosen one's hands. This human, named Artemis, had developed a close bond with his pet dragon and was often referred to as the dragon knight; and so he chose the word "dragoon" to represent this new title.

Goblin

It was believed that, eons ago, goblins once lived in peace with the rest of the races. However, somewhere down the stream of time, perhaps due to their putrid and stout appearances, goblins were casted out and looked down upon by races such as the humans. It is due to this theory that many believe this is the reasoning why goblins are so mischievous and vicious creatures. They are smarter than any indigenous race, as seen by the fact that they speak the common tongue. It is interesting to note that they do not speak their own language, thus they had to have been taught the tongue by another speaking race, such as humans. The hue of their skin is usually an olive-green or yellow color, which combined with their generally short stature and stubby features, makes them come off hideous and strange.

BESTIAL:

Dragon and Wyvern

A set of nearly extinct races not often seen anywhere in Caelestis. Oboro, Darkflare's pet and friend, is one of the last known remaining wyverns, but that does not mean somewhere in a far off continent that more do not exist, unbeknownst to the people of Caelestis. A wyvern differs from a dragon in the sense that it does not reach the sheer size and magnitude of the latter; they usually only grow to the size of common house pets. They have shiny scales all across the top of their head and bodies which act as a tough exterior defense for them. They have sharp claws and teeth for hunting, as well as some have barbs on the extent of their tails. Dragons and wyverns have two abilities that set them apart from other creatures; flight and magical breath attacks. They are able to channel the arcane magic that flows within their blood and call forth streams of elemental power from their mouths.

Golem

The origins of these strange creatures are unknown, but the root more than likely lies in magic. An observer can be led to believe that a small mountain has been given life due to how golems' exteriors are nothing but rock. Their arms, legs, and even bodies resemble large boulders that they have full control over. From the middle of a golem's chest, one can usually see two glowing eyes that represent something deeper within the outer shell. What lurks within the exterior of boulders is unknown, even to Caelestis's greatest researchers, but it seems to be the creatures' only weak spot. They are capable of churning out a high pitched, deafening screech, which seems unexpected to come from such lumbering brutes. This is said to be a self-defense mechanism to alert others of enemies and is made by grinding rocks within at such high speeds that the frequencies are piercingly loud.

Advanced Beasts

Because of the nature of the realm, how magic is common and vital in everything and seen everywhere, it has altered the evolution of some beasts. Magic has given rise to new strains of life that are highly aggressive when threatened; so much so, that they can become endangering to even advanced warriors such as dragoons. Some examples of creatures as these are snakes and birds; the average kind of each does not present much problem to people. The world of magic has influenced such groups as the kobraikan and zuu, respectively. Advanced beasts are usually larger than their pre-magic counterparts and tend to have more of a bloodthirst. To aid in this endeavor, they possess sharper claws and teeth, larger appendages, or even the aid of toxins such as venom and paralysis. These advanced beasts have become a part of everyday life for the people of Caelestis but tend not to appear in open environments, such as while the sun is out or on open roads. These creatures tend to wait until the dusk or when people stray off the path, so that they can catch their prey with the element of surprise in their own natural habitat.

Kobraikan

Normal snakes are usually vicious in their own right; coils, venom, fangs, all the deadly attributes. When you have all that on the body of a four to six foot long snake, that is what you would call a kobraikan. They have wide hoods with illustrious swirls of designs that have evolved to intimidate prey and lure them into a sense of security or confusion. They have been known to curl themselves up and then launch themselves at their prey, as well as binding them to suffocation. Kobraikans are not usually found in populated areas and usually travel in groups, out of fear of being intimidated by other species. The poison created internally that coats their fangs is so deadly that it can kill a mortal within seconds of contact.

Kraken

These eight-armed creatures are solely found in deep bodies of water, rarely ever coming to the surface unless disturbed. Whatever creature that would dare to bother this rage-ridden species would be sorely mistaken. Each arm is strong enough to snap a fully grown, thick bodied tree, and the suction cups on the tentacles ensure that the prey will not escape. The skin of a kraken is thickly coated and absorbs so much water that they are impervious to most attacks unless performed with superb force. Not many inhabit the waterways around Caelestis, but the few that do are not to be challenged.

Homers

Small rodent-like creatures that have mostly been domesticated due to their ability to travel quickly to a specific location. Homers usually stay to the ground and carry letters and small packages strapped to their backs. They have elongated, floppy ears that allow them to fly for short distances if they need to. Bandits try to steal the items that they carry, but the small creatures are quick enough to evade any that is not their target. It's unsure how the intelligent creatures know exactly who and where to home in on, but it is thought that magic has affected their brains, giving them a sort of psychic element. They always return to their point of origin after their delivery is complete.

Slugnar

Creatures that crawl across the ground at incredibly slow speeds. Originally created from lava, slugnars have a natural red hue to their slimy skin. Their underbelly is coated in a thick, viscous substance that allows them to move vertically up objects. When they get intimidated, the slime they leave in their wake can light aflame as a defensive tactic.

Armorilla

Burly ape-like creatures that have hardened scales across their body. They are slow moving, very defensive, but were not blessed with much intellect. Their scales allow them to curl into a ball; which in turn they can then roll away, attack in that form, or remain still and unable to be attacked. These creatures are usually found in jungles and are usually hunted because of how easy they can be slain when not paying attention. Their name is also used as an insult among humans.

About the Author:

Everybody's got their own story. I have my own tales and adventures that have made me who I am, just like any character I write about; but to tell all of that, I would need my own book. So let me just share the relevant information to writing that would make you want to read my literature.

I'm a strong believer that imagination is everything when it comes to writing. I grew up playing video games for hours on end – RPGs, mostly – and I'm proud to say that I'm a child of the internet and know everything about memes; but the world was also my playground. My grandparents had a huge house that my sister and I would run around in and just let our imagination guide us into what games we would be playing. An open backyard at a friend or family member's house was my stage in what character and role I would take on that day.

I did not go into any plays or get involved in any activities in high school. Instead, I was on my computer, roleplaying in chat rooms since I was about twelve. It was where I created and shaped the character that has gone through many iterations, known as Darkflare Omni. Online roleplays helped to harness my imagination, as I was able to interact with people from all over and connect my character to theirs. I brought all of the things that influenced me in television, games, and music, all to one central point of creativity. It's where I met some invaluable people that helped me to create some of the characters in my writing, most notably, The Dragoon Clan.

Besides that, I'm a graduate of Monmouth University and a longtime resident of Point Pleasant, New Jersey; proud husband and father. I have worked with companies such as Fantasy Flight Games, PostHill Press, and am a full time editor for Winged Hussar Publishing and Zmok Books. My time with WHP has led me to work with many different authors and build great bonds with men and women who share the same love of writing as I have.

My philosophy on writing has always been that just because dark fantasy has a tendency to more realistically mimic life, that doesn't always make it good. I read and write fiction to get away from reality. I treasure novels with happy endings; stories where I can get invested in characters and know that I won't be losing them.

Let me impart one life lesson that I think everyone, young or old, should know. Imagination is the key to everything and anything a person can do in life. Always follow your heart and dreams, and never stop believing in fairytales. The only obstacles stopping someone are their own fears and doubt.

Brandon Rospond

Look for more books from Winged Hussar Publishing, LLC – E-books, paperbacks and Limited-Edition hardcovers. The best in history, science fiction and fantasy at:

https://www. wingedhussarpublishing.com
https://www.whpsupplyroom.com

or follow us on Facebook at:

Winged Hussar Publishing LLC

Or on twitter at:

WingHusPubLLC

For information and upcoming publications